Mafioso

Mafioso

A HISTORY OF THE MAFIA
FROM ITS ORIGINS TO
THE PRESENT DAY

Gaia Servadio

A DELTA BOOK

A DELTA BOOK

Published by
Dell Publishing Co., Inc.
1 Dag Hammarskjold Plaza
New York, New York 10017

Delta ® TM 755118, Dell Publishing Co., Inc.

Reprinted by arrangement with Stein and Day.

ISBN: 0-440-55104-8

Printed in the United States of America

Second printing—June 1978

VB

FOR ORLANDO

CONTENTS

LIST OF ILLUSTRATIONS

ACKNOWLEDGMENTS

This book was suggested and nursed by Professor John Hale. It would not have been written without his editorial interest and his encouragement. My husband read it through as each chapter came fresh from the typewriter, one eye on the mistakes, another on the form. Steve Cox dedicated time and enthusiasm to it.

I used the British Museum, that almost unfailing and wonderful British institution, and the London Library, where I am especially grateful to the kindest of assistant librarians, Douglas Matthews. I used the *Archivio di Stato* in Palermo and the Public Record Office in London.

Professor Denis Mack Smith answered with patience, wit and immense knowledge, many of my questions. So too did Professor Eric Hobsbawm, who read some of the chapters.

Vittorio Nisticò, editor of *L'Ora*, Giuliana Saladino and Marcello Cimino (who also read my manuscript) assisted and helped me when I was in Palermo. Perhaps no one knows more about the Sicilian social phenomenon than these three people.

Many mafiosi talked to me and answered my questions; some of them have been quoted in the text.

Francesco Cattanei, former President of the Antimafia Commission, dedicated much time to me, and so did many Parliamentarians.

Gigi Petyx, who took most of the photographs reproduced, looked through vast numbers of files in order to provide me with documents.

To all these people, my most grateful thanks.

INTRODUCTION

I first wrote about the Mafia fifteen years ago. I have been dealing with the subject ever since, although, until recently, it was not very popular with editors or publishers, especially Italian ones. But I dealt with it episodically, often regretting having to simplify its problems or skip its implications. Now, after elaboration and research, I have come across so many pitfalls that I must point them out to the reader before starting to develop my material.

One of the many difficulties I encountered in writing about the Mafia is the enormous amount of literature on it published in recent years, especially since the 'Mafia boom' which followed the publication of *The Godfather*. But this accumulation of material is a healthy sign. It may sound absurd, but ten years ago the word 'Mafia' was hardly mentionable, nor indeed was it ever mentioned. Police, officials or Sicilians (who of course had nothing to do with it) did not say the word; it was even hard to find it in written documents—not only Italian, but British or American—even when the concept of the Mafia was described. It was considered a rude, offensive word, a taboo word, a word which could be mentioned only in extreme cases. Substitutes were found: sometimes it was 'that thing', or 'you know, here in Sicily ...'

On the other hand, and here is another pitfall, the word 'Mafia' is a compromise in that there is no such thing in Sicily as a secret organized society called 'the Mafia'. Whenever a mafioso says that he does not know what the Mafia is, he is not lying. The concept of a secret sect irritates him and perhaps he enjoys pronouncing at trials the only piece of truth he offers, and which is never believed: 'I don't know what the Mafia is.'

Mafia is a way of thinking, a way of life which is peculiarly Sicilian. Its code is based on traditions and customs which every Sicilian has inherited. The average Sicilian, even a great enemy of the criminals, could be described as mafioso because he naturally knows those laws just as the average Englishman has an introspective nature and a fair complexion. The word 'Mafia' is now used all the time, often out of context. It is printed daily, used as an adjective, or to describe special rackets like 'the real-estate Mafia', 'the Soho Mafia'. This custom has blurred the original meaning of the word.

But it is healthy that the word should have become part of our language, although the police complain that journalists and novelists alike have inflated the legend of the Mafia and portrayed it as a much more powerful 'organization' than it really is. After all, the police say, it is just a criminal association, or rather, a chain of criminal associations. But although the pattern of the Mafia is getting closer to straightforward gangster activities, the police view is oversimplistic.

In order to see the interesting phenomenon of the Mafia, in perspective, one has to look back at Sicilian history and seek help from sociology. The Mafia too is a result of class struggle, and it is impossible to reject a Marxist vision of history in dealing with this subject, as the social development is the result of economic causes.

Although the police accuse writers of inflating the reputation of the Mafia, it is often true that it is the Mafia itself that spreads legends about itself. These are pitfalls which may swallow not only writers but also the police. They are dangerous especially when there are no data against which to check the true story. The examples of legends spread by *vox populi* are many. There is a very popular story often mentioned in books which deal with the Mafia, and which has been told to me many times. It is about an old 'Capomafia', Vito Cascioferro, who reigned before the advent of Fascism. The only murder he ever committed, the story goes, was the one he *had* to perpetrate with his own hands. When Lieutenant Petrosino of the American police was sent to Sicily to investigate the links between criminal organizations in the USA and Sicily, Cascioferro felt that he had been personally challenged in his authority as Capomafia. As the ship was docking, Cascioferro, who was having lunch at a smart Member of Parliament's house, asked his coachman to drive him to the harbour. There he waited for Petrosino, who was arriving incognito. Cascioferro shot him and then was driven back to finish his lunch in the company of beautiful ladies, aristocratic gentlemen, and his host, the MP. No one ever dared to bear witness against Cascioferro, even though he had shot the policeman so openly, and in day-time.

In fact I recollect that the first time I heard this version of the story was when I was a child and my father, who had otherwise no interest in the Mafia, told it to me with a sort of admiration for the daring Capomafia.

What actually happened is totally different from the legend, yet has a few points which link it to the truth. Cascioferro had committed many murders, but not that of Petrosino, which he commissioned from two professional killers. Also Petrosino had been in Palermo for several days before he was shot, and unhappily, his presence there was no secret. Moreover, the American policeman was shot at night, lured into a trap by two men who had promised to give him evidence against several criminals, including Cascioferro himself. After the policeman's murder, which caused an enormous scandal on both sides of the Atlantic, Cascioferro went into hiding in the house of an MP friend of his.

One can detect in the false—and better-known—version of the story (one of many examples of Mafia legends) a desire to enhance the power and the nobility of the old mafioso who easily outwitted the experienced American policeman: an old mafioso who has never killed, but chooses to shoot Petrosino personally as a self-elected judge. Not only that, but he has to deal with the American policeman himself because they are on an equal level. Cascioferro is having lunch with an MP and beautiful Sicilian ladies: he is protected by the aristocracy, politics and society, and by participating in the social gathering he underlines the ease with which he attends to this piece of Mafia justice. Nobody bears witness against him, neither the Sicilians who are waiting for the ship, nor the foreigners on the ship, who understand Cascioferro's great power and authority. In this legend, the murder becomes a challenge to the Law, something dear to all Sicilians. The fabricated version of Petrosino's murder is, in synthesis, the apotheosis of Mafia glamour. The reality shows instead the Mafia's real face—the cowardly sheltering with an MP (elected to Parliament with Cascioferro's support), the hiring of killers, the old criminal at work, but well protected.

Written documents are few (especially before the nineteenth century) and even those are partial: no mafioso has ever written down his story in the past and when he has (in the present) he has naturally written a pack of lies. So every source of information hides a trap.

Sometimes the spoken word is a genuine expression of feelings, but facts are doubtful; the old mafiosi are not reticent in telling stories about the 'good old days', but they can be biased.

War and calamities have destroyed police files and archives; but often a popular revolt has been a good excuse for destroying records, a move which underlines the real nature of many a Sicilian 'popular' revolt. The *Catasto* (the Property Office) in Palermo, for example, was destroyed in 1820, 1837 and 1848; the *Registri della Pretura* were destroyed in 1943, and more recently other 'popular disorders' wiped away much evidence in the Records Office at Agrigento.

Both police and Carabinieri in Palermo are often generous sources of information, but since they receive their facts from informers who would never give their names or turn up at trials, they have no proof. Not only is the lack of evidence a serious obstacle for both police and writers, but also we often know who has ordered a specific murder without being able to understand the motive. To establish the motivation behind Mafia crimes is one of the most difficult tasks of the magistracy and of a writer, and far too often trials end in acquittals for this very reason.

Other important sources of knowledge are the so-called Mafia lawyers, many of whom know far more than the police and 'Mafiologists' put together.

In some cases Sicilian lawyers are conniving fabricators of alibis and even worse criminals than their clients. At times they give the wrong information to help their clients and to discredit the police and the judiciary. The most thriving trade on the island is crime: criminals are the richest people, and there are plenty of them. Becoming a 'Mafia lawyer' is therefore very lucrative. It is also true that since a successful mafioso's dream is to see his sons in professions like medicine, law or the administration, it is not uncommon for lawyers themselves to belong to mafioso families. Anyway the mafiosi, those who survive, are cunning, skilled at avoiding punishment and likely to win in the courts. They are also likely to pay most of their illicit gains to their lawyers. And the lawyers, being Sicilian, have a natural dislike of and disbelief in the Law, even if they should have been trained to believe in it.

There is another difficulty. As so-called progress moves ahead, the changes within the Mafia are so fast that whenever police and public grasp a situation the scene in the meantime has already changed several times: several 'generations' of Mafia-bosses have been killed, and what we consider 'news' already belongs to the past. For example, when I found myself with a group of mafiosi in 1970, I spent most of my time with those whom police and public opinion considered the real 'bosses' and disregarded the 'small fry', among whom was a tall man called Calò (now at large), always impeccably dressed in a camel-hair coat and smart suits. Now it turns out that Calò is one of the Mafia bosses of the 1968–72 period—something which no one knew at the time.

The Mafia's propaganda succeeds at times, and one encounters curiously glamorous visions of those men, but it should be remembered that the life of a mafioso is often miserable, even when it does not end in violence. And the difficulty in writing is sometimes to be found in oneself: at times the writer forgets professional impartiality and either leans too much on the side of the police or on that of the criminal. Of course so much depends on the individual mafioso or policeman one encounters, and at times there is a symbiosis between the two. It may be the cunning personality of the mafioso which fascinates, or it may be the honesty of a poor policeman fighting his battle with unequal arms. But the Mafia is not glamorous: the Mafia is a subcultural phenomenon which has sprung up from an intricate history of injustice, from unlawful practice of the Law, from misgovernment and mismanagement. That it should be so is a tragedy. But that the mafiosi should take such a large slice of the meagre Western Sicilian economy, is a waste. It is even sadder that the trade of crime employs a considerable proportion of a population which I regard as outstandingly alert, quick, and intelligent. Sicilian culture seems to bypass Italy; in literature this is very apparent: Pirandello's world is linked to German expressionism, Lucio Piccolo to Yeats, Lampedusa to Thomas Mann, Verga's realism to Dickens, and Sciascia's cultural world is French. The Sicilians are almost Anglo-Saxon in their restraint with gestures, in their sparse use of words and sense of privacy. Difficult as it is to generalize, I would say that their quickness in grasping people and situations in a flash is due to an atavistic need to observe, to steal information and see how to put it into use.

Given an outlet and a training, the Sicilians show what drive they have: if one looks up the names of the top men in Italian Northern business, one always finds a Sicilian gnome. A Sicilian working abroad, an emigrant, often avoids saying that he comes from the island because the popular belief is that Sicily is the Mafia and the Mafia is Sicily. But is this true?

PART ONE

Establishment

'Latifundia Trinacriam perdidere'
Pliny: *Historica Naturalis*, III

1 Genesis

When Sicily became part of the new-born state of Italy in 1860 it had been under continual foreign occupation for more than two thousand years. The administrators whose job it was to establish the untried liberal institutions of their brand-new country came up against customs, attitudes and unofficial institutions moulded by a long series of rapacious and frequently repressive regimes which had never succeeded in domesticating the people of Sicily but had bequeathed many of their own worst attributes. To the outsider, Sicilian society appeared brutal, corrupt and secretive. It was not difficult to lump these qualities together, and in fact it was during the decade of 1860–70 that the myth of a 'secret society' was born and baptized. Italy, and soon Europe, discovered 'the Mafia'.

The history of the myth can be traced quite accurately, and is one of the themes of this book. The history of the reality it conceals, both in its ancient roots and in its modern developments, is a lot more elusive. I shall not attempt to provide a comprehensive historical survey of Sicily, but I would like to point to some of the key episodes in its sociological and 'criminal' history and to offer an explanation of why Sicilian society followed a different course of evolution even from others which were temperamentally and geographically close (like Naples and Spain); how it remained a feudal society—one with a number of features in common with Ireland; and why it developed such a reflexive distrust for any kind of official, legal institution that illegality became the rule.

Sicily's wealth and strategic position gave the island vital importance in ancient times. It was a central point from which to control trade and warfare in the Mediterranean, and the Mediterranean basin was the centre of the old world. But Sicily was too small to maintain its

3

independence (it is less than half the size of Ireland). Consequently it
could never be secure, and could only be at best a prize possession and
at worst a bone of contention. Little by little its forests were cut down
to build ships for foreign fleets, its territory became a battlefield for alien
causes and peoples, and its inhabitants became the natural enemies of
any foreign rule, indeed eventually of any rule at all, even that of their
own feudal lords. A number of proverbs express their attitude:

> *A liggi e pi ricca*
> *La furca e pri lu poveru*
> *La giustizia pri li fissa.*

(The law is for the rich, the gallows for the poor, and justice for the
fools.)

> *Cu avini dinari e amicizia*
> *teni la giustizia.*

(He who has money and friends has justice too.)

Attracted by Sicily's position and wealth, Carthaginian colonies
settled along the west coast, while the Greeks concentrated mainly on
the south and east. It was Greek rule in Sicily which turned the word
'tyrant' into a pejorative. Forgetting the ethics of their homeland they
already showed that tendency towards brute force that the island seems
to have encouraged.

The Romans took Sicily after the first Punic war and turned it into a
colony and a granary for wheat. It was they who created the *latifundia*,
extensive landed estates, owned by absentee Roman landlords, which set
the pattern of land holding that has plagued the island down to the
present day. Sicily's inability to defend itself had already given rise to an
attitude of passive acceptance of any new domination. Although Roman
rule there was particularly harsh and corrupt it met little of the armed
resistance put up by Gaul and Spain, and there is only one reference to
an outbreak of banditry (around 260 BC), which was probably a peasant
revolt supported by slaves. Roman corruption is far better documented,
and the episode of the trial of Gaius Verres, known chiefly through
Cicero's five speeches at the trial, is not unique. Verres was governor
of Sicily from 73 to 71 BC. His story reads like those of some contemporary politicians whose strong backing in Rome enables them to
keep their seats and positions in Sicily despite strong evidence of mal-
practices, although they are not so unlucky as to stand trial.

While Christianity was spreading through most of the Mediterranean it made little impact on Sicily, and the island missed its first chance of developing an alternative to the pagan concept of the non-value of human life. As Carlo Levi put it in his famous book, *Christ Stopped at Eboli*—that is, in southern Italy. When the Arabs reached Sicily in 826, succeeding the Vandals, the Ostrogoths and the Byzantines, Islam made easy converts, particularly in Western Sicily, then as now much further removed from the influences of the mainland.

The Arabs stayed for two centuries, and left deep traces, again mainly in Western Sicily. They brought literature, art and sciences, irrigation, oranges, a civilization that the island had never known before. Even under their Christian successors they continued to occupy high positions in Palermo. Other Arab customs made further contributions to the island's growing store of damaging conventions: they reinforced the notion of the cheapness of life, of private violence as a means for redressing wrongs, and of women as an inferior species. The Arabs also left behind something of their own proud and exaggerated individualism.

The Norman conquest of 1060 brought Sicily 'back' to Europe after its African span of life when Pope Nicholas II authorized Robert Guiscard to govern as much of Southern Italy as he could conquer. Robert's brother Roger embarked on the conquest of Sicily, and was master of the north-eastern part of the island by 1064. During the long ensuing tug-of-war with the Papacy, which claimed suzerainty of Sicily, once again the native population proved more submissive to its immediate occupiers than to the mainland. Yet the Normans were hard masters, and murder, freebooting and slavery were rife.

Roger's first step was to seize the land: '*Ego dominus omnium locorum et totius insulae Siciliae.*' He resumed the process of colonization which had ceased with the Arabs, endowing bishoprics and monasteries and distributing fiefs to his own soldiers. In his book *The Mafia in a Sicilian Village*, Anton Blok describes how such feudal regimes contain the seeds of their own destruction:

... through grants of land in return for military services, vassals increase their independence from the central ruler ... the authority of the king, ultimately, depends upon the likelihood that vassals will remain loyal to their oaths of fealty: to control a rebellious vassal or to protect a loyal one, the king has to rely on the allegiance and support of his other vassals. We know that he was often unable to do so.

The crown gave away most of its land to the Sicilian barons in order to appease them, until no new land was available. As the barons grew progressively less dependent on their kings they succeeded in transforming the fief into a private domain with its own retainers, inheritable within the family, but not saleable without the crown's consent. Thus it was the barons who ultimately controlled the crown, whose weakness under the Norman and subsequent feudal regimes resulted in the absence of effective centralized government and the rise of a landowning aristocracy too powerful to uproot and with a vested interest in reaction.

Norman rule was succeeded by a brief Hohenstaufen interlude until Charles of Anjou was crowned king of Sicily in 1266. As Steven Runciman remarks in *The Sicilian Vespers*: 'It was probable that Charles, like so many conquerors of Southern Italy, believed the country [Sicily] to be naturally richer than it was and he underestimated the Southerners' individualism and their dislike of working hard for an alien master.' Resistance to Charles's heavy-handed absentee rule culminated in the uprising of 1282 known as the Sicilian Vespers, although there is evidence to suggest that this was no more a true revolutionary popular movement than earlier revolts under the Norman William I, which had been baronial moves to regain lost privileges or extort new ones.

The Sicilian Vespers have been characterized by Denis Mack Smith as 'one of dozens of popular revolts which shows that, even in the cities, many powerful forces existed of which central government had little understanding'. The Sicilians had grown used to welcoming new rulers, an opportunity for families or towns to seek to improve their private interests. History had schooled them in conspiracy and in conspiratorial groupings. The family itself, partly under Arab influence, constituted a tight-knit protective group with interests extending much further beyond the ties of simple affection than elsewhere in Europe. Private interest, the family, and later the guilds—it was through these kinds of institution that Sicilian society came to express itself.

Soon after the massacre of the Sicilian Vespers the island submitted to Aragonese rule. Now it was the turn of the Aragonese aristocracy to receive Sicilian feudal estates, and Spanish Viceroys stood in for another line of absentee kings. The Spanish presence meant that Sicily was to miss the tide of the Italian Renaissance, with all that it might have offered in political as well as artistic and scientific developments. Instead the island was to become a backwater: under the Spaniards, central power was further undermined, the annual Parliament was dropped, and noble landowners were free to enforce narrow sectional ambitions. In the struggle between them and the king, in the person of his Viceroys, the local, de facto power structure was bound to prevail, and any attempt to change it might easily stoke up discontent to the point of another rising and another change of rulers. Sicily was easier to have than to hold.

If the Aragonese failures in Sicily were mainly those of omission, however, their presence was to add a further ingredient to the island's growing stock of tainted traditions. In 1487 the Spanish Inquisition installed itself in Palermo. Naples had successfully resisted its introduction; the Sicilians accepted it and turned it into an institution whose methods and purposes identify it as a Mafia prototype. The 'relations of the Inquisition' (*i familiari*) held the power of life and death over ordinary Sicilians and used it to their private advantage. Viceroys protested that the Inquisition shielded 'all the rich nobles and rich criminals of the kingdom', but it retained the support of Spanish kings who found it a useful tool for keeping Sicilians in fear of one another by means of terror and a widespread network of informers. Its function in the machinery of power was as essential as that of the Mafia today, and just as invulnerable.

By 1525 the Inquisition was already strong enough to force the Viceroy to pass a law exempting those hundreds of privileged individuals from taxation and from the rule of law. They were responsible to no other institution—'*ab omnia alia jurisdictione exempti*'—and could be tried only by a special tribunal, whether for civil or for criminal matters. When these privileges were later extended to members of their retinue the Familiari could kill, steal or blackmail with impunity, and had the ultimate weapon of denunciation, which generally meant death and confiscation of the victim's property in favour of the Familiari themselves. In 1577 the Viceroy Marco Antonio Colonna estimated that the Inquisition had at least 24,000 'employees' in Sicily, 14,000 of them in Palermo, where the palace of the Inquisition still stands in the Piazza Marina. Although chroniclers suggest that the Sicilians enjoyed the autos-da-fé, there were several riots directed against the prisons of the Inquisition, and archives were burnt more than once. Even so, it is possible to see these incidents not as expressions of popular dissent but as planned operations to cover the disappearance of compromising documents—still a regular feature of administrative life.

Well into the sixteenth century and beyond, Sicily's special development of the feudal system continued to bedevil the reforming efforts of the few honest Viceroys who reached Palermo. Even Machiavelli described the Sicilian barons as *'uomini al tutto nimici di ogni civilta'*— men totally opposed to any form of civilization. It was a fairly pointless gesture for the Spanish authorities to forbid them to interfere in the elections of towns within the royal demesne: the barons were the only employers. A Viceroy who attempted to curtail their prerogatives would simply become 'unpopular'.

In 1611 the latest Viceroy, the Duke of Ossuna, wrote to the king that assassination was rife throughout the island, and that murderers were cheap to hire and protected from the law by their aristocratic employers. 'No one is safe,' Ossuna went on, 'even in his own house. This kingdom recognizes neither God nor His Majesty; everything is for sale, including the lives and possessions of the poor, the estates of the King, and justice itself ...' The sale of jobs and justice was as common then as now. Sicilians despised honesty and regarded public office as a source of private advantage, bribery and perjury as normal legal processes. Sicily was by no means the only country in Europe where a judge could buy his office as a hereditary property, but elsewhere there were the beginnings at least of centralized structures of law enforcement.

It was the power of the barons, the threat of the Inquisition and the total corruption of the legal system which determined the function of the city guilds, which became very powerful in the sixteenth century. Starting as the same medieval institutions which trained apprentices, protected guild members and represented the trade's interest as they did in the rest of Europe, the Sicilian guilds turned into societies to enforce their own justice and protect their interests by any means available. Because they were closed monopolies with inherited privileges (such as the right to bear arms), they never served the cause of the common people. They were to grow into an influential political force, however, whose power was felt in the revolts of 1647, 1708 and 1773. At the latter date they were used as an auxiliary police force, and their bullying methods administered rough, Mafia-style justice. Typically, their statutes contained provisions such as: 'The guild will pay for the expenses of a lawyer and the keeping of the family of any member who may be sentenced for some crime.'

The situation in the rural interior had been chaotic when Aragon took over Sicily. The peasants lived in a state of slavery. Many of them spoke

Arabic and dressed in Eastern style. Their masters, the barons, held every kind of feudal monopoly, whether for making bread, slaughtering animals or pressing wine and oil; they also had their own private courts and prisons. Again, these were standard practices elsewhere in Europe, but again there were no countervailing traditions. The *latifundia* tenures excluded village or communal rights and landholdings, the aristocracy were out of control of the monarchy and free to squeeze their peasants unmercifully. As the land grew ever poorer the barons' greed only increased. Unlike their opposite numbers in other countries they never considered it useful to plough any of their revenue back into the land.

Banditry was endemic in Europe. In Sicily it rooted deeper and lasted longer. When the Spaniards, unable to enlist Sicilian troops, organized a popular militia to maintain a degree of order, they paid only the captains and the sergeant-majors. The result was that these armed units designed to combat banditry became in effect a body of legalized bandits. The illegal rival bands were generally formed by farmers who had resisted extortionate baronial demands; this gained them prestige with the peasants, who saw in them the only feasible form of rebellion against their masters. The effect was to reinforce the system of Sicilian counter-morality.

In the sixteenth century we have records of armed men who committed murders and kidnappings and stole cattle. One bandit who operated around Palermo in 1560 was Agnello. He had his own flag, with a skull drawn on it. The peasants kept him informed about police movements, and he gave a certain amount to the poor, to keep them on his side. Another bandit was Saponara, whom I mention because his fate has exact parallels in the twentieth century. In 1578 he was captured and put into solitary confinement, where he died of poison. Some powerful individual must have been afraid that he would talk, because bandits had much to tell. At times they were used by the barons against other feudal lords, or to intimidate fractious peasants. When they outlived their usefulness or started to be troublesome, the barons would betray them to the law, or have them killed. The Mafia were to use the same tactics with Giuliano, and to exploit the Sicilian tendency to regard the bandit as a rebel against society, a fighter for his country's independence, a defender of the poor against the rich. The attitude persisted even though the bandits frequently aligned themselves with the exploiters of the poor. A similar misguided mythology continues to protect organized exploitation under a cloak of romantic resistance to authority.

But the real authority in rural Sicily was allowed to come into existence by the idleness and snobbery of the nobility, who lived mostly in Palermo to be near the Court. They were absentee landlords, unwilling or unable to manage their own estates, and therefore leaving a vacuum which was filled by the formation of a new class of *gabelloti*, or estate managers, to whom they rented their fiefs. The *gabelloto* emerged from the peasantry, and tended to be already established in his locality as a strong man—*uomo inteso*. He exploited the peasantry even more than the barons had done, asserting his new position with brute force and solving any complaint by habitual violence.

The *gabella*—the granting of leaseholds over large areas of land—became common in the eighteenth century after the Congress of Utrecht had confiscated Sicily from the Spaniards in 1713 and awarded it to the Dukes of Savoy. Sicily was to be ruled for five years by the Piedmontese, fourteen by the Austrians, and then by the Neapolitan Bourbons until it was unified with—in fact annexed by—Italy in 1860. These imposed changes of ownership could only confirm the Sicilian suspicions of central authority. They certainly had little effect on the real native power structure, in which the *gabelloti* gradually installed themselves in a central role.

As late as the eighteenth century, 282 out of the 367 Sicilian communities were still under feudal control, which meant that about a third of the island's population of just under two million were under the direct authority of the barons and their middlemen, the *gabelloti*. They in their turn recruited other personnel, naturally from among their kinsmen and friends. Their *uomo di fiducia* (henchman, confidant) was the *soprastante*, who combined the functions of overseer and tax collector. He dealt directly with the peasants, with the assistance of the *campieri*, armed, mounted field-guards, watching over the animals, the crops, and above all the peasantry. The *campieri* dressed and talked in a special way. Their violent methods were the main condition of their employment and made them *uomini di rispettu*, 'men of respect', which in Sicily does not mean that they were respectable but that they commanded respect by terror and murder.

By 1770 the *gabelloti* were being referred to as 'the tyrants of the countryside'. The nobles borrowed more and more money from them, and spent it on conspicuous consumption—to enlarge their palaces in

Palermo, or build new summer residences in the fashionably beautiful locality of Bagheria. Meanwhile their lands deteriorated by natural erosion and deforestation. The *gabelloti* had no interest in improving their leaseholds: they wanted land of their own, still the greatest emblem of power and status. Eventually they might buy it from their own bankrupt noble landlord, one of the 142 princes, 788 marquises and about 1500 dukes and barons still forming a crumbling upper crust at the turn of the century.

It is Sicily's historic disaster to have given birth to a 'middle' class between these feudal remnants and the urban and rural masses which was parasitic upon both. It was formed by the guildsmen, the *familiari* of the Inquisition, the *gabelloti*, the *campieri*, men who had been able to accumulate capital, certainly, but only by violence and extortion. And while it might be argued that most middle classes acquired their capital by dubious means, what is peculiar to Sicily is the rise to power of an alternative class created by passive, non-productive means, progressive neither economically nor politically. Lawyers became rich by delaying cases and fighting against reforms in a legal system discredited even then by complexity and inertia. Artisans merely perpetuated their own privileges by preventing others from joining their guilds. The *gabelloti* battened on the peasantry, middlemen took their cut from trade on pain of disrupting it. None of these had any interest in challenging the authority of the nobility or the corruption of the law. Quite the contrary: their positions depended upon exploiting the nominal power of the nobility, propping up the existing governmental structure and propagating an atmosphere of ignorance and mystery.

Consequently when the peasantry made genuine attempts to rebel it would find both the nobility and the middle class in its way. Often this middle class would deliberately foment peasant grievances into uprisings that undermined any government seeking to change the status quo. Thus in Sicily we find a growing class which was nothing like the French, Milanese, or even the Neapolitan 'bourgeoisies' as we have come to understand the term, new social groupings forced to precipitate change for their own economic and political purposes. The third Sicilian class was bound to use its power and remarkable energies to prevent such changes. The result was a kind of French Revolution in reverse, an enforced stagnation which went against the current of the age and was to keep Sicily isolated from the great waves of thought and action sweeping through Europe.

This was the experience of the Marquis Caracciolo, whom the Bourbons sent from Naples as Viceroy in 1781. He was a man of the Enlightenment, who had travelled to London and Paris and read Voltaire. Caracciolo wrote that Sicily was inhabited 'only by the oppressors and the oppressed'. He declared private armies illegal, complained that the Sicilian parliament was tyrannical and represented only the nobility, reformed the guilds and suppressed the Inquisition (1782). The advice he received from 'the highest people in the magistrature' was: 'Here they want to govern by themselves. Let them be. Follow the example of your predecessors.' Reforms in the interest of Sicily were seen as an enforcement of Neapolitan will, and Caracciolo was so unpopular that he was recalled after only five years, and his memory is still hated in Sicily.

But the Napoleonic era brought the wind of change even to the coasts of Sicily. With Napoleon threatening the Mediterranean, the only salvation for the Bourbons was to ally themselves with the British. When the French invaded Naples, King Ferdinand fled to Palermo on board Nelson's flagship. His Austrian queen hated the Sicilians, and it was his first visit to the island in forty years of rule. In 1812 he granted Sicily a constitution under which Parliament was given more power than the Crown. In an attempt to defeat the native landowning aristocracy, feudal rights and privileges were abolished and the peasants were offered better conditions and land of their own. In 1820 the Bourbons abolished entails and *maggiorasco*—primogeniture—which had exacerbated the island's problems by preventing division of the *latifundia* and channelling generations of landless younger sons into the growing stratum of unproductive parasites.

Ferdinand's actions turned the Sicilian upper class against himself and his descendants, even though when the peasants started claiming their new rights he authorized the formation of armed bands contracted to maintain public order, which meant keeping the peasants in their place. No full-scale Sicilian resistance followed the Neapolitan revolution against Ferdinand in 1820–1, except for isolated incidents during which official records were burnt, as usual. And while hostility to Naples did produce a new desire for political change, in Sicily this was always plotted by the two upper strata, and revolts and revolutions happened, as Lampedusa explains so brilliantly in *The Leopard*, in order that things should *not* change.

'Many authors,' writes Henner Hess in his sociological study of the

Mafia, 'continue to underline the fighting spirit of the Sicilian peasants against [the arbitrary rule of the barons] ... while it would be more important to turn one's attention to their usual passive reaction and their remissive state of subjugation; it is in this that we find the historical grounds which made acceptable to the mass of the arrogance of the single individuals: i.e. the mafiosi.' Instead of the stratum of smallholders which the Bourbons had sought to create to counteract the excessive power of the Sicilian aristocracy and their agents, what emerged in the nineteenth century was a totally impoverished landless peasantry. Between 1812 and 1860 the number of big landowning families multiplied from about 2000 to 20,000. It was the Mafia elements who thus clawed their way upwards, and the peasants who suffered. Their only outlet was brigandage, which became endemic, with severe outbreaks in 1820, 1837, 1848, 1860, 1893 and 1918.

The Companies at Arms (*Compagnie d'Armi*) were the Sicilian solution to rural lawlessness. Being made up of local individuals who did not wear the hated uniform of the Bourbons (and later of the Italians), these twenty-five armed bands had easier access to information and cooperation. They became part of the unofficial power network, and in their own right they extorted protection money and might form ad hoc alliances with criminals. One notorious practice was the *componenda*, an arrangement by which the Captains at Arms approached the criminal to restore part of the stolen goods, and the legitimate owner agreed not to denounce the theft. The criminal would escape prosecution and the Captain at Arms took a rake-off on the deal. This practice still survives, particularly in those provinces (such as Messina and Catania) where the Mafia is not established as the overseer of all transactions. Its worst aspect was that it turned the representatives of the law into criminal accessories, leaving the State without a formal role.

The all-pervasive nature of criminal activity in Sicily is described in a much-quoted report sent by the Bourbon administrator Pietro Callà Ulloa to the Neapolitan Minister of Justice in 1838. It is an accurate account of the kinds of activity and mentality soon to be dubbed 'Mafia':

There is not a single clerk in Sicily who is not ready to obey the whims of a dominating man and who has not thought of gaining illicitly from using public office. This general corruption has forced the populace to resort to exceedingly strange and dangerous methods.

In many villages there exist unions or Brotherhoods, kinds of sects which call themselves 'parties' without a political identification or aim, which do not meet, with no other link but that of dependence from a head who is here a landowner, there an archbishop. A common fund provides for their needs, at times to get rid of a civil servant, at others to defend him, or to protect an official or accuse an innocent man. All these are kinds of small governments within the Government. The lack of police has caused the multiplication of crimes; the populace has come to a tacit agreement with the criminals ... Therefore many landowners have chosen to become the oppressors rather than the oppressed, and they join these parties. Many high magistrates ... protect these brotherhoods with an impenetrable network. It is impossible to compel the city guards to search the streets, nor to find witnesses for crimes which happened in daytime. At the centre of such a state of corruption there is a capital with its luxury and its feudal pretensions, a city in which there live 40,000 proletarians, and their livelihood depends on the luxury and whims of the rich. In this umbilical capital of Sicily, public office is on sale, justice is corrupt, ignorance is encouraged ...

Palermo was then, and always has been, the centre of criminal activity, because wealth and administrative power was concentrated there. As the nobles drifted away from their estates to live near the Court, the peasants followed them. Palermo was, with Naples, the largest city in Italy—a real capital. Annexation to Italy was to reduce both the South and its two great cities to provincial obscurity. Palermo has retained its corruption but lost the beauty described by Goethe in his *Italian Journey*. It was cut off from other Sicilian cities because of the lack of roads, but open to the world through its harbour, through which passed writers and travellers, kings and queens. They found a city divided then as now into quarters whose inhabitants still speak different dialects and have a strong sense of identity. The quarters include the Punic-Norman Cassaro (from the Arabic *Al-Qasr*, castle), the Arab Kalsa, the Albergheria, the Amalfitano, Seralcadio, il Capo etc. They have their own markets—suks in spirit and appearance, and in name in the case of the Lattarini, which was once the Suk-el-Atarin. From time to time these markets become the scene of appalling murders as rival mafioso groups fight for control: peace means that the local boss is well entrenched.

1. 1875 The bandit Patti, shot by the police after he had outlived his usefulness to the Mafia (*Archives Museo Pitrè*)

2. 1890 A typical threatening letter from the Mafia: 'Friend, We have seen that you are not a man of your word, and that you made a mistake but take care. You are not dealing with the kind of people you think. We warn you that if on Saturday morning always at the same spot which we indicated. Take care not to miss the appointment because you will be followed and stabbed, you and any of your family. You have understood, you scum, do not fail on pain of death. Friends.' (*Archives Museo Pitrè*)

AMICO

ABIAMO VISTO CHE SIETE UN
BARABUTTO, E VISIETE SBAGLIATO
MA BADATE CHE NON AVETE DA FAR
E CON AGENTE COME VOI VICREDATE
VI AVVERTIAMO CHE SE SABBATO MAT
TINA SEMPRE ALL OSTESSO PUNTO
DA NOI DESENATO BADATE DI NON
MACARE AL PUNTAMENTO PERCHE
SARETE PEDENATO E PUGNALATO
VOI E CHIUNQUE DELLA VOSTRA
FAMIGLIA AVETE CAPITO GRA
SCHIFOSO

NON MANCATE PENA
DI MORTE

A MICI

3. 1902 Don Vito Cascioferro with his son: Don Vito was the first organizer of the Cosche (*Gigi Petyx*)

4. 1923 Prefect Cesare Mori, Mussolini's envoy to Sicily with instructions to eradicate the Mafia (*Gigi Petyx*)

The last Bourbon kings oscillated between repression and reform, neither of them welcome to those in power in Sicily. With the Risorgimento well under way on the Italian mainland, the island became ripe for another change of regime. But there was great confusion of aims among the Sicilians: some wanted annexation, others were separatists, others merely anti-Bourbon. Italian patriots were naturally few in a land which had seldom been in contact with the mainland and the North, and where the majority of the peasantry had never heard the word 'Italy', any more than had many of their descendants according to an inquiry conducted by Danilo Dolci in 1959. Different concepts of the new Italy also animated the driving forces behind King Victor Emmanuel II. His prime minister, Count Cavour, envisaged a bourgeois state achieved by diplomatic means. Garibaldi was for a democratic populist monarchy won by force of arms. He saw Sicily as an ideal base to start the liberation and unification of Italy, and his follower Francesco Crispi was sent to foment a rebellion. Any means justified Crispi's ends, as he was to show later when he became Prime Minister and armed bands, Mafia gangs and freed criminals became 'Italian patriots'. Cavour's contribution was to promise self-government for Sicily, even if annexed by Piedmont.

On 11 May 1860, five weeks after the initial Sicilian rising, Garibaldi landed at Marsala with a thousand men and proclaimed himself dictator of Sicily, ruling on behalf of King Victor Emmanuel. His thousand became many more, some fighting for new hopes, others for loot, others for the settlement of old scores. A Venetian officer wrote: 'The Sicilian revolution turns out to be little more than country bands ... composed for the most part of notorious bandits who fight the government just as an excuse to fight the landowners.' To many of the *picciotti*— 'brave young men'—Garibaldi seemed cast in a mould dear to Sicilians: they rallied to the image of the bold, flamboyant leader described in a contemporary song:

> *Quannu talia, Gesu Cristu pari,*
> *quanna cumanna Carlomagnu vero ...*

(When he appears, he looks like Jesus Christ. When he leads, a real Charlemagne ....)

As Sicily was liberated from Bourbon rule, Garibaldi nominated as district governors men who belonged to the upper strata. With a few exceptions they took advantage of the 'full powers' they received to back bullying methods and to install their own men in the new municipal jobs and key posts. There was a period of chaos which saw a growing incidence of looting, arson and murder.

Goodwin, the British consul, analysed the familiar characteristics of any Sicilian revolt in his diary, although he had not foreseen that the events of 1860 might become a class revolution. He noted how passion and excitement at the beginning were followed by disorganization in the absence of a sense of public self-sacrifice. The Sicilian attitude of cynicism and deceit remained unchanged: in the legal system, mal-administration continued, as did bribery and corruption. Road-building and public works in general came to a halt due to 'the monstrous centralization'. The clergy too were extremely corrupt, and the people ignorant and subject to grinding taxation. Their condition remained the same even though the coming of Garibaldi gave them a welcome Sicilian feeling of having no government. In the interior, bands of *picciotti* were becoming a 'nuisance', raiding the countryside without control. There was an eruption of large-scale cattle-theft (*abigeato*), always common in southern Italy because the scarcity of pasture necessitated migration of animals and ruled out fences.

A new kind of money, new laws, new weights and measures (although Sicilians talk to this day of *onze* and *salme*) and almost a new language were imposed on Sicily. Cavour's promise was broken, and self-government never came. Fourteen days after Garibaldi's triumphal entry into Naples, on the heels of the fleeing King Francis and his queen, a plebiscite was held in Sicily. Only the literate could vote. (In 1861 the national Italian electorate comprised less than two per cent of the population; in Sicily it was just over one per cent. The franchise was enlarged in 1882 to include five per cent of a Sicilian population of about three million, and Giolitti's introduction of so-called universal male suffrage in 1913 raised it to a mere twenty-five per cent. Real universal suffrage arrived in 1946.) An overwhelming ninety-five and a half per cent of Sicily's one per cent voted for unification with Italy under King Victor Emmanuel, and the chief of police at Modica (Ragusa) referred to the electoral abuses perpetrated on behalf of unification in a note to the central government dated 26 October 1860: 'It became legal to bring to the voters' houses documents carrying the names of those who had to be elected as deputies, with the threat that if others who were not mentioned were to be named they would suffer.'

The gentry and middle strata (*gabelloti* etc) deserted Garibaldi and sided with Cavour and the House of Savoy, who had an equally pressing interest in forestalling the social revolution which found in Garibaldi its symbol and hero. The historian Rosario Romeo wrote that 'if the Risorgimento in the North was the social revolution of a bourgeoisie active in the development of capitalism against the old landowning classes, in the South and Sicily, on the other hand, it was the old landowning classes *and their allies* which fought the battles of the Risorgimento, with notorious consequences for the structure of the ruling classes of united Italy' (my italics).

Today most historians insist that the Mafia was born in 1860 with the unification of Sicily and Italy. The foregoing pages, necessarily highly selective, are intended to illustrate an alternative account, and to show that every feature of Mafia philosophy and practice was present and functioning long before that date. Crime and exploitation had become the natural element and expression of the Sicilian power structure. Nevertheless the island's criminal networks and associations were bound to adjust their forms and methods to retain control in a changing society. They had bored into and occasionally undermined the institutions and administrations of centuries of foreign rulers. Now that a constitutional State and an elected parliament had been established, with their own assistance, these were to prove easier to infiltrate and manipulate than the more tyrannical regimes of the past. In 1860 the old wine was poured into new bottles; it did not change its nature.

Union with Italy was a crucial step in the rise to public power of Sicily's special kind of middle class. 'I have understood perfectly well,' says the 'Principone' of *The Leopard* to the mafioso Russo. 'You don't want to destroy us, your "fathers". You only want to take our place.' The barons and nobility as the source of protection gave way slowly to the parliamentarians, and Mafia groups were to infiltrate political power as far as parliament in Rome, while Palermo remained merely a centre of provincial administration.

Anton Blok traces the development of the Mafia in the nineteenth and twentieth centuries from a situation in which 'the modern State superimposed itself on a marginal peasant society which was still largely feudal in its basic features.' He argues that the mafioso must be considered as 'a variety of the political middleman or broker, since his *raison d'être* is predicated upon his capacity to acquire and maintain control over the paths linking the local infrastructure of the village to the superstructure of the larger society'. This control was and is ensured by the systematic threat and practice of violence.

Northern policemen and *prefetti* tended to arrive in Sicily quite ignorant of local conditions. They would see the various criminal groups and processes as evidence of a unified sect, a secret organization with a mastermind at its head. This interpretation was in keeping with the 'romantic' mood of the times, and with the undoubted fact that the Risorgimento had been furthered by the activity of true secret societies like the Carbonari. Therefore reports began reaching Rome from Sicily which talked about 'a kind of *camorra*'*, and in 1865 a dispatch from the Prefect Marchese Filippo Gualtino used the word 'Mafia' in this context for the first time. We are obliged to use the word for the sake of convenience, and before pursuing the history of the phenomenon itself its baptism in the 1860s provides the opportunity to investigate its birth as well as some of its associated terminology and structures.

* The nineteenth-century Neapolitan secret society.

2 Anatomy of the Mafia

Gualtino saw 'the Mafia' as an especially virulent kind of criminal secret society. It was a convenient hypothesis, and easy to arrive at. Naples had seen the rise and fall of the Carbonari, but continued to suffer from the activities of the Camorra till as late as 1911, when forty of its chiefs were tried and convicted. Furthermore, Sicily had always been a breeding ground for true secret societies. In the late eighteenth century the Marquis Villabianca had referred in his voluminous and fascinating diary to a 'vindictive' society known as the *Beati Paoli* and said to date back to the twelfth century. Its members 'prided themselves on dealing with enemies by themselves, with their own hands, evils which were the consequence of the notorious weakness of justice.'* Loose associations existed in various parts of the island, with names such as the *Cudi Chiatti* (Flat Tails), the *Birritti* (the Caps), the *Mano Fraterna* (the Brotherly Hand). Between 1812 and 1818 there had been a bloody political and territorial war between the *Stuppaghieri* of Monreale and the *Fratuzzi* of Bagheria, with thirty men killed.

For an administrator or policeman confronted with the complex criminal machinery of Sicilian society the conspiratorial notion of a mysterious secret entity made a kind of sense, and glossed over any more far-reaching speculations. They saw the symptoms, but diagnosed the wrong disease. If the Mafia were in fact a secret society, it would be long defunct. Even a weak police force would have uncovered names and

* This sect is the subject of the massive nineteenth-century novel *I Beati Paoli*, set in the seventeenth century, during the domination of the house of Savoy. Although it presents a faithful picture of the corruption of the nobility, it seeks to justify the activities of a secret group administering its own 'justice' by stealth and murder. As such it is a romantic glorification of the Mafia spirit presented as bold resistance. It is interesting to note that the novel enjoyed great success when republished very recently in Palermo.

details of its organization, and the Mafia whose rise we have traced is not secret: on the contrary, it thrives on publicity. It has received a great deal of it from successive parliamentary inquiries in the nineteenth and twentieth centuries. None of them located Gualtino's Mafia, but we shall see in their researches how the word 'Mafia' becomes a portmanteau term to describe an intricate network of historical, social and economic ways and attitudes.

'Mafia', then, can be understood as a convenient label pinned to a whole way of life, a living system that develops and changes in the course of time. The related word 'mafioso' can be similarly transcribed. As a noun, it applies to an active representative of that system; as an adjective, to his typical qualities, or to those of the system itself. Both words also present etymological problems, and although what they stand for is only too concrete, their usage continues to plague even contemporary investigators. Because the confusion they cause is quite useful to the Mafia, and characteristically Sicilian, it is worth putting the clock forward to the twentieth century to overhear the following dialogue, in which an official interrogation practically transforms itself into a theological debate. The dialogue took place during the latest and most thorough of the parliamentary inquiries into Sicily's peculiar institution, and the first to have dared include the word Mafia in its title. The speakers are Senator Li Causi, a Communist, then Vice-President of the Antimafia Parliamentary Commission, and the bandit Pasquale Sciortino. Both are Sicilians.

Li Causi: So Salvatore Chiaristi was the recognized head of the Mafia in San Cipiriello ... What does 'Head of the Mafia' mean?

Sciortino: You said something important, you said 'Head of the Mafia', and I ask *you* a question—what does the Mafia mean? Because remember that the Mafia, in our part of the world, is a small word, but it encloses an immensity.

Li Causi: Let's see then.

Sciortino: Because you too have been a mafioso at various times, haven't you? Haven't you?

Li Causi: On the contrary, I represent the Antimafia.

Sciortino: Yes, it's true, today you represent the Antimafia, but there have been times when you have been a mafioso, that is, *you wanted to impose your will on others*. [my italics.]

LI CAUSI: You say that 'Mafia' is a general word. No, Mafia means to organize oneself in order to get illicit gains.

SCIORTINO: I think you have the wrong idea of the Mafia.

LI CAUSI: Very well then, explain.

SCIORTINO: ... The Mafia, let us say, can be compared to God, something which exists, it exists, we know it by faith, but where is God? Everywhere: God is in the air, he is in front of us, God is in all things. But where is the Mafia? Where God is, we believe in it because of faith.

...

SCIORTINO: No, let's get this concept of the Mafia clear ... You make one person or another coincide with the idea of the Mafia; I have another concept of the Mafia, because as a child I heard people talk about it; because mafioso is an individual, let's say the individual who likes to show off in front of others. 'Look what a beautiful face like a *mafiosetto* he has,' for example—it was a popular way of speaking.

LI CAUSI: Yes, in any case these are folkloristic definitions. I was born in Termini Imerese and therefore I grew up in a Mafia environment. I know what the Mafia is because every week in Rome ...

SCIORTINO: Be precise: if you want to interpret the word Mafia as delinquency, then say delinquency, don't say the Mafia.

LI CAUSI: No, no, no.

SCIORTINO: If you want to say burglar then say burglar, don't say the Mafia.

LI CAUSI: No, let me speak. If the mafioso and the Mafia can gain their aims of supremacy by 'legal' means, that is by influencing the power of the state in Sicily, naturally the Mafia hides, but when the day comes when the Mafia does not get what it wants, it kills.

SCIORTINO: I would call such people delinquents. If you want to identify as a mafioso an individual who violates the law and departs from moral principles in order to commit a serious offence against an equal, I say that for me that person is a murderer. And then if you want to call a murderer a mafioso or if there are many murderers who want to associate together, I would call that a criminal association.

...

SCIORTINO: Look, I wanted to say this: as I'm always reading about the oil Mafia, the fruit Mafia, the fish Mafia, I ask myself this question: What is the Mafia? If it is an organization it must be possible to discover it. We would know who they are and who they are not. If there is an organization there is somebody, let's say a boss, an under-boss, associates, officers, under-officers and so on, that is the organization.

This conversation took place on 2 July 1970, when Sciortino had been eighteen years in prison. Like his brother-in-law Salvatore Giuliano, he was a bandit, not a mafioso, although he had continuous contacts with the Mafia of the 1940s, which was a paternalist, agrarian type of Mafia. Senator Li Causi had every right to claim that he represented the Antimafia. He was even shot at and seriously wounded when he dared to hold a political meeting in a village with particularly close mafioso connections. Several points emerge from their exchange. The bandit rightly denies that the Mafia is an organization—that could be unearthed and defeated. On the other hand by refuting the mis-conception he tries to suggest that in Sicily there is no Mafia, merely criminals like anywhere else. Yet he cannot help offering an illuminating definition of 'mafioso', or comparing the concept of the Mafia with that of God—something ubiquitous, a state of mind, a system of thought and action: 'the powers that be', in fact.

Sciortino also indicates that for him, to be 'mafioso' means showing off, playing to the gallery, and this is indeed the original meaning of the Sicilian adjective, which is still used in this sense. It can be heard in the poor districts of Palermo, especially at Borgo. Looking at a little girl who has dressed up and is aware of the power of her good looks, someone might call her '*mafiusella*': pert, but attractively so. One can be welcomed '*mafiosamente*': generously, with good food and a display of wealth. A dress can be '*mafioso*': magnificent. You can even ask the cook in a restaurant for '*un pasto mafioso*'. The adjective was first defined in print by a Sicilian scholar, Pitrè, in his *Usi e costumi, credenze e pregiudizi del popolo siciliano*, published in Palermo in 1899. Applied to a man, he saw the word as involving a sense of absolute autonomy, and con-sequently a refusal to be dominated by others.

'Mafioso' came to be widely used in the sense familiar to non-Sicilians in the mid-nineteenth century. In particular it gained currency with the success of *I mafiusi de la Vicaria*, a play written in the Sicilian dialect by Giuseppe Rizzotto and Gaspare Mosca in 1863. It was so successful that in 1875 it was staged three hundred times, and it is still often played in Palermo. The first two acts are set in the Nuova

Vicaria, the new prison built by the Bourbon King Ferdinand II in 1837, popularly known as the Ucciardone. Here the hero, Joachino Funciazza, is imprisoned. Funciazza was a real Mafia boss, and the authors did not even bother to disguise his name—in fact it was he who suggested the writing of the play and explained the jargon and customs of its subjects, the mafiosi, strutting, defiant bullies.

Inside the prison a mafioso group imposes law and takes a rake-off on all transactions. Funciazza intervenes whenever the rule of the *sucività* (the society, that is the Mafia of the prison) is flouted. The jailer goes out of his way to favour the mafiosi, allowing messages to be passed in and out, and even smuggling parcels of food, clothes and arms. There is also an incognito character, a politician persecuted by the Bourbons, and portrayed as a 'goody'. He was meant to be the Sicilian socialist leader Crispi, later to exploit the Mafia machinery in local and national elections as prime minister of the united Italy.

It is unlikely that the play disclosed anything new to its public when it was first performed, but it put into focus many details, such as the custom of giving nicknames to 'in' people, special slang and dress, the unwritten laws, the way a boss could be recognized as an authority, the rough justice he enforced and the silence (*omertà*) which surrounded him. All these are aspects of what came to be known as 'the Mafia'.

The third act is less interesting, and was added later, after the great success of the play. In it we see the mafioso back in his official job of innkeeper, leading a normal life after paying his dues to Justice. It has been suggested that the authors added this act in order to placate the Mafia, which had been offended by the amount of details given away. In fact it was written to play down the glamour of the Mafia, so as not to offend the police of the new Italian state. In giving away those details, Funciazza the man behaved in a typical mafioso manner: the play's description of defiant strength is just the kind of publicity the Mafia likes and needs to enhance its prestige and authority.

If the play crystallized the special use of the adjective mafioso, the real origin of the noun Mafia is controversial—assuming that the substantive precedes the adjective, and is not a back-formation. Some scholars have traced the word to the Arab *Mahias* (daring), or to the name of the Arab tribe *Ma afir*, which occupied Palermo in pre-Norman days. Others point out that the Arabic *mu* means 'safety' and that the verb *afah* means 'to protect': *mu afah* would therefore refer to the Mafia seen as a clan offering protection to its members. A host of more obscure or fanciful theories can be safely overlooked.* It is in fact likely that the word has an Arab ancestry. Certainly it is old enough to be found as the nickname of a witch, Catarina La Licatisa, '*nomata ancor Maffia*', who was burnt in an auto-da-fé in Palermo in 1658. But the most likely sources of the noun are the Arab 'mafie' (*maha* or *mahias hajar*), rock caves in the area of Trapani and Marsala, which were used by Saracens, later by bandits, and finally by secret groups and bands of anti-Bourbon volunteers. The local dialect transformed the sound *mahias* into Mafia.

In the guerrilla warfare against the Bourbons, many who were in trouble with the law saw the advantage of becoming 'patriots'; some were straightforward criminals who had everything to gain from a change of regime. Here we are brought face to face yet again with what Li Causi calls 'folkloristic definitions' in his debate with the bandit Sciortino. Outlaws in Sicily have always been regarded as heroes defying foreign rule, law-makers rather than law-breakers. The island never lost the medieval way of thinking which held that a man must protect himself and his possessions by his own personal influence and courage, regardless of the law's authority. Ruthless courage and self-assertive exhibitionism become admirable qualities in the light of such a belief. Add to this the romantic nineteenth-century respect for anarchic individualism and independence, and even murder and terror become glamorous. Many Sicilians still look up to the capomafia as the embodiment of Sicilian resistance.

It is as though the spirit of resistance reached a new level under Italian rule, and came to represent the actual mind and body of Sicily, with the mafiosi as the will and ultimate government. Every Italian

* There are also eccentric theories, many of which still find their way on to the printed pages of semi-serious books and newspapers. For example, the initial letters of the phrase: Morte Alla Francia Italia Anela, which is supposed to have been coined during the Sicilian Vespers (1282). But the Sicilians didn't speak Italian then and the concept of a United Italy hardly existed. Another motto of the same nature is: Mazzini Autorizza Furti Incendi Avvelanamenti. This would have been coined during the Risorgimento as an order sent by the exiled Mazzini to sabotage the Bourbon regime, and those who obeyed him by 'perpetrating robberies, arson and poisoning' became known as the M.A.F.I.A. Perhaps the latter was invented in the North, during the late 1850s. The Risorgimento had a mania for using initials as a sort of code which gave a different and secret meaning. For example, the cry of the Milanese, 'Viva Verdi', was meant to sound innocuous to the Austrians but was understood by the Italians as 'Viva Vittorio Emanuele Re D'Italia'.

legal institution was duplicated by their activities, and a protection racket is a form of taxation. Where the police could not guarantee immunity against burglary or kidnapping, or recover stolen goods, the mafiosi could. Where the slow, expensive process of the legal system could not ensure justice, they administered their own—rough, perhaps, but quick and effective. Work too was in their gift, and recently Fiat received a list of all the names of those to be employed before its factory at Termini Imerese had even been built.

The executives of the Sicilian counter-government obviously had different sources of revenue in the nineteenth century, but allowing for changes in technique, their character and methods remain much the same. A consistent psychological profile of the mafioso emerges, although it must be pointed out that many of its features coincide with those of the Sicilian character in general. In conversation he speaks little and carefully (small talk is almost non-existent), and like any 'big' politician or industrialist he prefers to ask questions rather than make statements. His stock in trade is information: I found that a 'boss' who had been isolated in banishment for some years had a detailed knowledge of my work, my husband, even my political views. In a book published in 1956, Renato Candida, a retired police officer, writes: 'The mafioso ... does not reveal his thoughts except to other mafiosi equal or superior to him; he wants, intends and pretends to know everything from the others whom he keeps in subjection ... even the smallest and most intimate family secret ... He talks little because he absorbs everything, like an insatiable sponge, without ever betraying his own thoughts.'

Candida goes on to describe the mafioso as a man who profoundly despises all legality and State authority but is always ready both to kiss the hand of anybody stronger than himself and to shoot him in the back at any moment. Mafiosi, he claims, 'are generally landowners, *gabelloti*, guardians of landed property, bodyguards, guardians of sulphur mines, mediators, real estate developers, solicitors, chemists, surveyors, occasionally doctors, and lawyers.' (In fact, the middle class.) Here Candida is describing the mafioso who has already 'arrived' and wants to legalize his activities and position, but he may well have started his career as a shepherd, a carter, or a hired killer.

The mafioso must be respected and revered, so he will display all the emblems of position. The Boss dresses with care, is generous, and has close relations with officials. Nowadays he drives fast cars. He has mistresses, but is morbidly attached to his family and children, and scowls at the mention of divorce. The modern mafioso needs greater flexibility and technical knowhow about his chosen fields of action than his nineteenth-century counterpart. Like him, he will be eliminated by his best friend, his lieutenant—the shot in the back is more common than the one in the chest, and he lives with this knowledge. So does his public. The name of an important mafioso is as famous in Sicily as a film star's. A popular Sicilian ballad glorifies the mafioso:

> *Iu sugno n'eriva cantuzzica a ttutti,*
> *eccu mi cogghi num mi po' mmanciari;*
> *mi metti nta la bucca e num m'agghiutti,*
> *eccu m'agghiutti li fazzu affucari.*

(I am a herb which poisons all, who picks me cannot eat me. Put me in your mouth and you won't be able to swallow me, and whoever swallows me, I suffocate.)

As a public figure, he must stand up for order. He is deeply religious—or pretends to be—and extremely conservative. Politically he is and must be a supporter of government. His enemies are on the far left, because they oppose the kind of government he needs and the methods he uses. In the nineteenth century the Mafia could not penetrate real peasant movements; in the twentieth it has been unable to infiltrate the Italian Communist Party. In any case no proletarian grouping could serve the Mafia's middle-class needs (unfortunately the same cannot be said of the Socialist Party). Even the Sicilian Communist Party has had some questionable people in its ranks, nevertheless, but it must be said that they were expelled.

Faced with really determined opposition, or a Mafia rival, the mafioso's final deterrent is murder. Like all the mafioso's actions, criminal or otherwise, this must ideally be committed with style as well as precision. Done with the right blend of expertise and calculated indifference it will be discussed with admiration by many Sicilians, as a display of native genius and panache. In fact this response is one of the objects of the exercise. The Mafia murder, which has come to mean 'an organized murder', has always had a function of prestige: it must express the authority and power of the person or persons for whom it has been executed. In Sicilian terminology the commissioner is the *mandante*, the killer the *mandatario*.

In the 'good old days' of the rural Mafia, which had no overall hierarchy, the *mandante* would most likely be the local *gaballoto*, while the *mandatari* would sometimes be bandits, sometimes men chosen from the poorest section of the population to kill in exchange for a meagre sum. Hired killers might be recruited from outside the boss's territory, so that there would be no obvious connection between the ordering of the crime and the actual criminal, or between him and his victim. Much the same pattern applies today, allowing for changes in management and personnel.

Yet a Mafia killing must be publicized as well as untraceable. Everybody must know why it was done and on whose behalf. Consequently grim signs on the corpse explained the reason for punishment. This convention was a necessity: while a legal trial can be followed by the population and the verdict understood, a Mafia trial has to be secret. Therefore if the dead man was guilty of talking too much (to the police) his tongue would be severed, or a stone inserted in the corpse's mouth as a sign of *'nfamita*. A severed hand placed on the chest: the victim was a *scassapagghiari*, a small thief operating against the wishes of the local boss. Testicles cut off and forced inside the mouth: the victim raped or tried to make love to the wife, sister or relation of the local *galantuomo*. Sometimes a card over the dead body would specify *infame, molle di pancia* (soft in the belly), *carogna* (carrion) — insults for the man who had betrayed names and secrets to the police. Eyeballs torn out of their sockets: guilty of having seen and then talked. The custom of amputating part of the victim's body is still practised by the rural Mafia, but it has also become a trick to mislead the police. A murder in 1972 had the conventional advertisement of a sexual offence, but it was common knowledge that the clues were false, although they successfully confused the police in their initial investigation.

What prevents 'common knowledge' from becoming incriminating evidence is a crucial Sicilian concept which reinforces the legal invulnerability of the mafioso and the active Mafia gangs. Founded partly on fear, partly on idealism, *omertà*, literally 'being a man' (*hombredad* in Spanish), is an extreme form of loyalty and solidarity in the face of authority. One of its absolute tenets is that it is deeply demeaning and shameful to betray even one's deadliest enemy to the *sbirri*, which is the contemptuous Sicilian term for policemen and guardians of order. It is the same familiar process by which Sicily's tenacious folklore turns the reflexes of an exploited people into the means of its exploitation. A traditional proverb runs: '*L'omu ch'e omu non rivela mai mancu si avi corpa di cortella*'—the man who is really a man reveals nothing, not even with a dagger through him. Sicilians, unlike Italians, are in any case a people of few words:

> *Cu e surdu, orbu e taci*
> *campa cen'anni 'impaci.*

(He who is deaf, blind and silent lives a hundred years in peace.)

> *L'omu chi parra assai nun dici nienti,*
> *l'omu chi parra piccè sapienti.*

(The man who talks a lot says nothing, the man who talks little is wise.)*

Folklore and convention apart, however, the barrier of silence surrounding every crime was and is more than understandable, since the denunciation of a mafioso by an ordinary citizen would have been suicidal. In any case the truth, from a Sicilian point of view, has no intrinsic merit, and is employed only when it has to serve some definite end. Even so, in recent years the custom of *omertà* has been maintained basically by the failure of legal justice to fulfil its responsibilities. Many would have liked to talk, to accuse—and some have—but no one in his right mind in Sicily or anywhere else would risk their life when the legal system all too often proves to be an ally of the mafioso.

In the long run it is the power and social position of the mafioso which preserve him. Yet his code and mystique are more than just an elaborate screen. They represent the ceremonial and discipline of office. The man of respect, the boss, is always 'Don' or 'Zu' (uncle) to his inferiors, and even if he addresses everybody using the familiar *'tu'*, others will address him as 'Voi', 'Vossia'. 'Don' derives from the Latin *dominus*, lord. The boss (*capo*) has a special status: people kiss his hands or say as a form of respect *'Baciammu le mani'*—we kiss your hands. Among themselves, the mafiosi often use a distortion of the local dialect (Palermo alone has five or six), very difficult for outsiders to understand. But the main way of communication is by using the eyes, tiny movements understood at once, and a few limited gestures.

* It is *l'omu* who is silent, not the woman, who does not belong to society and knows next to nothing about her men's secrets. One jailed Mafia boss was particularly angry when a magistrate arrested his wife to put pressure on him. 'What kind of magistrate is Mr X, to imprison my wife?' he asked me furiously. 'He should know that if I am the kind of boss he thinks I am she is not likely to know any of my secrets.' Yet in this most man-centred institution of a man-centred island, one of the first people successfully to break the 'law' of *omertà* was a woman, Serafina Battaglia, who informed on the murderers of her husband and son—both of them mafiosi. (See p. 158.)

In the eyes of many Sicilians, all this ritual and ceremonial is no less than the boss's due. After all the mafioso challenges and pays. He pays not with a prison sentence or by being condemned in court as he deserves, but with his life in the internal struggles of the Mafia. He has courage, and a pagan attitude towards life, which he takes away with ease. But his own life too is continually threatened, and he often has to kill in order to avoid being killed himself. The mafioso who emerges at the top therefore represents the best selection simply because he has survived—and one may be sure that his survival has involved a good number of assassinations. Nina Sardo Spagnuolo pays a fulsome tribute to the mystique and fascination of the mafioso, practically an apotheosis: 'The life of the body does not count for him, or counts very little, in comparison with what is considered as the real life, the real essence of one's own person, expressed in the overruling of all obstacles, in infinite liberty. We think we can distinguish two elements in this particular attitude, logical and moral: the human sacrifice and the anarchical individualism to which it is offered.' It is a striking account, even though it would be hard to choose a more misleading term than 'anarchy' for the rule of the Mafia in Sicily.

Dominance is the mafioso's objective. He achieves it through the only authority he recognizes, the Mafia group or gang, known in Sicily as the *cosca* (plural *cosche*). As we have said, probably the only time when we hear the truth from a mafioso on trial is when he asserts that he does not know what the Mafia is. He does not see himself as a mafioso because he sees himself as pursuing a career like anybody else, with the same motive—the accumulation of economic and social capital—and in a time-honoured Sicilian manner. But he is also telling the truth because he himself does not use the term 'Mafia': he expresses his social relationship in terms of the *cosca*. Outsiders may refer to the *capomafia*, the 'Mafia boss', but to his retainers and rivals he is the *capocosca*, whether he rules a particular area or whether he monopolizes a particular racket in an area carved up among several *cosche*.

The word *cosca* refers to any plant—such as the 'artichoke', or the thistle—whose spiny closely-folded leaves symbolize the tight-knit resistant nature of the group. Anton Blok's investigations showed:

As a noncorporate group, the *cosca* should be understood in terms of a set of dyadic ties linking each member to every other member. In turn, these dyadic ties were part of larger overlapping networks involving other mafioso, kinsmen, friends and many others. The *cosca* was thus an integral part of these networks, and cannot be understood in isolation from them. Each member, most notably the leader, was connected in a ramifying order with people outside the *cosca*, either directly or indirectly through intermediaries. The position of the leader depended upon his range of contacts with persons who were important to him and vice-versa: the smaller the number of steps that the leader had to take to reach these persons, the stronger his position. Yet this reachability accounts for only part of the leader's strength. The number of lateral linkages between these contacts, especially links between persons adjacent to the leader, should be controlled and kept to a minimum to ensure his monopoly as a broker: when people learn to make their own contacts, the leader will be out of a job.

Of course there are degrees of precedence even among *cosche* and their bosses. 'So-and-so is a nobody, just a little *capocosca* of a poor and provincial *coschetta*,' one mafioso remarked to me about one of his enemies. Sometimes one *capocosca* has such authority, and there is such a need for somebody who can settle disputes from the inside, that he is recognized by all as an over-boss. This happened in the cases of Don Vito Cascioferro and Don Calo Vizzini, but does not work if the man cannot command total respect. From such a position, a boss can make and unmake industries, politicians, and even Sicilian governments.

The *cosche* operate wherever there is economic production to be tapped or political power to be marketed. Where these have grown since the nineteenth century, so have the *cosche*, which are rooted in every zone of Western and Central Sicily. Some are active in a single village, and have overall control of the meagre economy. Others cluster around the richer pickings of the towns, which have developed numerous *cosche* and are particularly exposed to the struggle for power. A city like Palermo is especially exposed because it is the centre of credit and justice, the seat of the Sicilian parliament, and therefore the source of governmental contracts and permits. Specialist *cosche* also proliferate, each with its racket, in prosperous areas like the Conca d'Oro, the beautiful valley which surrounds Palermo, rich in citrus plantations and orchards. Water for irrigation, for example, is so rigorously controlled that its cost frequently multiplies by a factor of five the gross value of the product, according to an estimate from Danilo Dolci's Centre of Documentation.

Even cemeteries have their *cosca*, and anyone who fails to pay up may find the family tomb vandalized, or fresh flowers removed and sold back to the local florist. Traders of all kinds have to give a percentage the *pizzo*—to the controlling *cosca*. (In dialect, the *pizzo* is the beak of a bird; to wet the beak—*fari vagnari u pizzu*—is to make one's 'donation' to the 'friend' who is liable to become an enemy if you let his beak dry.) In Palermo even big stores, one of which is Swiss-owned, pay the *pizzo*, a racket said to have been invented and organized by Vito Cascioferro. Another of the *cosca's* services is to guarantee the trader the monopoly of an area. Wine, beer, fruit, transport, the wholesale meat trade, sulphur, public works belong to some *cosche* in particular; others specialize in dock labour, fishing or cigarette smuggling. Of course this makes prices in Sicily the highest in all Italy.

Sicily has such restricted fields of exploitation that the criminal groups cannot share their economic pre-eminence or make room for newcomers. If one *cosca* tries to expand in another's dominion, there is *burrasca*, war. Since anarchy is not their objective, stability requires some sort of 'order' and organization, especially as communications in Sicily began to develop and cities to expand demographically. Emigration to Canada and the United States also established long lines of com- munication across the Atlantic, and with the rise of the American Cosa Nostra, which *is* a sort of secret society, decisions sometimes had to be taken in consultation. Another change was the evolution of new and richer fields, such as the black market for cigarettes, hard and medical drugs, and real estate development. Eventually the Sicilian *cosche* were forced to come to a general agreement and a shared internal organiza- tion.

We know more about these later developments than about the *cosche* of the post-1860 era, during the period when they were settling into the legal and administrative structures of the new Italy. Nevertheless their better-documented successors were following a familiar beaten track. Long before Renato Candida comes to describe the Mafia of pre- Fascist Italy, the *cosche* had been an entrenched feature of Sicilian society, and murder so much their natural expression that it was its absence that constituted an event. At Favara, a town near Agrigento which still has a reputation for cruelty and *mafiosità*, an old man died at the age of eighty-three, of natural causes, in a year when there had been one hundred and fifty unpunished murders. The family duly recorded on his tombstone the miraculous epitaph: 'He died in the bosom of nature.'

Describing the 'mafias'—the *cosche*—of Palma di Montechiaro (the Donnafugata of *The Leopard*), Candida writes: 'Police and Carabinieri worked, but the law did not help them.' One fat local mafioso still complained to Candida of being ill-treated by the police, even though he himself respected them so much that once he had returned a gold pen to a policeman from whom it had been stolen the previous day. This man was the Public Prosecutor in 'the so-called Mafia tribunal'. These tribunals really existed and do exist; 'trials' take place only when a particularly delicate item has to be decided among different *cosche*. If the punishment involves one group alone there is no need of a common decision, but when a mafioso has offended another group his fate must be decided by the whole criminal community, so as not to risk a war between different *cosche*. That is why an overall *capocosca* is such a useful presence: he can be an impartial judge, as high kings used to be in primitive societies.

Candida also observed that the Palermo Mafia was structurally more complex since the sources of income were so many. Monreale, ancient seat of the powerful Archbishop, is situated in a dominant position above Palermo. From Monreale, a stronghold of the Church, the water which flows to the *giardini*—the orchards—can be cut off, and any goods arriving in Palermo from the interior can be controlled. That is why the Monreale Mafia has always been especially important. During the time of Giuliano, the *cosche* and clergy of Monreale protected the bandits until the Mafia decided to get rid of Giuliano.

The Church is not immune from the Mafia spirit. 'The Mafia shows itself by profiting from the superstitious beliefs of the population, obtaining money under the guise of charity,' an official wrote in 1874. In the 1940s a priest said to Candida that there were two Mafias, the good and the bad, and that the good Mafia made people vote for the Christian Democrats. It is also customary for a mafioso family to put some of its children into the Church, so that a boss will often have uncles, brothers or nephews among the clergy, and they can count on their families' protection. Father A. Coppola was unrated, in 1976, as a leading mafioso. In very recent times, churches have provided sanctuary for wanted mafiosi. Magistrates often deny the police the authorization to search churches.

But it would be unfair to single out the Church for special mention.

Vocations and professions must be adapted to the prevailing conditions in any society, and in Sicily these conditions are the Mafia. The mafioso and the *cosca* are merely their active expression—the executives; their kinsmen are in the Church as they are in the professions listed by Candida, and as they are in the police, the judiciary and the law.* An exhaustive description of the Mafia would correspond closely to a portrait of Sicilian society. This account focuses on Sicily's most prominent profession, but it is not separate. It belongs.

---

* However, since these are the bodies which non-Sicilians would reasonably expect to find heading the opposition even to socialized crime, they do deserve special attention. Chapter 7 contains a brief account of Italy's complicated police and legal systems, and their ambiguous role in Sicily.

3 Institution

The plebiscite of 1860 welcomed the new Italian state by a massive majority of the tiny electorate, but it did not bestow the monopoly of public administration upon Sicily's final inheritors. Instead they found themselves in constant competition with the Mafia, both as a loose association of power groups and as a prevailing mentality. In Sicily the mafiosi—and not the population in general—recognized the potential strength of legal institution and allied themselves to it. Therefore the Mafia, then as now, was a governmental force but an opponent of the state. Its objective was always to establish itself as an ally of the ruling power, while remaining an illegal autonomous force. The Italians realized that no Sicilian government had ever been able to stamp out criminality because the Mafia had for so long been the only form of stability. Alliance was the easiest way out for them too, and the *omertà* subsequently enforced by both government and Mafia was a necessary element to the stability of the dual institutions.

But first there was a period of adjustment and confusion during which the Italian administration was more disastrous than that of the Bourbons. The latter had sinned by omission, but at least they had understood something of the spirit of the South. The Neapolitan laws had been assimilated; the Piedmontese Northerners tried to impose theirs harshly, and often by force. Sicily was an enigma to them: Cavour had never been to Rome, let alone further south, and spoke better French than Italian.

A typical example of Piedmontese ham-fistedness was the report sent by General di Montezumolo to the Ministry of the Interior soon after the plebiscite. The population was in a ferment, he wrote, and this was the fault of the anti-governmental parties—the Mazzini, Garibaldi, Bourbon and Separatist factions. He advised waiting for the next uprising (there had been so many that another could be arranged) in order to imprison 'the leaders of the opposing factions'. The general also asked for reinforcements, and wanted 'to purge the interior with mobile forces and battalions of *bersaglieri*'. The political aim was to suppress any disorder in the South and attempt to confuse the expression of social needs with criminal disorders. The new state was worried about international reactions, and wanted to offer the spectacle of an orderly, peaceful Italy under the Piedmontese regime. Thus the wave of military repression that swept over Sicily and the South was due to a timid political vision.

The new government left local administration in the hands of the Dons, the *gabelloti*, the *galantuomini*, in return for electoral support. The middle stratum which had previously ruled de facto behind the barons was now the de jure ruling force. Elections were a fertile field for bribery and manipulation, a gift to the local groups. The Prefects often became responsible to the grand electors—those mafiosi powerful enough to deliver a majority vote to candidates of the ruling party. State jobs became the monopoly of local bosses, and credit institutions and public works contracts formed the basis of a system of patronage.

Meanwhile the island was in a turmoil. Benjamin Ingham, an Englishman who had settled in Sicily and made his fortune out of Marsala wine, wrote a letter to the British Consul about the unrest 'in the provinces of Palermo and Trapani, where assassination, robbery, burning of property, seizure of persons, and the so-called *componenda* are the order of the day and of the most frequent occurrence ...' The long series of political assassinations had already started. As early as August 1861 Domenico Peranni, former Secretary of State of the Garibaldi regime, an honest man and a democrat, was shot dead in a Palermo street in broad daylight. Rumours circulated connecting the murder with his supposedly scandalous private life: denigrating the victim is a traditional Mafia trick to deter and confuse investigation. In the same month Giambattista Guccione, a left-wing Republican and Councillor of the Court of Appeal, was shot in the back outside his home. His wife saw him fall, but 'nobody saw the three killers'.

In June 1861 Diomede Pantaleoni, a former colleague of Cavour, and envoy to Paris and the Vatican, had arrived in Sicily to observe the situation. He was a perceptive man, and his most striking observations are to be found not in the official report but in his letters to the Minister of the Interior, Minghetti, and to Prime Minister Ricasoli. He quickly discovered that the identity of Guccione's murderers and the men behind them were an open secret to which no one would testify, 'including the police, who were terrified'. He went on:

> The man who did it is known to everybody, and is called de Marchis, or something of the kind. He has taken refuge in a villa in the hills. It belongs to a solicitor, and I—a stranger in Palermo—got to know this on the first day of my arrival and passed on the information to Lieutenant Pettinengo. De Marchis did not know Guccione. He had two or three accomplices, of whom one if not two work at the royal palace in Palermo and, if I am not mistaken, are called Braggio and Valenza. It was one of them who—in Sicilian dialect—told the other to shoot and who recognized the victim.

Pantaleoni had even heard the name of the man who commissioned the murder mentioned 'by everybody, even the press: the deputy P—, of ultra-governmental tendencies'. It was at his house that the murder had been decided, and two days after the meeting the deputy left for Turin—'and these are the men who represent us in Sicily!' It was a typical Mafia assassination. The *mandatario* had never met the victim. The killers received immediate shelter and protection. The *mandante* was out of town and in a public place (what more public than Parliament?) at the time of the murder. And *omertà* was absolute. What particularly scandalized Pantaleoni was that the murder had been planned within the governmental party and was actually welcomed by authority. But a democratic system which allowed anybody to act and speak had to be controlled, and with the Mafia already well implanted in the new regime it was bound to protect its investment by eliminating or intimidating any left-wing enemies of Sicily's established order.

Considering how remote and dangerous the island was then, and how bad its communications were, Pantaleoni saw a great deal. He found that local administrators were dishonest and incompetent: 'The mayors are often those who lead the disorders and revolts.' Stressing that 'everybody stole a lot', he wrote: 'The fact is that public morality is in a deplorable state, worse than what I found in Greece—and which has made it impossible for that unlucky country to resurrect even under liberal institutions. Public security here, even in villages, is in a deplorable state.' From a letter dated 17 September: 'Assassination or attempted assassination is common and, I should say, almost an everyday event in the more populated rather than in the smaller towns.' Instancing the twenty-nine murders and attempted murders recorded in twenty-seven days: 'Justice cannot put a stop to that because the fear of revenge is such that no witness can be found, nor mayors or police officials to sign orders of arrest, and even when these do take place ... it is impossible to find judges to convict.'

Pantaleoni also stressed how beloved Garibaldi still was in the region, and in his final report he had the courage to recommend offering 'peace to honest men who belong to the *Partito d'Azione*' (Garibaldi's party). Lastly he noted that the police acted not against the mafiosi but against the reformists, the peasantry and the socialists. In this they had the full cooperation of the Mafia which, by destroying any popular will to change, was building its permanent highways within the Italian state.

Garibaldi had wisely avoided imposing military conscription on the Sicilians. His hard-line successors made it compulsory, although the rich could buy exemption. For an agriculturally backward peasantry whose women did not work in the fields, military service was a special hardship. In some provinces they simply failed to report for conscription (at Trapani, all but eleven out of 151). In 1861 there were 2952 deserters out of 4897 recruits. In 1863 there were 236,225 deserters. Some of these went to swell the bandit population:

> *Vulemu a Garibaldi*
> *C'un pattu: senza leva.*
> *E s'iddu fa la leva*
> *Canciamo la bannera*
> *Lallararera, lallarara.*

(We want Garibaldi with a pact: no conscription. And if he orders conscription we will change flags.)

But it was too difficult to change flags this time. In 1863 General Govone was given a free hand to suppress disorders; some were tried by military tribunals and executed on the spot, while others were held in prison without trial. Torture was common. At the same time prices were rising because Sicily was importing manufactured goods while exporting raw materials to the North. The island was becoming a colony of the new Italian nation.

In 1866 Palermo exploded in one of the few genuine popular uprisings the island had ever seen. It was supported neither by the aristocracy nor by the middle classes, who feared the changes threatened by the republican ideals of the revolutionaries. Palermo was shelled by the

Italian navy as it had been shelled by Bourbon ships a few years earlier. The clergy was an ally of the revolutionaries against the Italian government, which was anti-Vatican. The revolt was put down, but it offered a pretext for the Italian Ministry of Finance to request the immediate imposition of a law suppressing religious societies. Ecclesiastical properties representing more than a tenth of the island's land were confiscated and sold between 1866 and 1874.*

It was a golden opportunity lost by the poor and seized by the Mafia. Garibaldi's proposal to distribute the land as smallholdings among poor families was discarded, and instead it was auctioned off in units. Officially no buyer was entitled to more than a single unit; in fact this proviso was disregarded. 190,000 hectares were sold in the form of 20,300 shares, about seventy-five per cent of which were concentrated in illegal block-purchases. Powerful buyers eliminated competition and kept the prices very low with the help of the mafiosi, who excluded the peasants and intimidated the auctioneers. Not only did the state gain little from this operation, but the land fell into the hands of the *gabelloti* and *galantuomini*, still further weakening the position of the peasants.

On 25 April 1867, a Parliamentary Commission was set up under the chairmanship of the MP Pisanelli with the specific task of inquiring into the city and province of Palermo. It was a whitewash job, hurried through by 2 July. Although the word 'Mafia' had by then been used by civil servants and officials it was never mentioned, and the Palermitan MP di Rudinì (a former Mayor and Prefect, and future Prime Minister) was so angry that he resigned. His proposals for special antimafia legislation and temporary banishment of some notorious criminals were rejected. The Commission regarded the Mafia merely as a manifestation of delinquency due to the political immaturity of the Sicilian population. The economy had much improved, it claimed: the 3131 ecclesiastical properties had been divided into 6882 smallholdings (but it did not mention who held them); the nine primary schools in Palermo in 1860 had grown to 135, the 738 pupils to 8957.

The Pisanelli Commission had noticed the similarities between the Mafia and the landowning middle class, but did not venture to examine

---

* A few monasteries could retain their properties because they had been bequeathed by noble families with the clause that they were to revert back should the family become destitute. One such case was that of the princes of Lampedusa, which is why the Lampedusa heir has special rights to this day over the nunneries and convents of Palma di Montechiaro.

the phenomenon, or to distinguish it from banditry or genuine peasant dissent. It recommended the building of roads, and spending on public works, while advising against severe laws to counter crime and banditry —these might have embittered the population, and in any case the politicians did not want to alarm the Italians at the time of the very low point in national fortunes which followed the double defeats of Custozza and Lissa in the Austro-Prussian War of 1866.

During General Medici's five years of administration (1868–73), the Mafia tightened its grip and the practice of colluding with criminals so as to lay hands on other criminals became the rule. As in Bourbon times, the police were implicated with the mafiosi and the function of politics was not to cure the causes but to cover things up. In 1871 the Procurator General, Diego Tajani, a senior member of the Palermo judiciary (and a non-Sicilian), issued a warrant against the chief of police, Questore Albanese. Medici was involved with the Questore, and arranged a 'preliminary investigation'. Tajani's warrant was disregarded, some witnesses for his case were murdered, and it was decided 'not to proceed for lack of evidence'. His career, not Albanese's, was ruined, and when he tried to stand for Parliament in Palermo he was not elected.

Tajani stood again, at Amalfi, and when he eventually took his seat he spoke up in Parliament, publicized his case, and concluded: 'Now … I can suggest what are the lessons and solutions for the future. The first is that the Mafia which exists in Sicily is not necessarily dangerous, not invincible, but it becomes so because it is an instrument of the local government. This is the first real piece of truth.' The Parliamentary debate which followed enlightened Italian and foreign public opinion about the corruption of government institution in Sicily. However the left-wing Crispi minimized Tajani's accusations, although the Conservative party was then in power, and another Sicilian parliamentarian declared that the Mafia was an invention of Northern policeman.

Tajani later became Minister of Justice. Ironically, he did little to help Sicily, but he did repeat and stress that the Mafia was strong because it enjoyed political protection. How could the Sicilians be so bold as to attack the Mafia when police, magistrates and MPs were in collusion with it? If people like General Medici were involved with gangsters, the ordinary Sicilian felt that he could do the same.

Two reports sent to the Ministry of Justice in 1874 enlarged on Tajani's account. Rasponi, the Prefect of Palermo, wrote:

The Maffia [sic] ... invades all classes of society. The rich use it to safeguard their person and property ... or use it as an instrument to maintain that oppressive influence and weight that they now see coming to an end because of the development and progress of free institutions. The middle class embraces it and *is* it [*la esercita*] ... because it judges it a powerful means to acquire popularity, or in order to obtain money or to succeed in achieving its wishes and ambitions. The proletarian, lastly, becomes more easily maffioso through his natural hatred of whoever possesses anything or is in a higher position, not only because he is accustomed ... to react against the public authorities and their laws, but also for the hatred that they generally have for any work or occupation ...

Rasponi makes the point that the Mafia was many things, and that the middle strata were the Mafia. As for the proletarian form of 'maffia', that is how he describes banditry, a source of power for the Mafia because it could pose as the protector of robber and victim alike.

The other report throws light on the alarming electoral hold of the Mafia bosses and on their legal immunity. A group of Sicilian magistrates complained:

The same principle which was used in 1848 and 1860 to bring the impure elements of society among the revolutions, is to be found today: they intrude and become a weapon in the fierce struggle for administrative posts, and the maffioso is used and sought after to gain votes during elections, so that his authority grows and he is seen as more and more necessary; he imposes himself in all those daily happenings of social life, and when he is spotted by justice he finds protection and favour in the highest and most powerful classes. By artificial contrivance the Maffia gives and receives protection at the same time and it acquires strength as more and more often it sees people asking for its help instead of that of the local authorities. This is how ... it has grown powerful in the cities and in the countryside and, with its hidden power, has created silence where there is a crime, has rendered witnesses and victims dumb, has frightened jurymen and thereby ensured the immunity which is the greatest encouragement to misdeeds, convincing criminals that the law cannot touch them.

In 1875 the Conservative Prime Minister Minghetti set up yet another commission to examine conditions in Sicily, known as the Bonfantini

Commission, after the MP who wrote the report. It was overtaken by a number of events. Towards the end of the year, groups of peasants formed a union to fight the unjust conditions of their life and work. At Vallodolo one of these *leghe contadine* became a real force, with four hundred members who formed a cooperative by a regular legal process. Here, and at Villalba, Vallelunga and Santa Caterina a series of strikes showed that the peasants had learned a very un-Sicilian lesson—that individualism could be discarded and that unity of action was strength. This was the biggest threat ever for the *gabelloti*, Mafia elements in general and the central government. It warranted sterner measures than a commission. Bandits and peasant leaders were banished, jailed or killed, and the strikes were quelled with the help of the police, intentionally confusing social demands with crime. The republicans suffered particularly in this repression. Some were even accused (by Mafia elements) of being mafiosi, a weapon often used to discredit enemies even today.

The following year central government faced another kind of rebellion. This time it succumbed. The Sicilian MPs in Parliament became apprehensive that the Conservatives might try to undermine their position and that of their mafiosi grand electors. Out of forty-eight deputies, forty-four switched their allegiance to the opposition, and the government fell. The left gained power, and held it under various groupings until 1896. Peasants could be suppressed, but not the Mafia. It was a conclusion taken to heart by all successive Italian governments. The Sicilian MPs, who hardly ever talked in the Chamber and hardly needed to make a speech to be elected, could and can be relied upon to vote for the government, but become touchy on the subject of the Mafia and of any threats to Sicily's established order.

Parliament was almost empty when the Bonfantini report came to be discussed, but there was little cause to fear that it would offend the Sicilian MPs. Although the Commission had called 1128 witnesses they had been officials and landowners. There was no question of discreet interrogations and semi-secret visits to villages and poor districts. While the Commission did see the Mafia as evidence of the Sicilians' inability to free themselves of the old feudal system, it pointed to the many witnesses who had talked about 'the good Mafia', which had imparted justice where neither police nor legality had had authority. Others had seen it as a demonstration of courage. Naturally the landowners interviewed had been enthusiastic about the Mafia's good offices in keeping down the demands of the peasantry—about whose conditions the report was silent. There was no real problem in Sicily, it said. The peasant strikes were dismissed: 'It had been sufficient to send a police official to use his influence on those workers for the strikes to end and work on the fields to resume.'

Italy was still anxious for prestige abroad, and wanted to appear as a stable modern state. So the Bonfantini Commission concluded that Sicily was quite well off. No measures were recommended to stop or even to hinder the growing power of the mafiosi.

The next round in the battle of reports was fought by two Tuscan deputies, Sonnino and Franchetti, who conducted an unofficial investigation of their own in 1876. Both were familiar with problems of economics and agriculture, and they arrived in secrecy and talked to the lowest strata of the population. They produced one of the best papers ever written on Sicily, probing deep into the realities of the situation. In total contrast with the Bonfantini account, Franchetti saw the Mafia as an evil deeply rooted in Sicilian society and impossible to quench unless the very structure of the island's social institutions were to undergo a fundamental and revolutionary change.

Franchetti saw how Sicily's feudal structure had ruled out 'that transformation of habit and rights of which the French Revolution is generally considered the prototype'. Instead it was violence which had become a general prerogative, 'the only prosperous industry on the island'. Needing the support of a middle class, the Italian government in Sicily had turned to the mafiosi, who used violence as the landowners did, to protect their interests. The violence of the lower classes, on the other hand, was banditry directed against the status quo. Believing that the Mafia was a temporary phenomenon, the government had tried to repress it by sending to Sicily 'the worst administrative personnel in the kingdom, especially the police'. But the Mafia was neither an organization nor a passing development: its great effectiveness had come from infiltrating successive governments and cooperating with the police. Its main function was that of enforcing a rudimentary order in an anarchic situation, and crimes were a means to the end of winning respect, money and power.

'While the government quickly stamps out popular disorders,' Franchetti wrote bitterly, 'it is miserably impotent against brigandage and against the Mafia which is linked to the landowning classes.' Both men concluded that it was the criminals who had effective power, that the Mafia was 'the real reason for the crippling economic conditions in

Sicily'. Sonnino had focused on the peasantry, and been struck by the will of some of them to join in cooperatives, which he saw as the force that could eventually get rid of the Mafia.

The Sonnino-Franchetti report shocked both Italian and Sicilian society, and made the Bonfantini Commission look ridiculous. It was attacked, disbelieved, labelled as 'unpatriotic'. Left-wing Sicilians called the two Tuscans 'slanderers' who had gone to Sicily for a couple of days with preconceived ideas. Italian nationalism condemned them as 'worse than bandits' for the shameful interest they had aroused abroad.

From January to August 1877 Italy should have been ashamed of the terrible campaign of repression launched in Sicily by the Minister of the Interior, Nicotera. Perhaps never before had an occupying power displayed so much violence and injustice towards the poorest section of the island population. A first wave of emigration now took place, mainly towards the United States of America. Started on the pretext of a purge of criminals, this repression was also aimed at potential leaders of the generally discontented peasantry. Both the Conservatives and the Socialists were relatively immune: neither side intended to oppose boss rule in Sicily, nor could they afford to do so. Even the Prince of Galati (still one of the most aristocratic names of Sicily) could write:

Leone, Nobile and co. [notorious bandits], who were instruments and victims of the High Mafia, are no more. [They were executed in 1877.] Tomorrow there will be new instruments and new victims. Looking at the history of Sicily, has one ever found the case of a brigand who has not ended his life on the gallows, or been shot? All ... came to the same sad end ... The High Mafia, instead, has always been spared by all governments, beginning from that of Don Arrigo de Guzman, Count of Olivarez, and ending with that of the Rt. Hon. Nicotera ...

Blok points out that the repression came shortly after the admission to Parliament of the Sicilian elite: 'With this settlement, banditry lost much of its utility to the Sicilian upper classes. Thus deprived of protection by the latifundisti and their vast mafiosi clientele, the exposed brigands fell easy prey to the army.' The criticism of Sonnino and Franchetti about the treatment of peasant unrest compared with that of the Mafia is fully borne out by these events and by the proceeding during the elections called in the following year by the new Socialist Prime Minister, Agostino Depretis. 'Every kind of illicit influence was employed,' Denis Mack Smith states. 'The new Sicilian deputies reflected this fact: at Caccamo, for example, the election of Raffaele Palizzolo launched the political career of a notorious mafioso—though he sustained a momentary setback when it was discovered that in one area he had the suffrage of more than one hundred per cent of the eligible voters.'

Palizzolo was to become the most influential of all political mafiosi, controlling every seat of power in Western Sicily. The Mafia had made its point in 1876, and was now free to consolidate its position in local government, the police and any economic developments which promised easy returns. A series of 'socialist' governments cooperated, and Palizzolo's links with Crispi, Prime Minister in 1887–91 and again in 1893–6 were especially close. Crispi was to earn the description 'the worst mafioso of them all'. It was he who put a stop to the next serious attempt by the Sicilian peasantry to improve their conditions when in 1893 the Fasci Siciliani (Sicilian Leagues) mounted an impressive effort to organize agricultural workers around a programme of higher wages, improved leases and reduced taxes.

The Leagues differed from most previous expressions of peasant discontent, in which there had been a great deal of brigandage and even Mafia sponsorship. Socialist artisans and intellectuals provided a leadership which the peasantry had always lacked, and besides the draft had brought many men back to their villages with new experience, while emigration had helped to overcome the lower classes' sense of resignation. Each town had its own Fascio, and there was a central committee in Palermo. The movement was reformist rather than revolutionary, seeking improvements by legal means, demonstrations and strikes, but this did not placate the *gabelloti* and landowners. Crispi dispatched a massive military force of 30,000 men to quell the leagues, and proceeded to conduct a campaign of terror against the peasant cooperatives. The Mafia joined in, and in some places such as Gibellina and Lercara it has been proved that peasants were shot even before the arrival of the Carabinieri.

Crispi's premiership saw a general growth of corruption in Italy, and coincided with the spread of 'Southernification' as more Neapolitan and Sicilian lawyers, solicitors and bureaucrats entered the ranks of the national civil service. These posts appealed to a certain type of Southern mentality which saw them as requiring little or no enterprise yet enabling illicit gains to be won merely by passive obedience. Crispi also built up his electoral machine by practices such as releasing convicts from jail and excluding unsympathetic voters from the electoral lists on false grounds—university professors were struck off as illiterate. His anti-French, colonialist foreign policy damaged the Southern economy in particular. All these features smell very strongly of Fascism, and in fact Crispi was a proto-Mussolini, and behaved accordingly, even down to being forced out of office by the military defeat of his foreign policy. Italian forces invaded Ethiopia in 1895, but lost the decisive battle of Aduwa in 1896, and were forced to withdraw.

When the Sicilian Marquis di Rudinì succeeded Crispi in 1896 (the Conservative party having once again defeated the Socialists), he tried to destroy Crispi's electoral machine. One way to achieve this was to unearth scandals. And the murder of one of di Rudinì's protégés was a crime connected with Crispi's misuse of public funds.

On the evening of 1 February 1893, the Marquis Commendatore Emanuele Notarbartolo, former director of the bank of Sicily, had been stabbed to death in a railway carriage travelling between Termini Imerese and Trabia, in the province of Palermo. His mutilated body was found on the railway tracks. The news shocked Sicily and Italy and the assassination was the subject of a debate in Parliament. The Sicilian deputy Napoleone Colajanni, who was later to write several books on links between the Mafia and politics, talked openly of a political murder.

Magistrates, police and public opinion agreed at once that the murder was not motivated by robbery or private vendettas. Notarbartolo had been an honest administrator. After working on the board of Palermo's hospital, he had been made Chairman of the Bank of Sicily. Several bankruptcies had revealed financial irregularities, and when he took his post he found that private fortunes had been made by manipulation of credit and that the bank's funds had been irregularly used to contribute to Crispi's governmental party. Notarbartolo had sent a report to the Minister of Finance, Miceli, describing the anomalies he had found, in the belief that the new liberal state would support him.

Miceli forwarded the report to Crispi, and Crispi gave it to 'Don' Raffaele Palizzolo, by now a deputy in the Roman Parliament, a municipal councillor in Palermo, the chairman of several charitable organizations and a member of the board of directors of the Bank of Sicily. Having succeeded in ousting Notarbartolo, he had embarked on a series of speculations which threatened the very existence of the Bank of Sicily. It was he and his friends who had been misusing the bank's money.

After Notarbartolo's denunciation, the board of the bank was changed and Notarbartolo dismissed from his post (Crispi was still Prime Minister). Colajanni wrote (in 1900): 'Since the very first day [of the murder] there were talks in Palermo about the reasons which had led to such a crime: all lead to the deputy Raffaele Palizzolo as the organizer of the murder. People recognized his criminal capacity, he was known to be closely associated with the underworld of Palermo and the countryside around; people also said that, besides the old motivation of hatred against Notarbartolo, Palizzolo feared to see him return to the chairmanship of the Bank of Sicily.' As a trusted friend of di Rudinì, and an honest administrator, Notarbartolo was indeed on the point of being appointed Director of the Bank once again.

A slow inquiry started—it was to last seven years—and although police and magistrates were well aware of Palizzolo's guilt, he was not even interrogated. 'The truth is this,' Colajanni wrote, 'although they were convinced that the basic material out of which to build a trial pointed towards Palizzolo, all magistrates cooperated to put him in the clear, and were more than satisfied if they could wind everything up with the formula "impossible to proceed for lack of evidence".' But the Marquis' son Leopoldo, who was an officer in the navy, dedicated his life to the achievement of justice, and worked as a private detective with the help of his brave lawyer, Giuseppe Marchesano. He was even assigned to duty in the China Sea to make it impossible for him to have justice done, and later he had to go on leave in order to pursue the matter.

Although everybody mentioned the killer's name, Palizzolo was awarded a decoration by King Umberto. Then certain mafiosi were arrested, among then the notorious Giuseppe Fontana, and accused of having carried out the murder. The trial ended in an acquittal. Inquiring magistrates who had been shown to be on the right track were either dismissed from their posts or sent away from Palermo. A Lieutenant-Colonel of the Carabinieri advised a Captain to abandon his investigation and follow a track which did not lead to Palizzolo as the *mandante*. Documents disappeared, fake minutes replaced the real ones in the files. Witnesses against Palizzolo, even if they could read and write, were declared illiterate. Police chiefs, simple policemen, inspectors, Carabinieri, bore false witness and contradicted each other. Authorities who were convinced of Palizzolo's guilt continued to receive him with signs of respect. The whole magistrature proved corrupt.

5. 1930 A token success in the Fascist attempt to repress the Mafia – the capture of a handful of small fry *(Gigi Petyx)*

6. 1943 American armoured cars entering Villalba, Don Calò Vizzini's village *(Gigi Petyx)*

7. 1946 The emergence of the Sicilian separatist movement in the first post-war elections (*Gigi Petyx*)

8. 1947 Passatempo, Giuliano and Pisciotta wearing the uniform of the separatist army at Monte Sagana (*Gigi Petyx*)

9. 1948 Giuliano's own election poster, advocating union with America (*Gigi Petyx*)

10. 1949 Giuliano's body on display at Castelvetrano (*Gigi Petyx*)

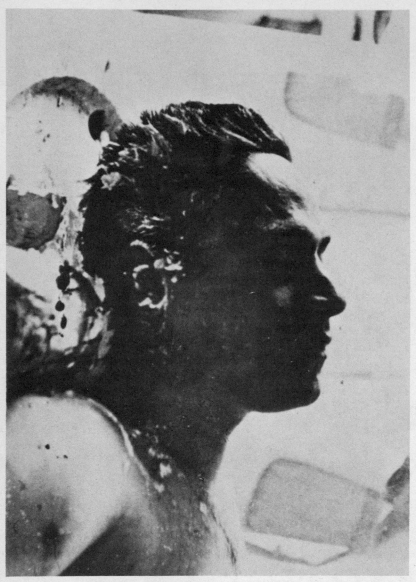

11. 1949 Giuliano's body in the morgue at Castelvetrano before the autopsy

(*Gigi Petyx*)

By a decision of the High Court of Rome, Notarbartolo's son managed to have another trial staged in Milan, and not in Sicily, for 'legitimate suspicion' that the courts in Sicily might be corrupt. Although the trial was of two henchmen and Giuseppe Fontana, Leopoldo Notarbartolo openly accused the deputy Palizzolo of having ordered his father's murder. Such strong evidence emerged against Palizzolo that the Chamber of Deputies granted the authorization to proceed against him, and the deputy was imprisoned (8 December 1899). Every merchant closed his business in Palermo that day, for 'civic mourning'.

The trial of Palizzolo and Fontana finally took place at Bologna, starting in September 1901 and ending in July 1902. It sentenced both men to thirty years' imprisonment, but the verdict and sentence were overthrown on appeal. A second trial opened in Florence in September 1903. Newspapers in Palermo carried such titles as 'A magic hand protects the guilty'; 'The police are Palizzolo's ally'; 'Palermo Police refuse to hand over documents to the Court'. Many witnesses retracted. A high-grade civil servant in Bologna had declared that Palizzolo was a well-known member of the Mafia, and quite capable of killing. In Florence the same witness called Palizzolo a gentleman and an honest man. When the President of the Court underlined the contrast with his previous evidence, the civil servant answered: 'The President of the Bologna Court asked me to give witness on the results of the inquiries, but your Honour asks me my personal opinion.'

A foreign observer, Bolton King, described the corruption underlying the Notarbartolo trial: 'Where the Mafia is strong, it is impossible for a candidate to win a parliamentary or local election unless he promises his protection ... The gangs are allowed free rein; they have licenses to carry arms, while honester citizens are denied them: they know that there will be no interference with a discreet blackmailing, provided that they terrorize the opposition voters at election time.'

In his book on Petrosino, Petacco writes:

In the intervening ten years since the crime various witnesses had died (naturally and otherwise); others had emigrated; still others had 'lost their memories'. In short, on 25 July 1904, the Florence jury acquitted Palizzolo and Fontana for lack of evidence. The release of Palizzolo created a sensation. While the mainland newspapers, and particularly *Avanti*, analysed the outcome of the Florence trial in bewilderment, all Palermo was on holiday. The steamer *Malta* was chartered to sail for Naples to bring Palizzolo home; the procession in honour of the Madonna del Carmine was postponed to enable the former jailbird to take part; the members of the Florence jury were proclaimed honorary citizens of Palermo; The Honorable Di Stefano, who had succeeded Palizzolo as a deputy, resigned his seat in favour of his predecessor.

There was even a reversal of Italian public opinion, which had started by being against Palizzolo. The usual voices began to spread alleging that the Notarbartolos were dangerous socialists, that Leopoldo Notarbartolo hated his native Sicily. What the Sicilians really could not understand was why Leopoldo Notarbartolo had been so stupid as to seek revenge through legal justice. For not revenging his father's death in a direct and personal way, he was even thought to be a coward, and certainly a fool, *un fesso*. And indeed his search for legal redress had been lengthy and fruitless.

There was also a Northern campaign of hatred against Sicily, Italian papers claiming that the Sicilians had an inferior and criminal nature; so much so that Sicily saw in Palizzolo its hero and martyr. But not all of Sicily. In the Chamber of Deputies, the Honorable De Felice Giuffrida angrily underlined the political connection of the Mafia, and their responsibility in the Notarbartolo murder:

Since there has already been mention of the *Camorra*, of hooligans, and of other associations with criminal purposes, I, who am talking about the Mafia ... ought to make an essential distinction. And this distinction is that, while the other associations for criminal purposes are formed only from the lowest depths of society, the sick part of the community, the Mafia, on the other hand, has various levels that shape it and sustain it. The lowest stratum, which is the best, is recruited in the working classes, which fear and more or less tolerate the influence of the Mafia. Above this there is a very dreaded stratum: the police. Then comes the highest level: the arrogant bourgeois, the gentleman, the Mafioso in kid gloves.

In this distinction I perceive the reason why in other parts of Italy it has been possible to crush some of these criminal associations that have appeared there and why it has not been possible to overcome the Mafia in Sicily. It has not been possible because in Sicily the only aim, in all periods, of all governments, has been to strike at the weakest and least responsible part. Contrariwise, those who support it and make use of it have been left in peace, secure, powerful: un-disturbed the public safety forces, undisturbed the arrogant middle class in whose homes the Mafia meets ...

You have tried new methods, restrictive laws, violence; you have had special legislation from the Chamber; you have abused all the laws, including the previous summary laws, but the result has always been the same: negative.

Do you see? The Notarbartolo trial teaches the lesson!

Look at the peasant, the peasant in the two or three provinces plagued by the Mafia. He does not have truly criminal tendencies, but he is dominated by the Mafia because he is not protected by the laws.

It was in Palermo, and in Palermo's province, that the Mafia was flourishing. And it was flourishing because Northern politicians had found a secure electoral machine which, they thought, they could control and operate. In a minor way the Mafia type of criminality was also doing well in the provinces of Trapani, of Enna (then called Castrogiovanni), Caltanisetta and Agrigento (Girgenti).

Although the individualistic tendency to ignore community rules and the State was stronger in Western and Central Sicily, the 'Mafia spirit' did exist in the provinces of Catania and Messina. But it did not express itself with extreme forms of criminality, such as murder, because that part of Sicily was richer and the fight for property and wealth was less hungry. Besides, Palermo was the centre of administrative power and the centre of corruption. Properties in the Eastern part of Sicily were not all latifundia, and so the *gabelloto* figure had not risen to dictatorial power. Cut off from Palermo (road communication was almost non-existent), the nobility of the Eastern provinces had never been attracted to Court life there (or to build large villas at Bagheria). Landlord absenteeism was much rarer and villages were closer to each other and linked by a social and civic life. In the nineteenth century there were industrial and economic changes, mainly due to the increased activity of the ports of Messina and Catania.

The Eastern side of Sicily had never accepted Arab rule and had never absorbed that mentality. It had the social background to enable its population to profit from the new liberal regime and from the expansion of trade. A middle class was springing up from the new industrial and liberal conditions, a class which successfully fought the interests of the landowners, which invested its income in trade and industry and which wanted to be genuinely represented in Parliament. Messina and Catania were following the social and industrial development of the rest of Europe, while Central and Western Sicily clung to the mood of the Middle Ages.* This middle class did not share the Western Sicilians' dislike of appearing to work hard, or their preference for living off unearned income: it had an interest in changing the old feudal system. The Western Sicilians call Eastern Sicily '*provincia babba*', in dialect 'the daft province': no parasitic classes there, but hard work.

Eric Hobsbawm has observed that the Mafia was the only form of bourgeois revolution which Sicily could ever have had. 'The theme of the Mafia means the theme of political power,' the Sicilian writer Leonardo Sciascia commented in a lesson which he gave on the subject at Palermo University. Therefore the Mafia, which before the nineteenth century had acquired a role in filling the gaps left by the State, and in running parallel services to those offered by the State, later became the very source of the administration of power. Just as the European middle class rose to power and government, so did the middle class of Western Sicily, which is the Mafia. Otherwise it would have been easy for the police, and the many Parliamentary Commissions which gave the police special powers, to fight it successfully. There will always be necessary compromises in the 'fight' against the Mafia, since a government cannot fight itself—it is a contradiction in terms. In this light one must see the Mafia from the 1880s onwards (when the liberal State with its mechanism of elections and free trade had been introduced in Sicily), and in this light one must understand the subsequent history of Sicily, its chronicle of assassinations and political victories.

* It is interesting to note that in a city like Catania today there are many more thefts than in Palermo. This is precisely due to the lack of Mafia control. Catania—at the time of writing—is predominantly Fascist. In this too, it does not follow the Mafia's technique of being a source of votes for the party in power.

PART TWO

Transformations

'A nation of acute and suspicious genius, born to controversy'
Cicero on the Sicilians

4 Links with the United States

Crispi's colonial policy led to friction with France which, in reprisal, no longer bought wine from Sicily. The economy also suffered as cheaper ways of mining sulphur were devised in the US and Sicilian sulphur could not find a market. The Nicotera repressions had created an army of deserters, bandits and paupers. The farmers who tried to survive on smallholdings did not have much chance of surviving. Emigration to North America, which had started in 1870 with only 130 emigrants, had grown by 1892 to 967, by 1896 to 15,432. In 1902 the figure was 127,603, and in 1913 emigration reached its peak of 146,061. Although emigration caused a lot of suffering to the Sicilians, by 1907 the Italian economy was gaining: 100 million lire a year in remittances sent by émigrés to their families at home.

A tremendous wave of immigration, which had originated in the southernmost, poorest, parts of Italy, had poured into America within a few years, creating problems that were often insoluble. While the growing industries of America urgently needed an army of cheap workers, the country as a whole was absolutely unprepared for their arrival. In consequence, the first contacts between the Italians and the New World were extremely harsh. Lacking schooling, rendered blind, deaf and dumb by their inability to express themselves in the language of the country, the immigrants wound up clinging together, so that in every city they formed a ghetto in which they lived under conditions that are difficult to describe.

In New York, for instance, the half-million Italians who had decided to stay in the city were crammed into the crumbling wooden houses of the Lower East Side, beneath the Brooklyn Bridge, which earlier immigrants to New York had long since abandoned. The Italians' settlement of the Lower East Side, of course, made fortunes for speculators and landlords, but also it transformed the neighbourhood into a kind of human antheap in which suffering, crime, ignorance and filth were the dominant elements.*

A certain number of Sicilians (in 1908 the American police estimated a hundred a month) left illegally. All sorts of ways were devised—besides that of false papers—to get to the 'promised land'. Some are known to have travelled in coffins, as dead former emigrants who wanted to be buried in the States. The 'corpse' would be fed at night, when 'it' took a walk as well. Some travelled as 'women' joining fiancés already in the US. Once they arrived they would change into suits and find jobs on the waterfront. The emigrants knew that it was easy to vanish into that large territory and those overpopulated cities, and in the US it was not a crime to change one's name, as it was in Italy. Moreover, the Italian police secretly encouraged criminals to go, giving them a clean record and a passport: anything to get rid of them. Not all those who left were criminals or potential criminals, and around the emigrants yet another repellent Mafia industry grew up: those who left were compelled to sell their few possessions for next to nothing. Obtaining documents and passports also became a speciality of some *cosche*.

Before the First World War, 40,000 Italians arrived in the United States every year, mostly from Sicily and from the South. They were escaping from an overpopulated territory, unemployment and poverty. It was not until 1920 that the American government, alarmed by the wave of crime and gang rule, imposed a quota, showing an understandable bias in favour of the North Italians. From 1930, not more than 12,000 immigrants per year were accepted from the whole of Italy.

The first wave of Italian immigration in the United States found an established underworld of Irish and Jews which prospered in a society with a higher standard of living. At first the Italians did not penetrate this underworld and operated within the circle of the immigrants. But the emigrants from Naples, Calabria, and especially from Sicily, brought a tradition of contempt of the law, clanship and a talent for the organization of crime which eventually led them to dominate the racket

---

* Lucky Luciano: 'When I looked around the neighbourhood, I found out that the kids wasn't the only crooks. We was surrounded by crooks, and plenty of them was guys who were supposed to be legit, like the landlords and store keepers and the politicians and cops on the beat. All of 'em was stealing from somebody. And we had the real pros, the rich Dons from the old country, with their big black cars and mustaches to match.'

network in the United States. (The word 'racket' soon became part of underworld slang; although its meaning in English is different, the word sounded like the Italian *ricatto*, extortion.) While the Jewish and Irish elements little by little showed themselves capable of being absorbed into a more advanced civic society, most Southern Italians did not. It is still so today, and it is apparent in the many 'little Italies' in the States which show the Italian need for living together in districts where the local dialects are spoken and local customs maintained, and where modern civic ideas penetrate with great difficulty. Even in London, small Sicilian communities are crammed into single blocks of flats, only the men learn to speak English, funerals retain the pomp of Sicilian functions and children are often not sent to school.

When the potential criminal arrived, he first started his career in becoming the executioner (and later the brain) in one of the various 'Murder Corporations' which existed in the States. There was great talk of a society called the Black Hand, with criminal ramifications, but in fact each 'Black Hand' was just an unattached *cosca*.

The first time that the word 'Mafia' appeared abroad was in *The Times* of London in October 1890, in connection with the murder of an American police official in New Orleans. A gang of Sicilians had gained control of the New Orleans waterfront. No cargo moved on or off without paying a tribute to the Sicilian families of Provenzano and Matranga. A 'war' broke out between them and was won by the Matranga, leaving many corpses on the streets of New Orleans. David Hennessey, a police chief who was probing too energetically into these activities and had prepared a dossier on a number of *cosche mafiose*, was murdered on 15 October 1890. Before dying he whispered to a police officer 'Dagoes', which at the time meant Italians.

Nineteen members of the Matranga gang were brought to trial, and the well-known pattern began to develop: the best criminal lawyers were hired and won acquittals for all but three of the defendants. But after the verdict a furious crowd murdered eleven of the mafiosi—two were hanged and nine shot. The incident almost caused a diplomatic break between Washington and Rome. When, during the following days, several ships brought some four thousand new Italian immigrants to New Orleans, the crowd would not let them disembark and the police had to be called to give them protection. The Italians were so unpopular, because of their criminal reputation, that many more were lynched. For example:

1895: three Italians were lynched in Walsemburg, Colorado, after they had been acquitted of a homicide charge.

1896: in Hanville, Louisiana, three Sicilians accused of murder were taken from the jail in which they were being held for trial and were hanged in the public square.

1899: in Tallulah, Louisiana, five Italians—Francesco, Carlo and Giuseppe Difatta, brothers, and their friends Giovanni Cerani and Rosario Fiducia, all from Cefalù, Sicily—were lynched after a bloodless quarrel with a certain Dr Hodges, who objected when the Sicilians' goats strayed onto his land.

In the beginning, the Mafia, or the Black Hand as it was called in the States, preyed almost exclusively on the hardworking Southern Italians who had settled there. Then it became such a problem that a special police squad—the Italian Branch—had to be assigned to try to fight it. One of its best officers, Joseph Petrosino, said: 'The Black Hand, as a large organization, does not exist.'

A report in the archives of the New York State Department of Justice (Organized Crime and Racketeering) states:

The Italian criminal arrives in the States in three different ways: 1) As a 2nd or 3rd class passenger—or a passenger in the emigrant class—with a passport which has been obtained through political help or money, because it would be impossible for a criminal to have a passport granted from the Italian Government. 2) With a passport issued to a different name. 3) Embarked illegally without a passport in one of the Italian ports with the help of those who have made this into a profession.

The same document went on to specify that the Italian criminals in the States could be classified as those who had been previously condemned for a crime in Italy and, after serving their sentence, wanted to escape the *sorveglianza speciale* (special surveillance); those who had committed a crime in Italy and had escaped before the Italian law could catch them; or those who were considered notorious criminals but against whom it had been impossible to find evidence. They came to the States either to escape hostility from the public, or to escape possible arrest or revenge from local enemies.

To these notes, Lieutenant Joseph Petrosino, a tough policeman whose methods were often criticized as unethical, added that while

Italian criminals were subject to the *sorveglianza speciale*, which they loathed, 'here, police control is almost non-existent. Here it is easy to buy arms and dynamite for criminal aims. Here there is no punishment for giving a false name and address.' In the same document Petrosino complains that, in order to escape the law, criminals finish up in 'political gangs' from which they receive unlimited protection. 'Nothing to do against So-and-So', Petrosino repeats as a normal comment, 'he is one of the Tammany Hall men.'

The New York police decided to send a trusted man to Italy, somebody who was familiar with the problems of the Mafia and the rackets, who could speak Italian and knew both American and Italian criminal codes. This was because, towards 1904, the Black Hand had reached the status of an organization, and it had branches in every part of the United States and a tie to Sicily as well. One of the aims was to find out how many Sicilians had emigrated illegally, and then to ship them back as fast as possible; another to find evidence for their incrimination or extradition. The ideal man was thought to be Joseph Petrosino who, in four years, had arrested or repatriated over six hundred Italian criminals. His visit, which was meant to be secret, was immediately publicized and articles were printed by American papers. So, when Petrosino arrived in Palermo and was seen and recognized by two Palermitans, they commented: 'That man is Petrosino who has come to Sicily to be bumped off' (note from a police file, 1909).

Many Sicilians had come back home from the States, some bringing a higher standard of living, new ideas, but some bringing back also a more sophisticated form of crime. One of these was Vito Cascioferro. A contemporary report written by the Royal Carabinieri reads:

In 1900 he had left Sicily for North America where he went to live with his sister Francesca who has a shop on 103rd Street in New York. He immediately took an important position in the criminal group of the Black Hand. The Italian police of New York judged him responsible for the murder of an Italian whom he stabbed, cut into pieces, and then stuffed the pieces inside a barrel. But before being arrested he left New York, taking residence in Brooklyn; then for six months in New Orleans, in Royal Street. He fled from the United States and returned to Palermo. Through confidential sources, we know that he always carried with him the photograph of the American policeman Petrosino.

Cascioferro was illiterate but, when very young, he married a teacher from his village of Bisacquino who taught him to read and write. A gambler and a lady-killer, he was an adventurous man. In the photograph from the police file, Cascioferro looks at one with a languid, innocent expression. Round brown eyes and dark moustaches; a short, white beard made his round face look a little longer and more severe than its otherwise jolly expression. A round nose completes the portrait of somebody who could easily have been a Naval officer or a high school teacher.

He had been born in Palermo on 25 June 1862, the son of a *campiere* of the Baron Inglese at Bisacquino, and the Inglese family were to protect him always. He was first attracted by anarchism, a movement that in those days was shaking Europe and the States. It is significant that the young and brilliant Sicilian, who was to develop into the most intellectual of all criminals, first sought liberty and individual idealism. Cascioferro's criminal record started very early and can still be consulted. 1884, assault. 1893, bankruptcy, threats against public officials, arson, attempted extortion. 1899, taking part in the kidnapping of the Baroness di Valpetrosa. In America, Petacco takes up the story:

> His first task was to establish an organizational structure for the Palermo–New York circuit, which until then had consisted of relations between persons rather than between groups. Because of his influence both in Sicily and in America, Don Vito very quickly became the pivot in the alliance between two criminal associations: the Mafia and the Black Hand. In a word, it was he who created the vast empire of crime, with permanent, solid interconnections, that exists today and that comes out into the open every now and then when the newspapers disclose that the mafiosi on both sides of the ocean have equal power and influence in the management of specific illegal operations.

Cascioferro had perfected the links between the Black Hand and some of the Sicilian *cosche*. One man was in his way: Petrosino, the one policeman who had also connected the murder of the man in the barrel (Benedetto Madonia, otherwise known as Morris) with Cascioferro and had caused his flight from the States. There was open war between the two. Petrosino's dream was to incriminate Cascioferro, undo his American connections, and send him to prison. After Petrosino's murder, the American consul in Palermo, Mr Bishop, found in Petrosino's suitcase a piece of paper written in Petrosino's handwriting: 'Cascioferro, Bisacquino, a terrible criminal.' The policeman carried Don Vito's name, the criminal the policeman's photograph. Of the two, who had a certain amount in common (they were both violent and used illegal means, even if one of them was a man of the law), the brighter was to survive.

Cascioferro's criminal genius was in organizing all channels of Sicilian trade. Since violence was 'Sicily's most successful industry', crime had to be organized as well. Businessmen, traders, shopkeepers and even beggars became part of a regular organization. The criminals gained domination over anyone who wanted to run any kind of business: the mafiosi offered them 'continuing protection' in exchange for the *pizzo*, the system devised and exported to the States by Cascioferro himself. 'You have to skim the cream off the milk without breaking the bottle', he used to say, 'But you're operating like two-bit punks. Try a new system. Don't throw people into bankruptcy with ridiculous demands for money. Offer them your protection instead, help them to make their businesses prosperous, and not only will they be happy to pay but they'll kiss your hands out of gratitude.' He who did not pay lost his customers, went out of business, or saw house and crop go up—literally—in smoke.

Before and after his return from the States, Don Vito's power was huge; he was at the same time the *capocosca* of Bisacquino, Campofiorito, Corleone, Contessa Entellina, Chiusa Scalfani, Burgio, Villafranca Sicula and of some districts of Palermo. In fact, he is known as the first *capomafia* of Sicily, although he would have been the first person to be flattered but surprised by such a 'title'. His influence was certainly great over *cosche* which he did not control, but there is a lot of fantasy connected with the figure of Don Vito and the colourful piece from *The Italians* by Luigi Barzini contains a lot of purely apocryphal items, besides a vivid and semi-factual portrait:

Discipline was such that when a *uomo rispettato* from the country, an important politician from Rome, or a distinguished foreign guest of Sicily was robbed within Don Vito's jurisdiction, he gave an order and, in a matter of minutes, the suitcase, the watch, the wallet or the lady's jewellery was returned with apologies. Palermo was not Catania, in the East of the island, where there was no Mafia to control things and anarchy prevailed ... Don Vito brought the organization to its highest perfection without undue recourse to violence. The Mafia leader who scatters corpses all over the island in order to achieve his goal is considered as inept as the statesman who has to wage aggressive wars. Don Vito ruled and inspired fear mainly by the use of his great qualities and natural ascendancy ... His manners were princely, his demeanour humble but majestic. He was well loved by all. Being very generous by nature, he never refused a request for aid and dispensed millions in loans, gifts and general philanthropy ... When he started on a journey, every mayor, dressed in his best clothes, awaited him at the entrance of his village, kissed his hands, and paid homage, as if he were a king. And he was a king of sorts: under his reign peace and order were observed, the Mafia peace, of course, which was not what the official law of the Kingdom of Italy would have imposed, but people did not stop to draw too fine a distinction.

In fact, this is the picture of the Mafia that the mafioso would like to project: mayors would have been very unwise to go and kiss the hands of one who was watched by both police and Carabinieri, and by the American police. Cascioferro was generous with some, but horribly cruel with the weak. He was certainly not loved by the relations of his victims. But he had the appearance of a nobleman, he did go to the elegant houses in Palermo and could 'rescue' stolen goods as the contemporary bosses still do.

Don Vito Cascioferro had succeeded in organizing rackets and criminality, and it is in that period that one can begin to consider the Mafia and the Black Hand as organized groups of associations. (This of course does not mean that there were not other *cosche* which had never heard the name of Cascioferro.) He had become a legend even when he was alive, and he is partially responsible for creating the image of the gallant gentlemanly *capomafia*. But one thing should be clear: emerging in the criminal worlds of Sicily and Brooklyn meant—and means— murder, violence, crime and cruelty. There is no such person as the kind, loyal and good *capocosca* or *capomafia*.

Lieutenant Petrosino had come to Sicily to investigate the network of criminal activities between the USA and Sicily. He had already been able to find incriminating evidence, although he had received little assistance from the local authorities. But he was on the right track and there was no question as to what caused his execution. It was a lesson for others, a warning not to poke one's nose into that kind of business.

Therefore it must be executed openly, like all Mafia killings, and receive maximum publicity. It certainly did. Petrosino was too smart a policeman to be shot in daytime, so he was tricked into meeting two informers at night: he was killed in the Piazza Marina, the very centre of Palermo. A contemporary police report gives away an important detail which has never previously been reported: Petrosino was shot 'when, walking by the fence of the gardens, the poor detective had stopped to satisfy a corporal need'. The mafiosi had wanted to humiliate him, choosing an undignified moment to kill their enemy. It is vulgar and odious, but it gives a faithful and non-romantic idea of Cascioferro's world.

Had Cascioferro just wanted to get rid of Petrosino, an 'accident' could easily have been arranged, but this was an execution, planned in all its details. Twenty-one days after the murder, the police officer Cavaliere Ponzi found Don Vito Cascioferro at Bisacquino. It was late in the afternoon of 3 April 1909, and Don Vito was coming off the train and walking towards his coach which had been waiting for him. 'Had I known you were looking for me,' he said smiling, 'I would have felt it my duty to come and see you, Cavaliere.' Even before being asked about the murder of Petrosino, Don Vito declared sarcastically: 'One thing must be clear, my dear gentlemen. From the sixth to the fourteenth of March I was staying, night and day, at the house of the Rt. Hon. de Michele. Ask him to confirm this, if you like.' And of course he had: and of course it had not been he who had shot Petrosino, but hired killers, one of whom was probably the same Fontana who had murdered Notarbartolo and who was already safe in the States.

Don Vito was immediately sent to the Ucciardone prison in Palermo, where he was questioned at length. He said nothing, and refused to sign anything. He declared that what there was to say, he would have said at his trial. Many anonymous letters came to the police; two, sent from New York, are particularly interesting. The first, dated 13 March, had been written when the news of Petrosino's murder had appeared in American newspapers, but before any names had been connected with it. It read:

Illustrissimo Signor Questore ... I want to tell you that the organizers of such a murder were: Giuseppe Morello, head of the Black Hand, Giuseppe Fontana, the killer of Marchese Notarbartolo, Ignazio Milone, Pietro Inzerillo proprietor of the dive 'Stella d'Italia' [in

Brooklyn]. And the two Terranova brothers, stepbrothers of Morello. All of the Black Hand, all very dangerous individuals. The job was given to them by their colleague Vito Cascioferro, from Bisacquino, whose photograph Petrosino, who wished to arrest him, always carried with him. All this is as much as I can tell you. Secrecy and nothing but secrecy.

It was signed by 'An honest citizen'. The same person sent a second letter three days later. It confirmed names while giving more specific details and added that the decision to kill Petrosino had been taken in New York, and that the mafiosi had each contributed a certain amount of money in order to pay the hired killers. 'Today in New York all this is no mystery for anybody. Many of the Black Hand talk about this with pride.'

After Petrosino's murder, both New York and Palermo police gave the following account of Vito Cascioferro's activities: '... he is notoriously affiliated to the "high" Mafia; he has wide links in the provinces round Bisaquino and in the province of Bivona, Sciacca and Palermo where he controls the worst criminals.' Although the police could not find out where his income came from, the report describes Cascioferro as leading a life of luxury, going to the theatre, cafés, gambling high sums at the Circolo dei Civili. Therefore they thought that during his journeys, when it was highly difficult to keep track of him 'for his uncommon cunning', he was able to organize thefts and robberies. He was a 'grand elector' for the deputy De Michele, the police report goes on, and at election times Cascioferro would go to those villages (Burgio, Bivona, etc.) where De Michele was a candidate, and organize his elections for him.

Cascioferro was arrested in 1926 by the Fascist Prefetto Mori, the policeman charged by Mussolini to wipe out the Mafia. He was condemned by the Court of Assizes of Agrigento to life imprisonment for the murder of Francesco Falconieri and of Gioacchino Lo Voi. After the sentence had been read out, Cascioferro answered that he had been guilty of many crimes, but he was being condemned for the only ones he had never committed. This was his sarcastic comment on legality and Fascist justice. It was probably the only time Cascioferro had told the truth.

When in 1945 he asked for a pardon, it was denied on the grounds that relations of the many people who had been killed by Don Vito might take some form of private revenge. He died in prison, an old man. At the Ucciardone his former cell is still said to be reserved for important criminals, but these legends must be taken with a pinch of salt. On the cell wall he had carved an old Sicilian proverb, 'Prison, sickness and necessity reveal the real heart of a man,' but recently a coat of paint covered Don Vito's last message.

Petrosino's murder underlined the strong links which had been woven between the 'American' Sicilians and the locals: a bridge, a 'black bridge', was to plague both nations—but especially America. When Petrosino had paid a visit to Mr Bishop, the American consul in Palermo, he had told him: 'I don't trust the Italian police at all, I've learnt things here that would make your hair stand on end.' The mistrust was reciprocal: both bodies were corrupt since both police forces depended on politicians who—on both sides of the Atlantic—often asked for the Mafia's electoral support. Petrosino himself had written in a report: 'Another factor to be taken into consideration is that, within a short time following their arrival in America, many of the most hardened Italian criminals become associated with certain political cliques for which they work and from which they receive unlimited protection in return.' The Italian investigating magistrate—who was to be dismissed before completing his work—saw at once that Petrosino's arrival in Palermo had frightened those Black Hand chiefs threatened with deportation, such as Vito Cascioferro, Giuseppe Morello and Giuseppe Fontana, against whom extradition proceedings had begun.

When Morello was convicted in New York (witnesses suddenly recovered their memories), it was because a new criminal generation was pressing for power; these men had already changed their first names into American ones, and the 'Mafia slang' was taking shape. They were Diamond Jim Colosimo, Giuseppe Masseria, called 'Joe the Boss', and Johnny Torio, whose godson was a little boy called Alfonso Capone, known as 'Al'.

Organized crime is America's biggest business. Recent (1965) estimates of the Department of Justice give it as forty billion dollars a year. It pays no taxes except the bribes for corrupting public officials, which are a form of taxation. Besides illicit rackets, it has taken over legitimate business and labour unions. Valachi said that 'Cosa Nostra', which was the name by which the various Black Hand associations were to be called, is a state within a state, a 'second government' as Joe Valachi himself explained.*

The Italian criminals did not begin to be a national American force until 1920. The catalyst was, of course, Prohibition, besides prostitution and gambling. The most powerful figures were Alfonso Capone, a Neapolitan, and Giuseppe Masseria. The latter had powerful allies whose names will continue to figure in police documents for many years to come. They were 'Lucky' Luciano, Vito Genovese, William Moretti (William Moore), Joe Adonis, and Joseph Doto.

Salvatore 'Lucky' Luciano (Salvatore Luciania, from Lercara Friddi in Sicily) earned his nickname when he was kidnapped by a rival gang who were after some narcotics he had hidden. Luciano was taken to a deserted section of Staten Island and hung up by the thumbs from a tree, tortured with razors and lighted cigarettes. But he refused to talk. Believing him to be near death, he was left, but he lived and the legend of Charley Lucky was born. He was to become one of the most powerful bosses Cosa Nostra ever had, holding court in a suite in the Waldorf-Astoria Hotel where he resided as Mr Charles Ross.

In the beginning there was a traditional tension between the Neapolitans and the Sicilians (Vito Genovese was a Neapolitan too) and they were fragmented according to those who had emigrated from a particular Italian village or region. The largest single unit came from Castellammare, a lovely port in the province of Trapani, near Alcamo. Even dispersed throughout the territory of the United States, the Castellammaresi retained strong links, and were under the rule of one single boss, Salvatore Maranzano, who lived in New York. Bidding for supremacy, in 1930, Joe the Boss Masseria decided to eliminate Maranzano and his group, which included Joseph Bonanno (Joe Bananas) and Joseph Profaci of Brooklyn, Stefano Maggadino in Buffalo, Joseph Aiello in Chicago. Masseria also tried successfully to eliminate Gaetano Reina, who was in his own group, because Reina controlled the ice

---

* Valachi, who had committed at least thirty-three murders by his count, had a $100,000 price tag placed on his head by Cosa Nostra and became its first major defector. Robert Kennedy said of him: 'For the first time an insider—a knowledgeable member of the hierarchy—has broken the underworld's code of silence. The picture is an ugly one. It shows what has been aptly described as a private government of organized crime, a government with an annual income of billions, resting on a base of human suffering and moral corrosion.' Peter Maas's summary of Valachi's story, *The Valachi Papers*, is still the most interesting and accurate book about Cosa Nostra.

distribution in New York (this was before refrigerators). Reina was shot in February 1930 by 'unknown persons'. But Reina's murder united his gang in the war against Joe the Boss. (All these facts form the background of Puzo's book *The Godfather*.)

During the 'Castellammarese war' murders were everyday events: they were commissioned 'under contract', and the henchmen knew very little about their target or the reasons for killing him. They always had with them 'the base', a man who knew the person who was to be murdered and knew his habits. Throughout 1930 and 1931, sixty bodies were left on the streets of America. Valachi describes the lavish funeral for a nephew of the boss Terranova who had been shot dead by 'Maranzano's boys'; the coffin was of solid bronze, and it had cost 15,000 dollars. Five funeral directors had been asked to share the work, and more than ten thousand people turned up to watch the cortege. There were forty cars to carry the flowers alone. The most impressive was a crown of white and red roses thirteen feet high, sent, as usual, anonymously.

Carlo Gambino, who was in the 'Masseria family', went over to Maranzano's side; finally Lucky Luciano and Vito Genovese turned against Masseria, because he was losing. In return for their promise to murder Masseria, Maranzano said he would end the war. On 15 April 1931 Masseria was invited by Lucky Luciano to lunch in a Coney Island restaurant called Scarpato. This is such a famous scene, many times reconstructed in films, that it has become difficult to describe it.

Joe the Boss Masseria had a good meal, and died, shot around 3.30 pm in the back and head by 'persons unknown'. When the police arrived, Lucky Luciano was in the restaurant. He said that he could not help them as he knew very little. After lunch, he and Joe the Boss had played cards for about forty-five minutes while the restaurant emptied. Then Luciano had to go to the men's room but, as he was washing his hands, he heard some noise, rushed back to the restaurant and found Masseria dead. The staff could not help the police either: nobody had seen a thing.

Maranzano became the boss of the bosses. Their meetings used to take place in a huge hall in the Bronx. 'Religious pictures had been put up on the walls and there was a crucifix over the platform where Mr Maranzano was sitting,' Valachi recalled. 'He had done this so that if outsiders wondered what the meeting was about, they would think we belonged to some kind of holy society ...'

Maranzano had been born at Castellammare and had emigrated to the United States after the First World War. In Sicily he had studied to become a priest, had a passion for Julius Caesar, and was quite well-read. Valachi described him: 'I was led to the other side of the table ... and the other guy said "Joe, meet Don Salvatore Maranzano. He is going to be the boss for all of us throughout the whole trouble we are having." This was the first time I even saw him. Gee, he looked just like a banker. You'd never guess in a million years that he was a racketeer.'

At a large meeting in which he talked Italian, Maranzano set down the foundation for the thorough organization of Cosa Nostra. He said that there was to be no more killing; he was going to be *Capo dei Capi*, and each *Capo* would head a family. Family units would each be supreme in its area. These areas included Boston, Buffalo, Chicago, Cleveland, Detroit, Kansas City, Los Angeles, Newark, New Orleans, New York City, Philadelphia, Pittsburg, San Francisco, Miami, Las Vegas. Pre-Castro Havana was 'open'; any family could conduct operations there.

The ruler of a family was known as the *Capo*, boss. Next, *subcapo* or underboss. *Caporegime*, or lieutenants, each in charge of a *regime*, a crew. A crew was composed of soldiers. When the soldier wanted to see the boss, he had to ask through his lieutenant, who would judge whether his request was important or not. Death was prescribed for anyone who told his wife about the secrets of Cosa Nostra. An order which came from the boss to the lieutenant and from the lieutenant to his soldier had to be obeyed, otherwise again the death penalty. At this meeting, it was decided that New York was to be carved up between five families: Frank Costello/Lucky Luciano, Tom Gagliano, Joseph Profaci, Joe Bonanno and Vincent Mangano. As underboss Luciano had Vito Genovese, Mangano had Albert Anastasia. It became a tightly knit secret criminal society, difficult to attack because of its political and police connections, and because of the brilliance of some of its leaders.

Being 'Boss of the Bosses' went to Maranzano's head. Maranzano in fact wished to control all the rackets himself and he decided to 'go to the mattress': moving from one apartment to another—in other words, 'war'. It was the wrong decision, because his enemies this time were the cunning Lucky Luciano and the terrible gangster Genovese, as well as Al Capone, Frank Costello and Joe Adonis. A few months after arranging Masseria's murder, Lucky Luciano set up Maranzano's. On the night he was shot, about forty leaders who had sided with him died as well. 'I was lucky I wasn't in the office,' said Valachi, who was with

Maranzano and who had received a warning. 'But a lot of others around Mr Maranzano who got caught sleeping, slept forever.'

The young generation had eliminated the old.

The names of Luciano, Genovese and Costello were to become household words. Their links with Sicily were to be interrupted during Fascist times, but, when the American authorities imitated the notorious practice of their Italian counterparts, by accepting the Mafia's collaboration and help, Cosa Nostra became an official institution which knew too many secrets about too many important people, many of which are secrets even today.

To go to America became the dream of all Sicilians, and when they saw those 'undesirables' coming back to their island rich and respected—sent back because not even American law had succeeded in convicting them—America became the dream of all the criminals.

The American Mafia, from a loose group called vaguely 'The Black Hand' (a name borrowed from a Corsican sect), became the organized Cosa Nostra. It had all the characteristics of the Sicilian Mafia, but differed in its need for a 'constitution' and formal 'membership'. This was because the mafiosi in America had to deal with a population who lacked the Mafia mentality, did not naturally respect the law of silence, of personal revenge, and did not feel contempt for the State and its institutions: on the contrary, the Americans believed in their country. Therefore Maranzano, who claimed to have borrowed his ideas for the semi-military organization of the American Mafia from Julius Caesar, gave a face to the new monster whose construction had been the work of men like Morello, Cascioferro and Masseria.

5 Competition

Notarbartolo and Petrosino had died in obvious Mafia killings. Palizzolo and Cascioferro, unquestionably the men responsible, had gone free. The state decided that organized crime had been successfully erased and the word 'Mafia' was eliminated from the vocabulary. No one questioned the methods of the Liberal Giolitti, five times prime minister between 1892 and 1921. His use of patronage and support of 'grand electors' were similar to Crispi's, if more sophisticated. 'Not knowing the nature of the Mafia,' Candida observed naïvely, 'he considered that organization for the number of votes it could gather for the government ... it is well known how elections are conducted there.' And no one questioned the fact that one of the most powerful and popular Sicilian MPs, Nunzio Nasi, from Trapani, was a mafioso.

The Mafia's own union with Italy had been consummated by institutionalization. Now that it had successfully negotiated the hazards of the post-1860 period it had also reached the other objective identified by Mack Smith when he wrote of that era: 'Far from Rome being able to improve the South, it was rather Southern methods of clientelage and political sharp practice which would soon be seeking further areas of profitable employment in the national capital itself.' The electoral struggle of an anti-governmental candidate was almost impossible because he did not have jobs to offer or favours to grant in return for electoral support. This Sicilian feature of *clientelismo* applies in Italian politics to this day.

The socio-economic investigation into Sicily by Professor Giovanni Lorenzoni, started on behalf of the Italian Parliament in 1907 and finished in 1910, was the last official inquiry until 1962. Lorenzoni made two visits to the island, and travelled on horseback to hamlets and villages in order to see the problems of the peasantry for himself. After studying how the land had been distributed, he disclosed that in the process there had been 'terrible injustices': the peasantry had been kept away with threats and violence. Landowners who succeeded in buying land near villages had immediately divided it into smallholdings and sold it back to peasants who were always 'hungry for soil'. While Franchetti had come to the conclusion that those responsible for the Sicilian social conditions were the nobles and the middle classes, Lorenzoni thought that real responsibility lay with the politicians.

An earlier report of 1877 by the Jacini commission had concluded that the Sicilians were 'an immoral and perverted race', racially inferior, and in need of some good Northern blood, 'as suggested by science'. Lorenzoni countered this proto-Fascist view:

> For the greater part, the Sicilians are good and noble. They are tenacious in their affections, make sacrifices for friends; profoundly attached to the land where they were born, they face the risks and the toils of emigration, living in a foreign country as poorly as possible in order to spare a little money to send back to their families. They keep their word, easily get inflamed by noble ideals, and if they are well led, they can behave heroically.

Private revenge, Lorenzoni thought, 'increased murders because, if the offence is remedied by the State, the cycle closes; but if it is remedied by the individual, a new cycle is opened.' The Mafia came into being from the lack of trust in justice, from which followed the principles of private revenge and *omertà*. It was 'an exaggeration of the feeling of the self and had become a *modus vivendi*.'

Lorenzoni underlined the reactionary and conservative nature of the Mafia, its hatred of peasants' cooperatives, and made a distinction between Mafia and delinquency (banditry). The Mafia, he said, was a central group which extended towards the upper echelons of society to obtain protection and towards the lowest for the execution of its crimes. Not all the protectors of the Mafia (which was difficult to hit for this very reason) were mafiosi, but among those were authorities who in a moment of weakness had asked for the Mafia's help in having a candidate elected, thus giving an example. 'This is more damaging than the deeds of one thousand mafiosi, because it nourishes the source of the Mafia spirit: the contempt for authority and justice and the State which, in making use of the mafiosi, becomes itself mafioso.'

The Lorenzoni report was perceptive, but had little practical effect. To remind the government and public opinion that conditions in Sicily were still far from ideal and that the Mafia did exist, Duke Colonna di Cesarò called a congress 'against criminality and illiteracy' at Agrigento from 21 to 25 May, 1911. It was an 'intellectual' affair, just like the congress that Danilo Dolci was to promote in the 1950s at Palma di Montechiaro, near Agrigento. It took place in the Margherita theatre, and gathered scholars of many denominations and political leanings. One of them was a priest, Don Sturzo, the organizer of Sicilian Catholic labourers. The MP Napoleone Colajanni presided.

In the province of Agrigento, both the phenomenon of criminality (Mafia) and that of illiteracy were and are particularly acute. But the peasantry, among the poorest in Europe, had shown itself capable of organizing into cooperatives so that the retaliation of the Mafia against the social leaders (many of whom were compelled to emigrate) had been particularly intense. On 16 May a few days before the opening of the conference, the trade unionist Lorenzo Panepinto had been murdered. By then, Sicilian public opinion was convinced that the Mafia was linked with the government, and this gave the mafiosi respectability and power. In fact, this well-founded belief was one of the reasons why so many emigrated; they were convinced that nothing could change in Sicily because some individuals were too powerful.

On opening the Agrigento conference, Colajanni pointed out that illiteracy in the province reached seventy-five per cent (Palermo sixty-two per cent) and that there had been 38.75 murders for each 100,000 inhabitants (in the Veneto the comparable figure was 2.31). Many different opinions were aired about Sicily's problems; again some blamed the biological inferiority of the Sicilian race, which made it difficult for the rest of Italy to advance on the road of progress. Since many politicians (including the Minister of Justice) were present, the links between the Mafia and the government were discreetly left unmentioned. Nevertheless the Congress was a kind of success, as was shown by the enormous crowd that gathered to see the important men who had come to derelict Agrigento to discuss such unmentionable topics as poverty and illiteracy.

The conquest of Libya under the premiership of Giolitti in 1912 consumed money and energies which could have greatly helped the Sicilian peasantry. During that period the young Calogero Vizzini, who was to become one of the leading mafiosi, devoted himself to the black market. As the boss of Villalba he came to exert such authority over the whole area that it became one of the most important Mafia centres. After only ten years of rule he was accused of thirty-nine murders, six attempted murders, thirteen acts of private violence, thirty-six robberies, sixty-three extortions, thirty-seven thefts and various other minor crimes.

Poverty, blackmail and disorder, which were a consequence of the perpetual state of war, were fertile ground for the Mafia. Many Sicilians refused conscription (always a bugbear) and became deserters, bandits or Mafia pawns. The requisition of horses, mules and donkeys in a region without roads, and where cultivated land was generally far away from houses, made life particularly hard, and the Italian government particularly hated.

On the other hand the fact that many young Sicilians had gone to fight at the front meant that their vision was enlarged, and socialist ideas were brought back to the island. After the 14–18 war the Socialist party grew stronger and larger. Also the Partito Popolare under the priest Don Sturzo was standing on advanced radical positions, organizing labourers in the countryside. While in the North workers occupied factories, in the South peasants occupied the land (there were almost no factories to occupy). It was the century's great opening to the Left, and at last Sicily took part in the great European movement which might have meant the de-provincialization of the island and the overthrow of its social and mafioso structure. When in 1918 the Sicilian peasantry formed once again into cooperatives, the government had to behave better than under Crispi just because many peasants were ex-combatants.

The peasants took over large latifundia, some of which had been left uncultivated. At times they occupied the land carrying a red flag and singing the International. Others were led by the Catholic party of Don Sturzo, who demanded land reform.

Suffrage had been extended in 1913, and in the post-war elections Sicily did not return to Rome the usual number of solid pro-government MPs. The Sicilian Liberals were cut from forty-two to twenty-one, and instead of one Socialist MP, seven were sent to Central Parliament. It was an insult to the ruling class, represented by the new Prime Minister, the Sicilian Vittorio Emanuele Orlando, one of Giolitti's disciples. He had built his career at Partinico, a town so notorious for its poverty and Mafia rule that Danilo Dolci chose it as his centre.

Partinico is in the particularly crowded coastal area behind Palermo, surrounded by villages and towns. It controls a lot of votes. The post-war *capocosca* in Partinico was something more than just a boss controlling trade and political power: he was a real kingmaker. Just as many MPs today owe their election to Frank Coppola, the Partinico boss, so Vittorio Emanuele Orlando owed his strength to the Partinico king-makers. As the latter felt more and more protected, their henchmen became arrogant. Two of them even wrote to *Il Giornale di Sicilia* declaring that they were the killers of a certain Desiderio Sorge. This man had so antagonized them by not answering two letters of extortion, they wrote, and even by denouncing them to the police, that he had deserved the lesson. What is extraordinary in this episode is that the two killers obviously felt outraged by the poor man's behaviour.

Yet it was the new peasant militancy that worried landowners, and often the latifundia were divided, not by law but by that kind of pressure. When he went back to Sicily, Professor Lorenzoni, the author of the leading study on Sicilian agriculture, remarked that where land had been divided among peasants there had been amazing improvements; better crops, drainage, irrigation, crop rotation, and a natural elimination of the *gabelloto* and of parasitic people, followed as the peasants formed into cooperatives. Three ministers of agriculture from 1919 to 1920 had to legitimize what had happened spontaneously. (But in 1920 alone four peasant leaders were murdered by the Mafia.)

In 1922 the Sicilian Socialist party returned twenty MPs to Rome out of the fifty-two Sicilian deputies, an unprecedented number, and no Fascist MP was elected in Sicily. This was partly because Sicily had no industrial working class and no militant labour movement, but even more relevant is the fact that Sicily had no industrial middle class to be scared by Socialism and to support Fascism. The industrialist class, which in the North gave total support to Mussolini, was nowhere to be found in Sicily and, anyway, as Denis Mack Smith remarks, 'Sicily had more traditional methods of intimidation.'

But as hunger grew and rage boiled, violence repeatedly swept the island. In the province of Palermo there were 223 murders in 1922; 224 in the following year, 278 in 1924, and 168 in 1925. Internal wars among Mafia families were increasing as sources of wealth became even scantier and cities were carved up between the *cosche*.

But after the March on Rome in 1922, which brought Mussolini the premiership, many of those who had followed Giolitti and Vittorio Emanuele Orlando switched to the Fascist party. The party hierarchy and administration was a source of the kind of jobs which appealed to the Southern mind. In 1924, thirty-eight Fascist MPs were elected in Sicily (out of fifty-seven) and Orlando, who had supported Mussolini's party, only discovered too late that Fascism would not collaborate in the old system based on respect for the coalition.

For twenty-one years Sicily was to be under Fascist rule, but for twenty-one years it remained forgotten; little was spent on roads, reforms and agriculture. The only large expenditure went into suppressing the Mafia which, once again, was wrongly assumed to be a single entity, an organization, a society which could be exterminated by sheer repression and brutal force. Mussolini used the bosses' influence until 1924, but after the Liberal party machine (with all its Mafia undertones) had helped him to power, he abolished the electoral machine on which the Mafia had flourished. Two such similar systems could not survive together (they used the same methods, and they had the same aims), and it was good publicity to stamp out criminality and the Mafia. Mussolini rightly saw in the Mafia a force of independence, of separatism, and therefore a threat to the Fascist objectives of national unity and 'totalitarianism' (a word invented by Mussolini himself). Specially printed school textbooks underlined Sicily's 'strong ties' with the mainland.

Mussolini's first journey to Sicily was on 4 May 1924. He stayed only five days, visiting the main centres, Palermo, Agrigento, Piana dei Greci, Trapani, Marsala, all of them strongholds of *cosche mafiose*. This was before his takeover (which took place on 3 January, 1925). In Palermo Mussolini spoke reproaching the Sicilians of *sicilianesimo* (Mussolini went in for invented words), which for the Duce meant separatism, feudalism and Mafia. He added that he wanted to go 'towards the population', but any actions against the regime could not be tolerated—nations had to be governed with a will of iron and a wrist of steel (another of his sentences which was to become famous). At Agrigento he referred more openly to the Mafia, and said that he 'could not tolerate that a few hundred criminals held down a population as magnificent as yours'.

His visit to Piana dei Greci is famous (well described by many authors, including Denis Mack Smith, Renato Candida, Michele Pantaleone, and by the Antimafia parliamentary documents). Mussolini was treated by the local boss Don Ciccio Cuccia, a powerful source of votes, just like any other visiting politician who, ultimately, would have to ask his help on many things, including votes. But Mussolini resented being bracketed with Vittorio Emanuele Orlando, or Crispi or Giolitti; his strong egocentricism was offended. Cuccia, who was also mayor of the town, accompanied Mussolini by car, and seeing all the policemen who were escorting the Prime Minister, said: '*Voscenza, signor Capitano, viene con mia e non ha da temere niente. Che bisogno aveva di tanti sbirri?*' ('You're coming with me and there's nothing to worry about. Why do you need so many cops?')

The Sicilian dominant class was given by the Fascist state an effective replacement for the methods of the Mafia in matters like the repression of the organized peasants' movement. Fascism was seen as a regime which would not seek any agrarian reforms which would benefit the peasantry. The 'criminal' Mafia could not work in harness with the Fascist state.* Fascism could not admit any coexistence with the Mafia, which not only gave a 'bad name' to the glittering image which Fascism wanted to give Italy under the new regime, but used its own methods of pseudo-legality. When elections were abolished in 1925, the Fascist party deprived the Mafia of its major instrument of alliance with the government and of control over the politicians. Besides, Italy was becoming more and more a police state, and the Fascist police could not take long in attacking the criminal manifestations of the Mafia.

Under the jurisdiction of Prefect Mori, repression became savage. Many mafiosi were sent to prison, killed or tortured, but also many left-wingers were called 'mafiosi' for the occasion, and were disposed of. Some people used the eternal Sicilian weapon of the anonymous letter to get rid of personal enemies who had nothing to do with criminality. In many cases the landowners provided Mori with information against the mafiosi they had so far employed, who had been their means to safeguard their interests against the peasantry. This was logical because they saw that the regime would provide a better and cheaper substitute. During Fascist times the number of murders diminished, although it is risky to trust Fascist figures any more than contemporary official statistics. (For example, a person who can just

---

* But the 'High Mafia' succeeded in penetrating the party hierarchy. Dangerous criminals like Vito Genovese, who had escaped from the USA where special prosecutor Dewey wanted to put him on trial for murder, easily infiltrated the Fascist structure, and were even given honorific titles. In Luciano's own words: 'He (V.G.) found out that Mussolini's son-in-law took cocaine, and that was all Vito hadda know. From then on, he was Ciano's personal supplier.'

write his name is considered literate, so that one should always double the official number of illiterates.) In fact, compared with today, criminality under the Fascist regime was higher, which shows that repression is no cure.

	murders	attempted murders	kidnappings thefts extortions	association to crime	thefts
1926	294	241	1,097	133	11,013
1972	52	101	197.6	55	37,915
Ratio of crimes to inhabitants, 1926	$\frac{1}{6,472}$	$\frac{1}{7,816}$	$\frac{1}{1,734}$	$\frac{1}{14,300}$	$\frac{1}{173}$
Ratio of crimes to inhabitants, 1972	$\frac{1}{43,430}$	$\frac{1}{22,360}$	$\frac{1}{66,300}$	$\frac{1}{41,061}$	$\frac{1}{59.5}$

In 1926, the population of the four provinces was of 1,902,000 people; in the census of 1971, 2,258,381, an increase of about twelve per cent.

A new law of 1926 laid down that 'people described by *vox publica* as bosses, partners or sympathizers of associations which have a criminal character or which are in any way dangerous to the community' could be denounced, immediately arrested and sent to the *confino*. The island was outraged. Even Vittorio Emanuele Orlando, who had retired from politics, spoke out in defence of the population—and of the Mafia. Nevertheless Fascism tended to hit the small *mafiosetti*—the henchmen, the small fry—and not the powerful, although the latter found themselves in isolation, since the substructure was missing. But the conditions from which the Mafia had sprung up were left untouched: with the Fascist and mafioso practice of official jobs imposed from above, *mafiosità* flourished.

Mussolini had given emergency powers to the 'Superprefetto' Mori, a veteran of the post-war campaign against workers and peasant agitations. Mori tried to kill the legend of the Mafia's courage and sense of honour, and to dismantle the myth of the necessity of the Mafia as a substitute for an efficient state. He showed that the regime meant real business by concentrating arrests in villages where up to one hundred people would be imprisoned on the same night. He also wanted to 'humiliate the island': under a special order all the high walls in Sicily had to be pulled down. This changed the landscape and the Arab-like aspect of Sicilian towns, but it did not change the practice of shooting people from behind a wall. It was certainly the first time that the bosses came under attack. Don Ciccio Cuccia was imprisoned and so were Vizzini, Genco Russo and Vito Cascioferro, all of whom were suddenly treated like ordinary criminals. But protection was of some use, and Calogero Vizzini and Genco Russo were released for 'lack of proof', just as in the good old days.

Firearm licences were withdrawn, cattle were efficiently branded and all citizens had to carry an identification document. Mori even instituted a prize for the best Sicilian school essay on how to destroy the Mafia. A new law made sure that the *gabelloto* had to be a person with a clear police record. All crimes must be denounced at once. Within a month from the diktat, all landowners had to report on all grottoes, caves and disused mines in their territories (to avoid their giving refuge to bandits). While Vittorio Emanuele Orlando had always done everything possible to say in his speeches that the Mafia hardly existed, that he did not know it, the Fascist regime blew it up sky-high. On 26 May 1927, in a speech called *'L'Ascensione'* (as with Papal Bulls, every speech had a name, so that one could quote from them), Mussolini praised Mori's repressive methods. He couldn't care less, he said, if there had been criticism about the way the repression had been conducted, and he praised the 'Fascist surgery'. He reminded his listeners of his encounter with Don Cuccia: '... and many of you will remember that ineffable mayor who found all means to be photographed on every important occasion: he is in prison and he will stay there for a long time!'

By 1928, Mori declared that the Mafia had been cleaned up, and from now on the Sicilians would look on the Fascist state and law as supreme. Many believed him, and it must be said that the propaganda about the Fascist eradication of the Mafia was so intense that it was difficult not to believe it. Countries which have not been subjected to the hammering of political propaganda forget how difficult it is to resist it mentally. The *Resto del Carlino* wrote: 'The extirpation of the Mafia will open the way to the rise of a middle class, based on the modern technical development of Sicily, which feudalism, served by organized crime and its network of political corruption, has always debased.' But when Cesare Mori, who was by no means an intelligent or subtle man, began to understand where the responsibility had lain, and denounced aristocrats and landowners, he was dismissed. And although Mussolini was proclaiming outright victory over the Mafia, mafiosi were still being arrested in 1935.

An interesting account occurs in Tina Whitaker's diary for 1930 (from *Princes under the Volcano*):

> I must allude to the great work being done against the Mafia which hitherto held Western Sicily in its mesh. The Mafia came originally into being, though not at first by that name, long before the unity of Italy, as an assertion of self-defence against government tyranny and oppression, but gradually it degenerated into an association of evildoers spread over the greater part of the island. Murder, rapine and total lawlessness prevailed unchecked, while landed proprietors, in order to be able to visit their estates, were obliged to pay a heavy toll for safety—not only for their own persons, but for the fruits of their lands and cattle grazing on their fields. In pre-fascist days the worst class, the scum, was protected by the government to secure its votes for the elections. These elections were the bane of the country and have now been done away with, swept aside by Mussolini as a mere heap of rubbish. First the local administrative elections were abolished, and now the Parliamentary ones are controlled through the Grand Council ... The fascist methods have been extolled by some of the most prominent of British journalists, but it should be realized that an evil of such long standing as the Mafia cannot be scrapped in a few short months or even years. Grave injustices have been inevitable in the wholesale imprisonments that have taken place under this repression, and the trials have been totally inadequate. The innocent have been left lying one or even two years in lurid prisons, owing to the insufficient number of judges ... The sparing of the upper classes has led to grave discontent, and important mafiosi have been left at large, some actually in power—while underlings and their dependants, far less to blame, receive heavy penalties and long years of imprisonment. So the Mafia is not yet destroyed ...

A brilliant piece of insight.

Mussolini was back in Sicily in 1937. 'Sicily is the geographical centre of the Empire,' he proclaimed (an empire which, of course, included Africa). The island might have been the centre of an empire, but it was still abysmally poor. The war in Ethiopia and commitments in the

Spanish Civil War drained the already dry funds. Mussolini's 'Battle of Wheat' had been disastrous—no expert had been consulted. Later, when the discontent against the regime grew, new laws for agricultural reclamation were passed: one of 1940 forced the owners of the latifundia to create houses for the peasantry on the land they were to cultivate. Farmhouses and hamlets were built in central Sicily to designs created for Tuscany, which took no account of the needs of a Sicilian peasantry. They were isolated, and without water or plumbing. Many of these empty, sad agglomerations still stand in central Sicily. They were never used.

In trying to win over the lower strata of the population, Fascism lost its grip on the upper class too, and the Mafia began to assert itself again. Local frustration was such that, in 1941, the Fascist government had decided to transfer all Sicilian-born officials to Italy because of suspected disloyalty. Like all Italian laws, this too was fortunately ignored and disobeyed. The Sicilian temper was rising high. The island could hardly wait for yet another change of regime.

12.   1950   The growth of the Giuliano legend (see Appendix Two for the ballad version)
(*Gigi Petyx*)

13. 1954 The last photograph of Don Calò Vizzini, last of the old-style Mafia bosses (*Gigi Petyx*)

14. July 1954 The funeral of Don Calò Vizzini at Villalba (*Agenzia Scafidi*)

6 The Mafia and the Sicilian landing

'There has been to date no element of official United States policy explicitly directed to Sicily ...' The Americans, as this quote from a Top Secret document from the Special Military plan for Psychological Warfare (WO 204/3701 X/J 9867) shows, had not prepared themselves for landing in Sicily. When Sicily was chosen as the first stepping-stone to Europe, they quickly collected intelligence reports, some of which make very interesting reading.

The landowning class and the mafiosi, for their part, had clear-cut goals: separation from Italy, independence and possibly a new role as a new state of the United States of America. Once again, the two Sicilian ruling groups had the same aim and acted together. Both American and British intelligence played up these political aims. Agents were parachuted onto the island.

Their reports were inaccurate—perhaps intentionally—about the amount of German forces stationed in Sicily and on the amount of resistance that the Italian army would have mounted. 'The presence of great masses of German troops stationed in Sicily draws heavily upon the scarce food resources of the country ...' It is interesting to note that a pencil mark queried this sentence when the top-secret document, sent from the USA (28 April 1943), reached the British War Office. The agents who were giving these pieces of intelligence to the Americans were Sicilians, most of them mafiosi.

British Intelligence, rather than the War Office, had always indicated Sicily as the ideal landing place, the best first approach to Europe. There had been two rough plans for the landing in Sicily, 'Influx' (1940) and 'Whipcord' (1941), before the final and definitive 'Husky' plan. As late as January 1943, at the Casablanca conference, Winston Churchill had finally talked Roosevelt into approaching Italy—and Europe—

from Sicily. Sardinia would have been a better base for planes to bomb the Italian mainland and support future landings, but Sicily offered other advantages. These were political and psychological rather than strategic—the Psychological Warfare Branch had an extremely important role in the Second World War: 'Sicilians consider themselves as distinct from continental Italians ... A good many Sicilians have been in the US and have picked up some English. They are highly individualistic and vengeful.' (W.O. 204/10096).

Sicily was, first of all, ready to surrender. The Fascist regime, which had caused the arrest of so many, was hated; its unpopularity with the lower classes, which had suffered most by Mori's repression, was now extended to the two upper classes, the mafiosi *gabelloti* and the land-owning nobility, since the regime had made land concessions to the land labourers. The American secret document already mentioned (X/J 9867) points out that 'tens of thousands of Sicilians emigrated to the United States during the first thirteen years of this century ...' Many had returned with savings, settling in their home towns—'Their attitude towards the United States is generally very favourable.' There were links between Sicilians in America and their relations in Sicily which had been maintained in spite of the war through 'mutual assistance associations which customarily bear the name of the Sicilian town from which its founders emigrated.' The social pattern is briefly summarized: 'The nobility, people of wealth, and those of the learned professions who stand at the top of the social pyramid, are regarded with fear and treated with deference. The continuing pattern of poverty, exploitation and governmental corruption has resulted in frequent uprisings ...' Many Sicilians had connections in the United States (not all criminal connections) and spoke some English; there had been commercial and political links with the English from Nelson's time onwards, and many Sicilian noblemen had married English ladies.

Two protagonists of Sicilian political life were in London: one was the priest Don Luigi Sturzo who took refuge in London from 1924 to 1940; the other was Andrea Finocchiaro-Aprile. The latter, leader of the Separatist movement, had been a minister in a pre-Fascist cabinet (1910), and had made polite noises to Mussolini and the Fascist regime, but when he arrived in London in 1940 he had just stayed on. As early as 1942, Finocchiaro-Aprile came back from London. Many Separatist meetings took place, and the Fascist regime by then had so little hold on Sicily that pamphlets were written, meetings took place, and speeches were made almost publicly. It was decided that Sicily was to become 'the Switzerland of the Mediterranean'. 'Sicily and liberty' was the motto.

The parliamentary report on the Mafia (1970) states: 'After the landing in Sicily of the Allies, those responsible for the military government gave 90% of civic administration posts to Separatists. Such a choice had obviously been pre-planned by the American and English branches responsible.' These men, the report goes on, were needed for counterbalancing the Italian government and were thought to be capable of organizing a resistance movement had it been needed. The Allies gave importance to the Separatists because they needed to lean on the traditional leading Sicilian classes. 'The movement for Sicilian independence was principally inspired by landowners.'

The leaders of the independence movement were Antonio Canepa, Andrea Finocchiaro-Aprile, Lucio Alessandro and Giuseppe Tasca, Concetto Gallo, the brother Dukes of Garcaci Baron Stefano la Motta and Antonino Varvaro. These men belonged either to the landowning aristocracy, or were of very recent *gabelloto* heritage. Some of them were intellectuals and taught at university. There was also a left-wing element among the Separatists, which was to play a minor role, since it did not accept the Mafia and *gabelloto* component of the movement. As it became clear that the Separatists were going to be the party of power, it was natural for all the mafiosi to change sides. This was the main reason for which the American forces allowed so many former bosses or future bosses to take the jobs of mayors or civic administrators. The Americans did not necessarily know that behind the Separatist mask hid many racketeers and *gabelloti*; nor did they care. If many appointments show a definite hand in scheming and putting back into power people linked to the Cosa Nostra 'Families', this hand was generally a Sicilian one.

American policy was quite straightforward: 'The infiltration of Americans (civilian and military of Sicilian origin who know the dialect and have personal contacts within the island) to obtain information, both combat and psychological, and to establish communications between Sicily and our own headquarters on the African mainland. Part of this personnel has already been requisitioned by the theater commander and is now en route to North Africa.' We know what 'civilians of Sicilian origin' had kept contacts and had power on the island. The document goes on to say that the training of personnel 'with

proper language qualifications' was under way, and that these were to be
sent to Sicily as 'organizers, fomenters and operational nuclei' (28 April
1943—3701 X/J 9867). The Appendix is even clearer (Appendix C,
point 4):

> *To organize and prepare dissident elements for active resistance:*
> (a) Establishment of contact and communications with the leaders of
> separatist nuclei, disaffected workers, and clandestine radical groups,
> e.g., the Maffia [*sic*], and giving them every possible aid.

On 24 June 1943, the plan became more detailed (F.O.R. 6317—
Allied Force Headquarters. Psychological Warfare Branch—American
Draft—Secret. Equals British Top Secret):

> ... d) That at once American and Britain be considered for this type
> of personnel suited to work with AMGOT [American Military Govern-
> ment of Occupied Territories]* in the event of a sudden collapse.
> For this contingency nothing but an elite of really high-powered
> men will do. They have got to assume immense individual res-
> ponsibility, take decisions quickly and be men of action as well as
> experts ... A group of 12 topnotchers and 50 men of second rank
> should be aimed at ... It will probably be said that it is impossible to
> find 72 'bodies', to this there is only one answer. The phase of the
> war has now come when, cutting our home base staff to a minimum
> essential to maintain the service, we must send out into the field
> the best men we have got. But if we have not got them, we must find
> them.

This American document states quite clearly that for this sort of
operation the Department of War was ready to enlist anybody at all

---

* Quoting a War Office report by Sir Harold Alexander: Birth of AMGOT:
Psychological Warfare Subcommission. AMGOT, Allied Military Government of Occupied Territories, was first established in Syracuse (late July 1943),
and then in Palermo (7 August 1943). It was first established and 'invented' on
1 May 1943. Its objectives were: (*a*) To ensure the security of the occupying
forces and their lines of communication, and to facilitate this operation. (*b*) To
restore law and order and normal conditions among the Civil population as
soon as possible, procure the necessary food supplies for them and, where
necessary relief and maintenance for destitutes within available resources.
On 10 February 1944, South Italy, Sicily and Sardinia were transferred
from AMGOT to the Italian Government (while the Allied Council Commission remained the organization which had the jurisdiction of law and civil
order).

who might be of help, including those notorious but certainly highly intelligent men of action, strategy and business, the racketeers.*

In a secret dispatch to the Foreign Office, Lord Rennell pointed out that many mafiosi had been given responsibility in local administration. He stressed that 'over half of the Sicilian population in many villages of the interior is illiterate' so that there was not much choice of candidates for jobs which were not even paid. Many of his officers 'fell into the trap' and chose those who had made themselves available for the jobs, people who talked some English, and had been anti-Fascist.

The alleged role of some Cosa Nostra criminals and Sicilian *cosche* in the war effort is and will always be controversial. There are several versions, many of which come from the same sources (like Moses Polakoff, Lucky Luciano's lawyer, who told conflicting stories). The truth is probably somewhere in the middle. There are some hints in the War Office and Foreign Office secret documents, but obviously most references to collusion between US officials and Mafia criminals would have been erased before the papers were released to the public in 1971.

While I strongly doubt that there were ever big deals between American officials and gangsters, it is more than possible that promises and exchanges of favours happened somewhere in the middle ranks. 'Lucky' Luciano, who appears as a protagonist of these stories, was not the overboss. He was second to Frank Costello in one of New York's Families, but not powerful enough to avoid being caught and sentenced. On 7 July 1936, he was condemned to thirty to fifty years in prison, and was sent to the penitentiary of Dannemora, near the Canadian border, known for its bleakness, maximum security and called 'Siberia' by the convicts. There he remained until 1942 when he was transferred to the more comfortable open prison of Great Meadows,

---

* I must immediately state here that if the Americans made semi-official use of the mafiosi, I find nothing shocking or scandalous about it. I am aware that in this I will be disagreeing with all the Italian scholars who have studied this question, but Italy was an enemy, it was a difficult moment for the Allies, and their main preoccupation was the lives of their own men. The American Psychological Warfare branch had already used similar techniques in operation 'Hurricane' (Tunisia) and the British were well aware of it. Organized or semi-organized groups of gangsters were natural enemies of the Fascist regime, and could be counted upon as leaders and organizers. In fact, one leading Italian industrialist who was complaining about the Italian political class once told me: 'I would get all the mafiosi, send them to Harvard for five years, and put them in Parliament to lead the country.'

near New York. What he did afterwards has never been pinned down, and is not really explained in Luciano's memoirs. In 1945 Polakoff pushed for his parole because of his 'contribution to the war effort'. It was granted.

In rehearsing the various versions of Luciano's wartime role, we should not forget the Mafia's inclination to exaggerate or invent stories which might enhance its importance. If some of the new bosses could fabricate the legend that they were in contact with the rulers, the Americans, the occupying forces, even with the President of the United States (it may sound a joke, but gossip of that kind was circulating), so much the better for their local prestige. Simpletons would have believed in them. As it turned out, most believed in the official American backing of the mafiosi.

Senator Estes Kefauver, who was chairman of an inquiry into the activities of Cosa Nostra, wrote:

During World War II there was a lot of hocus-pocus about allegedly valuable services that Luciano, then a convict, was supposed to have furnished the military authorities in connection with plans for the invasion of his native Sicily. We dug into this and obtained a number of conflicting stories. This is one of the points about which the committee would have questioned Governor Dewey, who commuted Luciano's sentence, if the Governor had not declined our invitation to come to New York City to testify before the committee.

One story which we heard from Moses Polakoff, attorney for Meyer Lansky, was that Naval Intelligence had sought out Luciano's aid and had asked Polakoff to be the intermediary. Polakoff, who had represented Luciano when he was sent up, said he in turn enlisted the help of Lansky, an old associate of Lucky's, and that some fifteen or twenty visits were arranged at which Luciano gave certain information.

... On the other hand, Federal Narcotics Agent George White, who served our committee as an investigator for several months, testified to having been approached on Luciano's behalf by a narcotics smuggler named August Del Grazio. Del Grazio claimed he 'was acting on behalf of two attorneys ... and ... Frank Costello who was spearheading the movement to get Luciano out of the penitentiary,' White said.

'He (Del Grazio) said Luciano had many potent connections in the Italian underworld and Luciano was one of the principal members of the Mafia,' White testified. The proffered deal, he went on, was that Luciano would use his Mafia position to arrange contacts for under-cover American agents 'and that therefore Sicily would be a much softer target than it might otherwise be.'

One version of the Luciano story goes that when at the beginning of 1942 the German submarine *Doenitz* endangered American cargo ships outside territorial waters as far down as the Gulf of Mexico, it was believed that the Italian and Greek underworld was helping the Germans with petrol and intelligence. The Navy was also said to be alarmed by possible sabotage at Brooklyn harbour, which was in the hands of the Italian organized underworld. Naval Commander Haffenden investigated, and it was thought that Joe Soks (real name Giuseppe Lanza) was organizing the sabotage. The underworld made it known that all the sabotage operations were controlled by 'Lucky' Luciano, so he was transferred from Dannemora to the Great Meadows prison, and the sabotage ended. The story goes that the district attorney, Frank Hogan, took part in the delicate operation of diplomacy. On the other side were Joe Adonis, Frank Costello and Luciano. And it was then that Luciano got in touch with Calogero Vizzini in Sicily, *gabelloto* of the Miccichè estate, reputed *capomafia*, who was able to organize a movement of non-resistance to the Allied forces in Sicily.

But 'Lucky' Luciano had been too long in prison by then to be able to control the New York 'families', and everybody was out of touch with Sicily because of the Fascist regime. Calogero Vizzini had no overall power, since Mori's operation had actually succeeded in disconnecting the Sicilian underworld network. The semi-official story was probably meant to cover something else up. Charles Haffenden turned out to work not only for the Navy, but was also a 'clandestine' detective, illegally tapping telephones on behalf of private individuals. He later confessed to the Kefauver Committee that the initiative for the first contacts with him had not been taken by a solicitor or by a Cosa Nostra man, but by a man from Dewey's staff, Murray Gurfein.

When 'Lucky' Luciano had been arrested at Hot Springs in 1936, it was because the ambitious Republican lawyer Thomas E. Dewey wanted to arrest a Cosa Nostra gangster. In so doing he wanted to hit Tammany Hall, the Democrat headquarters where Frank Costello and the other bosses played a major role. Dewey wanted power and wanted to become the national hero fighting vice and racketeers. The Democrats were deeply involved with the Cosa Nostra bosses, and many of their votes came from the trade unions and the Italian section of the New York area.

'Dewey was such a goddam racketeer himself, in a legal way, that he crawled up my back with a frame and stabbed me. If he'd hauled me into court for anythin' I done, I'd have taken it like a man,' Luciano said later.

Dewey, who had become Special Prosecutor for Organized Crime, picked on Luciano (and not on the too highly protected men like Costello or Lansky) and fabricated the evidence against Luciano for his 1936 trial (Court of General Session of New York), where he was accused of rackets for the control and exploitation of prostitutes—something that would shock the puritan general public, and even more so his own people, the Italian and Sicilian community. There was no evidence against him on any murder or major crime (which he certainly had committed). That girls were bought by the prosecution and testified against Luciano is a fact.

Dewey exploited to the full his victory against vice (and against Democratic corruption) when he tried to become Governor of New York in 1938. He almost made it, but for the personal intervention of President Roosevelt, who came to help the Democratic candidate by playing down Dewey's campaign.*

To get Luciano out of jail, his friends had to seek Dewey's own intervention. It was important for men like Costello and Lansky, and for their reputation, to show that they were able to rescue one of their lot even from Dewey's hands. If the subordinates were to think that Costello had lost his political power and was not able to protect his men, he would have lost many faithfuls and it would have been difficult to recruit new people. In order to placate Dewey, Costello, Lansky and Co. began to adopt a friendly attitude towards their former enemy. $250,000

---

* It is extraordinary that Dewey still enjoys an undeserved reputation. In Dwight Smith's book (*The Mafia Mystique*) one can read that 'Dewey did not annihilate rackets in New York City, but what he did accomplish represents the one relatively successful attack on organized criminal activities in the thirties ... but his efforts were aimed beyond them, at the collusion and corruption that lay at the heart of racketeering.'

was given by the Lansky group* for Dewey's electoral campaign. In 1942 Dewey won with over 600,000 votes, many of which came from the Italian Democrat faction, and from the trade unions under Cosa Nostra control. 'I repeated my promise that Dewey would get all our support and we would deliver Manhattan, or come damn close, in November which would mean he'd be in, as soon as he got into office, he had to make me a hero. The only difference would be, a hero gets a medal, but I'd get a parole.' The assistant DA, Hogan—who in the other story figures as an envoy of the American Navy—in this much more likely version of the events was Dewey's assistant in the election campaign.

Only now could Dewey's special prisoner be freed. But, as Lansky wrote in his biography, an excuse had to be found. Dewey could certainly not let it be known that he had been elected with the help of those he had previously fought. 'We could say,' Lansky wrote, 'that new proof had emerged, or that doctors had declared that Luciano suffered from an incurable disease, or that somehow, the prisoner had given "some services for the State".' So in February 1946 Luciano left the prison of Great Meadows and sailed for Italy on board the *Laura Keene*. 'The bastard was willin' to let me out,' said Luciano, 'but he wanted me far, far away—that meant I'd have to agree to leave my own country, because I was a legal citizen ever since my old man took out papers when I was a kid. They couldn't deport me even if I didn't agree to it.'

Luciano did not want to live in Italy where he had no friends, and where he (wrongly) suspected that economic sources for exploitation were going to be few. He tried to escape to Havana, but was immediately shipped back.

Another saga starts in Italy. Luciano was said to be already in Sicily in July 1943, when the Allies began their operation 'Husky'. From the USA he had already got in touch with Calogero Vizzini who, in turn, had gathered the forces of the Church (he was related to two bishops, and his brother was a priest). Some versions said that Luciano flew over Villalba, Vizzini's home town, flying an American Army helicopter, and dropped a yellow scarf with the double letters 'L L' printed in black. Don Giovanni Vizzini, Calogero's priest-brother, picked up

* Meyer Lansky was an intellectual. *Making Profits* by a Harvard professor, became a sort of gospel: the law of supply and demand was good for legitimate and illegitimate business. The 'Buy-Money Bank' was for 'greasing' officials.

the scarf: it was the signal for action. But which action? The *cosche mafiose* were too weak to be able to organize a semi-military operation, or even any resistance. Moreover, if Vizzini was a man of local 'respect' he was unknown in other parts of Sicily at that time. He became a prominent figure only after becoming Mayor of Villalba, Honorary Colonel of the US army, and 'king' of the post-war black market. It was only after the liberation that Vizzini's criminal dossier disappeared from the Palermo Questura. Vizzini is said to have handed Luciano a list of 850 'secure' persons and, after the legendary arrival of the helicopter, to have run away. His mythical trip had taken Vizzini to the other Sicilian 'capomafia', Genco Russo in the nearby village of Mussumeli. Vizzini's journey, some authors wrote, was made in armoured cars (American) and took place one month before the landing of the Allies.

Separatists and mafiosi 'friends' had already helped the clandestine landing and parachuting of agents who had come from the American headquarters in Africa. This happened between January and February 1943, and later in June 1943. All the agents spoke pure Sicilian, and only one was arrested. One of these American agents was Charles Poletti who, before the war, had been Lieutenant Governor of New York under Dewey's predecessor, Herbert Lehman. He was to become Military Governor of Sicily (and later of Rome), friend of the Separatists and of American bosses like Vito Genovese, who was to be his aide. 'As it happened,' Luciano wrote, 'the Army appointed Charlie Poletti, who was *one of our good friends*, as the military governor in Italy, and Poletti kept that job for quite a long time.' It may be that the role of Poletti in organizing and linking the Separatists and in alerting them to the Allied landing has been confused with a supposed role of Luciano's.

The Allies were worried about what kind of civic administration they would have to organize in occupied Europe after its liberation. Sicily was their first experience and AMGOT was founded in Sicily:

Foreign Office.   R6308
Most Secret cypher telegram.   From: J.S.E. (Joint Staff Mission)
                                      Washington
                               to: War Cabinet Office, London
1 May 1943
Position here in regard to planning organization of Civic Administra-

tion of Huskyland is becoming complicated ... (2) The Secretariat of War and Navy recently agreed that the US War Department 'be designated as capacity to plan handling of Civic affairs in the territory about to be occupied and to coordinate activities of civilian agencies in US in administering civil affairs in hostile and liberated territory during the period of military occupation.'

There were contrasts between the Americans and the British for the allocation of civic administration. A British candidate (no name) was judged not fit for the post:

Most Secret and Personal
Cypher
From Resident Minister, Algiers, to Foreign Office
9 July 1943
Someone is found in his place who has superior experience and qualification i.e. knowledge of Huskyland and its language. The latter advantage would make a special appeal.

It is said that after being parachuted into Sicily Charles Poletti went to live in the house of the Counts Tasca, leading Separatists, under the disguise of being their manservant.* The Tasca family name, which means 'pocket' in Italian, came from the nickname given to their grandfather, who was a greedy and notorious *gabelloto*. (After the liberation of Palermo, Lucio Tasca was to become Mayor of Palermo and later his role in the bandit Giuliano's saga ended with the double kidnapping of himself and his grandchild, also called Lucio.)

F.O. Staff and organization
4) With the 7th Army assault a group of 17 officers was landed on D and D+1 day under Colonel Charles Poletti ...
Charles Poletti and his second in command of the AMGOT personnel in the 7th Army area, Lt.-Colonel P. Rodd, were themselves alone trying to cope with the problems of Palermo city. Some assistance was afforded by Group Captain Benson staffing the West part of Ragusa province which had been previously staffed by Colonel Poletti. Black market: this is rampant throughout the island. All appropriate steps are being taken to curb it.

---

* This is very likely: even my father—who is Jewish—was hiding in a house and pretending to be the family butler.

Mafia is not dead.
(Report on the working of AMGOT—Secret)

In another cypher telegram (M 8027—19 August 1943) for Colonel Rickards, for Civil Affairs, the British disagree with the Americans who want to give local government to civilians.

In 1943 Sicily was ready. The Separatists (grouped around the Tascas in Palermo, the Carcacis in Catania, Stefano la Motta at Nicosia, and the Left around the Communist Antonio Canepa—who had been interned in a lunatic asylum by the Fascists, but freed just before the beginning of the war—had the trust of the Allies. (Canepa, from 1940, worked for British Intelligence, and so did an elegant, distinguished lawyer, Vito Guarrasi, who was said to be present at the signing of the armistice, and was to be a dominant figure in Sicilian political life. He is probably the person referred to in the dispatch from the Resident Minister in Algiers.) Only the Communist wing wanted to take up arms against what remained of the Fascist-Italian regime, but the other discouraged them because 'everything will happen by itself'. The Communists were not sure either of their Italian and Soviet leadership's attitude to the idea of a separate Sicilian entity.

On 10 July, Patton and Alexander landed their forces on the South coasts of Sicily.

Draft: Account of Operation Husky—15th Army Group—Phase One—W.O. 204/6896
The wind rose sharply in the central Mediterranean on 9 July as the top convoys of the Seventh and Eighth armies closed in on their rendez-vous area to the East and West of Malta ...
W.O. 204/6894 Narrative of Husky Operation—D Day 10 July 1943
By nightfall advances inland had proceeded sufficiently to give reasonable assurance that all beachheads were safely held. Considering the magnitude of the landing operations, the supposed strength of the enemy defenses and the rather unfavourable weather, the indications pointed to amazingly small losses of men, craft, planes and material.
The Italians continue to fight poorly whenever found.
14 July: Italians continue to surrender in large numbers.

Colonel Charles Poletti, Chief of AMGOT, saw to it that the majority (85%) of Sicilian towns and villages had a civic administration formed before the actual arrival of the American forces. He made various gangsters into mayors: Calogero Vizzini at Villalba, Genco Russo at Mussumeli. In official eyes they were acceptable people since they were anti-Fascists and Separatists. Lord Poole, who was Liaison Officer, remembers: 'We ourselves took weeks to form a civic council. The Americans had them all ready.' Poole says that at meetings with American Staff Officers he would encounter men 'with black moustaches and American military uniforms who hardly spoke any English'. He also recalls that it was believed that 'Lucky' Luciano was on the island at the time of the Allied landings. He never met or saw him, but a massive rumour campaign indicated that Luciano was somewhere in Western Sicily—and this was certainly not so. The French Ambassador in London (1974) described to me the signing of the peace treaty: Charles Poletti was always present. He took the future Ambassador and Vishinsky out sight-seeing, or to dine ... every day he was in their company. There is something symbolic about the Mafia being present as a major power with none else but the official representatives of Soviet Russia, America, Great Britain and France! Italy had lost, the Mafia was one of the victors—a victory which was to be dramatically important for its future role in society.

On 25 July 1943 came the coup d'état which deposed Mussolini. Marshal Badoglio was in close contact with the British (Foreign Office papers give a fascinating account of this confused period), and an armistice was signed on 8 September. Italy became an enemy of Germany, and until 25 April 1945 Central and North Italy experienced the full weight of Nazi Germany as an enemy force, and built up an active Resistance movement. Sicily never went through the important and constructive Resistance struggle which shaped many men and gave them a much needed democratic and anti-Fascist experience. The Sicilians, in fact, were turning out to be quite a problem for the Allies:

R8/308/G

Minutes. Report—20 April

Lord Rennell:

Sicilians count themselves as quasi-allies. On the political side, the chief feature is the activity of the Sicilian Separatist Movement ... the leaders have drawn up a programme for a Sicilian Republic in grandiloquent terms, which provides, inter alia, for a seat at the Peace Conference! ... Another element which will want watching is the Mafia, which is likely to be associated with the Separatist Movement. Apart from these two Movements, the Communists are the only active political party.

Lord Rennell also observed:

> Generally speaking these men [mafiosi] will be reputedly, and really, considered anti-Fascists; but they are not people to whom clemency can safely be extended on the ground that they are political prisoners. While the Mafia is primarily a 'racket' organization for blackmail, protection and robbery, it formerly also played a considerable political part in elections. I would expect the Mafia to be associated with the Sicilian Independence Movement ... The aftermath of war and the breakdown of central and provincial authority provide a good culture ground for the virus [Mafia].

The resurgence of Mafia power is illustrated by the activities of Vito Genovese, who was aide to Charles Poletti. According to Valachi, when he left the US in 1937 (to escape the attentions of Dewey) he had taken $750,000 with him. He had given money to the Fascist regime, became a prominent member of the party, and was rewarded with honour and respectability. Genovese was based in Naples, his native city, and was a liaison official in an American unit. He was the closest of Poletti's collaborators and gave him presents (including a de-luxe white car) and shared part of his profits with him. The end of his Italian postwar career, based on the black market and smuggling, came at the hands of an honest and stubborn American soldier. Sergeant Orange C. Dickey, of the US Army's Investigation Division in Italy, was assigned to look into the black-market operations behind Allied lines in Southern Italy. In 1944, he interrogated an Italian criminal who boasted that he had nothing to fear from Dickey, since he was under the protection of Don Vito Genovese, who had powerful connections with the Allied Military Government. Later Dickey broke up a gang of Italian civilians and Canadian deserters who were stealing US Army supplies and channelling the black-market operations. Vito Genovese was identified as the mastermind of the operation.

In August 1944 Sergeant Dickey arrested Genovese. He found that he had had unlimited permits to travel in occupied areas of Italy, that he was very rich, and that he had personal letters from various American officers praising his virtue and honesty. Genovese had been interpreter to the Allied Military Courts when Naples was taken, and had ample opportunity to jail anyone he disliked and to free his friends. Sergeant Dickey sent all the information he had about Genovese to the American FBI, and received a letter saying that Vito Genovese was wanted in the States for murder. But while all this was happening, Dickey was under strong pressure for 'treating Genovese well'. And Genovese was not being tried for his black-market activities. Finally Dickey received a note from the Brooklyn police saying that a warrant for Genovese's return was forthcoming: it never arrived.

The naïve but persistent sergeant went to Rome to see Lieutenant-Colonel Charles Poletti, who was Chief of the US sector of AMGOT, but Poletti (unsurprisingly, except to Dickey) refused to discuss the matter. Therefore Sergeant Dickey decided to take the matter into his own hands and bring Vito Genovese back to the States to face trial. Now, seeing that Dickey was quite determined to see him convicted, Genovese offered a bribe of $250,000 in cash to the Sergeant, who earned $210 a month. 'You are young,' he told Dickey. 'There are things that you don't understand. This is the way it works. Take the money: you are set for the rest of your life. Nobody cares what you do. Why shouldn't you?' (Cf. *The Valachi Papers*.) Finding that it was the sergeant who did not care what and who was behind Genovese, the gangster told Dickey, as a final warning, that he might regret taking him back to the States. After that his attitude changed totally and he thanked his captor warmly for 'taking me home'.

In fact, having failed to prevent Genovese's return to the States, Cosa Nostra began to move quickly. Peter La Tempa, the key witness against him, had asked to be kept in protective custody. He knew Genovese's cruelty and power. On 14 January 1945, while La Tempa was being held in Brooklyn jail, he swallowed some tablets which he used to take for stomach disorders. He died soon afterwards, and the autopsy revealed that he had taken enough poison to kill eight horses. The death of Peter La Tempa ended the proceedings against Vito Genovese.

One year later another man, Assistant District Attorney Julius Helfand, tried to find more evidence to incriminate Genovese, who had once again become a prominent member of the American protection rackets. But Helfand had to announce that he had not found any corroborating evidence against Genovese. Two witnesses were needed to convict him of murder, and send him to 'the chair'; Helfand had found only one, Rupolo 'The Hawk' who, as a reward for his collaboration, was given back his freedom, although advised not to use it. Rupolo led a terror-stricken life for a few years, hiding and changing his name all the time. In 1964 his mutilated corpse was found in Jamaica Bay, having broken loose from some concrete weights.

Finally, Genovese was convicted for minor crimes. Valachi met up with him again in prison, and since Genovese was convinced that Valachi had 'talked' to the police, he tried to have him killed. 'You know, we take a barrel of apples, and in this barrel of apples there might be a bad apple. Well, this apple has to be removed, and if it ain't removed, it would hurt the rest of the apples,' Genovese said to Valachi. That was how Valachi murdered somebody else (in self-defence; or, in fact, in what he thought to be self-defence, since he killed the 'wrong' man) and then began 'to sing' to the police. When Genovese was due to be released he died. Lucky for many that he did, as he had a score of death sentences in his head.

Of the other Mafia representatives active in post-war Italy, Charles Poletti went back to the States, where Professor Mack Smith met him, by chance. When Poletti realized that Mack Smith knew about Sicilian affairs and history he avoided talking about the war, and vanished. As for Lucky Luciano, he was to become a major gangster in Italy running the drug-smuggling business from his base in Naples.

7 The post-war Period: the Mafia and Separatism

First in Sicily and then in Italy, the end of the war provoked more social changes and upheavals than in any other European nation, excluding, perhaps, Germany. Socialism was the promise, the great new faith, the hope for an Italy where work and a just reward would finally be everybody's right. At that time, Communism was symbolized by the victorious and heroic face of the Soviet Union. Stalin was still the symbol of a better way of life. The slogan '*A' da veni' Baffone!*' —'Big-Moustache must come!'—had been adopted by all Italy, and was painted on walls and on river embankments. Only a handful of people knew what Stalin really stood for; one of them was Togliatti, who in fact kept Italy firmly in the democratic system. And no one then knew that Europe's fate had already been decided and its territory politically carved up at Yalta—a decision which went over the heads of many who had fought for a better future, not for a return to the past 'order'.

The Seventh and Eighth Armies (made up of Canadian, English, Poles, Moroccans, Americans, Australians, Scots, etc.) had brought with them a new way of life. The Americans were the most admired. American affluence (white loaves of bread which had never been seen in Italy before, colourful clothes, big cars, canned food, shiny packaging, chocolate bars) was a distant and enviable dream which impressed and attracted the Italians. Of all the European nations, it was Italy which was the most influenced by the American 'Coca-Cola' philosophy, and not by the more creative and scientific aspects of American culture.

It was a revolution in the way of thinking and of seeing life. The war had left most people distressed and penniless. The incredible inflation of the lira had destroyed many fortunes. Only those who were quick starters and without scruples were able to profit from a post-war situation in which the black market was the easiest and quickest way of amassing wealth. In the North, the war profiteers were many, had few scruples and acted against a more sophisticated background. Because the Allied liberation had been slow there, the Resistance movement had had time to organize itself into fighting units, and into a political movement with which the *pescecani* (sharks), the war profiteers, had to reckon. Their fellow-predators in the South had had longer to organize their black-market operations. Those in Sicily acted within the Sicilian code and were therefore mafiosi.

There was a great evolution in the ways of accumulating capital and the Sicilian middle class—the Mafia—showed its vitality in this process. As in all European countries, the Second World War swept the old landowning aristocracy away, leaving Sicily's new 'class' to gain overall control in all those fields which, in other healthier environments, were becoming the stronghold of a more conventional bourgeoisie.

The arrival of the Allies in Sicily had made prices rocket. The soldiers could pay higher sums for commodities which only those Sicilians who were profiting from the black market could afford. There was no shortage of arms: the weapons of four armies were yet another black-market commodity. Those were days of violence, intensifying the dream of every Sicilian, which is to possess a gun and a coffin. (The peasant generally buys them as soon as he can afford both. Sicilians have an atavistic horror—rather like the ancient Greeks—of being buried without honour and without a coffin.)

The Sicilian post-war desire for political separation from central Roman government and for self-rule was familiar and understandable. The Sicilians were used to changing their rulers after the loss of a war, and to being 'acquired' by the winners: some genuinely expected and wanted to become a possession of either England or the United States. Besides, American and British propaganda had done everything it could to foster the Separatist movement, to secure cooperation against the Italians and the Germans who were garrisoning Sicily.

Andrea Finocchiaro Aprile, the tiresome leader of the Separatist movement (described by Lord Rennell as 'somewhat garrulous and not very outstanding in ability') had friends in England. He sent a message to General Alexander after the meeting of the Central Committee for Independence which took place on 23 July 1943, asking for independence from Italy and a federation with the Italian mainland. The Allied forces, which had favoured and complied with the Separatists in the organization of civic administration, were deluged under the verbose demands of Finocchiaro Aprile. As it became clear that the Separatist movement was sponsored by the victorious Allies, all sorts of people flocked to the party. First in the queue came the Mafia bosses, naturally attracted by whoever held power.

In the Separatist movement there were several trends. Genuine popular discontent with the Italians and their Fascist creation formed a left wing. The middle classes (Mafia, *gabelloti*) feared that the aftermath of the war might destroy the shaky foothold of privilege acquired during the crisis of the regime. The landowners were anxious not to lose their estates.

After the fall of the Fascist government and the arrest of Mussolini, which happened only a fortnight after the landing in Sicily, the position of the Separatists became weaker because the Allies did not need them any longer. Marshal Badoglio was conducting secret (and messy) negotiations for an armistice with the Allies. When the Allies, in 1944, handed over Sicily to the Italian administration, extremist groups formed a secret army, the EVIS, whose flag showed the three-legged symbol of *Trinacria*—the Latin name for Sicily—and declared war on Italy. Bandits were freely recruited for the campaign and the Mayor of Palermo, Count Lucio Tasca, the prominent Separatist, declared that the recruiting of criminals was justified, recalling that the same thing had happened in the 1860 Garibaldi campaign. In fact it was to be the Mafia who would exploit both the bandits and the Separatists, while most Sicilians had no intention of going to war again to fight for the independence of Sicily.

Many hundreds of 'undesirables'—notorious gangsters—were expelled from the United States and repatriated to Italy. This meant that relationships with the more sophisticated American criminals became stronger as those modern racketeers began to organize a network of crime. From this period onwards it becomes difficult to talk about the traditional Mafia (although the patriarchal and archaic type of mafioso continued to exist in the centre of the island). In fact the intermediate class—the Mafia—was changing along with the times. But 'archaic' rackets, such as interference with water supplies, levies on transport and marketing, etc., went on influencing the already high prices of post-war Sicily.

A prominent figure of this period was Calogero Vizzini, known as Don Calò. Vizzini, who had been imprisoned and bankrupted under Mussolini, and had an extensive criminal past, was immediately appointed to a position of civic influence. He was the *gabelloto* of the latifundium 'Feudo Micciche'. His 'lieutenant', Genco Russo, from Mussumeli, was *gabelloto* of the 'Feudo Polizzello'.

Immediately after the war we find that all the Mafia bosses were *gabelloti*. They were entrusted with the administration of large estates by the aristocracy who were terrified of the mounting wave of peasant discontent. In the Mafia town of Corleone, Carmelo Lo Bue was *gabelloto* of the property called 'Feudo Donna Beatrice', Francesco Liggio of 'Feudo Sant' Ippolito', Biagio Liggio of the 'Feudo Patria', Luciano Liggio of 'Feudo Strasatto'. Vincent Collura, who arrived from the United States as an 'undesirable', became the *gabelloto* of the 'Feudo Galardo'. The most lucrative sector of the Corleone black market was *abigeato*, clandestine slaughtering, transport and the selling of meat on the Palermo market. (In 1952 when the Carabinieri made a surprise visit to the nearby wood called 'la Ficuzza', they found two hundred stolen pigs, one hundred cows and six hundred sheep—a vast number for such a depressed area.)

Understandably the Mafia was fiercely anti-Socialist and anti-Communist. Its aim now was to stop the new wave of the Left and to promote a 'liberal' regime which could give it ample ways of exploitation and political infiltration. It is generally reported that there was a planned strategy between the Sicilian aristocracy—as represented by certain Separatists—and the Mafia, although it seems more likely that since both these social groups had the same natural aims and would be threatened by the awakening of the proletariat and a victory of the Left, the 'strategy' was more a common fight for survival than an actual plan. The Separatists and the Mafia had a solid network among the administrators and politicians in charge—all of them being either Separatists or mafiosi or both. They were in a position to intimidate the peasants' movement. But neither the Socialists nor the Communists were as weak (or as corrupt) as in Crispi's time, and they did create solid cooperatives which, led by heroic *sindacalisti*, peasant trade-unionists, pressed for land reforms. The left-wing parties wanted to fight the growing power of the Mafia, which once again was bidding to become the depository of electoral power and votes. And the peasantry began to identify the Mafia as its real enemy, a new important step.

In fact after the fall of Fascism, the landowners fell back on the mafiosi to control the peasantry—which was even poorer for the flourishing black market—and to safeguard their properties. In many parts of the island the peasants occupied large estates or joined forces with armed bands of outlaws. The occupation of the land was often symbolic: large crowds of peasants carrying red flags would arrive at a large estate and ask for the implementation of the Gullo laws. The Gullo Land Act authorized peasant cooperatives to occupy poorly cultivated estates and regulated a more just partition of land produce. (The agrarian reform of 1950 invalidated all transfers of land after 1948. Land from extensively cultivated properties larger than 200 hectares was to be expropriated, holdings exceeding 100 hectares to be transferred by intensive cultivation. Woodland was exempt from expropriation.) But the representatives of the law were always on the side of the land-owners and of their mafiosi retainers, who often asked for and obtained the intervention of the Carabinieri against the peasants.

On 16 September 1944, the Communist leader Girolamo Li Causi challenged the prestige of Don Calò, the boss of all bosses, when he went to speak to the landless labourers at Villalba, Don Calò's own village and private domain. The powerful mafioso let Li Causi know that Villalba was his own territory and that intrusion could not be tolerated. He 'advised' him not to speak there. But Li Causi, recently emerged from fifteen years of Fascist prison, dismissed the warning. 'I started talking to the half-empty square,' he told me years later at the Senate, 'but people were listening behind the semi-closed windows and doors.' The little alleys which led off the small square of the wretched village were also choked with people who listened as Li Causi reminded the peasantry of the unjust exploitation of the Mafia. When Don Calò, surrounded by his bodyguard, shouted 'It's not true', machine-guns opened up and hand-grenades burst around him. Eighteen people, Li Causi included, were severely wounded.

Don Calò and his bodyguard were accused of attempted man-slaughter. The trial started in 1944, but dragged on until 1958. By 1946 reports and documents had already disappeared from the Caltanisetta *tribunale*. Don Calò was never condemned because he was dead.

One week after the attack on Li Causi, on 24 September 1944, a lawyer from Castellammare, Bernardo Mattarella, a future Christian Democrat MP and minister, closely linked with all subsequent Mafia events, wrote an article in the Christian Democrat official newspaper *Il Popolo*. He invited the Separatists to join the Christian Democrat ranks, as they all had the same common cause: 'It is beyond doubt that the inspirers of the Separatist Movement are the landowners who are worried and want to protect their privileges.' But those forces to whom Mattarella was appealing were not yet ready to move to a party like the Christian Democrats, which was hardly known and was feared to be a populist party. In fact, in the uncertainty of post-war Italy, from 1943 to 1945, the mafiosi did not at once forecast which was going to be the winning party, and they therefore flirted with several.

The Separatists guaranteed the large estates and stated that the Mafia was an acceptable Sicilian necessity. Finocchiaro Aprile announced: 'If there were no Mafia it would have to be invented. I am a friend of the mafiosi although I am personally against crime and violence.' But even before Sicily was granted regional autonomy in 1946, Separatism was to lose influence as the Christian Democratic party opened its ranks to the large estate owners and their men. As they realized that the wave of Communism had to be stopped, many more changed sides. It was the Christian Democrats, with the Church and the Allies supporting them, rather than the Separatists (or the Monarchists who had also competed for the favours of both landowners and mafiosi), who were able to check the peasants' struggle for land and the demands of the Left.

On 27 April 1945, Mussolini was again arrested, and was executed on the following day. Before the end of that week, the German armies surrendered. No Allied help could any longer be expected, and the Separatists had to act before the Italians got total control of Sicily. The Committee of the Separatists sent lengthy messages to the ambassadors of the USA, UK and USSR, concluding with the slogan 'Independence or death.' They feared that unification with what they thought was going to be a left-wing Italy would mean the end of boss rule on the island. The possession of land would be threatened by the future Italian constitution which was being drafted and by new promises for agrarian reforms.

'Well, General, was there an alliance between the Mafia and the Separatist leaders?' Paolantonio, the general of the Carabinieri, was asked in 1971 by the Parliamentary Committee of Inquiry on the Mafia. 'Yes with the Separatists when those leaders had power,' he answered. 'Calogero Vizzini was a Separatist, but let's not consider Don Calogero, he was the *capomafia* of Sicily.' The inquirer concluded: 'Of Sicily, that's it. There was a relationship with Lucio Tasca, who in 1943 wrote a pamphlet "in praise of latifundium". It is clear that these groups of reactionaries, of great landowners, were connected with the Mafia.'

Finocchiaro Aprile sent the Allies a message, one of many, that the Separatists would go to war on 15 October 1945. The Allies suspected that he was bluffing as he had so often done before, but were glad to let the Italians deal with this provincial problem. It was known that a pact had been made between the Separatist movement and some gangs of bandits, notably the Avila gang in Eastern Sicily and the Giuliano gang in Western Sicily. Banditry was once again raging over the mountains and communications were impossible except for those mafiosi who had come to some form of 'understanding' with the bandits. The outbreak was once again due to the extreme poverty and to the conflicts with the Italian police forces, who were trying to put a stop to the traffic in black-market goods.

It was on one such occasion that the young Salvatore Giuliano from Montelepre, who was smuggling goods like so many young men, had been stopped by the Carabinieri and had shot one of them dead. He and his men came to control the area behind Palermo and Monreale, where the valley of the Conca D'Oro ends in high ridges and bare mountains. On the other side, the valley towards Castellammare del Golfo, which included mafioso towns like Partinico, Borgetto, Montelepre, Alcamo and Castellammare itself, became Giuliano's territory. Only the Mafia had free passage there, and Giuliano came to control all transport of goods and men going to Palermo from central Sicily.

As the clandestine Separatist radio called for Sicilian officials to leave their jobs, often accompanying the request with personal threatening letters, both Italians and Allies realized that a civil war was imminent. The Allied arms supplies for use against the Germans went to Giuliano, the Avila bandits and to the Separatist general of the EVIS (the Voluntary Army for the Independence of Sicily), Professor Antonio Canepa. At this point the Separatist movement and the EVIS became an Italian problem. It also became a criminal party. Since it lacked funds, it was suggested to Giuliano that he should raise money by kidnapping and ransom. This request happened at a well-documented meeting between the Separatist leaders (Carcaci, La Motta and Giuseppe Tasca) and Giuliano at Ponte Sagana, near Montelepre, in which the young bandit was also dubbed Colonel of the Western Separatist Army. He and his boys were given a uniform, made 'legal soldiers', and promised an amnesty for their previous crimes.

Italy and regular Italian troops were sent to help the Carabinieri in the area of Palermo and Monreale. After a few months of civil war, Professor Antonio Canepa died in very mysterious circumstances. The Italian Prime Minister came to Sicily incognito and decided that the Separatist leaders should be arrested and banished. Aprile was shipped to the island of Ponza. By the end of 1945, all had been arrested, the party had been proscribed and Separatist propaganda banned.

With all finances closed to him, Giuliano had initiated a policy of terror; trains and buses were held up in broad daylight, and kidnapping became an almost everyday event. In December 1945, the new Italian Prime Minister, Alcide De Gasperi, was saying that if the Separatists were to be eliminated by force rather than by election (which might go against Italy), Giuliano's army had to be attacked. Throughout 1946 Giuliano's gang carried out almost daily ambushes against the Carabinieri. General Branca of the Carabinieri wrote, 'The Separatist movement and the Mafia have now made common cause . . . the Chiefs of the EVIS must be found more and more among the *capomafia* of the island.'

The referendum in 1946 on whether Italy should be a monarchy or a Republic naturally touched Sicily as well. King Umberto came to campaign, and since the most powerful 'grand elector', Don Calogero Vizzini, had already moved to the Christian Democrats, Umberto sought the help of several mafiosi, among them Nick Gentile, an American gangster who had been working with AMGOT until he was jailed by the British. From recently published documents (State Department, CIA and FBI) it appears that a high-powered Mafia meeting took place on 21 November 1945. Vito Guarazi (*sic*) and both Cattones were there. The decision was to remain neutral, to use inertia as a political weapon. But in spite of support from part of the Mafia (and from Giuliano's gang) the referendum went against the King. Slogans like 'Whoever votes Republican votes for the Communists' did not have the hoped-for effect on the simple Sicilian peasantry. In fact, the abolition of the monarchy made them take heart: if the old monarchy had been rejected, perhaps things were really going to change. In the mines, the countryside, and the island's few factories, the popular forces renewed their fight against the landlords, the bosses, the Mafia. It seemed a miracle that the Monarchist party had lost in spite of Mafia support. Perhaps the Mafia and the landlords could be defeated by united popular action.

In May 1946 Sicily was granted a large measure of autonomy: a legislative assembly of ninety regional MPs was set up in 1947 in Palermo with a cabinet and ministers; it had control over Sicilian agriculture and industry and all fields of public life. The central government also decided to make special grants to the region to make up for the past. Now that Palermo had once again become a bureaucratic capital, the city offered precisely the kind of job which is the dream of the Sicilian: red tape, offices, bureaucracy, devious ways of earning money. From the hall porter who looks after the least important corridor of the regional office, to the telephonist, the Sicilian—happy to have finally abandoned the meagre soil—sees his work in terms of saleable power, exerted to grant or block an interview, to delay or forward a letter or document. The bureaucratic system easily leads to these practices, and while the system is not peculiar to Sicily, the further southward one travels the more one finds it magnified.

Except in those territories under Giuliano's grip, and despite the Mafia, the police and Carabinieri who seemed always to intervene on the side of the landowners, the occupation of the uncultivated estates began again. In September 1946 the prefect of Caltanisetta gave in and enforced the law by signing a document by which five uncultivated estates were handed over to the peasants who had occupied them. Within a couple of months another fourteen estates were occupied, cleared of stones and ploughed. Six thousand peasants turned up at the town hall of Sciara in the province of Palermo when land which was due for legal expropriation was being held back. The new show of strength was answered by the landowners and by the middle classes in the usual way: intimidation and murder. Over forty peasant leaders, Catholic, Socialist, but mainly Communist, were to be killed.

In 1947 the first Sicilian electoral campaign to choose its chamber was conducted with the usual methods of intimidation and corruption. Danilo Dolci records some typical comments in his book *To Feed the Hungry*: 'The nuns came to every house at Petralia with presents of food and 1000 lire notes. Yes, the vote is bought, all right—with packets of pasta.' 'If you don't vote for our party, you'll be kicked out ...' 'The scrutineers check the slips as they come in, so they know whether you've voted or not.' The Left, gathered in a united front—*'Blocco del Popolo'*—of Socialists and Communists, could not hold meetings in Mafia territory. Its leaders, trade unionists and its followers were threatened and intimidated. On the day of the elections, men with guns and *coppola* of no uncertain provenance stood before the polling stations.

The results were a surprise for all. Fewer than ten per cent of the deputies elected were Separatists, and the Socialists and Communists together outnumbered the Christian Democrats. The results were (out of a total of 1,948,460 voters): Blocco del Popolo 29 seats, with 591,460 voters; Christian Democrats 400,084; Monarchists 185,423; Separatists 171,470; Agrarian block (centre-right) 287,698.

A campaign of terrorism followed the success of the Left. Trade unionists were murdered, and their assassins were always acquitted for 'lack of proof'. On 1 May 1947 left-wing peasants became the target of a massacre (see Chapter 8) which was central to the intimidation of the peasantry. The police took severe action against peasants ploughing uncultivated land, but were much more lenient to their murderers.

A State Department document (86500/11-2395) reported that 'the Mafia has no prejudice against any party, with the exception of the Communists,' and another (86500/12-145) quotes Cattone as saying, 'The Mafia is ready to fight Communism with armed force.' While the Communists and Socialists failed to unite, their victory alarmed both landowners and middle classes enough to make them concentrate their votes on the Christian Democrat party.

In the 1948 general elections which followed the 1947 election for the Sicilian Assembly, the Christian Democrats doubled their representation. They have remained in power ever since, both in Sicily and in Italy. Regional autonomy and a large budget opened up new possibilities for men like Calogero Vizzini, to attach themselves to the party in charge of contracts for public work, licences, import permits—the sources of income and power. The Christian Democrats became increasingly polluted by Mafia interests.

In 1948, the secretary of the trade-union centre of Corleone, Placido Rizzotto, was murdered by Luciano Liggio, who was acquitted several times for lack of proof. The murder of the trade unionist Accursio Miraglia was decreed by the Mafia of Agrigento. Giuseppe Montalbano told the Antimafia Commission: 'At the trial for the murder of Miraglia there were two contradictory conclusions. The first trial acquitted Miraglia's murderers because the judiciary had decided that their confession had been forced by way of torture. Then there was a trial against those policemen accused of having tortured the henchmen, but they were acquitted for "not having done the deed".'

A peasant told Danilo Dolci that when the Labour Exchange was opened in 1944, Miraglia became its secretary:

There had never been one. It was in order to organize a party for justice and for our rights. He used to say: 'Get organized, form cooperatives that, if it goes like that, can have land for all.' Everybody agreed. In one year we had 1800 members. He was really loved by all ... He looked like the Paladin Orlando riding his horse, it was a pleasure to see this great man riding a horse, he was a person who one had to look at, he was a wonder to look at, his presence was a loving one. Children would throw flowers, all the mass of people was for him but, when he was murdered, all backed away, got frightened, because of what had happened, and each tried to hide the fact that he belonged to our group. ...

It was always like that for those killed by the Mafia. Just around here: Montalbano's son has been kidnapped and has disappeared; Spagnolo from the Labour Exchange, murdered. Even among those in politics who sometimes kill each other: the lawyer Campo, from Agrigento; they shot Leonardo Renda, then they stabbed him, and then they put a stone in his mouth ... And also Almerigo, mayor of Camporeale; Giglio, mayor of Alessandia della Rocca; Vito Monteaparto, mayor of Campobello di Licata, all these murdered in our province alone ...

Rizzotto's father told Dolci that his son had clashed with people who wanted to have posts in the municipality and be the deputies in the Regional Assembly and since 'he knew what kind of people these were, persons from the High Mafia, who also had links with the headquarters of the police and with the magistrates, and since they had become rich with the war, he started this work of trade unionist in favour of the peasants'. He then described the evening of 10 March 1948, when his son was murdered: 'He came in to get his coat because it was cold. And I said: "Where are you going? We are having dinner in a moment." "I'll be back in a moment. I'm meeting the Mayor who is coming from Palermo by bus." This was the way he went out. He was thirty-three years and seventy days old. I waited and I waited and he never came back. He never came back ...'

We know what happened after Rizzotto left the house. With two other henchmen, Luciano Liggio stopped him as he was walking along the sad main road which cuts Corleone into two. At the point of the gun, Rizzotto was made to follow the three for a *ragionamento* (discussion). A Mafia *ragionamento* generally means death, and Rizzotto knew that well. Everybody saw them at Corleone; all those who loved Rizzotto and considered him as their only hope, closed their eyes and let the three criminals lead the trade unionist to his death.

The Antimafia Parliamentary Relation (published on 2 July 1971) had hard words for the 'anomalies' which had occurred during the inquiry on the murder of Placido Rizzotto, and the Commission cast 'heavy doubts' on the judiciary and the police:

> The Palermo court acquitting Luciano Leggio (called Liggio) for 'lack of proof' for the murder of Rizzotto, doubted the confessions taken from his accomplices before the trial and also doubted the words of Rizzotto's relations who had recognized the poor remnants of his body and clothes, and even doubted the cause of this horrible murder ... The first trial for the murder of Rizzotto in March 1948 was in 1952 and the second in 1958, eleven years after the deed!

The peasants had a trustworthy leadership and a record of successes. It is sad, and perhaps surprising, that they should have been so quickly intimidated by the murderous assault of the Mafia. Perhaps too many centuries of virtual slavery were behind them, but it is a bitter comment on Sicilian fatalism that the cooperatives failed to avenge the murders of their leaders.

Not all the trade unionists were killed; some are still here to tell their stories. Girolamo Scaturno recalled his experience in the peasant movement which took place in the province of Agrigento.

> In that province there were clashes with the police, threats from the landowners and from the mafiosi. I could describe hundreds of episodes, but one which happened at the Feudo Cattà of Raffadali explains the great strength and endurance of the peasantry. On that estate there were violent armed encounters with the mafiosi and *campieri* who defended the landowners, but finally the estate was given to the cooperative 'L'Agricola'. After that, the Council of State revoked the decision and restored the land to Baron Parciuta. We occupied the estate again for a whole week and at the end there was a meeting with the baron at the municipality. The baron ... was defended by the provincial secretary of the Christian Democrats; he affirmed in front of the Prefect that the peasants who had occupied the Catto' estate were armed with guns and machine-guns, so all had

to be arrested. The Carabinieri came to the estate, but they found the peasants armed only with spades and hoes.

Scaturno also remembered a particular morning of October 1948: 'I was a member of the Provincial Commission for uncultivated estates. As the representative of our cooperative, I was called to have a *ragionamento*, a chat, with Baron Stefano Agnello. The baron asked how old I was, whether I had a wife, in other words a lot of hints that I'd better mind my own business.'

From 1946 to 1972 in Sicily, 2500 people have been either murdered or have disappeared. From 1947 onwards, with the money they received by selling their land or from the expropriation of their estates by the State, the landowners invested in the cities, mainly in Palermo. Much of the land was already in the hands of the *gabelloti*, the mafiosi who had bought it cheap from the original landowner. The years after the war had enriched the latter, and the aristocracy were selling everything they had. After the tragedy of losing their land, their prestige, their serfs, their villages, the landowners realized that they now had a better deal, and the rush for urban building began. Palermo had been heavily bombed, and was attracting many new people from the surrounding villages.

The Mafia infiltrated the process of social change, operating through newly-formed societies or in a parasitic way by acting as mediators in building operations and in getting permits for building areas. New capital was arriving for the industrialization of the island. In its report for 1946, the Italian Treasury announced gross receipts of 22 billion from Sicily and expenditure of 38 billion in the island. For the year 1947–8, 18 billion were received and 69 billion spent. This was a stimulus for new kinds of Mafia infiltration within the regional authorities. 'The Mafia of real estate', 'the Mafia of petrol', 'the Mafia of building cooperatives' flourished like the 'Mafias' in all those areas of operation which should have been the foundation of a new Sicily.

On 14 September 1948, two Communist MPs and one Socialist proposed a Parliamentary Commission to inquire into the problems of the Mafia in Sicily. The ranks of the Christian Democrats reacted immediately against the proposal: the party was already too heavily involved and infiltrated. It was an unnecessary insult to Sicily, they said. The Minister of the Interior, Scelba, himself a Sicilian, talked about 'propaganda which I would venture to call shameful'. The Christian

Democrat Senator Umberto Merlin said that 'charity towards one's motherland and love for the Sicilian region should have been enough to prevent such a discussion'. But it was not only the Christian Democrat party which objected: the centre parties had been penetrated as well. The Liberals and Republicans talked about 'the mortification of the island', their 'horror for such a proposal'. Vittorio Emanuele Orlando, who had reappeared after the Fascist period and had been elected as a Senator for the town of Partinico, a centre of Mafia interests, said: 'Even if the electorate, as an entity, might include some mafiosi, I could never turn aside from the loyalty which links me to the electorate, even if, as a result, I run the risk of being called a mafioso.'

At Partinico, Orlando was supported by Frank Coppola, a native who had just come back from the United States to become grand elector of the whole area, the densely inhabited valley which was Giuliano's territory. Coppola, much more than Calogero Vizzini or any other '*capomafia*', was the criminal overlord of one of the most populated areas of Sicily, a constant source of votes. Several times implicated in drug traffic, he has been involved in every major Sicilian criminal incident. Many *capocosche* reach no further than their own locality; Coppola was the controller behind the scenes, the maker of Sicilian and Roman deputies. He was also the *deus ex machina* of the Salvatore Giuliano saga. But, before proceeding, one's attention should be focused on some of the protagonists of the story, the police and the judiciary.

Because the Mafia coincides with, and is the same thing as, the System, power, politics, government (and it is the government which can stop or promote an inquiry), the Sicilian police and Carabinieri find themselves in a very difficult position. While knowing that their duty is to fight unlawfulness and recognizing in the Mafia a source of criminality, orders from above invariably emasculate any effort to eradicate one or another group of *mafiosi*. The police are successful if the *cosca* is weak and unpopular with the others—and with the politicians. In fact it is often the Mafia itself which hands people over to the police. Carabinieri and the police successes in fighting banditry have always come from an agreement with some of the *cosche*. Small thieves and bandits are anyway an embarrassing presence to a *cosca* because they work outside its control. In fact banditry has now been eradicated in Sicily, but not in Sardinia where there is no Mafia to help the police. 'Experience demonstrates continuously that the *mafiosi* and the State institutions collaborate in the struggle against banditism,' writes Hess, 'and that the *mafiosi* are accepted by the officials as a body of order.'

The police and carabinieri have an ambivalent role, the role of defending those very persons whom they should attack. But when the Mayor or the High Magistrate, Prefects, MPs in both regional and national Parliament are part of the Mafia mechanism, how can the police force possibly fight the very people whom it is meant to serve? Since in Italy the police forces have a rather complex structure, a few words of explanation will be useful.

The Corps of Guards of Public Security, which we call the PS, or *Pubblica Sicurezza* or, much more often, simply 'the police', are responsible to the Ministry of the Interior (Home Office). On the other hand, the *Corpo Carabinieri* (CC) are responsible for the greater part of their work to the Ministry of Defence as they are part of the Army. The carabinieri are a 'bequest' of the Piedmontese kingdom. For various activities (duties of public order and security) the CC also come under the Ministry of the Interior. In 1814 Victor Emmanuel I of Savoy formed a new police force which were to use the *carabina*, a kind of gun, and therefore took the name of *i carabinieri*. During Fascist times, Mussolini did not want to rely on the carabinieri, who were noted for their obedience to the crown, so he initiated two more police forces, one of which is the PS, the *Pubblica Sicurezza*. (But Mussolini was said to trust the very efficient intelligence branch of the carabinieri more than the OVRA, the Fascist secret police). When the king gave orders to put Mussolini under arrest, it was the carabinieri who executed them. After the war, the Allies allowed 60,000 carabinieri to remain in office and they were given the special task of controlling and repressing the Socialist and Communist movements of post-war Italy. The force of *i carabinieri* is also called *L'Arma* (it came from the army and it still is part of the army) and '*La benemerita*'. (It earned a gold medal for its wonderful work at Messina's earthquake). Both bodies have a repressive, rather than protective disposition.

In 1967 the carabinieri were some eighty thousand strong. The CC also form part of the judiciary authority for special duties: execution of warrants, transfer and escort of prisoners, attendance at debates. They have to furnish information, generally requested by military commands, government offices, the ministries, the judicial authorities (more than twenty million pieces of information on private citizens each year.) The PS, or police, has the task of repressing and preventing crime, maintaining the security of citizens, and the re-establishment of order. The structure is complicated and divided into units, groups, according to territories. The *Squadra Omicidi*, the Murder Squad, is part of the police 'mobile' forces (the notorious *Celere* which is a real assault army). Especially in Sicily, the Murder Squad and the non-mobile Criminalpol investigates Mafia crimes. Its counterpart in the CC is the Investigation Bureau—*Il Nucleo Investigativo*. These two are comparatively modern institutions, modelled on the American bodies of investigation, and keep in close contact especially with the FBI, the Narcotic Bureau, Interpol, and the French police. The Murder Squad and the Investigation Bureau are in fierce competition and frequently investigate the same crime without passing information to each other. In fact, they often have totally opposed theories about the background of a crime.

Apart from various police forces (eight: road and traffic police, frontier and maritime police, *la Guardia di finanza*, the railway police, etc.) there are 2086 civil officials of PS.

Their Record Office contains the secrets of all the Italian citizens, and the keys to blackmail are in the hands of the head of the police in Rome, who is always very close to the Minister of the Interior (the Carabinieri have a similar and lethal service). Most of the big shots in the police are Southerners and, in particular, Sicilians. This is due to the fact that sixty-three per cent of the policemen come from the South (twenty-two per cent from the Centre, and fourteen per cent from the North of Italy). Wages are incredibly low (at the time of writing, 122,000 lira a month). Work is tiring—sometimes a policeman is on duty for twenty-four hours—and often dangerous, but for the poor Southerner, the job of policeman is often the only solution. The police are more subject to political intrigues than the carabinieri—who rather snub the police—but the one serious attempt to overthrow the present Republic in favour of a Neo-Fascist rule came from the carabinieri (General De Lorenzo). In one of its concluding reports, the Antimafia Parliamentary Commission (doc. XXII—2 July 1972) had strong words to say against both the police and the CC: 'The difference of orientation among the various police forces, noticeable in many reports, is such that one may suspect that both police and carabinieri in Western Sicily become at times two dented wheels which don't engage and each spin by itself. Before 1963, it was not infrequently the case that police and the CC totally disagreed on the context of informative reports. If, according to the former, one is facing a dangerous criminal, for the latter the image is instead that of an honest citizen who thinks only about his home, his family and his work. Then, when the reports are used for the purpose of granting a passport or a permit to carry arms, these are always modified, even very laboriously, in order to allow the police (*la questura P.S.*) to grant the requests. There are some minutes of these reports in which one can observe the effort of the writer in his attempt not to say what in fact appears clearly in the documents. Also in this case there emerge the most disquieting questions. Could one answer that the *maresciallo* of the CC is guilty, or the *brigadiere* of the PS when we know that they often have to obey superior orders? In that case, the corrupted officials would really be too many.' (*Atti Parlamentari*, p. 30). The Parliamentary Commission tells us how corrupt the police and the carabinieri are. In fact, they are not; they are doing exactly what they are required to do. Their job is to obey, and power is the network of the *cosche mafiose*.

All too often the honest policeman, the one who is actually gathering proof and information against the powerful *mafioso*, is moved to another city or is demoted, while the policeman who obeys the rules arrives at the top. And so it should be: the government must trust its forces, and if by the government we mean the *cosche mafiose*, it is all too clear that the unfortunate policeman who is honest fails in his job of serving his employers. The anomaly in the police force therefore is not the police-man who has come to some form of arrangement with the local *mafioso*, but the other way round. In fact it is still amazing to find how many truthful reports have been written confidentially by the individual policeman or carabiniere, many of which concern regional administra-tors, prefects, the judiciary, or members of parliament. Even when the PS and the CC succeed in gathering proof, often the instructing Magis-trates put the documentation away and nothing more is heard about their work. Only rarely—and recently—the police and carabinieri have worked together in an operation of mass Mafia arrest which was kept secret from the magistrates on the justifiable, but illegal, fear that the operation would have been delayed and information would have leaked out. By keeping the judiciary in the dark (although they should have signed the order to arrest) both corps underlined that they did not want to lose the element of surprise, declaiming openly that they did not trust the magistrates.

I know some honest policemen and carabinieri in Sicily (that is, the ones who don't comply), and I also know many dishonest ones. There is also the policeman who just knows, sees, and lets things happen. The lowest policeman's life is rather tragic. He is helpless and over worked; he knows far too many scandalous facts about his superiors; he also knows lots of things which he cannot prove. He is embittered by seeing trial after trial ending up in acquittals and seeing the worst criminals walk in liberty. In Sicily he is in the limelight: journalists go and see the 'good' policeman, and he has become accustomed to a civilized exchange of opinion—something new in the Italian police force. On the other hand, he also knows too much about each individual journalist: there is a police file on all of us, and this may be either because we know the actual criminals, or because we know many things. There is also the usual process of symbiosis between the best policeman and the best criminal: the initial attraction is the same and both are in the same game. In Sicily, then, the game becomes even closer than in other countries. Most policemen (I am talking here of high-grade and intelligent officials, and always of the rare honest type) make the mistake of considering the Mafia as an ordinary criminal association, understanding infiltration inside politics, but not grasping the fact that the Mafia is power. On the other hand, were they to recognize that, they would probably leave. Many of them are not bright enough to fight highly skilful and clever criminals. Many are ignorant and know too little about the Mafia, although there is a special course in the police. Both corps should have ample and easy access to the Antimafia Parliamentary secret and published reports, while it is not part of the routine to send copies to the various departments, let alone to the single officers who work in Western Sicily. The largest part of the police and the carabinieri is corrupt, i.e. they have understood where power lies; those are the ones who get to the top in Palermo and in Rome. If they happen to get into trouble (like Questore Albanese in Tajani's times, and so many others in more recent days) ministers will come to their rescue: these policemen know too many secrets about politicians, and they have the power of blackmail. Either they'll be promoted, or they'll be sent to some other city. Some have been shot dead. The fact that a magistrate and a policemen may come to the same end as the *mafioso* is the best indication that he has become a *mafioso*. Many authors and observers talk about the Mafia's infiltration of power. But to understand the Sicilian—and often Italian—political mechanism, one should reverse the concept to the infiltration of honesty, of legality inside the structure of power, an infiltration which, on the other hand, is easily kept at bay.

Police and carabinieri not only get no help from the State, but are considered enemies by the Sicilian population. They are the *sbirri*, representatives of a foreign occupation force, and are disliked by all strata of society. Both police and the cc have been unable to gain the trust of the population, even of that honest section which could have been their greatest ally. And this is the result of political motivations: the proletariat which is the natural enemy of the *mafioso* tends to be on the left, and the police forces have both been used as a repressive weapon against them, just as much as the Mafia was. Too many criminals are acquitted for the population to trust the police; besides, the local *capocosca* is too often seen walking side by side with the police official. The press has often been sensitive to these aspects, even in the past.

All this remains true today, and the police work in isolation, receiving no sympathy and no help from the citizens. Many high police officers know a lot, but they have no proof. When people talk to them they say 'Here I say it, and here I deny it' (*qui lo dico e qui lo nego*), by which formula it is meant that the person who has leaked the information will always deny having said it, and will never testify at a trial.

What has been said about the police and the carabinieri is even more valid for lawyers and magistrates. Since financial power and active rule lie within the *cosche*, the non-mafioso magistrate and lawyer in Sicily is an anomaly, and it couldn't be otherwise if the System is the mafioso. And while the police ranks are composed largely of lower-class men, the lawyers come from the middle class which has no interest in fighting the Mafia, i.e., itself. Besides, since the 'active' mafioso's aim is to assure respectability for himself and his family, often uncles and nephews, brothers or cousins study and practise the legal profession.

Unsuccessful attempts to try mafiosi and bring them to justice have been, and are, all too familiar. In 1970 the Antimafia Commission analysed the failures of such trials, showing the conflict emerging between the magistrature and other institutions, mainly the police, when the person on trial is a mafioso. It discovered that judges tend to dismiss the evidence offered by the police, while giving too much weight to the retraction of witnesses in court. On the other hand—and this is not stated in the report—the magistrates often are following higher instructions.

(Recently in London I received a telephone call from a mafioso who was to be tried for a considerable number of crimes and murders. He told me that he had decided to tell me 'certain things' and that he wanted to see me as soon as possible. He would ring me up again. When I began to think about the logic of such a telephone call, I thought that it was highly unlikely that he wanted to tell me anything about his own deeds or those of his friends and enemies, which would have meant to create evidence against himself, but that he was clearly alleging that he had 'political' secrets to tell me. Having access to the English press, I could guarantee publication of items which could not be printed in Italy, and therefore I could become an element of blackmail. In fact, I do not know whether the telephone call 'helped' him or not, but he got off very lightly: five years instead of the twenty-two he had been sentenced to in the previous trial.)

The legal procedure in Italy is particularly inefficient, and a slow judiciary machinery favours the *mafiosi*'s methods of operation. In any Italian court case, a person can be tried three times on the same indictment, and on the same evidence: first trial, appeal, high court. The accumulation of paperwork alone that results from one case going through several trials inevitably leads to an overloaded system and to delays. There are three possible verdicts: guilty, not guilty and non-proven. A person in Italy has to be proved not guilty; that is, he is detained and tried until proved otherwise and acquitted. If a defendant is acquitted on lack of proof (non-proven)—a standard verdict in Mafia trials—a new trial is generally called by the Public Prosecutor. If he is found guilty, the defendant will call for it. Years can elapse before the retrial. During these delays the *mafiosi* have opportunities to 'prepare' their defence. Witnesses are bribed, coerced, even silenced. Compliant lawyers are a contributory factor in the breakdown of the trials. They earn well (big 'bosses' generally employ three) and often it is in the counsels' interest to see that these trials go on for years without a conclusive verdict. The same legal faces appear at one Mafia trial after another; the same pattern of retraction by witnesses develops as trial succeeds trial. In fact, the money acquired illegally by the *mafiosi* finishes up, legally, in the pockets of the lawyers, whom the *mafiosi* call the 'vultures'. (Italian judges—*la magistratura*—are a group unto themselves: they must be lawyers first, and the road to becoming a judge is paved with mountains of rhetorical speeches.)

Norman Lewis, in *The Honoured Society*, points out: 'Insufficiency of proof is the standard formula under which cases brought against mafiosi are eventually committed to oblivion, and nine times out of ten it covers up the fact that essential witnesses have suddenly decided to retract their damaging evidence.' On the other hand, *omertà* is no longer the same phenomenon as that which existed in the past when Sicilians were actually on the side of the mafioso. 'Against the spirit of the mafia (*il sentimento di Mafia*) which should keep me silent, I shall speak,' said the bandit Angelo Pugliese in 1868. But then he withdrew in court. Today the man in the street is no longer keen to defend the mafioso, but as trials fail to convict, the potential witness proves himself right in not trusting his legal institutions. The mafioso instead has every advantage to gain from keeping silent and respecting the laws of *omertà*; to talk would mean to betray other *cosche*'s secrets as well as his own, disclosing evidence which might convict him; as long as he keeps silent he has a good chance to get away, literally, with murder. But recently there have been a surprising number of people who have testified, often in vain. *Omertà* is really alive only because of the justified mistrust in the efficiency of the law.

It often happens that in Mafia trials it is very difficult to find people willing to act as 'popular judges'. During a recent trial, in 1969, against the mafioso Liggio, all the members of the jury received threatening anonymous letters: Liggio was acquitted on lack of evidence, an acquittal which shocked Italy. It is even difficult to find judges or public prosecutors; not only is the paperwork of Mafia trials such that it scares even a civil servant accustomed to this Italian weakness, but counsels are generally highly skilled in finding any small procedural error, so that trials can be annulled or delayed. The formula of acquittal from lack of evidence generally scandalizes part of public opinion, which often suspects judges (whether rightly or not) to be corrupt. If in the past it was the mafioso who crept around the judges and blackmailed them, in recent years something new has happened, it is the mafioso who is blackmailed by police chiefs and the judges. These facts leave observers speechless with anger unless they realize that the Mafia is itself 'the establishment'. The spectacle of the mafiosi complaining that high magistrates do the same things that they do themselves is humorously paradoxical; yet one's laughter is bitter.

Since respect for civic institutions does not exist in Sicily, the representatives of those institutions also conform to this disrespect. So that people who are to be arrested are warned even before the order for their arrest has been signed, and the policemen find that they have left two or three days before.

In Sicily the *Tribunale* has the role of administering the *ammonizione*. There is no need of evidence for such a preventative measure. The *ammonizione* is a judicial proceeding which imposes specific restrictions —not always identical—on offenders or potential offenders. With the coming into effect of the Penal Code of 1938, the Mafia is juridically considered an association formed to commit crimes which, in itself, can be punished with up to ten years imprisonment. Also a new 'Antimafia law' (575—article 4) allows the arrest of Mafia suspects even when there is no legal need for detaining the person. For these groups of 'preventative laws' (30 May 1965—law no. 575) at the time of writing 593 people are under police control (*sorveglianza speciale*): 996 have been sent to *confino*, banished to some remote village. Since 1962, 18,846 Sicilians have been hit by the *diffida*, which is like the *ammonizione*. These measures, a Parliamentary paper states, have been successful, and the police can use them against people who are judged (by the police) as being 'socially dangerous' (*pericolosità sociale*).

After being released from prison or acquitted by the courts for lack of evidence, many mafiosi finish up in *confino*, *il soggiorno obbligato*, for a limited period of time. Some sources give the number of Mafia suspects who live in banishment as 672, of which 495 are from Sicily and the rest from Calabria. But with the existence of long-distance calls, motor roads, aeroplanes, the idea of isolating a person has become a farce. In fact, the *confino* has proved to have been a way of spreading Mafia activities to the North of Italy. On the other hand, it is certainly humiliating for a Mafia boss to be displaced from his area 'of respect' and from his family, but this applies particularly to the rural mafioso linked to agrarian communities and villages. The mafioso who deals in drugs can operate from anywhere. In 1970, the carabinieri declared that some 20,000 Sicilians had been hit by the various antimafia laws. But five years later it cannot be said that the situation has improved. Once again repressive methods have proved not to be the answer. I need not stress, besides, how dangerous laws can be which permit a citizen to be deprived of his liberty without evidence. In fact, the *confino* was used in Fascist times against mafiosi, but also against 'enemies of the state'—anti-Fascist democrats, many of whom died in remote and barren places.

Every day the *confinato*, i.e. the banished mafioso, has to pay a visit

This map, prepared in 1974, shows the numbers of mafiosi from Palermo alone held *al confino* in mainland Italy. The effect of such regulations is to diffuse the Mafia message: note especially the concentration in the industrial north.

to the police station, cannot be outside in the street after dusk or in the morning before a time fixed by the local police station, cannot go to 'inns', *osterie*. It is impossible to enforce these rules, especially in the South: houses are hot at night, and the only place where a breath of fresh air can be enjoyed is in the street; the local inn is the only place where the bored mafioso can go and drink a cup of coffee. The local *maresciallo* of the *carabinieri* generally opens his arms and says 'They are human beings as well as ourselves' and lets things go. The mafioso at the *confino* lives by the telephone. Genco Russo, a *capocosca* who had been sent to Lovere, near Bergamo, spent 125,000 lira (about £90) a week in telephone calls. The most dangerous, or rather the less highly protected, mafiosi have recently been banished to faraway islands in groups of fifteen or twenty: the law of the *confino* specifies that a Mafia suspect should have no contact whatsoever with another Mafia suspect.

Another new law, called 'the Valpreda law', which was passed in 1970, suspends the detention of prisoners appealing to a higher court. It was a just law which prevented innocents from remaining in prison for years before they could be proved not guilty, but it was also paradise for the mafiosi. It meant that a mafioso who had been convicted but had appealed to a higher court, could not be detained. The Chief of the Palermo police, Questore Li Donni, said: 'Even with the help of the magistrates, our hands are tied by the procedure. We know a lot, we could find the guilty ones as public opinion demands, but the respect of the law paralyses us. Some norms which guarantee the citizen's liberty, here, in this context, become favourable to the Mafia.'

The mechanisms of the State—the legal structure and the police forces —are still lamentably weak, and invite the contempt of the Sicilian population at large. Possibly exaggerated by the post-war confusion and by the after-effects of Fascist education and 'philosophy', the collapse of the State machinery is dramatically exemplified in the 'saga' of Salvatore Giuliano.

8 The Sicilian puppet-theatre: Salvatore Giuliano

Salvatore Giuliano is the embodiment of the tragedy which Sicily has lived through these last decades, unable to adjust to the present century. Giuliano was the very Paladin Orlando, the legendary protagonist of the Charlemagne epic represented in the Sicilian puppet theatre, held by invisible hands, on a colourful but limited stage. Even his character seems less his own than a stereotype of one kind of ultra-individualistic, semi-paranoiac Sicilian mentality.

Il Teatro dei Pupi, the puppet theatre, a popular form of entertainment in Sicily, is a key to understanding the Mafia. Every district of Palermo has a theatre in which each night the story of the French Crusaders is told in instalments, ad lib. The paladins always kill their enemies who have wronged them or their gentlewomen. These stories were introduced into Sicily in Norman times, but were transformed by the Sicilian temperament (the Normans and the Sicilians more or less ignored the Crusades anyway) and the heroes are bullies who continually kill on stage. When there are few murders the public won't turn up. The noble crusaders who kill Moors and Infidels justify the sanctity of personal revenge and of violence. The *teatro dei pupi* became a popular form of entertainment only in the nineteenth century and ended its real functions after the Second World War. The *teatro*, a small sordid room or a tent, was a place where no ladies would or could go, and if a noble family wanted to watch the spectacle, the *puparo* would be warned and he would keep out all the *picciotti*. The *picciotti*, the young men of the poor districts, those who dressed and behaved *mafiosamente*, really came to the '*Pupi*' in order to shout, to bash each other up, to give way to that energy which in Sicily often explodes in violence. Many can still recollect those scenes.

Salvatore Giuliano was conceived in New York, but born in Sicily.

His father had lived in the United States for eighteen years, and the young Giuliano must have heard many a glowing reminiscence of America in his childhood, which was spent in the grim town of Monte-lepre. All his life he looked to the US as to a promised land, writing to President Truman asking that Sicily should become part of the US, and finally hoping to escape across the Atlantic to start another life.

In 1943, at the age of twenty-one, Salvatore 'Turiddu' or Turi Giuliano killed a Carabiniere. Now he was an outlaw, and the only 'career' left for him was banditry. He went to live in the caves of Calcerama, overlooking Montelepre, and gradually mustered a group of men with similar backgrounds. 'Turi' Giuliano was handsome and had a strong personality. He was certainly loved by the inhabitants of Montelepre, who gave him shelter and protection. The Italian police were behaving so abominably towards the Sicilian peasantry that Giuliano was seen as the rebel, a symbol of liberty and an expression of popular discontent. As soon as he achieved power he was respected by the Sicilians, who always bow to might. But Giuliano was also a megalomaniac and very naïve. He could easily be convinced about panaceas for Sicily's and his own problems, and in fact his own safety and legal pardon became the mainspring of all his actions, however horrible these might be. Selfish, and pleased with his own importance, he gave interviews and acted like a king. But he was not a king, not even a regent: he was just a puppet.

One of Giuliano's companions, the bandit Terranova, remembered:

I already knew Giuliano before all the events because we came from the same village, we were friends and we were more or less the same age. At a certain moment the war came and with the war, disaster, black market; and Giuliano was one of those who got caught for a black-market offence. They wanted to take a sack of wheat from him, and for him that was a lot. He resisted and escaped, but a guard opened fire and he thought it was the Carabiniere who was shooting. He turned back, killed him and fled. In Palermo they were forming the Separatist party. With the Separatists there was the Volunteer Army for the Independence of Sicily, the EVIS. Political personalities invited Giuliano to join: Concetto Gallo, Baron La Motta, the Duke of Carcaci and many others ... and they made him commander of our area in Western Sicily, begging him to form a small army, which he did ... There were several meetings ... and we were waiting for the moment when we were to receive orders and attack the barracks of the Carabinieri so that we could separate Sicily from Italy. Because we *were* to separate Sicily. They said that in Sicily there was too much hunger; this hunger came because Italy stole all the wealth of Sicily. And since at that time I knew hunger very well ... I was convinced of what they were preaching. Just think, at that time I worked and earned 200 lire a day [about 10p.]; 200 lire, and I had nobody to support, neither father nor mother, nobody. I used to buy a piece of bread for 90 lire: I ate two pieces and 20 lire were for cigarettes. Nothing was left ... In that period they took three politicians who had been banished to Ponza, and then they came back, like Finocchiaro Aprile. At a certain moment they ordered us to lay down our arms and quit the struggle. Giuliano said that for him the fight was going on at all costs; and it did.

Giuliano was territorially well placed. His band was protected by the important *cosche* of Monreale and Partinico, which judged it useful to keep the small army of bandits in their area. This is the reason why Giuliano's nest of bandits was the only one to survive the fierce struggle against banditry carried out by the Italian police which destroyed all other Sicilian gangs. He did not have many men—a hundred at the most—but they were disciplined and obeyed orders, not so much his as the Mafia's. They had the advantage of being able to live in their homes in town, which was totally on Giuliano's side, and withdrew to the mountains only when the police were around, in which case the network of intelligence would let the bandits know in advance.

For the Sicilians (and for many English writers) Giuliano is still a romantic figure, a martyr of Sicilian independence.*

Ballad singers would tour Western Sicily and sing stories in praise of Turiddu 'Turi' Giuliano. The public delighted in these stories of Giuliano robbing the rich who had 'wheat, jewels and land', a Robin Hood who was gallant with the ladies and gave money to the poor. But what went to the poor were actual bribes, and most of the loot was for his men for buying arms and for survival. For the Italians Giuliano

---

* When I wrote an article for an English magazine in which I talked about Giuliano as a weapon of the Mafia, a Sicilian woman wrote a letter of protest: Giuliano was a good man, and the Mafia was good; in London she had always been helped by the Mafia against the Jews who had tried to exploit her. I was obviously ignorant if I could speak ill of both Giuliano and the Mafia.

is a bandit whose hands were drenched in blood. His criminal career was full: he killed 430 people.

In the three years between 1943 and 1946, the largest part of the Mafia (the middle class and the landowning class) stood by the agrarian structure which could guarantee its power, and organized the Separatist Movement (the only party which had not promised any agrarian reform). As we saw, Giuliano's political involvement started with his meeting the Separatist leaders at Ponte Sagana, where he was made a colonel of the EVIS. The Antimafia Report records:

> The Mafia needs banditry and common criminals who are necessary instruments for its criminal actions; bandits enjoy its protection and help until the time comes when they become dangerous for its survival. Those arrested by the police are criminals no longer needed by the Mafia, or they have betrayed or are going to betray ... And so, once again in Sicilian history, the circle of collaboration between the Mafia and politicians closes: politicians who from the Separatist and later from the Monarchist party, defend strenuously the economic logic of the latifundia and use the Mafia and bandits engaged by the latter to spread terror and death ...

It was from the day of the Sagana meeting that Giuliano became no ordinary bandit because the local *cosche* protected him and guaranteed him an amnesty. Fighting Italy, the common enemy, Giuliano's previous crimes would have been pardoned by the new ruling class. The war against Italy was going to cost money, and the Separatists needed a Giuliano who was prepared to kidnap those who still had 'land, wheat and jewels'. A list of names was drafted: those who agreed to give money would be spared, and given a certificate indicating the sum handed to the cause. There followed a long series of kidnapping, attacks on the barracks of the Carabinieri, murders of policemen and civilians.

In June 1945, Giuliano organized a series of night attacks on Carabinieri barracks: a war blew up between Giuliano's EVIS and the *Arma dei carabinieri*. When the leader of the Separatist movement, Finocchiaro Aprile, came back to Palermo from banishment, the Separatists publicly denied all responsibility for what Giuliano's gang was doing, and insisted that he was no longer their agent. Giuliano himself felt betrayed as he was demoted from official colonel to ordinary bandit. His official pardon seemed to be further and further away.

In December 1945 the Italian army attacked the EVIS in Eastern

Sicily and Concetto Gallo, the commander of the Separatist Army in Eastern Sicily, was imprisoned. Gallo was accused of revolt against the State, but was to receive a pardon, and was elected as a deputy the following year. After Gallo's imprisonment, Salvatore Giuliano's was the only nucleus of the EVIS left in Sicily. But while in Eastern Sicily the Italian army had easily overpowered the two hundred volunteers under Gallo's leadership, it seemed as if the Italian government was not interested in getting rid of Giuliano's bandits. No army was sent there, only small groups of Carabinieri. At one stage there were only twelve stationed at Montelepre.

When Giuliano felt betrayed by the Separatists, the bandit declared that he would have gone on fighting for the annexation of Sicily to the United States of America. He held up cars, trains, gave interviews to leading newspapers, had foreign mistresses, but he was too highly protected to be caught by the Italian State. Popular fantasy thrived on Giuliano's conquests, his women, his successes:

> ... *Era Svidisa e bedda ppi natura,*
> *comu na rosa 'ntra la primavera,*
> *e 'nta ddi munti, chini di friscura*
> *Turiddu amuriggo' ccu dda stranera.*
> *Ma mentri Turi sintia felici,*
> *sintiti ca successi, cari amici ...*

('She was Swedish, and she was beautiful like a rose in spring, and Giuliano made love to her in the fresh mountains, but, while he was so happy, hear my dear friends, what was happening to him ...')

There were even curfews at Montelepre, house-to-house searches, mass arrests of small fry. There were odd episodes like that of the driver who tried to warn the police when his employer was kidnapped by Giuliano in the centre of Palermo. Not only did the police not help him, they detained him for over a month 'for questioning'.

Giuliano was cut off, again reduced to the status of an ordinary outlaw. He could not have survived without the full support of the Mafia. Any informer against Giuliano became an informer against the Mafia: policemen and Carabinieri who were quite capable of eliminating bandits could do nothing against a man backed by the most powerful *cosche mafiose*. The police were under the direct control of the Minister of the Interior, the Sicilian Mario Scelba, who was to become Prime Minister in January 1954.

Prince Alliata, a monarchist, and his lawyer Leonardo Marchesano (who administered Alliata's properties), sought Giuliano's electoral support. But as we have seen, after a reign of less than a month King Umberto II was dethroned as a result of the referendum of 2 June 1946. The greater part of the nearly eleven million votes which had been polled for the monarchy came from the South, while the industrialized North was mainly responsible for the thirteen million votes in favour of the Republic.

From the Parliamentary Inquiry on Mafia and Banditism 8.1.1971: text of the statements of the former General of the Carabinieri, Dottore Giacinto Paolantonio (p. 730—*Relazione tra la mafia e il banditismo in Sicilia*)

AZZARO M P (Christian Democrat): ... I am interested to know about Giuliano and which were the powers who backed him until his last days. Because, you see, at a certain moment, in 1949, at the end, everybody washed their hands of Giuliano because this man was no longer of any use, because, by then, political patterns had already been established and there was a political stability for which Giuliano could no longer be an instrument. Whereas in 1945, 1946, 1947 and 1948, until ...

LI CAUSI M P: Until the elections of 18 April 1948.

AZZARO: ... until the elections of April 1948 there was still hope of being able to determine ...

PAOLANTONIO: To determine what? But ... I haven't the electoral results here: it's enough to have a look at the results at Montelepre year by year, election by election, in order to see ...

LI CAUSI: The evolution ...

PAOLANTONIO: The many evolutions ... One day a judge went with two Carabinieri to pay an unexpected visit to a farm and at that moment Giuliano was there; the Carabinieri were asked to stay on the ground floor. Giuliano, with two or three of his men, was upstairs. The owner didn't fear the judge and the Carabinieri, but he was scared of Giuliano. You can interpret this story in many ways. Once Giuliano had died, the phenomenon was over, it was he who had such a strong personality!

AZZARO: Certainly, as a bandit; you see, there have always been bandits similar to him, at all times.

PAOLANTONIO: After the war we had a list of thirty-three nests of bandits and, in the Giuliano period we didn't fear Separatism any longer. We were far more bothered by the gang of the 'Niscemesi' than by Giuliano's nest in the period when the Mafia was ...

AZZARO: ... protecting him.

PAOLANTONIO: ... when it closed in, closed in around him! So much so that we used to ask ourselves: is Giuliano still alive?

The Carabinieri knew that Giuliano's survival was due solely to the Mafia's protection. And Giuliano was still of some use for those interests represented by the Sicilian middle class. In the regional elections of 20 April 1947, Montelepre (and the region around it) voted as Giuliano had asked. The Separatists (MISDR) polled 1521 and the Left 70 votes. In the general elections of 1948 Montelepre, following Giuliano's political switch, voted almost to a man for the Monarchist party. The bandit Giovanni Genovese, from Giuliano's gang, told the examining magistrate who was preparing the trial against him:

On 27 April 1947, in the morning, at Saracino, near Montelepre, Salvatore Giuliano came to see me, with the brothers Pianelli and Salvatore Ferrari ... They had something to eat with me and then stayed on to talk. At about three o'clock, Pasquale Sciortino arrived. He had a letter for Giuliano and called him on one side. The two went and sat down behind a wall where they read the letter and they discussed it. It must have been an important document because, after reading it, Giuliano burned it with a match. After that, Sciortino went away ... Then Giuliano said to me: 'The hour has come.' I asked: 'What's that?' Giuliano said: 'We have to go into action against the Communists; we've got to go and shoot them on May the first, at Portella delle Ginestre.

On May Day 1947, Giuliano committed his most infamous crime, the massacre of innocent people at Portella delle Ginestre, near Piana degli Albanesi, traditionally a left-wing stronghold (in the 1947 elections it had voted overwhelmingly for the Left, with 2739 votes against 13 votes for the Separatists). The peasants living in the area had resumed a custom which had been suppressed during the Fascist era: the celebration of Labour Day, 1 May. Whole families in their best clothes, with their Sicilian carts, donkeys and mules, picnic baskets, children, set off on the winding *trazzere* which took them to the picturesque locality of Portella delle Ginestre. Mountain ranges on both sides made Portella a bottleneck. The bandits took up position on the lower slope of Monte Pizzuta, overlooking the site of the *festa*, and as the local Socialist leader —a cobbler—started speaking, machine-guns opened fire on the people. Men, women, children and animals were mown down by automatic rifles: eight people died, thirty-three were wounded. Panic seized the merry gathering, donkeys and mules fell covered with blood: it must have looked like Guernica as seen by Picasso. Some eight hundred empty cartridge cases were found on Monte Pizzuta.

This popular ballad is unwilling to accuse Giuliano openly:

> ... *A Purtedda Ginestra, si cci iti*
> *truvati ancora petri 'nsanguinati*
> *E deci 'nnomi ci morti liggiti,*
> *ca 'ta grossa petra su stampati*
> *Tannu si dissi ca fu Giuliano*
> *ca simino' ddi morti 'nta ddu chianu ...*

(If you go to Portella delle Ginestre / You'll still find stones stained with blood / And you'll read ten names of people killed / Engraved on a large stone / They said it had been Giuliano / who killed those people on that ground.)

Giuliano's offensive against the Communist party did not stop there, and party offices in towns which were in 'Giuliano territory' were bombed and burnt. On 22 June 1947, two people died when the Communist offices in Partinico were destroyed by hand-grenades. One hour later, grenades and two Molotov cocktails were thrown at the Communist offices in Carini. At 11.30 in the evening, two men dressed as Carabinieri attacked the Communist offices at Borgetto; five minutes later, at San Giuseppe Jato, the offices were wrecked and a woman was wounded. Next day it was the turn of the Communist party at Cinisi. The whole operation had obviously been planned, and was meant to intimidate. At Partinico nearly ten thousand anti-Communist leaflets were scattered around, and anti-Communist slogans were painted on hundreds of walls.

Giuliano's war against the Left and against the peasantry had been dictated from high places. We have mentioned names like Alliata, Tasca, Mattarella, Vizzini; police files were full of names of local mafiosi in league with Giuliano (and with the police), like Minasola, Fleres, Miceli. But these orders to Giuliano had come from further up, in fact from the 'High' Mafia. The names of the MP Mattarella and the lawyer

Girolamo Bellavista were mentioned over and over again, but those of Frank Coppola, Judge Scaglione, the Rimi family were never uttered. Giuliano never betrayed them, and when there was a danger that he might do so or that he might kill the employers who had not kept their promises, Giuliano died.

Italian public opinion was shaken by the slaughter at Portella delle Ginestre. In Parliament the Communist party accused the Monarchists, the Liberals, and with them the Mafia. Many were mentioned too, among them Girolamo Bellavista—a man close to Christian Democrat Minister Mattarella—and Mattarella himself. Alliata, Leone Marchesano and a man named Cusumano were accused of having ordered the attack. Alliata has recently (1974) been linked with the neo-Fascist groups who had planned a coup in Italy. But the accusation begged too many questions. Could it be that only a few reactionaries would risk such a scandal? Who had really unleashed Giuliano against the Left? And who had the power to promise the bandit legal pardon in exchange for the bloody deed?

Scelba, the Minister of the Interior, denied that Portella had been a crime motivated by politics. But a few days later he was proved wrong by the burning of so many Communist offices in Giuliano's territory. At the same time the *cosche* were reinforcing Giuliano's anti-Left operation with the murder of several peasant leaders. In December 1947, at Baucina, Nicolò Azoti; in March 1948, at Petralia Soprana, Epifanio Li Puma; and at Corleone, Placido Rizzotto. In April at Camporeale, Calogero Cangelosi, and at Partinico, Vincenzo Lo Jacomo and Giuseppe Casarubea. The campaign of terror worked: the elections of 18 April 1948 went very differently from the previous ones, with the Christian Democrats polling 47·87% of the votes (from the previous 20·52% in 1946). There was a Sicilian middle-class logic in all this: killing is the Mafia's usual way of getting rid of obstacles and of intimidating would-be rebels. In 1948, four hundred and ninety-eight people were murdered in Sicily.

But the slaughter of Portella had been too brutal and ugly. Giuliano who had certainly perpetrated it on behalf of a third party, was abandoned by everybody. More reinforcements were sent to Montelepre and some members of the gang took refuge in North Africa. Sensing the shift in the situation, Giuliano's brother-in-law Sciortino fled to America with a case of documents which were said to be compromising for some Italian politicians. They disappeared, like all documents concerning Giuliano. (Sciortino married an American girl, claiming that his first marriage to Giuliano's sister had been annulled. He was later arrested and is still in an Italian prison.)

In Parliament the Communist Girolamo Li Causi proclaimed that police inspector Messana had been in league with Giuliano, and he denounced Scelba for allowing Messana to remain in office. Later on documents were to prove the accusation. In fact, it was not only the specifically criminal Mafia which had something to gain from Giuliano's intimidation of the Left. It was also in the interest of the Centre-Right parties, the politicians whom it enabled to remain in power. In fact, those who had most of all to gain were all the representatives of that middle class which, especially in Sicily, had not moved with the times, which believed in repression and identified with or shaded into the Mafia. One member of Giuliano's gang, Salvatore Ferrari, was Inspector Messana's informer inside the nest of bandits; whether he had told Messana in advance about the Portella slaughter was never made quite clear. Ferrari was arrested later on, then killed by a Captain of the Carabinieri while in captivity, and the suspicion that he had things to tell about his connections with the police has always remained.

Inspectors were changed quickly, but intrigues kept growing. Another police inspector, Ciro Verdiani, was meeting Giuliano and his closest collaborator (Giuliano's cousin Gaspare Pisciotta) through the Miceli mafiosi from Monreale. The inspector had drinks and cakes with men whom he should instead have arrested at once. Maresciallo Lo Bianco, a jolly Carabiniere who was in the forefront of the fight against banditry, told the panel of M Ps of the Antimafia Committee:

> I already knew that Giuliano was in the hands of some mafiosi of Monreale [the Micelis]; in fact I remember that one man—not a mafioso, a good sort of person—who knew that I wanted to catch Giuliano at all costs, told me one day: 'Listen, the difficulty is not catching Giuliano, it is to get the Mafia to agree; because if the Mafia liquidates him, it will give him up to you; but if the Mafia says no, you will never get Giuliano ...'

At the trial for the massacre at Portella delle Ginestre, Gaspare Pisciotta said: 'Those who have made promises to us are called Bernardo Mattarella, Prince Alliata, the monarchist M P Marchesano and also Signor Scelba, Minister for Home Affairs ... it was Marchesano, Prince Alliata and Bernardo Mattarella who ordered the massacre of Portella delle Ginestre. Before the massacre they met Giuliano ...' But the MPs Mattarella, Alliata and Marchesano were declared innocent by the Court of Appeal of Palermo, at a trial which dealt with their alleged role in the deed.

On 19 August 1949, Giuliano and his men killed seven Carabinieri and wounded eleven at Bellolampo, between Palermo and Monreale. Parliament decided that a new body for the destruction of Giuliano was to be created. The CFRB (*Corpo delle Forze per la Repressione del Banditismo in Sicilia*) was answerable only, and directly, to the Minister of the Interior, and was to be under the leadership of Colonel Ugo Luca. Luca was a Carabiniere and came from the Secret Service of the Italian army; he trusted nobody. He had full powers. The new force was intended to be overpowering.

'You have no idea,' a former CFRB told me. 'We were given food for a week and it was enough for a day. So we ate it all, and the rest we stole. I joined that force because we were paid a little bit more as the job was dangerous. The population hated us and loved Giuliano. We respected Giuliano too; our real enemies were the policemen [PS]. We shot at each other, and killed each other, ourselves against the police. Many casualties ascribed to Giuliano's gang were in fact caused by armed encounters between the CFRB and the police.' The former General of the Carabinieri, Giacinto Paolantonio, told the Antimafia Commission: 'The situation of the Carabinieri was alarming—undermanned, sleeping in haystacks. We got our first machine-guns by confiscating them from Giuliano's gang. I remember that at Montelepre, in the beginning, there were twelve Carabinieri who had six pairs of shoes between them; they went out on duty in turn, using the six pairs.'

The police resented the creation of the new body, and Police Inspector Ciro Verdiani 'didn't give a single piece of information to Luca, not even a piece of paper, and didn't tell him who his informers were inside the Giuliano gang. So that the CFRB had to start from scratch' (from the text of the 1950 trial). In fact Ciro Verdiani, of the *Ispettorato di Polizia* which was dissolved with the creation of the CFRB, had entered into negotiations with the mafiosi of Monreale. After the arrival of the new force, some of Giuliano's men began to melt away. Giuliano realized that not only had the politicians abandoned him but also the Mafia—or part of it—was letting him down. He counter-attacked in the only way he knew: violence. In July 1949 the powerful *capocosca* of Partinico, Santo Fleres, was shot dead. Leonardo Renda, a Christian Democrat official from the Alcamo Mafia, was found dead. On 7 August Giuliano tried to kidnap the Minister Bernardo Mattarella and his family. Even Don Calogero Vizzini's life was threatened by Giuliano: bodyguards armed to the teeth escorted the old man whose power had always been such that he had never needed to carry a weapon.

To fill the chair involuntarily vacated by Santo Fleres, the criminal *cosche* of Partinico needed a 'big shot', especially at such a crucial moment, when Salvatore Giuliano had to be got rid of at all costs. The big shot came from the States. In January 1950 Frank Coppola took up his position of supreme authority, immediately recognized by all. Action was called for: the trial of thirty-two men for the massacre of Portella delle Ginestre was due to start at Viterbo in that same year. Giuliano had to be silenced before he could be caught alive by the Law, but the Mafia must not appear to betray him directly.

It was difficult to arrange the destruction of Guiliano because actual politics, Mafia and legal power were involved. The operation was masterminded by Frank Coppola, a man who had left Partinico poor and illiterate. 'Three-fingered Frank' was aided by the powerful *cosche* of the Trapani area, a Mafia which has traditional links on the other side of the Atlantic, especially through the town of Castellammare. The Mafia of the *Trapanese* were for a long time more respectful and respected—i.e. more powerful—than any other. Its bosses lived on, were not regularly shot down as in Palermo or Agrigento. In Alcamo, just above Castellammare, lived the 'Royal' family: the Rimis.

Giuliano was offered safety in the United States: the promised land was finally going to materialize. He had to relinquish his *memoriale*, a sort of diary in which 'everything' was written down, and which had often been used by Giuliano as a threat to blackmail Mafia and political circles. While waiting for the final arrangements for his departure, Giuliano was given shelter in the house of a so-called *avvocaticchio*, 'petty lawyer', De Maria. This was at Castelvetrano (far from Montelepre), where Giuliano had no support.

It was Giuliano's cousin Pisciotta who began the final act. 'He understood that by then there was almost nobody left in the gang,' said Maresciallo Lo Bianco. 'He told me, "Look, I have decided to give you Giuliano." ' When Colonel Paolantonio was about to capture Giuliano, he saw his superior, Ugo Luca, and his driver sneak away unescorted from the Palermo headquarters. Paolantonio and Maresciallo Lo Bianco, suspecting that Luca might have wanted to prevent others from capturing the big prize, followed him unseen past Monreale, towards Partinico. There was one person only whom Ugo Luca might have wanted to see at Partinico, and this was Frank Coppola. At around six o'clock in the morning, Maresciallo Lo Bianco recalls that his friend Paolantonio woke him up by telephoning: 'Guess what?' There was no need to say. For Lo Bianco it was obvious: Luca had tricked them, but the High Mafia had out-manoeuvred Luca, in masterly fashion. Later that day (5 July) Luca sent a message to the Ministry of the Interior: Giuliano was dead, he had been accidentally shot in an armed encounter at Castelvetrano, a town in the Trapani province. His cousin Pisciotta had been able to escape.

Pisciotta had betrayed his cousin to the Carabinieri, Paolantonio and Lo Bianco, but in exchange for his own liberty he had promised to give Giuliano up alive (he was to be allowed to flee to North Africa or North America). The moment was ripe, but Luca, wanting to reserve the big prey for himself, went to see Coppola. And that was what Coppola was there for: to give Giuliano to the Carabinieri, making sure that he had been silenced forever before he did so. It may even be that Luca's motives were not as simple as that; corrupt alliances of interest and protection have been a feature of Coppola's career.

The official version of Giuliano's death was disbelieved from the start, and not only by men like Paolantonio and Lo Bianco, who knew too much of the story. Journalists flocked to see the body, and photographs which appeared in all the newspapers two days later bore witness to the impossibility of the official version: Giuliano was lying face down, his vest stained with blood, a machine-gun next to him. His body had been riddled with bullets: no blood had come out of some wounds, as if he had been shot again when already a corpse. Bloodstains from other wounds clearly ran upwards, which contradicted the version by which Giuliano had fallen on the ground in that position. Plainly he had been killed earlier, and the body had been taken to the courtyard to stage a clumsy, hurried scenario.

Ugo Luca said that he had been warned that Giuliano was somewhere at Castelvetrano, and was about to leave the country. Captain Perenze of the Carabinieri, who was in the village at dawn, claimed that he saw two men running. He asked them to stop, but one of them started shooting. Perenze fired back, and hit one man who took refuge in a courtyard. When Perenze reached him he found that the man was already dead, and was none other than Salvatore Giuliano. The courtyard belonged to the house of the *avvocaticchio* De Maria: the 'other' man had been Pisciotta. The only piece of truth in Perenze's version was the last statement.

Everybody realized that Giuliano had not been killed by the legal forces of the State but by the Mafia, and the Mafia was quick in leaking information—an occasion to discredit the State even further was not to be missed. From this operation the Mafia emerged more powerful than ever, with an aura of infallibility. Pisciotta's agreed role was to give Giuliano a sleeping potion and hand him over to the Carabinieri. But at the Viterbo trial, in 1951, Pisciotta alleged that he had killed Giuliano himself. Ugo Luca did not want to share the success of the operation with Paolantonio and Lo Bianco; he therefore acted foolishly and by himself alone. Questioned by the Antimafia Commission, the Carabiniere Captain Perenze declared:

> We hoped to take him alive: in fact, we were aiming for that goal. When Pisciotta killed him it was a total suprise for us. It was also a surprise for Pisciotta.
> TUCCARI MP: I too am surprised by what you are saying, since Pisciotta was acting in agreement with you.
> PERENZE: Pisciotta didn't have to kill him. His role was to get him out of his hideout, first to find where he was and then to get him to go out.

De Maria spent a few years in prison, and emigrated to the States. Today he is back in Sicily and a frightened destitute. Interviewed, he will only speak a few terrified words: 'The Mafia is powerful, it frightens one.' A small figure after years and years of silence, he said that he had to comply. 'There wasn't a word said between myself and the bandits. I was petrified by fear; I took them to a room to the upper floor without uttering a sound.' De Maria had testified that on the night of the murder he was woken up by the noise of shotguns. When he entered Giuliano's room he found the bandit already a corpse, with Pisciotta beside him.

There was another witness who never talked for the justified fear that he might be killed, as what he had seen was quite different from the official version. Pietro Lo Bello, a young baker, was trying to sleep in the hot summer night away from the baking oven. He was lying on the floor of the bakery under the half-closed shutter, when the noise of a car woke him up. 'We knew that in De Maria's house there was a strange guest, a tall man with dark hair who always wore a white trenchcoat, but we would never have guessed it was Giuliano.' The sole witness to the Giuliano affair did not feel safe enough to speak out until 1974. His evidence is important because it shows that Giuliano was actually killed at Castelvetrano. (Many had begun to say that he had been shot at Monreale and then taken to De Maria's by car, then a journey of two to three hours. This was unlikely anyway, since the slaying of Giuliano had become the Trapani *cosche*'s responsibility.) It also indicates that when Pisciotta arrived with the Carabiniere Perenze, Giuliano was already dead. Pisciotta had arrived too late. Lo Bello, who was not alone on the bakery floor, recalls:

At about three o'clock in the morning we saw a dark Fiat 1100 which proceeded slowly along Via Mannone, its motor to minimum power in the last hundred metres, and stopped by the pavement opposite the courtyard of De Maria's house. Two men got out of the car, one tall with moustaches, a canvas jacket on [Perenze], the other in a rather old dark suit [Pisciotta]. They went towards the house. Pisciotta had the keys of De Maria's house, he opened the door without making any noise, and entered, followed by Perenze.

Lo Bello, who had previously heard the noise of shooting, also saw two other men, fully armed, descend from the car (two plainclothes Carabinieri). A few seconds later, he saw Perenze come out of De Maria's courtyard and call over the driver of the 1100. In a matter of seconds Pisciotta jumped into the car and disappeared towards Palermo. So Pisciotta and Perenze together had entered Giuliano's room. Had Pisciotta killed his cousin, he would have had to shoot him in front of the Carabiniere. Pisciotta had entered the house and had gone out almost immediately. Nobody has even asked Perenze if Pisciotta had shot Giuliano in front of him (which he certainly did not), or whether there was a third man in the room, and nobody asked Lo Bello when exactly he heard the shooting. It is very likely that the person who killed Giuliano did it when he heard Pisciotta and Perenze come into the house. The two Carabinieri in plain clothes, armed with automatic weapons, and Captain Perenze started firing around them at once, shouting that there were bandits. 'Had I said this at the time of the Viterbo trial, I mightn't have been believed, and I might have been killed. Now it is all different.'

In December 1950 (the Viterbo trial had started) Gaspare Pisciotta was arrested. Not by the Carabinieri, who had promised him a safe conduct, but by the police. Inspector Carmelo Marzano arrested Pisciotta in Palermo, where he lived in peace under the protection of the Carabinieri. According to Frank Mannino, a prominent member of Giuliano's gang, during the Viterbo trial his lawyers assured him that although Pisciotta was going to say that he had killed Giuliano, he had not actually done so. 'Pisciotta is a traitor,' Mannino said, 'but not Giuliano's killer.'

Pisciotta had no great interest in killing his cousin because he had promised the bandit alive in exchange for a pardon and safety. The Italian state, as such, needed Giuliano alive at the Viterbo trial, and wanted his *memoriale*, his famous diary. Certainly not all the authorities concerned were corrupt and in league with the Mafia. But the Mafia represented by those who had sought their interests in different political parties, by those who had used Giuliano as a weapon to gain power and to intimidate the Left, had every motive for silencing him. And the *memoriale* could in the future be a weapon for blackmailing those authorities who had been too close to Giuliano.

The Carabiniere Paolantonio told the Antimafia Commission (Parliamentary Report on Mafia and Banditism, page 478):

> Yes, Giuliano had some papers on him where there were written names. He also had a letter from the Police Inspector Verdiani, and a five-lire note torn in two; he had photographs of the room where he lived at the *avvocaticchio*'s [the mafioso De Maria's] and what for us was more interesting, he had a list of names: I asked Luca for those ... But as soon as Giuliano was dead, they got rid of all of us saying that banditry was over. Instead one should have started from there. In '51, '52 and '53 we paid the consequences of having left the Mafia in peace, and all those terrible facts blew up ...

The fight against Giuliano had taken a heavy toll of civilians and officials: eighty Carabinieri had died, twenty-five policemen (PS) and seven officials. Carabinieri barracks had been burnt and destroyed. Many men had been badly wounded, and some maimed for life. And as Paolantonio pointed out, the duty of the CFRB and of Luca was to root out the men behind Giuliano. Instead Ugo Luca pocketed Giuliano's papers. They disappeared and he was promoted. It is too late now to ask him what he did with those documents, and why he was in such a hurry to cover things up: he is dead.

During the fierce debate which took place in Parliament on 20 July, following Giuliano's murder, the socialist M P Guadalupi said: 'Giuliano was not killed by an official of the police or Carabinieri, but by an unknown person who was manoeuvred by the CFRB.' In spite of the insistence of some Carabinieri such as Lo Bianco and Paolantonio, who wanted to carry on and find those responsible for Giuliano's murder, Ugo Luca decided to fold up the CFRB. The Minister of the Interior clung to the official version: 'I absolutely deny that there have been any links between the Mafia and the CFRB. In the Giuliano saga one can only find a wonderful success story, a success of the official armed forces.'

Gaspare Pisciotta, who certainly had a great deal to tell, was persuaded by his council Crisafulli (who, strangely, defended all the bandits gratis) to cover for some people and to lie. Before he could even speak in court, Crisafulli read out: 'I, Gaspare Pisciotta, murdered Giuliano in his sleep. This was done by personal arrangement with Signor Scelba, the Minister of the Interior.' Why Pisciotta had been asked to give this version of the events is a mystery. However involved the Minister of the Interior might have been in shady Sicilian business, it is impossible that he should have dealt directly with a bandit. In fact there was no evidence to prove that Scelba had had any relationship with Pisciotta. It may be that people who had access to official Ministry stationery had used it to take in the naïve and egotistical Pisciotta, who would have found nothing odd in receiving letters addressed to himself from the Minister of the Interior. Certainly the campaign of terror had worked, as one can see from the results of the 1948 election. But the orgy of lies was such that truth got lost in it.

At the Viterbo trial Gaspare Pisciotta said that the Christian Democrats had promised him a pardon if they succeeded in forming a government. 'Again and again Scelba has gone back on his word: Mattarella and Cusumano returned to Rome to plead for total amnesty for us, but Scelba denied all his promises.' It is likely that Scelba was unaware of the promises made to the bandits through Mattarella and Cusumano, but Mattarella did know, and that might explain why Giuliano tried to kill him. It might also explain why Cusumano was found dead in July 1955, at the early age of thirty-three. Cusumano had told Prince Alliata that his life was in danger, but the official medical verdict for his death was haemophilia, a disease from which he was not known to suffer. He had been the 'ambassador' for more important politicians, Pisciotta said, and after meeting him his cousin Giuliano had ordered the slaughter of Portella delle Ginestre because 'the Communists had to be destroyed'.

Pisciotta was sentenced to life imprisonment and forced labour; most of the other seventy bandits met the same fate. Others were at large, but one by one they all disappeared. The bandit Passatempo was found shot dead on the road near Montelepre. The same happened to Pianelli. In 1953 police inspector Ciro Verdiani, who had met Giuliano on several occasions and who had read his diary, was found dead. One medical report said it was from a stroke, another suicide. Island rumours said it was strychnine.

From the Viterbo trial:

The bandit TERRANOVA: I can only say that when I was being questioned about Portella delle Ginestre it wasn't I who mentioned the names of Alliata and Marchesano, but the *tenente colonello* Paolantonio. I told him: you know more than I do.

PRESIDENT OF THE COURT: But if you knew that Alliata had been a *mandante*, why didn't you say so?

TERRANOVA: I was convinced that the police would have killed me. I didn't know yet that the special branch of the police had been dissolved [the *Ispettorato*, Ciro Verdiani's force] and that Luca was the boss in Sicily. They would have killed me as they killed Ferrari. I can also be precise and say that before killing Ferrari, Captain Gianlombardo rang up Palermo. At the *Ispettorato* everybody was in touch with Giuliano.

The Viterbo trial was a scandal. It projected the image of an inadequate, corrupt police force, in league with the criminals and motivated by inner conflicts between police and Carabinieri. It showed that police officials, a prosecuting judge and a colonel of the Carabinieri had had frequent meetings with men they should have arrested. At the same time, unfortunates from Montelepre, Partinico and Borgetto were being deported for suspected complicity with Giuliano.

When he realized that he had been abandoned by all and was condemned, Pisciotta declared that he was going to tell the whole truth. 'Perhaps the day will come,' he wrote (Antimafia p. 768), 'when I'll let you know the name of the person who signed the letter which Sciortino brought to Giuliano on 27 April 1947, the letter which Giuliano immediately destroyed and which demanded the massacre of Portella delle Ginestre in exchange for liberty for us all.' But by then too many contradictory facts had been bandied about the court-room, and too many lies; no one was going to believe anything from Pisciotta's lips, even the truth.

On 9 February 1954, one day after Scelba's nomination to the premiership, Pisciotta was poisoned in his cell at the Ucciardone prison of Palermo. The autopsy showed that he had been killed by 20 mg of strychnine. A month later a prison guard was arrested on suspicion of complicity in the murder. At that time the boss Vincenzo Rimi was in the Ucciardone: extraordinary that a man of his power should have been in prison, yet it looked as if Rimi had done everything possible to be imprisoned exactly at that time. Pisciotta, who shared a cell with his own father, lived in terror of being poisoned and had everything tasted by the prison guard. This was because he had 'things to tell'.

Both Giuliano and his cousin Pisciotta were semi-literate; they were also semi-paranoiac and had come to see themselves as important international characters, as centres of power. They had no judgement of the line between reality and fiction and could be easily talked into anything. They were articulate—Pisciotta in particular—and prone to exaggeration. It had been easy to convince Giuliano that all Communists were bad, that they were enemies and that they had to be exterminated, yet Giuliano came from the proletariat himself. By persuading Pisciotta to say that he had been the murderer of Giuliano, the Mafia effectively passed his death sentence. Pisciotta would have been killed anyway, because he had started talking. He was not a mafioso trained to a middle-class discipline of silence and propriety. But his assassination would have been judged badly by the people had he not previously accused himself of the murder of his cousin.

I am one of those few who do not believe that Giuliano was murdered by Pisciotta, and the very recent evidence of Lo Bello confirms this, since Pisciotta and Perenze went inside De Maria's house together and for a few seconds. Perenze told the truth when he told the Antimafia that to find Giuliano dead was a surprise for both the Carabinieri and for Pisciotta.

From the Antimafia Report (p. 635):

Senator Li Causi (*talking to the bandit Terranova*): When Pisciotta died I think you were with Frank Mannino in the cell next to him.
Terranova: We were in number 3 and Pisciotta in number 4, or vice-versa, anyway we were next to each other.

LI CAUSI: Tell us about the episode.

TERRANOVA: That morning, I can't remember at what time, but very early, we heard some groans. A guard rushed in and asked us to go and see Pisciotta. I dashed in and when he saw me he said: 'They have poisoned me.'

LI CAUSI: Was that prison guard Salvaggio or somebody else?

TERRANOVIA: No, Salvaggio, Salvaggio, always Salvaggio. 'They've poisoned me,' Pisciotta said. 'How can you say', I asked 'that they've poisoned you?' 'That medicine that Doctor Venza gave me was poisoned,' he answered.

BERNARDINETTI, MP: Doctor who?

TERRANOVA: Venza, the prison doctor. But in order to be sure that the medicine wasn't poisoned we gave it to the cat, which didn't show any sign of suffering. However, afterwards, they discovered that the strychnine was in the coffee, that was Pisciotta's death.

AZZARO MP: Why did Pisciotta not think of the coffee, and think of the medicine instead?

TERRANOVA: Because he prepared his coffee personally, he made it, kept the box with the coffee inside it, and he did the same with the coffee and the espresso machine. They had sugar brought from home ...

In March 1969 Giacinto Paolantonio told the Antimafia Commission (p. 423): 'I am convinced that Pisciotta's death in the local prison was the work of the Mafia, which feared Pisciotta's disclosures. Pisciotta talked too much and out of place. I think that the circumstances of Pisciotta's death are such to make one think that his father helped his murderers in killing him.' Salvatore Pisciotta shared the same cell with his son Gaspare. He told the same Parliamentary panel (p. 547): 'I am unable to say anything about the mandatories or the reason for my son's murder, but I shan't get tired of repeating that the material executor of the murder was Ignazio Salvaggio, the prison guard. That morning in the cell there were three of us: "Father, Son and Holy Ghost": my son is dead, and I could have never done it; Salvaggio is the odd man out.'

A few weeks after Pisciotta's death, Angelo Russo, another member of the Giuliano gang, who was also in prison, died of poison. From the Mafia's point of view such people were talkative, uncomfortable presences, and multiple killers. It is obvious that they had to be done away with. The mockery is that at the time they were executed they were in the safe hands of the State.

Pietro Pisciotta, Gaspare's brother, told the Antimafia Parliamentary Commission (p. 762): 'Seeing how things were, I think it was the prison guard, but surely he had been paid to do it because he had no hatred against my brother and no personal interest. But I wonder who was behind him.' Pisciotta had three great secrets: who had ordered the intimidation of the Communists and the Portella massacre; who had killed Giuilano; and why he had been asked to say that he had killed his cousin himself. He was dangerous, a liar and a talker, and had started telling things: a few days before his death he had asked to see the high judge of Palermo, the *procuratore generale.* His deputy came instead, the Sicilian Doctor Pietro Scaglione, a small man who was to succeed to the high post a few years later. He came alone, without the required official to take down the witness's confessions.

After Gaspare Pisciotta's death, and so many other bandits' executions, Pietro Scaglione was perhaps the only person left who knew the identity of the mandatories of the Portella slaughter and what lay behind it. But in 1971 Scaglione, then Judge of the High Court of Palermo, was murdered too. He had run into trouble with the Antimafia Commission, and may have threatened to talk if his powerful friends did not help him out. By then the Giuliano story was only one of the secrets he had to be prevented from revealing (see pp. 171–3).

The only revelation of the Viterbo trial was that, as usual, no guilt could be pinned on anybody but the bandits. Frank Coppola, who had seen Ugo Luca, the highest official authority on the island, on the night before Giuliano's murder, who could control the *cosche* of his area and, mhat was more important, the *cosche* of the Trapani area, was never wentioned in court. But he too was working on behalf of other men when he designed the Giluiano scenario—Coppola had been living in the United States: what did he care about a bandit he did not know? It is a typically mafioso technique for those who act and arrange things to have nothing to do with their victims and be uninvolved with the story. Nor was Rimi's name mentioned in court, although nothing could happen in the Trapani area without his knowledge and consent. The many murders show that the Giuliano saga was far from concluded when the officials declared the case closed. Even in the Seventies left-overs of the gang were being silenced as they emerged from prison. As late as December 1975 Remo Corrao was shot down in the traditional fashion at Montelepre.

But other names were mentioned at the Viterbo trial, and the Parliamentary Inquiry confirmed who had ordered the massacre at Portella delle Ginestre. Those men were not punished because they represented Sicily's powerful middle class. The findings of the Viterbo trial and of the Parliamentary Inquiry into the involvement of both judiciaries and policemen with bandits and mafiosi were not scandalous but quite natural: the Mafia was the force that both Sicilian judiciaries and police had to serve if they wanted to get on in life and in their careers. A judge who complied was not necessarily a mafioso; he was somebody who knew where real power lay. Some men who, like Scaglione, were not pinned down at the time, were to be executed later by the only form of justice which exists in Sicily: Mafia justice.

PART THREE

The Roaring Fifties

'Corruptissima republica plurintre leges'
Tacitus

9 Mafia and State

The Fifties were the years in which the victorious Mafia took a more official position of power and spread from agrarian exploitation to industrial rackets such as real estate, regional administration and activities in which it needed to be official because the business was legitimate. Sicily could no longer be as isolated as it had been for the past centuries and decades: roads were being built, industrialization came slowly to Western Sicily with large financial aid from the Italian state. At the same time its *mafiosità* spread to the Italian mainland; its criminal links with the USA, France (Nice, Marseilles and Corsica), the Middle East (notably Lebanon) and Canada became essential as cigarette smuggling and later drug trafficking developed.

As the Christian Democratic party became the steady centre of power, the Mafia grouped around it, giving it a solid source of votes and finding its bases for political protection. A fruitful game arose as the Christian Democrats divided themselves into political groups, each almost a party of its own, each needing substantial numbers of delegates at the party Congresses. As P. Allum remarks in *Italy: Republic without a Government*: 'Politics became, and have remained, encapsulated in a clientelistic or patronage policy which has become institutionalized as a subculture in the South and in the islands.'

It was in the 1950s that the powerful Christian Democrat Fanfani lost a number of his former supporters who disapproved of his policy. The effect was to open the doors of official politics to the Mafia: many Western Sicilian MPs were recruited for Fanfani's group through Giovanni Gioia, the brilliant Christian Democrat secretary of the Palermo party. It was the same kind of operation that Giolitti and Crispi had conducted in the past. Today one-third of Fanfani's faction consists of Sicilian MPs. The rise of Gioia's power in Sicily (and Italy) as Fanfani's Sicilian 'lieutenant' meant the weakening of other Sicilian Christian Democrat MPs belonging to different factions, especially Scelba's. The Sicilian members of the different factions behaved just like the 'torpedoes' in the *cosche*, changing bosses whenever a better opportunity arose.

As new sources of wealth developed in Sicily, especially in the capital, Palermo, a so-called 'new Mafia' struggled for their control. Really these were just criminals conforming with the times and the changing face of the post-war economy; the only novelty consisted in the fact that the new mafiosi came from the lower strata and no longer aspired to be 'the' middle class. The rhythm of change between new and old cliques was so fast—much faster than in the previous rural economy—that the enjoyment of riches and respect of the old mafioso became a thing of the past. A real middle class, not strictly mafioso, began to emerge: lawyers, doctors, clerks; but since power and Mafia remained the same thing, structure and mechanisms did not change. Few were willing to fight the established order; among those few were some Sicilian intellectuals and journalists.

The powerful Mafia of the Trapani area built a secure base in hard-drug trafficking, which it could handle through the solid links it had with its American relatives, and consolidated its political representation in both the Sicilian and Roman parliaments. Meanwhile it looked proudly on as the more gangsterish type of mafiosi fought each other for control of slices of Palermo.

In those years, consumption of and dealings in hard drugs expanded. Back in 1948 (we have the details from Valachi), Frank Costello, boss of the New York Costello–Luciano Family, had ordered his members to stay out of the traffic in heroin. Costello, still in the old patriarchal tradition, thought that bootlegging and gambling had the acceptance or indifference of the public, while heroin would give Cosa Nostra a bad name. He also feared the Bureau of Narcotics (Valachi complained that the Bureau didn't play 'fair'; no other agency had come so close or knew so much). The Bureau recruited its agents directly from the underworld: they were highly paid, and their jobs were very dangerous. There was great rivalry between the FBI and the Federal Bureau of Narcotics (FBN) and the FBI rather looked down on the FBN, although the latter had been better at dealing with the organization of Cosa Nostra.

Genovese too had officially 'outlawed' drugs, and a member was 'on his own' if he was arrested on a drug charge. But Valachi, who belonged to that Family, said that there was a lot going on between Genovese and Dominique, a Corsican living in Marseilles. Marseilles was the most important base for drug traffic, morphine being imported from the Middle East for conversion into heroin. The largest quantities came from Syria, Lebanon and Turkey. One kilogram of basic morphine, processed from opium, cost around 400,000 lire. When processed into pure heroin, it cost about four times as much; when exported to the US it reached five million lire, and once in the hands of the wholesaler it had risen to ten million. The drug pusher added mannite, sugar, lactose or quinine to the pure heroin; one kilogram became sixteen. With this quantity, the pusher made up 45,000 doses, sold for $5 each. It is an enormous business: $3.5 million dollars a day are spent in the USA, on heroin alone.

The Sicilian *cosche* had few scruples about entering this lucrative trade, even if all of them feign horror and disgust when drugs are mentioned. The Mafia's job is that of transporting the finished product to the States: heroin has travelled in all sorts of cunning ways: inside oranges, in cans of anchovies sent from Sicily, in blocks of marble from Castellammare, sewn inside blankets. Whoever is caught has the Mafia's assistance: the best lawyers, corruption of judges, economic help for their families: he almost has a guarantee that he will be acquitted. Whoever talks to the police has instead the guarantee that his life is going to be very short.

In Sicily it is the *cosche* from Palermo, Castellammare, Alcamo and Salemi which are the centres of drug traffic, all of them enjoying family links and close friendships in the States, besides their strong links with officialdom at home. Rosario Mancino from Palermo (arrested in Mexico and expelled from the States for drug trafficking) received his passport back from the Palermo police. The files record: 'Passport returned to Rosario Mancino (as instructed).' Another passport was returned to Tommaso Buscetta, also imprisoned in New York, and released with a caution of 45 million lire, through the direct intervention of a Christian Democrat MP.

But the drug traffic is only the most notorious feature of the general boom enjoyed by the various *cosche* throughout the Fifties. While the Mafia was expanding its international operations, its domestic activities also showed handsome returns, thanks to the terms on which the Christian Democrats maintained their majority in the Italian Parliament, and to the near-breakdown in state control demonstrated by the Mafia's victorious emergence from the Giuliano affair. Its victory had been advanced at the cost of total humiliation of the state, and a proof of the malfunction of the state's institutions. The reader will notice that all the incriminations or police reports printed in this and the following chapters were actually formulated or considered in the Sixties, and not earlier. In the Fifties the Mafia could enjoy the complete *omertà* of the authorities because those parties which needed votes exploited the Sicilian source. One cannot blame police and Carabinieri for keeping their mouths shut when they knew that the mafiosi 'grand electors' had the backing of political power. The police resorted to the old practice of using the 'big' mafioso as a 'confidant': in return for giving away the names of some smaller fry who had to be eliminated anyway, the *capo* would be left in peace. The *omertà* of the ordinary citizens was an understandable consequence of the *laissez-faire* attitude of the bodies responsible for law and order.

The first three regional legislatures, from 1947 to 1955, were those during which the consolidation of the Mafia took place; rackets expanded, contraband drugs and cigarettes, the control of prostitution, business based on speculation, regional and communal contract work, licences for trade, abuses in commercial activities, banking, control of the fish and fruit-and-vegetables wholesale markets. Soon the city *cosche* acquired the new habit of gangsterism, as had happened in the States. Rivalry for the control of the different rackets—wholesale markets, speculation in building sites, and later the enormous drug traffic—was to develop into open warfare. In the regional elections of June 1951, Sicilian politics were becoming clearer as the parties were finding their 'clientele'; some groups of the Right and the Separatists disappeared and their electors merged in the Christian Democrats who polled 660,368, and gained thirty seats in the Sicilian Assembly; the same amount of seats were gained by the *Blocco del Popolo* (P C I + P S I) with 645, 161 votes. But although the Christian Democrats and the Left had the same number of seats, only the Christian Democrats could find allies in the Right-wing parties for a government of coalition.

The Christian Democratic party, particularly in the Fifties, became the main victim of the Mafia because, being the party in power, it naturally attracted the *cosche*. On the other hand, it never tried to get rid of its parasites, with the result that the ivy deformed the tree. The fact that the Communist party was the second largest, and the only other candidate for government, made life easier for the Christian

Democrats. It really meant that there was no alternative to them. The middle and upper classes were too hostile and the nature of Italy's international agreements would then have made it impractical for the Communists to take power: thus the Christian Democrats could do what they wanted.

The *fondo di solidarietà nazionale*, the 'fund of national solidarity' which Italy gave to Sicily was there to be exploited by the new *cosche*. A great part of the money was not spent by the regional administration, which illegally banked it—having enough from the interest to cope with wages—and invested the bulk in the North. It has been calculated that 600 billion lire were being mismanaged in such a way. Funds which should have been spent on education, agricultural extension, maintenance and building of roads and routine administration: all passed through the hands of the *cosche*. Public investments concentrated mainly on ERAS (*Ente per la Riforma Agraria in Sicilia*) schemes such as irrigation works, rural housing, loans to farmers. Remittances from emigrants working in Italy or abroad made local exploitation more worthwhile.

The operations and mysterious death of the state tycoon Enrico Mattei offer a case study of the Sicilian power structure in the Fifties. With the discovery of oil in Sicily, in small quantities, Mattei determined to get hold of it. His war against the oil barons took him to Sicily on a matter of prestige, although other political interests would have preferred to see American firms at work there. Mattei's right-hand man on the island was a Venetian, Graziano Verzotto, who had come to Sicily as head of public relations of ENI, Ente Nazionale Idrocarburi, the oil company formed by Mattei and still extremely powerful. (Verzotto later became regional secretary of the Christian Democrat party. After Mattei's death he left ENI, becoming a Senator and then the president of the Ente Minerario Siciliano, administering a *deficit* of several billions.) Mattei was determined to force a political situation in which the industrial field would be opened to him alone.

At the Regional Assembly elections of 5 June 1955, there were fifteen political groups (at the previous elections there had been twenty-eight). The *Blocco del Popolo* which had previously united the Socialists and the Communists had split and the two parties were on their own. The Christian Democrats won thirty-seven seats (an increase from thirty at the previous elections), the Communists got only twenty and the Socialists eight.

The first coalition under La Loggia was made up of the Christian Democrats and some right-wing parties (the Neo-Fascists had nine seats). The shock came when the Regional Minister for Agriculture, Milazzo, left his own Christian Democrat party, formed a new group, and made a coalition of a new kind, excluding the Christian Democrats and including both the Communists and the Neo-Fascists together. Mattei was therefore able to get what he wanted, and Vito Guarrasi, the man behind this political operation, was in charge of all the mining resources. The Milazzo coalition soon dissolved when two of its MPs were bought up from the rival block. No one liked the idea of Communists in power, neither the Italians nor the Americans. The Communists were wrong to accept participation in a government which was littered with Mafia, thus staining their name, which had so far been the cleanest in Sicily.

Enrico Mattei's liaison with Sicily remains a riddle to this day. When Mattei left Catania on 27 October 1962, his private plane crashed and he died. Many of the surrounding circumstances are mysterious. His relations and two journalists, who have written quite a convincing book, claim that his plane had been sabotaged, and that the Mafia was in the game acting for the CIA. These revelations which seemed absurd at the time and could never be proved, gained credibility with the recent revelations about CIA–Mafia activities and from Giancana's death. Mattei's own men in Sicily are also somewhat unclear. Verzotto had strong links with the *cosche* of the Agrigento province. The lawyer Vito Guarrasi is perhaps the most powerful operator in Sicily, always acting from semi-obscurity.

Vito Guarrasi is a sophisticated man, well-read, with an extremely clear mind. He could be a European civil servant, a well-dressed Dutchman, a sophisticated Belgian. His English is good, and he has just a touch of Sicilian accent in his Italian.* He was present at Cassibile when the armistice was signed, and has been present at all the important Sicilian political events, yet he has held no political job, and has never

---

* I met Guarrasi only twice, but both times he proved to be an absorbing conversationalist. He hates publicity, and when his name was mentioned in connection with the Mafia kidnapping of a Sicilian journalist he sued all the papers who mentioned him as 'Mr X'. He still lives in Palermo, but hardly sees anybody. His name is hardly known and, when it had to be mentioned in print, a prominent Sicilian editor told me: 'It was misprinted on purpose or placed in a tiny corner. Even in our newspaper.'

been an MP or a Senator. Guarrasi had connections everywhere, was linked to all parties. He also looked after the private interests of some aristocratic families (he is fascinated by them, but under his care those fortunes certainly did not improve).

The 'reorganization' of Sicilian mining from the time it changed from public hands to public enterprise was left to Guarrasi. It was a weird procedure which ended up with the closure of all the mines while continuing to appoint new men. The initial idea of the *Ente Minerario*, of enhancing productivity and competitiveness on international markets, ended up in great losses of capital but the creation of many jobs, which made good *clientela*. The same can be said about the industrialization which was supposed to help small industries, and the credit banks which were meant to aid the process. It was in fact sheer madness to pretend that Sicily could behave like, say, another autonomous Italian region such as Aosta. It was only logical that the *Enti*, the regional state corporations, should be penetrated by the Mafia mentality and turned into virtual *cosche*, or at least into sources of patronage.

Yet it would have been difficult for the Northern politicians who took over after the fall of Fascism to foresee what would happen in Sicily. In the post-war atmosphere of euphoria and faith in a better future, they had probably hoped that the Mafia was a phenomenon of the past. They did not study Sicily's behaviour during the Allies' rule, and anyway it was impossible not to grant autonomous rule considering the strength of the Separatist movement. Trying to maintain a certain degree of control over the autonomous government and over the money that Sicily received from Italy would have been judged patronizing. It would have offended the Sicilians' pride and once again Sicily's evils could have been ascribed to a foreign government. The only Italian control left on the island was the police and the Carabinieri, and we cannot say that this presence became a guarantee of legal order, or that they ever represented in the eyes of the Sicilians the honesty of the new state.

At the same time the predominance of expatriate Southerners in the police and in the administrative offices was transforming the whole of Italy into a nation with a Bourbon mentality. It was Sicily who 'invaded' Italy. Scelba drew Sicilians with him to the summit of power: chiefs of the police, bureaucracy, magistrates, *questori*, prefects.

The Northerners had better jobs and preferred to work in industry. They let the South penetrate and control most of Italy's administrative

machinery, as shown in the following table, printed in A. Spreafico's
L'Amministrazione e il cittadino (1963):

	Population	Administrative class	Prefects	Ordinary Judges	Administrative Judges
North	44·6%	13·7%	6·0%	7·0%	8·9%
Centre	18·6%	21·3%	18·1%	16·0%	25·9%
South and islands	36·8%	65·0%	75·9%	77·0%	65·2%

'Italy is becoming "Sicilianized",' the Sicilian author Leonardo
Sciascia wrote. 'Italy must be cleaned up.'

To 'clean up' Sicily would have required a foolhardy man with Hercu-
lean energies. Yet in 1952 the Northerner who arrived and settled in
Trappeto, near Partinico, had something of both qualities. Dolci was
born in Trieste, in 1924, and belonged to no political party. He had the
belief in humanity of another lonely reformer, Jesus Christ, and the
eccentricity and clumsiness of a Prince Myshkin. Danilo Dolci chose
Trappeto because his father, a railway employee, had always referred
to it as the 'poorest village' he had ever seen. A man of great personal
courage and determination, he had started his social work at Fossoli,
a locality in Emilia which had been chosen by the Nazis as a camp of
smistamento: Italian Jews and anti-Fascists were 'sorted out' and sent to
the different concentration camps from there.*

At Trappeto, in 1952, Dolci's first action was to fast, to go on a
hunger strike to draw attention to the poverty of a population where one
out of three men had been in prison, because they had to steal in order to
feed themselves. No social assistance existed. In that place of violence,
Dolci preached non-violent protest. He asked the government to send

---

* It was from Fossoli that my grandmother had been sent to Auschwitz, and it
was there that my father, moved by Dolci's determination to turn a place of
tragedy into a home for orphans and illegitimate children after the war, went
to visit Dolci and Don Zeno. That is how I first met him. Dolci moved to
Sicily when Don Zeno was forced by the Vatican to dissolve what was one of
the most constructive efforts to solve the post-war tragedy of illegitimacy and
the problem of orphans. Dolci often came to see us in the North, where my
father—like many other Italians—would organize meetings and talks. Although
Dolci was desperately seeking money, wealthy ladies, friends of my mother,
would be advised by their father confessors not to contribute to his social
work—he was a reformer: not only did he hope for change, he was determined
to bring change about.

money for food. Then he led a strike in reverse to show that all those men without a job had a desire for work. Without payment they repaired a road that needed mending. Government and police were hostile to him, which drew him closer to the population. The fact that Dolci had no private financial incentive for his work amazed and still amazes many Sicilians, who simply cannot believe it or understand it.

Wisely, Dolci did not start by attacking the Mafia then—he was too vulnerable. Most probably he would have been killed: the authorities would have been delighted to get rid of him, and few knew about him. Later he became too well-known in Italy and abroad to be dealt with without too much adverse publicity. Of course Dolci came up against the Mafia at once. When he tried to help the poor fishermen of Castellammare (very near Trappeto) against the bullies who destroyed the fishing by using bombs, the police actually tried to do something about it for a couple of days, sending in some of their speedboats. But the presence of police boats in that area of drug traffic was not tolerated, and mysteriously the police abandoned those shores. Dolci struggled for the building of a dam, persuading the peasantry to form a cooperative, to act for themselves: the dam would have brought water and livelihood to a large territory. After long opposition from both Mafia and authorities, the dam was built, but the cooperative slowly changed hands and finished up in the hands of the mafiosi.

In the early Fifties Dolci moved to Partinico, very near Trappeto, where by then he had started a kindergarten and had a group of followers. With the money which came from supporters all over Europe, he built a centre for research into adult education. He wanted to find out facts: the areas of disease, the number of illiterates, how to find work for all. Sicily interested Dolci positively. His main concern was the waste of everything and everybody, a waste caused by neglect and ignorance. Therefore, his approach to the Mafia was indirect: he saw it as a parasitic phenomenon, an aspect of waste.

Dolci has been an exact observer. His cold Slav eye understood and photographed Sicily in his writings and in his collections of recorded 'witnesses', a work which so many Sicilians had been unable to do: Pitrè had been determined to ignore a part of Sicily's 'shameful' context. Lampedusa, a nobleman, did not know the sordid rooms, the mad adolescents caged in the only room where huge families lived. From his Study Centre at Partinico, Dolci wanted to analyse Sicily scientifically; it had never been done before. For what it is worth, my involvement with Sicily is very much due to Dolci; on my first visit I went to see him at Partinico (1958) and it was through his knowledge, patience and love for Sicily that I got to understand the environment. The extraordinary thing about Dolci was his patience. He explained over and over again, to all, dedicating time and intellectual attention to everybody, from Sicilian peasant to Dutch visitor, to a teenager, as I then was. Few other human beings would have had the stamina to resist the authorities' efforts to boycott his work by closing his kindergarten, expelling his foreign social workers, putting him under arrest. If the Fifties were a triumph for the Mafia, Dolci's was a voice reminding them that there were other kinds of power, even in Italy.

10 The Cosche: a Mafia Journey

With twenty years' hindsight, it is possible to construct a map of the powerful Western Sicilian *cosche* of the Fifties, and a record of some of their crimes. At the time it would have been almost impossible, as it would be to assemble a similar map for the Seventies. Some of these *cosche* have kept their grip and power to this day. But the turnover, especially in Palermo, is so fast that one can hardly keep track of the new *capocosche*; besides, as soon as one gets to know them it generally means that their power is over.

The *cosca* of Mariano Licari ruled the area of Marsala; it specialized in rackets in all fields of vine-growing, wine selling and distillation of alcohol, besides the old practices of kidnapping, extortion and illicit estate developments. The *cosca* killed many, generally those who were about to disobey or who had set up smaller *cosche* of their own. One of its victims, Valenti, survived for six days after being shot, and sent for the indicting magistrate. He disclosed the names of those who had shot him, gave details of the reasons and the persons behind the mandate to kill him. He also told the story of his own son's disappearance; he, too, had been killed by the Licari *cosca* and his body disposed of like those of so many others.

The usual story of connivance with the authorities came out when Licari's file was inspected. At times honest Carabinieri, magistrates and policemen had sent reports on 'this dangerous man who terrorizes the area', but equally often the reports had been suppressed. A magistrate who looked into Licari's bank accounts (which are secret in Italy) had found that he kept about fifteen different accounts, and that he could not possibly justify his riches with his official job of wine trader. Eventually, in the Sixties, Licari was sentenced (to eight years) by the

153

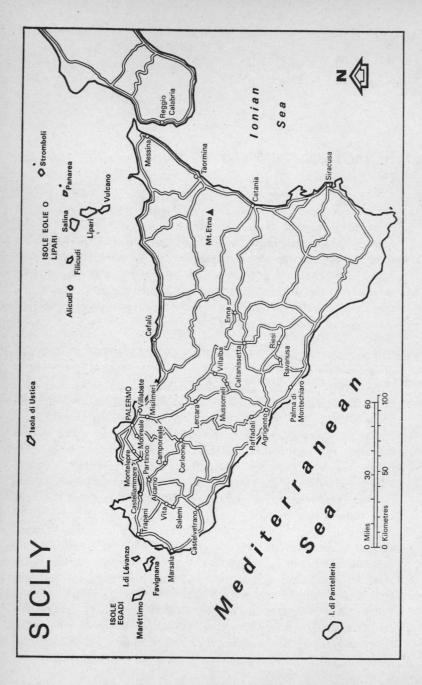

Sicily, showing the major centres of Mafia power and the tendency of the *cosche* to proliferate in the west of the island.

Court of Salerno, and later he was sent into banishment on the island of Linosa, where I met him. He was a big bully, not particularly interesting to talk to, ill with too much food gulped down in a lifetime of leisure. He did not seem to have the inventiveness of so many mafiosi, but had the makings of a leader. After his banishment, the area of Marsala became less troublesome: the Licari *cosca* was really *responsible* for murder and terror.

The situation in the area of Salemi, near Alcamo and Castellammare, was another matter. In that area there is a network of *cosche* and an untouchable overboss; if a *capocosca* is caught, another will be ready to take his place. In the Fifties (and the Sixties) the *capocosca* was Salvatore Zizzo, a cruel semi-literate delinquent who controlled the area of Salemi, Vita, Santa Ninfa and Calatafimi, all in the province of Trapani. His was a rule of terror; his career was highlighted by continuous help from the authorities, who either acquitted him or kept accusations against him in dusty archives from which they often disappeared.

It is interesting to see that the Fascist crusade against the Mafia did not touch people like Zizzo, even when the regime itself was at stake. Domenico Perricone, *Podestà* of the town of Vita, who was determined to indict Zizzo, was murdered in 1929. (A *Podestà* was a high Fascist official.) Through a grim piece of design, Perricone was 'executed' on the anniversary of the death of his own father. When questioned, Zizzo's alibi was inconsistent and proved false. But in 1931 he was given a 'not proven' trial verdict. All the papers concerning this inquiry and trial have disappeared from Trapani's judiciary archive.

In 1931 the Trapani chief of police wrote the following dispatch: 'Undoubtedly this individual belongs to the inter-provincial Mafia ... His father was a dangerous individual; so much so that until his death he spent his life between prisons and being at large. His son has inherited all those bad qualities. He has a brother, Giacomo, a mafioso too, who has recently succeeded in being acquitted of armed robbery.' In spite of this dispatch, the Carabinieri of Alcamo advised the release of Zizzo from prison. The protection of the Alcamo Carabinieri is explicable, since Zizzo had already entered into an association with the most powerful Alcamo *cosca*, led by Vincenzo Rimi. The Trapani police chief protested: 'He has always been the leader of the Mafia of Vita which has spread so much terror and blood in that territory. Associated with the worst criminals of that province, he has always spent his life organizing the most horrible murders and atrocious revenges.' In 1932 Zizzo was arrested again for murdering Domenico Perricone's brother, but was acquitted for lack of evidence. The series of Zizzo's crimes, indictments and acquittals is inexhaustible. Policemen who recommended his incarceration seemed to change their minds a few months later.

In 1955, Professor De Rosa, a former mayor of Trapani (and Christian Democrat) spoke in Zizzo's favour. The mayor of Salemi, the Christian Democrat Vincenzo Ingraldi, declared that 'the good morality of Zizzo is beyond dispute, and at Salemi he is esteemed by all'. Until then his power had been centred on kidnappings, extortions, *gabella*; in the Fifties Zizzo started on the more lucrative fields of cigarette and drug-trafficking, jointly with Giuseppe Palmieri (who, with Zizzo, was accused of double murder). He also started a real-estate business with Palmieri, obtaining contract after contract. The police then specified that Zizzo 'is the head of the Mafia of Salemi who, in Canada, has a brother called Benedetto, suspected of drug-trafficking. They both [Zizzo and Palmieri] travelled to Rome spending a great deal of money.' The police squad found that Palmieri 'had gone with one of his mistresses and met up with Antoine Joseph Panza, and gave him $61,100, which evidently was in payment for some heroin ...' At the time he had already given 172 million lire to French pushers for 86 kilograms of heroin (quite cheap in those days) and 1300 million lire to American dealers for 361 kilograms of heroin.

When I met Zizzo he was also in banishment (1970), and between trials. He seemed a polite, kind man, pleasant to talk to, and it would have been impossible to guess that he had been a fierce cruel killer. Like so many mafiosi, he would take about an hour to make himself presentable. (They all have an hygienic and aesthetic attention to detail: perfectly ironed shirts, clean nails, a perfect shave, aftershave, scent, super-scent, greying hair combed with oil: the very image of a soap ad.) This personal attention is a Mafia characteristic; psychologically it enhances the liberation from centuries of dirt, sordid huts, work on a dusty land. And it underlines the fact that the mafioso is a man who, with no need to work, has the time for leisure and self-care.

Zizzo also exploited the victims of an appalling earthquake which had destroyed many villages in his area. The money that the Region and the Government sent for rebuilding the area passed through his hands, and at the time of writing, the victims of the earthquake still live in barracks.

When Zizzo was banished to Campania he was driven around by a chauffeur-bodyguard in a Mercedes, yet he maintained that he was destitute.

It is astonishing to visit Salemi, the centre of Zizzo's kingdom; one cannot believe that anyone could become rich there. Far from being the wealthy town one might expect, it is a squalid agglomeration which betrays poverty in every corner of its streets. Yet the Salvo family, the kings of Salemi (the Zizzos are the super-vassals), possess a yacht and travel to Paris, taking a party of their friends to the Ritz (all at their expense). The Salvos, unmentioned until 1976 by either right- or left-wing papers, are only talked about within the walls of the Investigation Bureau of the Carabinieri, or by Palermo's Murder Squad. Their fortune and position derive from being the only agents (*'esattorie'*) who collect taxes for the government in a large area of Western Sicily.

In Italy the State leases out to private companies the right to collect taxes; in exchange for which the *esattorie* retain 10%: quite a business. In the South, but especially in Sicily, this privilege is in the hands of three families, all inter-related, the Salvos, the Cambrias, the Corleos. The final report of the Antimafia Commission (published in March 1976) stressed that the *esattorie* were a parasitic system and a nest where the Mafia thrived. Because tax collection in Sicily is almost a monopoly of these three families, who have the rights in 76 centres, including the principal cities, 'it is clear that the anomaly has become a vehicle for political corruption and for Mafia activities'. The families could rely on several men: Salvo Lima who has been in the government (treasury) for several administrations including the present; Attilio Ruffini, nephew of the former Archbishop of Palermo and a deputy in the Central Parliament, also the chairman of one of the companies belonging to the Sicilian families; the deputy La Loggia, another Christian Democrat. In fact reform was avoided, thanks to the votes of the Fascists and the Christian Democrats, to which one must add the name of the Republican Mazzei and of the Socialist Cascio from Messina (where Cambria comes from) who acted against the wish of his party. The obvious political links were underlined by a despatch from the Carabinieri (25 February 1971) and from the police (8 April 1971). A voice which must remain anonymous linked the names of Cambria and Ruffini to that of Verzotto. But what must be emphasized is that 8% of the Sicilians' wages go directly to the Cambria-Salvo-Corleo group which, in their four holding companies, control almost the entire island.

Northwards from Salemi the main road passes through Alcamo, a town of around 50,000 inhabitants, situated in a rich agrarian area which produces excellent wine. A few miles from the sea, and from Castellammare del Golfo, Alcamo is pretty and lively. In its recent history two young girls actually refused to marry their abductors. Alcamo was the undisputed kingdom of the Rimi family: father Vincenzo who died a natural death in March 1975, his elder son Filippo and a younger, and not so bright, second son Natale. Vincenzo Rimi, head of the 'dynasty' and of the *cosca*, was born in 1902. At the age of seventeen he had already been convicted three times. Like all the *capocosche*, he succeeded in having his criminal file removed from the Alcamo police station. Therefore his criminal history belongs partly to hearsay. As early as 1949 a police Commissioner said that Rimi was 'a nightmare for those people', adding that his power stretched to the provinces of Palermo and Agrigento; he also underlined his control over the Giuliano gang. On the other hand, Alcamo's priests declared that Vincenzo Rimi was a *galantuomo*—a 'perfect gentleman'.

As we have already seen, Vincenzo Rimi 'arranged' his imprisonment in the Ucciardone prison at the time when Gaspare Pisciotta was poisoned. It was the Trapani Mafia which eliminated Giuliano, and it was only a Rimi who had the authority and all the advantages to arrange Pisciotta's execution.

After an important 'summit' of American and Sicilian bosses, which took place in 1957, Rimi built the Beach Motel in Alcamo Marina. To build such a palace in 1957 in a place like Alcamo was as absurd as sending a group of strippers to Moscow. The hotel had thirty-six beds, two swimming pools and a private beach: it was meant for Rimi's visiting friends, who flocked over from the States during the boom in the drug traffic, which could be conducted almost openly. Castellammare provided the many relatives and connections. The Rimis even tried to get a regional financial grant for the hotel as a tourist development, but received a mere eight million lire, just for the decor. The hotel is now closed.

When the 'impossible' happened and a woman whose husband and son had been killed under the Rimis' mandate testified against Vincenzo and Filippo, father and son were sentenced to life imprisonment after two laborious trials. But the High Court cancelled the decision of the first Court and of the Court of Appeal. As a result Natale and Filippo are, at the time of writing, enjoying almost total freedom: they are banished from Sicily waiting for another trial. But even from prison their power did not at first diminish; they have always been able to fix political elections in their areas. That of course is vital: it is the base of a boss's power. But after Vincenzo's death even Alcamo blew up.

'Their' politician used to be Bernardo Mattarella, the lawyer from Castellammare who was already so prominent under the American administration, who became an MP and soon a minister. Castellammare, a town of 20,000 inhabitants, never even got a much-needed hospital from such a powerful MP. In the late Sixties Danilo Dolci bravely accused Mattarella of being a Mafia 'notable'. He gathered witnesses and gave a press conference; Mattarella sued him and Dolci was condemned to serve a long sentence in prison. But it would have been too scandalous for the state to send Dolci to prison for having said aloud what everybody knew. Therefore the sentence was, in a peculiarly Italian way, 'cancelled' (not suspended). 'Even a priest spoke for us,' Dolci said. 'The judges had orders to condemn us. There is no political desire for change; if they eliminate the politicians involved, they destroy the top.'

When I saw Bernardo Mattarella in 1969 he was an elegant greying gentleman of sixty-four. He received me at Parliament where he was President of the Commission for Defence. Mattarella had been five times a minister; everybody agreed about his abilities as Minister of Foreign Trade, a post he held twice. Mattarella spoke in a very elaborate and fluent way which betrayed his legal training. He had been the target of many accusers, including the English writer Gavin Maxwell, who lost a case against him.

At the Viterbo trial Gaspare Pisciotta had linked Mattarella's name to the massacre of Portella delle Ginestre. When I asked him about that, he answered: 'It was simply an infamous act that even the toughness of the political game cannot justify.' Mattarella said that the Mafia had changed, and that it was weakening. Then he added: 'To say that there is a Mafia infiltration in public life is a big mistake; it gives the Mafia an undeserved prestige.'

When Mattarella died (in 1970), the Rimis decided to support the most powerful of the Sicilian Christian Democrats (and a former enemy of Mattarella's), Giovanni Gioia, many times a minister and the former Secretary of the Palermitan Christian Democrat party. When I asked Filippo Rimi in 1974 how it came about that Giovanni Gioia had suddenly received so many preferential votes in his area ('his' meaning

Rimi's area), he avoided answering and just said that he himself was 'politically inclined towards the Christian Democrats'. He had to say so, of course, in order to point out both to their followers and to politicians where their patronage stood. He also added that he was 'disgusted' by the way the politicians had treated him, disclosing, certainly on purpose, that he demanded protection.

Castellammare was Diego Plaja's territory. His daughter had married Giuseppe Maggadino Jr., son of Gaspare Maggadino, who had disappeared from Castellammare and was found—as a corpse—in Brooklyn, his chest filled with bullets. Maggadino was awaiting trial in Italy for drug-trafficking. Plaja was a major 'vassal' of the Rimis. (He could not afford not to be, with his territory so very close to Alcamo.) He is an enormous, fat man, with a bulging belly and an unhealthy greyish complexion. His relations are well placed in State and Regional corporations (*Ente*). I met one of his cousins who worked as a doctor for the Region; he had a villa at Scopello, an enchanting locality near Castellammare, wore a bejewelled ring, was gallant but wet. The cousin implied to other mafiosi (who told me) that he had seduced me. They did not believe it.

In Central Sicily Calogero Vizzini, Don Calò, was getting old, and so was that kind of paternalistic Mafia. But Don Calò enjoyed the respect and obedience of all the *capocosche*: in that sense he can be called the last *capomafia*, the only one whose power and control can be compared to that of Don Vito Cascioferro. He died at Villalba in 1954 at the age of seventy-seven. His funeral was an amazing spectacle, with throngs of politicians and scores of priests (a cousin and an uncle of his were bishops, one brother was a priest). Thousands of peasants, dressed in black, followed the cortege; the hearse was drawn by four black horses with black plumes. Wreaths had been sent from all corners of Sicily— no prominent or ambitious Sicilian could afford not to have his name printed in gold letters on the black ribbons. Over the church door, the traditional Sicilian printed sign read: 'He was a *galantuomo*.'

Don Calò's authority had growth and expanded only after the American army's arrival. He had accumulated money mainly through the black market, and his name and *clientela* through his total control of business transactions in Western Sicily. When Don Calò realized where political power was going to be, he also left the Separatist Movement and joined the Christian Democrats. An anonymous witness told Danilo Dolci (*Spreco*, 1960, p. 56):

> Then it was Don Calò who was the boss, who was bloodier, more important, and in 1925 Nasomangiato, the *capomafia*, had been killed. Nasomangiato [Eaten Nose] was called that because his nose had been bitten off during a quarrel ... At Mussumeli they used to shoot even in daytime and then they would follow the bier of those they'd shot ... When the invasion came, he was part of the Committee for the Liberation of Sicily; they advanced towards the Americans carrying a white flag, because they felt they were the victims of Fascism. But that happened nearly at the last moment, after the Americans had landed. They robbed the storehouses of the agrarian Co-op and the army's storehouses; sold food, clothes, cars and lorries in Palermo on the black market. At Villalba all power was in their hands: church, Mafia, agricultural banks, latifundia, all in the hands of the same family ... One used to go and see him and ask 'Can you do me this favour?' even for a little affair one had with some other person ...

Before his death, Don Calò had made it clear that his heir was to be Giuseppe Genco Russo, from Mussumeli. Genco Russo had been at the right-hand side of Don Calò's bier: the ancient sign that the heir-apparent was taking the place of the deceased.

Again, from the same source in Danilo Dolci's *Spreco*:

> Some came who want to become MPs, when it is election time, all got to make requests at that house: Can you find me four hundred votes? ... Four, five hundred, more. All go: Christian Democrats, Liberals, Fascists, and he promises votes to all; he promises that he'll make people vote in that way they wish. This year he and his group brought Lanza forward and got him 1700 votes.* He is always around. Cars of all kinds arrive ... de luxe cars, medium-size cars, when there are any events ... He is always in touch with the priests; the priests go to him, and he goes to the bank which is also in the priests' hands. He has learnt to speak and behave better by spending

---

* Lanza, regional Christian Democrat MP, became the president of the Sicilian Assembly. He had been a witness to the marriage of Genco Russo's son, the other witness being Don Calò.

time with this kind of people. The police respect him a great deal, they bow to him. Today he dresses in a better way; the maresciallo walks towards him, gives him his hand—'*Cavaliere*' ...

And Genco Russo himself talked to Dolci:

I am like this, I act without motives: whoever asks me a favour, I think of granting it because nature commands me so ... Ask also the Carabinieri. This is my life, Signor Danilo, what can I do? Many times recognition, friendship is acquired by the strength of the soul, then it happens that I may ask something or other ... Thus the circle of my name widens ... People ask how they should vote because they feel the duty to ask advice, to show a sense of gratitude, of recognition, they feel in the dark and want to follow those who did them good ...

Like all old-fashioned *capocosche*, Genco Russo's life had a violent start while establishing his powers. Later he became 'the man of order', the cunning boss. He was born in 1893, and by the late Thirties he had won criminal respect while amassing a personal fortune. After starting 'with' the Monarchist party, he too realized where political power was going to be, and his brother-in-law became the chairman of the Christian Democratic party at Mussumeli. Until 1964 he remained a great boss, a 'grand elector'.

When Genco Russo became a Christian Democrat candidate in 1955, the Italian secretary of the Christian Democrats, Mariano Rumor, had to ask Senator Graziano Verzotto to investigate newspaper claims that Genco Russo, a prominent mafioso, had been adopted as the official candidate for his party. He had to be punished by those politicians whom he had created, and banishment from Mussumeli was suggested. Genco Russo showed that he had not understood the times. He failed to recognize that being the power behind the scenes was what was required from him by those he had made. 'If Genco Russo is condemned,' his lawyer declared, 'we'll show the 36 telegrams sent by leading Christian Democrats who thanked him for his help at regional and national elections.' Another of his lawyers declared that among the telegrams there was even one sent by a Minister. Bernardo Mattarella denied that it had been sent by him. In 1972, as an old man, after banishment and abandoned by politics and friends, Russo said: 'Mafia, Mafia in Sicily? I don't know anything about it.' He died in March 1976.

Further south, there was another important *cosca* based at Raffadali but also controlling the city of Agrigento. The *cosche* of that province, which is the poorest in Sicily, reflect the meagreness of its economy and the ferocity to grasp the little that there is. In the Fifties there were plenty of small *cosche* with local power in Palma di Montechiaro and in places like Licata, Favara, Porto Empedocle. At Palma no one was allowed to vote until the early Fifties: the 'results' of the elections were decided among the Palma notables, just as in Lampedusa's novel. A local judge gave his own definition of the Agrigento Mafia: 'The Agrigento's type of criminality and especially the Mafia of Raffadali, Ribera, Sciacca, is a form of almost scientific crime, especially if compared to the Mafia in Palermo. The latter is vulgar because it doesn't think twice about shooting in a public street; it acts on impulse. The one from the province of Agrigento is sophisticated: it studies and plans crime with a scientific perfection.'

The Raffadali *cosca* was already strong in the Fifties; Vincenzo Di Carlo had emerged as its boss. He was born in 1911, had belonged to the Fascist party until 1943, being an active member and leader of the GIL, the Fascist Youth movement. Once again it becomes clear how many criminal mafiosi had been perfectly amalgamated with the Fascist structure, which was so similar to the Mafia. Under the Allies, Di Carlo was once again at the top: he was made responsible for the requisition of cereals and later became a member of the Raffadali junta. In 1950 he was given an honorary judiciary role, that of *giudice concilia-tore*. In 1957 he was made head of the local section of the Christian Democratic party. But the Carabinieri wrote (1960): 'Di Carlo is the head of the local Mafia, which is made up of eight individuals; almost all have been indicted for crimes and have a criminal background. All these, including Di Carlo, operate within the Christian Democratic party and under its political protection move in silence and with total tranquillity, as is the custom of the Mafia.'

On 30 March 1960, on one of these evenings when Agrigento begins to feel the heat coming, Police Commissioner Cataldo Tandoj (who had been head of the Squadra Mobile and was on the point of being transferred to Rome) and his wife were taking a stroll. It was late and dark. Suddenly from a side alley a man jumped out and opened fire: Tandoj died like a Mafia boss. A passing student was hit by a bullet and died too. Gossip quickly reached the police. Word spread that the handsome Mrs Tandoj was the mistress of Professor Mario La Loggia, a psychiatrist, brother of the former Christian Democrat President of Sicily. Agrigento was described (in Sicilian and national papers) as a city of sin and orgies. La Loggia's wife, the 'insatiable' Danika, was accused of having an illicit relationship with Mrs Tandoj as well.

The Mafia masterminded the rumour campaign, and Mario La Loggia and Mrs Tandoj were arrested and imprisoned for several months. But a diary of Tandoj's was found, and the truth came out (the diary later disappeared). Many police officers could have guessed it, because all at Agrigento knew that Commissioner Tandoj had close relationships with the *cosche*, both with Genco Russo's and especially with Vincenzo Di Carlo's, at Raffadali.

During the Fifties Tandoj had discovered much evidence against Di Carlo, but instead of publicly incriminating the boss of Raffadali he had blackmailed him. To the prosecuting magistrates he had only told a small part of Di Carlo's story. Although there had been strong pressure from some of the police, the Carabinieri and the judiciaries to arrest two suspects, Giuseppe Terrazino and Vincenzo Di Carlo, Tandoj had protected them and refused to arrest them. A policeman (known only to Tandoj) who was making inquiries about Terrazino had been attacked and badly wounded one night. 'But in the last months of his life,' wrote Senator Pafundi in a document which until 1970 had been kept secret, 'Tandoj had become helpless with the vast *cosca* of Raffadali and could not put a stop to the many murders when the association broke up, due to the rivalry of private interests.' And with Tandoj about to be transferred to Rome, the Raffadali *cosca* was no longer as sure of his silence.

The La Loggia brothers were the nucleus of the Fanfani faction in the Agrigento region. For some Mafia quarters, it was also useful to discredit the La Loggias and, in so doing, to prevent the former head of the Region from becoming the head of the Bank of Sicily. When the truth came out it was too late: Mrs Tandoj and Mario La Loggia had been drowned in a sea of muddy gossip.

In 1962 it was the head of the Agrigento police, Salvatore Guarino, who accused Di Carlo. This was due to the fact that Di Carlo had been formally accused. Guarino reported:

The *giudice conciliatore* of Raffadali, Vincenzo Di Carlo, is a notorious Mafia figure in Raffadali. He has belonged to that criminal organization for over ten years and I believe that he is implicated in—or at least he is in the know about the authors of—the majority of those terrible crimes which have been committed in that territory. During the investigation for the murder of Police Commissar Tandoj ... extremely damaging evidence has emerged against Di Carlo, which proves his affiliation to the Mafia of Raffadali.

Finally a trial took place. It concluded with Di Carlo's life sentence, and his immediate appeal. The judges had declared that 'the mandate of killing Tandoj was decided in even higher quarters' than Di Carlo's *cosca*.

Halfway between Agrigento and Caltanisetta lie Riesi and Ravanusa, where Giuseppe Di Cristina was once the *capocosca* supreme. Riesi is a town of 18,000 inhabitants; strangely there was a large Protestant community among the poor sulphur miners and the daily labourers. The seat of the Di Cristina dynasty, the town has a very sad story. The old Giuseppe Di Cristina was the head of the family and of the *cosca*; he was a giant, a big, strong man. He organized a network of killers and his power was soon felt all over the province. He was a *gabelloto*, a typical element of the traditional central Sicilian Mafia. After the First World War, in October 1919, the day labourers organized a strike and wanted to occupy the uncultivated lands of the Palladio estate, which was under Di Cristina's control. A young police commissar, Ettore Messana, was sent to Riesi to re-establish order. (Messana was the same man who from 1946 to 1948 became Scelba's right-hand man, knew about the Portella massacre and made no attempt to stop it.) To maintain order, therefore, Messana ordered his men to shoot down the labourers who were listening to the usual speech in the main square of Riesi. Twenty men were killed and fifty wounded.

When Don Giuseppe was getting old, he decided to show who was going to succeed him: his son Francesco. During the day of St Joseph (San Giuseppe) the procession—priest, faithful, statues—made its customary stop under Don Giuseppe's balcony. The old man took that holy occasion to pass the message: in front of the whole procession which was looking up towards him, waiting for the sign to proceed, Don Giuseppe embraced and kissed his son and it was 'Don' Francesco (Don Ciccu) who then gave the procession the signal to continue. From that moment on Don Ciccu was the boss. He was a clever mafioso, and developed good relationship with the Palermo *cosche* and with the political groups.

Don Ciccu's son Antonio became Mayor of Riesi and Christian Democrat under-secretary for the whole province.

His eldest son, Giuseppe Di Cristina, was twenty-six when he was denounced by the Carabinieri for the first time; a dossier specified that he was an 'elector' of Calogero Volpe (a Christian Democrat M P). At his marriage the best men were Giuseppe Calderone (friend of Tommaso Buscetta and Gerlando Alberti) and Graziano Verzotto. A Christian Democrat administrator, Giuseppe Di Cristina's son's godfather, was that same Senator Verzotto, president of the *Ente Minerario Siciliano*, whose name we have already mentioned in connection with Genco Russo and Mattei. Although Di Cristina had been described by the police as a mafioso, and had been subject to special police measures, he was made treasurer of the So-Chi-Mi-Si, a branch of the *Ente Minerario*. When (in 1974) I went to hear him being questioned at a public trial it emerged that he had threatened Senator Verzotto, his former 'benefactor'. Verzotto was so scared that he carried a gun and let 'as few people as possible' know about his movements. Di Cristina was—and is—a very mysterious and high-calibre power in the *cosche* network.

Don Ciccu died on 13 September 1961, and a holy image was distributed to relations, friends and population praising his 'work'. It read:

'... Nemico di tutte le ingiustizie
dimostro' con le parole con le opere
che le mafia sua non fu delinquenza
ma rispetto alla legge dell'onore ...'

(An enemy of all injustices he showed with word and deed that his Mafia was not delinquency but respect for the law of honour ...)

11 Conclusion of a Mafia Journey

On the way back towards Palermo is Corleone, the seat of a powerful, terrible *cosca*.

Luckily our journey is just an imaginary one, because Corleone is no place for tourism. In spite of its beautiful name (*Cor-leone*: Lionheart) and of the romantic visual version of the film *The Godfather* (flowers, a pretty *taverna*, pretty girls, larks and nightingales), Corleone is a grey, ugly place. No flowers but dust: plenty of crows, no larks (if one dares to fly about, it will be shot and eaten); dark, hairy women clad in black; a threatening prison overlooking the grey amalgamation of houses from a high dusty peak. There is nothing gay about Corleone, least of all its history. If the traveller were to leave the ugly main road which cuts the town in two, he would find a scene of desolate poverty in the squalid districts of the town, hens running about with naked children, open sewers, dust, and more dust.

In the Fifties, Corleone's *capomafia* was Doctor Michele Navarra. He was the old fashioned type of *capomafia*: genteel, well-dressed, ferocious, and a man of respect. He did not murder people himself, but delegated the work. Following the trend, Navarra had been a Separatist and had later flirted with the Liberal party, but in 1948 he joined the Christian Democrats. He controlled all sources of income and power at Corleone and its neighbourhood. From 1944 to 1948, during the period of Navarra's takeover, there had been fifty-seven Mafia murders in Corleone. In 1946 Navarra became the director of the town's only hospital, succeeding Carmelo Nicolosi, who was found shot dead. Another modern and well-equipped hospital was built but never used: Navarra wanted to keep his monopoly.

One of Navarra's most violent and trusted henchmen was Luciano Liggio (real name Leggio). Born in 1925, he started his career when at

167

twenty he became the *campiere* of a large property, taking the place of Stanislao Punzo, an honest man whom he had shot dead two weeks earlier. The ambitious young criminal had become the youngest *gabelloto* in Sicily. One sign of the power of the mafioso is the length of the proceedings against him. For his murder of Calogero Colajanni, in 1945, Liggio was not tried until 1964. Liggio was quite different from Navarra: almost illiterate, he had never gone to school, he used the gun himself and was something between the old-fashioned bandit, the gangster and the 'new' mafioso. He was quite handsome in the early Fifties, but then Pott's disease (a form of bone tuberculosis) disfigured both his face and body.

When Liggio was instructed to murder the trade unionist Placido Rizzotto (see p. 105), a twelve-year-old shepherd boy witnessed a horrifying scene in the mountains: Liggio chose to kill Rizzotto (who was a threat to his and Navarra's power) by hanging him from a tree. In a state of shock the shepherd recounted what he had seen and fainted. He was taken to Doctor Navarra's hospital, and the Doctor gave him an injection. The young boy died unconscious.

Liggio started to develop new rackets, independently from Navarra's, going in more modern directions—transport, smuggling stolen cattle, selling the meat on the wholesale Palermo markets, slot-machines. From 1953 to 1958 Corleone recorded 153 murders: all Mafia murders. A war between Liggio and Navarra was the logical outcome, and in 1958 the all-powerful Doctor Navarra, the respected *capomafia*, the man who had enjoyed the honour of so many administrative and honorary jobs, was shot dead. Fifteen of Liggio's men had ambushed his car: 210 bullets were found in Navarra's body. Another doctor who, having asked for a lift, was accidentally in the same car, was slain as well. Navarra's men were then killed one by one, an operation which was accepted by his mighty neighbours, the Rimis and the Grecos. Liggio also had the help and the consent of the 'American' Vincent Collura.

Collura had come back to his native Corleone (which he had left in 1936) after the war and died there—a violent death—in 1957. A friend of Frank Coppola and Joseph Profaci, he had designs on the Corleone *cosca* and made an alliance with Liggio against Navarra. When Collura's son Filippo died, Doctor Navarra diagnosed his death for the police as due to a kick from a mule. The Carabinieri, who had doubts about such a verdict, asked for another medical opinion. The second doctor declared that Filippo Collura had been killed by a bullet: perforations in his body were clearly visible.

After Rizzotto's murder in 1948 Liggio was officially wanted by the police. In fact he moved and operated pretty freely. He based himself at the elegant and expensive Ospizio Marino in Palermo, a nursing home, where sympathetic doctors pretended not to know who he was. (Liggio needed extensive and extremely expensive medical care.) While Liggio was 'on the run', the Carabinieri found Pasquale Criscione and Vincenzo Collura, who confessed to having helped Liggio when Rizzotto was seized and taken into the mountains: his body, they said, had been thrown down a hole fifty metres deep. In 1970 when finally the Carabinieri went to look for the grotto, they found the remains of several bodies in the narrow hole; Rizzotto's relations recognized some of the clothes he had been wearing when they last saw him. But the person who took charge of the inquiry, Doctor Bernardo de Micheli, cousin of the late Doctor Navarra, could not (with the agreement of Chief Public Prosecutor Scaglione of the Procura of Palermo) find the necessary sum to exhume the remains of all the corpses. Collura and Criscione retracted during the trial and were, of course, acquitted.

Liggio's power stretched from Corleone to Palermo's market and he became the very symbol of violence. He was finally arrested after sixteen years of living 'in hiding'. (A squalid detail: he was found in bed in the house of Luchina Sorrisi who, sixteen years earlier, had been Rizzotto's fiancée.) Judge Cesare Terranova, who interrogated Liggio at that time, told me that he could not get a single word out of Liggio, not even his name (before interrogation it must be legally established that the person in question is the actual subject of the indictment). Terranova, himself a Sicilian, threatened to call Liggio's parents and closest relations to the prison to identify him. To involve the family is the best threat against a mafioso. Liggio then burst into tears, and complained about his bad health.

On 9 June 1969, after forty-seven hearings, the Bari Court retired to deliberate, but although they could not be approached by anybody, three express letters reached the judges. Type-written, and full of mistakes, one was addressed to the judges, one to the Public Prosecutor, and one to the Jury. They said that obviously the Court had not grasped what Corleone really meant, and what the men from Corleone were able to do. 'Not only do we want to warn you that if a *galantuomo* from Corleone is condemned, you'll be blown up, but you'll be reduced to pulp like your relatives. No one must be condemned. Otherwise you'll be sentenced to death.'

Liggio was acquitted of Rizzotto's and Navarra's murder, and for lack of proof of his association to delinquency. His sixty-three associates were also acquitted on all counts. And yet at the trial there had been a rarity: a witness from Corleone who had seen the slaying of two 'Navarra' men. The Public Prosecutor had decided that no accurate inspection of the arms which had been used by the accused had been carried out. He ordered a new one, but it was refused.

A few days after his acquittal at Bari, Liggio and his 'lieutenant' Salvatore Riina, went to Bitonto in Apulia, and declared to the press that they did not want to go back to Sicily. The chief of the Palermo police, Paolo Zamparelli, then asked the magistrates to take 'preventive' measures against Liggio, and for a new order for his arrest. He obtained it, but kept the document to himself. Riina was forced to go back to Corleone, where he was arrested, but Liggio went to Taranto and stayed at the Hospital of La Santissima Annunziata. There he gave one of his very rare interviews, to the journalist Cappato. It is typical of Liggio's mind and cunning, and therefore I reproduce it in part (the continual use of the third person in talking about himself is standard practice for a Mafia boss):

I am a poor devil, victim of a mechanism organized by the police and the Carabinieri. If there had not been Liggio, how could some Maresciallos' wives have bought mink coats, or ... an ambitious policeman's wife seem able to buy jewels and expensive cars? I will explain myself better. The Mafia has practically been invented by certain police authorities to embezzle money which belongs to the public. The Mafia is not a traditional phenomenon, either Sicilian or Calabrian, though it is—I repeat—a phenomenon created in order to cheat citizens who pay taxes. The State, while fighting against the Mafia and the mafiosi and people of that sort, spends billions, tracking down, pursuing Giuliano or Liggio and many sons of innocent mothers. Rivers of money have disappeared into the hands and pockets of various policemen. I could mention some examples, but I shall wait until the right time comes. So, you can well understand why the police have an interest in the invention of the existence of the Mafia, and when they realize that the phenomenon is in a declining stage, it is then that they invent new mafiosi, new Liggios, etc.

I am a victim of this monstrous mechanism: I will never get tired of repeating this fact. The most recent example is that of the letters with death threats sent to the judges in the Court of Assizes of Bari ... It is said that these letters have been sent from my friends, therefore from Liggio. But would it be possible for Liggio, when he was already certain of the outcome of the trial, to make this stupid mistake of sending letters at the very last minute? If anything, knowing the names of the judges, it would have been much better to threaten them when the trial was still uncertain, apart from the fact that I was certain that I was innocent and I have always believed in justice. Those letters were sent by those who had an interest to cast an even more sinister light on Liggio, and it is easy to find out who they are. [He means the Communists.] Until the very end they tried to make me appear as one who can do anything and one who can buy anybody. All this is terrible. And also I have been on trial eleven times, I have been condemned for two mild sentences (for theft and association to commit a crime), while nine, I say *nine* Courts of Assizes have absolved me from infamous and very grave indictments.

Liggio, who was suffering from an infection of the bladder, then went to Rome and was operated on in a private nursing home, Villa Margherita. On 19 November he left Villa Margherita and never went back. The police got to know about his disappearance two days after he had fled.

When Zamparelli was questioned by the Antimafia Commission on his responsibility for Liggio's 'flight', he blamed Pietro Scaglione, the highest judge in Palermo. Scaglione had given orders that Liggio's arrest could be carried out only at Corleone (where Liggio had already specified that he would never return). But Zamparelli did not explain why he obeyed an order which was clearly illegal. Finally Scaglione, the plump little High Court Judge, was also interrogated by the Antimafia Commission. In 1964 he had allowed Father Francesco Capillo, the chaplain of the Ucciardone prison, to keep his post, in spite of the fact that he was proved to be the messenger of the Liggio gang. Scaglione had been the last person to talk to Pisciotta before the latter had been poisoned. It was the first time that this powerful man had found himself on the other side of the table, being interrogated rather than interrogating. He was angry and denied Zamparelli's allegations. But besides Zamparelli there were other witnesses to testify to Scagilione's order specifying that Liggio was only to be arrested at Corleone.

During Scaglione's interrogation, the MP Tuccari remarked on 'the difficulty and slowness' with which Scaglione had dealt with 'all situations of clearly determined Mafia interests'. The President of the Antimafia Commission, Cattanei, talked of 'grave responsibilities on the part of Zamparelli and Scaglione' and went on: 'It will be now the job of the magistrates to establish whether the behaviour of Scaglione and Zamparelli was due to ignorance or guilt. In any case it is obvious that the two officials cannot go on retaining the posts which they now occupy.'

Evidence emerged on how Liggio could come and go without any police control: had they wanted, the police could have arrested him at any time. Zamparelli's 'punishment' consisted in being recalled to Rome, promoted and sent to Naples, a better posting for a policeman. A tribunal in Florence examined the behaviour of Judge Scaglione, but decided that the dossier should be shelved. A special council of magistrates took one year to decide what to do with him—one year, in spite of continuous pressures from the Antimafia Commission. On 26 February 1971, with fifteen votes in favour and three against, Scaglione was declared innocent and was promoted to General Procuratore—Chief Public Prosecutor—but to another seat, at Lecce, in Apulia.

Pietro Scaglione had followed a long and distinguished career. Born in Lercara Friddi, like Lucky Luciano, he became a magistrate in 1928. In forty-three years he succeeded in leaving his favourite seat, Palermo, for only two years, which were spent in Rome. In 1949, he was deputy General Chief Public Prosecutor of Palermo, and from then on all the important indictments passed through his hands. He became Chief Public Prosecutor of Palermo in 1962, while the *cosche mafiose* warfare was going on, and while Lima and Ciancimino were controlling the city. Among his close friends were Bernardo Mattarella, Ciancimino, the millionaire Caruso from Trapani, and a mysterious Palermitan figure, Signor Jalongo.

Scaglione allowed the dust to gather on many police and Carabinieri indictments—notoriously, for four years, the dossier from the Narcotics Bureau against all the *cosche* involved in drug smuggling. When the Narcotics Bureau insisted, the entire Mafia of Castellammare was imprisoned, from Frank Coppola to Frank Garofalo, the Plajas, the Maggadinos, the Bonventre, but after a long trial all the bosses were acquitted for 'lack of proof'. In 1965 an indictment against the Palermo administration (the Bevivino Dossier) was shelved. For years Scaglione held up scores of indictments against politicians, banks and administrators, waiting to make them public at the opportune political moment. It was Scaglione who had taken down Gaspare Pisciotta's last statement about the Portella massacre, years before. He was also one of the last men to talk to the journalist Mauro de Mauro, who stumbled across lethal information in 1970 and was never seen again (see p. 262).

The 'Law' acquitted Scaglione on 25 March 1971 but the posting to Lecce still stood. To him it was a demotion to be forced away from his power base. He must have lost his patience and made threatening noises —the last thing a mafioso ever does. 'Don Petruzzo, he should have waited,' somebody told me later. 'He would have spent a few years in Apulia and kept silent, and then he would have been back.' On 5 May 1971 he paid his daily visit to his wife's grave in a Palermo cemetery. On the way back, he and his driver were shot dead by 'persons unknown' whom nobody in the district saw, knew or heard. With twenty-three years of Mafia history for leverage, he had tried to prevent the humiliating transfer to Lecce by using what he knew, backed up by dusty documents and dossiers which had been closed for ages. Safer instead to close the file on 'Don Petruzzo'.

In the direction of Palermo, Frank Coppola had his electoral hold on Partinico; no candidate belonging to the entire political spectrum (except for the Communist party) could be elected without his help— which is well documented. But Coppola was a cosmopolitan of crime, and kept Partinico only as the base which gave him power. Otherwise he maintained close connections with the hundreds of 'undesirables' who, after the publication of the report of the Kefauver Crime Commission, had been repatriated to Italy in the early Fifties. They immediately fitted into the network, bringing new techniques of gang warfare, and tending to live in towns rather than villages, where the new methods could be better employed. In those years, the mafiosi fought industrialization fiercely, seeing it as a threat to their power; the concentration of workers would educate them into a realization of their rights and power—it would make life too difficult.

Vanni Sacco was the *capomafia* of Camporeale, another beautiful name for another ugly town. Camporeale is right in the middle, between Palermo, Corleone and Alcamo: the very centre of Mafialand. Sacco had been in prison during Fascist times, but with the arrival of the

Americans in the area he had become the *gabelloto* of the large Parrino estate, a latifundium often used by the bandit Giuliano for important meetings. Like so many mafiosi, Sacco had got it wrong and joined the Liberal party that had dominated the area before Fascism, but when elections all over Italy showed that power was going to be in the hands of the Catholic party, he too changed his tune. Before that the Christian Democrats had polled very poorly in the 'Liberal'-controlled area: 180 votes in the first and 87 in the second election. But Pasquale Almerico, a determined honest Catholic, reorganized his local party and succeeded in polling 1156 votes at the 1948 elections.

Almerico was that rarity in Sicilian Christian Democrat politics, a man of integrity who did not believe in compromising with the mafiosi. He was popular with the peasantry at Camporeale, a Mafia-ridden area, so much so that he was elected mayor of his town. In 1952, Almerico was forced to accept three of Vanni Sacco's 'Liberals' in the municipal administration, but Sacco wanted total control of Camporeale and the money coming in through the regional corporations. Almerico would not allow this, and refused to accept any of Sacco's men in the Camporeale branch of his party. When Sacco offered his protection, he dared to refuse it.

The Sicilian leadership of the Christian Democrat party now began to put pressure on Almerico. The party needed coalitions and new men. Its new 'philosophy' was that of 'not putting any obstacles to patterns of compromise', which in Italian political jargon meant: get the Mafia's help. The honest mayor could not believe it, but when he went to Palermo he was horrified to be told by the secretary of the Palermo party, Giovanni Gioia, that he had to 'follow the trend of political coalitions.' Gioia invited Almerico to leave Camporeale and offered him a job at a bank—La Cassa di Risparmio—at a nearby town. Considered as an obstacle by his leaders, Almerico asked for a vote of confidence, which he did not receive. He was forced to resign.

A Christian Democrat MP, Raffaele Russo Spena, in the sixties, testified at a trial that Gioia told the Sicilian Christian Democrat MPs that the Camporeale branch of the party had to be dissolved because it was unwilling to collaborate with the right-wing parties. The same MP said that Gioia had helped Sacco's nephew to get a job in the Bank of Sicily in exchange for Sacco's support of the Christian Democrats during elections.

15. 1955 The Mafia's involvement in open politics: Genco Russo's election poster
(*Gigi Petyx*)

16. 1957 Genco Russo, Don Calò Vizzini's successor (*Gigi Petyx*)

17. 1960 The emergence of the new regime: Salvo Lima on the right hand of Cardinal Ruffini at the head of the Corpus Domini procession in the centre of Palermo
(*Gigi Petyx della Agenzia Scafidi*)

18. 1963 The recovery of bodies from the triple murder in the Liggio-Navarra feud; police technology at work in the barren foothills near Corleone (*Gigi Petyx*)

But Vanni Sacco was not content with this. The very presence of Almerico at Camporeale was an irritating symbol of honesty, and Almerico's stubborn resistance could be a dangerous example. At that stage, Almerico knew that his life was in danger: he wrote desperate letters to Giovanni Gioia and to the Secretary General of the Christian Democrat party in Rome, Amintore Fanfani. He even sent a detailed typescript of the events, explaining how the Mafia was penetrating the party at Camporeale and why he knew that his life was in danger. His appeals remained unanswered. Almerico and the few like him were an acute embarrassment to people like Gioia and Fanfani, who were working towards a grand coalition. 'The so-called Liberal party', said one witness at the trial, the Carabiniere Francesco Belghieri, 'promised the Christian Democrats to switch en masse to their party if Almerico were to be deprived of all his party and civic responsibilities. It was then that Almerico himself began to worry about his own life.'

In 1957 Almerico was shot dead in his own town, where for the past months he had been living in terror, despair and humiliation. He was returning home with his brother (they had been watching television at a café) when five masked men who had been waiting for him fired a hundred bullets into him and wounded his brother—just wounded him: he had to be alive to tell the story. As the men made their escape, the electricity supply in the town broke down. Vanni Sacco, a friend of Navarra, Genco Russo and Vizzini, could now control the town, the municipality and the local Christian Democrats.

When Almerico had threatened Giovanni Gioia with making public the liaison between the Christian Democrats and the Mafia, he answered that 'the matter doesn't impress anybody'. By 1969 Gioia had moved to Rome. When I asked him about Almerico, he lost his usual self-control. 'The Left spread such rumours', he protested. 'Not a very civilized way to play politics.' Many times he had tried 'to persuade Almerico to avoid a split and to follow the general political directive'. Seated beneath a heavy Crucifix, he added that the Mafia 'is not eliminated, but progress will kill it off.'

Gioia's name has been linked to the Mafia many times. He has always sued and mostly won. But in 1974 he sued the Sicilian newspaper *L'Ora* and later Senator Li Causi and lost. Gioia (and Fanfani) were certainly responsible for opening the doors to the Mafia inside official political arenas, but Gioia is no outright mafioso; he is a wealthy man by birth, and he has never made illicit gains (unlike many other Sicilian leaders); he is too intelligent for that. His mentality is typically Sicilian, and his links and blood relations are mafiosi.

Vanni Sacco was the old type of mafioso, the patriarchal figure. He used the methods of slow intimidation and punished rebels such as Almerico. It was rare for somebody like him to kill outside the Mafia, and he made a mistake by shooting Almerico. He was to be tried (but in the Sixties) and acquitted for lack of proof. Gioia had to give evidence, answering embarrassing questions, and denied having even met Sacco, although Sacco had declared that there had been an agreement regarding Almerico between himself and Gioia.

One episode is indicative of Sacco's methods. One of his *campieri* was sentenced to seven months in prison, which he started serving at Alcamo prison. There he began threatening to name people unless he were freed. And so he was: one night, armed men gagged the prison's guards and freed the *campiere* and the man who shared his prison cell. A day later their bodies were found on a *trazzera*.

Palermo is the last stop in our Mafia journey. In the Fifties the land-owners were getting rid of their estates or sulphur mines, or what was left of their properties, to invest in the growing city. The land reforms which they had fought so fiercely during the previous decade turned out to be to their advantage. The State expropriated the worst part of the land, paying far too much. Model villages began to grow up under the auspices of ERAS (church, houses, monuments); like those built by the Fascist regime, they stayed uninhabited. Often there was no water, or the villages were too far from the land where the peasants worked, or there was no road: the locality was always chosen to please notables and not the populace. The villages are still there: ghost places, the windows broken, the wood splintered. But Palermo was booming. It had doubled in size between 1861 and 1921. It trebled by 1961, although it had been heavily bombed during the war. Not only did capital invest-ment concentrate in cities (though especially in Palermo) but new peasant cooperatives were formed, working the land in intensive, rather than extensive, culture, and thus changing the social structure of Central Sicily. The rule of the *gabelloto* was almost over.

The regional administrative offices in Palermo were a source of jobs and corruption, of *clientela* and raccomandazioni; many new autono-mous enterprises, the *Ente*, financed by the State, became sources of easy money. 'The reason for the higher preference votes in the South,'

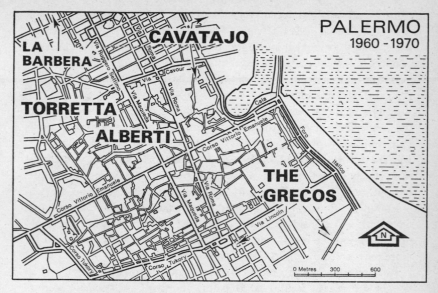

The distribution of Mafia power in Palermo in the years 1960 to 1970.

writes Percy Allum, 'is the "Southern system": the fact that patronage is the fundamental link between the *clientela* and the politician.' Anyway, to take advantage of the State is part of the Sicilian (and Italian) mentality; the State, especially in Sicily, is an absurd concept. A man who turns down the chance to profit at the State's expense is a *fesso*, a fool. The Sicilian's pride is at stake in outsmarting the State—an easy occupation there. The Ente Minerario, the Ente Riforma Agraria, the Ente Bonifica, etc., etc. became niches where all the *capocoshe* feathered their nests, and especially in Palermo.

But if the new situation was enriching some, the largest proportion of the Sicilians went on living in exactly the same miserable conditions as before. In the Fifties, and especially towards 1955, many discovered that jobs in Turin, Germany, Switzerland were not only available but better paid. Around half a million (out of a population of nearly five million) left in ten years. Emigration, one of the saddest sagas of the Southern peasantry, robbed Sicily of its best men. It was a process of self-selection: those with initiative and those who genuinely wanted to earn an honest living went away, depriving Sicily of a possibility of social evolution. Young men left behind villages inhabited by old men and women and small children. But emigration relieved the pressure of population and the lack of jobs. Those staying behind had increased wages, and the money that emigrants sent back to their families became a source of income and enriched the island. So the long exodus went on.

In 1955 the murder of Gaetano Galatolo (Tanu Alati), shot in the vegetable markets of Palermo, started an open war for the control of the city's food market: twenty-nine murders in one year were to settle the leadership of one particular *cosca*. Some villages just outside Palermo, like Bagheria and Villabate, flared up with the same kind of warfare for the control of irrigation, transport, and the wholesale markets. During that year in Palermo and its province sixty people disappeared. One day some builders made a frightening discovery: a corpse in the flow of liquid cement. By then, many other bodies must have been sealed inside the new concrete buildings which were growing up in Palermo like fungi. New activities in the shipyards coincided with more murders and with Mafia control of the waterfront.

Palermo's *cosche* were established in the different Palermo districts. On the South, at Ciaculli and Giardini, the two Greco cousins were a nucleus of formidable power. Since both were christened Salvatore Greco, I shall refer to them by their nicknames, 'L'Ingegnere' ('The Engineer') and 'Ciaschiteddu' ('Little Flask'—he has narrow shoulders and broad hips). These two were the heirs and survivors of a savage family history. Their fathers had bossed neighbouring *cosche* on the south-eastern outskirts of Palermo. Piddu u Tenente (Giuseppe the Lieutenant), father of L'Ingegnere, was *gabelloto* of 'I Giardini', a property of about 300 hectares, whose citrus orchards were a profitable concern. His brother-in-law, also named Giuseppe, was head of the *cosca* of nearby Ciaculli. The depressed circumstances of the late Thirties forced each to eye the other's territory, and after a period of friction the first murder occurred in October 1939.

Eleven members of the two families died and several others were wounded in the resulting feud. In 1946 Giuseppe was shot and killed from ambush, but the war went on, and in 1947 it was the turn of Antonio Conigliaro, a very close friend and adviser of Piddu u Tenente. Realizing that he himself would be next on the list, Piddu asked for assistance from Antonio Cottone, the boss of Villabate, a mafioso village close to I Giardini and Ciaculli. Cottone was influential in Palermo as well as in his own village, and had relations and connections in the us. He could also call on the Profaci brothers, well established in the Cosa

Nostra hierarchy, who had been deported as 'undesirables' soon after the war and were now living in Villabate.

The peace between the two branches of the Greco family was settled by giving the rights of *gabelloto* of 'I Giardini' jointly to L'Ingegnere and Ciaschiteddu, born respectively in 1924 and 1923. Piddu u Tenente withdrew from the active life of a Mafia boss and went to live in a modern house in Palermo, where he consolidated his friendships and made new ones in the 'accepted' section of society, making it easy for him to protect his younger relations when they got into trouble with the law. As descendants of the old, established Mafia, the Greco cousins soon learned how to ride the neo-capitalistic wave which was preceding the Italian boom. The partnership was welded together by the rise of *cosche* elsewhere in Palermo which were to become their natural joint enemy.

To the North—the opposite side of the city—the two La Barbera brothers were emerging from a childhood of poverty and an adolescence of violence. Pietro Torretta came to power close by, in the district of L'Uditore. Other smaller *cosche* came to recognize the supremacy of these bosses—a supremacy achieved, of course, by sheer violence. Men who were starting their 'careers' in their shadow were forming into dangerous criminals; they had initiative, and the road to the leadership of a *cosca* had suddenly become quicker and available to those who were fast with their tommy-guns. One of these upstarts was Tommaso 'Masino' Buscetta, another was Gerlando Alberti.

The La Barberas, Torretta and their henchmen formed the so-called 'New Mafia' which had adopted the new gangster techniques: tommy-guns instead of sawn-off shotguns; quick executions instead of slow revenge; daytime killing in crowded streets rather than ambushes in dark alleys. These new men had to form a new political base of their own, pushing forward new politicians through whom they could control the regional corporations and the credit banks and avoid building regulations. The new politicians began to take the place of the old guard. Little by little men like Bernardo Mattarella and Calogero Volpe were pushed aside by the new school of toughs who had grown up in parish churches playing mini-football and pinball machines.

But this new school of Mafia had little support from Sicilian public opinion. This was a Mafia which did not go in for the old amalgam of granting favours, dispensing justice, settling quarrels. Favours and jobs were only given in exchange for votes. The respect commanded by the new gangsters—both killers and politicians—was entirely bought, and the Sicilians began to see the Mafia as a straightforward parasite. The Mafia was losing its patriarchal organizational element, its social context which had partly come from the necessity of filling the gap in public rule in desolate parts of Sicily. The new criminal mafioso was therefore developing into a straightforward gangster, leaving behind the traditions which had made his forerunners part of Sicilian society.

What developed from this rule is a network of political protection and criminality (as had already happened in the States) which was to involve not only the Sicilian regional Assembly but the Italian Parliament, the parties, the administrations, the institutions all over Italy. The 'evolution' of the Mafia was tragic because it was to spread, physically and psychologically, to the whole of Italy. The already fertile ground for corruption blossomed when groups of Sicilian emigrants imported their mentality, and mafioso sent to banishment in the Italian mainland found a platform from which to build richer rackets.

In a large city like Palermo, the problem of corrupt officials became more intricate. It was no longer, as in Don Calò's village, a question of corrupting one *maresciallo* or influencing the small fry in the administration. The institution had to be conquered; partnership with the administrators had to be extended to higher levels.

The two Grecos abandoned the old code, and in 1955 L'Ingegnere's name was connected with drugs when a truck containing 6 kilos of heroin sent by him to Frank Coppola was found by the police at Alcamo. Tightly linked with Liggio, the Rimis, the 'Americans', the Grecos had so much power that when the mafioso Stefano Leale asked L'Ingegnere's protection, he was told: 'Don't be afraid, my consent is needed for killing you.' He gave his consent in 1959.

Both 'Ciaschiteddu' Greco, based at Ciaculli, and 'L'Ingegnere' (also called *Toto il Lungo*, Toto the Tall), from I Giardini, started drug-smuggling early in the day. Apart from their many 'American' connections they developed a real industry, not only smuggling but distributing. They owned a clandestine fleet, mainly Corsican boats with mixed crews. (Boats and ships changed name and appearance, the police explained: a boat would leave Tangier with a certain name and superstructure, and arrive in Marseilles or Malta with another.) The Grecos' alliance with the Rimis could guarantee the use of several miles of coastline around Punta San Vito (between Castellammare and

Trapani), where there is no road and where no road has been planned or wanted for these reasons.

Judge Terranova, who investigated the Grecos and indicted them (in the Sixties, when they were already at large) wrote about L'Ingegnere:

> His relationships with the worse characters of the international underworld became clear by reading the reports sent by the Tributary Police. He is linked to Serafino Mancuso, Frank Coppola, Peter Giardino, Joe Picci, Frank Callace, Antonino Sorace, Lucky Luciano, Sam Corollo, Salom Golas, Elio Forni, Marcello Falciai, Jean Gomez, Paul Poli and many other individuals belonging not only to the Sicilian underworld but to the American, Spanish, Corsican and Tangerine, all people notoriously involved in the smuggling of tobacco and hard drugs.

Interpol believes that L'Ingegnere (who in 1968 was condemned to ten years only, but as he had been on the run since 1963 he did not serve a day) lived in the Lebanon, whence he controlled a slice of the international smuggling channels. In the Fifties, tourism was a privilege and taste of a few, certainly a very few Sicilians, but L'Ingegnere was already travelling: France, Morocco, Tangier, Gibraltar, Milan, Genoa.

Of the two cousins, L'Ingegnere was the more accomplished and, according to both Interpol and the Narcotics Bureau, the more powerful operator. A real cosmopolitan of crime, L'Ingegnere (whose brother Nicolò disappeared—his corpse is probably in quicklime) had his hands not only in the local, Mediterranean basin drug traffic but also in South America. If the Trapani Mafia had actual power in Sicily, the Grecos showed that their political protection, their international contacts, their basis at home (Piddu' u' Tenente) were a stronger platform: they have never been caught, although the Narcotics Bureau, Interpol, the Criminalpol etc. have both the cousins on their priority list.

Salvatore Greco, 'Ciaschiteddu', 'is a top man of a *cosca mafiosa*', Judge Terranova stated, 'operating in drug and cigarette smuggling.' In 1968 he was condemned in his absence by the Court of Catanzaro to only four years; and in 1973 both cousins were given the maximum period of banishment—five years—at L'Asinara, one of the most remote of Italian islands. But of course both cousins live in much better places than L'Asinara, and although it is said that from time to time they come back to Italy to take part in Mafia summits they are very unlikely to end up in an Italian prison. There is only one blurred photograph of one of them (at a Mafia wedding), but by now they have probably changed their features with the help of those Brazilian plastic surgeons who developed their skills thanks partly to years of practice on former Nazi officers.

The Grecos almost 'had' to choose the more lucrative (as it turned out) field of drug-smuggling, because the building rackets and the markets were in the hands of the 'new' *cosche*, on the opposite side of the city. It was on the Northern side, in fact, that the building boom exploded: gardens became districts made of cement, apartment blocks were crammed one next to the other, pretty *art nouveau* villas, orchards and parks were bulldozed away. No building regulation held, almost no law was respected. Palermo never recovered: from being one of the most beautiful cities in the world, with a breathtaking panorama and large green areas, it is now an ugly hazy jungle of cracked cement.

The La Barbera brothers, Salvatore and Angelo, the men mainly responsible for this disaster, had started from nothing, but soon acquired a position as wealthy and respected real-estate operators. Their men were everywhere: at the regional assembly, in the city municipality. Needless to say, their road to the top was paved with corpses. The Grecos and the La Barberas were not the best of friends, but accepted each other's presence and activities. The Grecos' links with the other Sicilian *cosche* were stronger than the La Barberas' and their relations with the 'Americans' better. Things couldn't go on in the same way after Angelo La Barbera became involved in drug-smuggling. That was a field which the Grecos and the Rimis reserved for themselves.

The La Barbera brothers went into 'partnership' with Lucky Luciano, who lived in Naples and had the best possible connections with the American underworld, and with Rosario Mancino, who was Luciano's friend. Mancino had left for the States in 1915, and had come back to Sicily after the war. He was also a man who had 'friends' on both sides of the Atlantic. But Palermo was too small to have two groups of over-bosses, and the trade in narcotics was too specialized for the La Barbera brothers, who had shot their way up from the very bottom of the underworld to a position of prominence.

The *casus belli* came from a deal which had 'gone wrong'. The La Barberas refused to obey a decision taken by all the overbosses together (the so-called Mafia tribunal) and considered themselves cheated. Their protest was expressed by a series of bloody killings: people were shot in the streets of Palermo in broad daylight; cars filled with gelignite exploded. This was a new kind of Mafia warfare which scared Sicilian and Italian public opinion in the early years of the Sixties. On the Grecos' side were the Rimis, Liggio, all the 'provincial' and rural *cosche*. On the La Barberas' side were the small but cruel Palermitan *cosche*.

As the casualties on the La Barbera side became more conspicuous, the brothers' former allies began to defect: Buscetta betrayed and probably killed Salvatore La Barbera himself. The police think it was L'Ingegnere Greco who arranged the deal. Salvatore La Barbera's corpse was dissolved inside the furnaces of Buscetta's glass factory. Angelo La Barbera himself was shot, but did not die, and was sentenced to twenty-two years in prison. He appealed against the decision of the Court, and when a new law—the Valpreda law—was passed in 1970 suspending detention of prisoners appealing to a higher court (if detention had been longer than eight years), La Barbera was a free man but was sent to the *soggiorno obbligato*. The anomaly of Italian law which can put a person on trial three times (or more) upsets the police: 'Many mafiosi waiting for a second or third trial acquire the right to come out because of the slowness of our legal machinery.' La Barbera was first banished to Northern Italy, and later to a remote island where I first met him.

Although he had spent the last five years between banishment, trials and prison, Angelo La Barbera had been accused by the police of having organized a new *cosca* in Calabria which dealt in kidnapping. Certainly the former boss still enjoyed financial wealth, respect and privileged treatment. When, in July 1975, he was moved to Perugia prison, he was interned in the prison's hospital (although it had been officially closed for a year), had various rooms at his disposal on the third floor, windows without bars, could ring up—he talked to his mother every night—and gave banquets (sometimes even champagne was served) to the inmates who readily recognized him as the man 'di rispettu'. The meals came from a restaurant nearby. But lately La Barbera's men, eight of his bodyguards, had been transferred to another prison and the boss was on his own. An odd arrangement. When three killers left their isolation cell with surprising ease and knocked out the prison guard who was on duty at La Barbera's building, the boss only just had time to ask 'What's the matter, picciotti?' La Barbera was stabbed eight times by the three Sicilians and died immediately.

The Corleo case is a classic example of how the Mafia can exercise power and maintain its control. The kidnapping of Luigi Corleo, tax collector from Salemi, a member of the all-powerful Salve family, was too big an insult for the Sicilian *cosche* to stomach. The provocation had in fact come from outside, the Calabrians had kidnapped the 'untouchable' (who, thinking he had nothing to fear, was alone, driving his Mercedes). The police were soon informed and made thirteen arrests. Again the Mafia had used the State by giving the police precise information—thus safeguarding their own order. The Sicilian Mafia knew, but did not give consent. A day before the kidnapping, Salvatore Zizzo came back to Salemi. Not a coincidence; nothing is a coincidence in these stories. Was La Barbera the mastermind behind the Calabrian clan who committed many of the kidnappings which disturbed the Mafia's operations? The police are still looking for the 'mastermind' but it might well be that the Mafia saw to it that a yard of earth would cover that mind, who was too clever, too knowledgeable and too untrustworthy.

I knew Angelo La Barbera well. He was the symbol of the quick, clever gangster, the new mafioso who, having perceived best ways to arrive at the top, became the victim of the many politicians he himself had built up, had made. In a way, he represented the proletariat who tried to become mafioso, middle-class, and ultimately did not succeed. This Sicilian *canto* is an account of a conversation between a Mafia boss and somebody who, although understanding the language and the power, is essentially out of his league: '*Ti dicu: tira manu, sudd'hai cori, e duna a cura ri nun truppicari. E quannu parri, pisa li paroli: n'omu r'anuri ha sapiri parrari.*' '*Tirannu manu, nun trovi tisori! L'agghienti ri stu mannu 'un semu quali: ni trovi ncunu cu'pochi paroli, ca ti nzigna a cingati a ragghiunari.*'

('I tell you, use your gun if you don't fear, and be careful not to trip. When you speak, be careful about your words: a man of honour has to know how to speak.'—'By using your gun you don't find treasures! Men in this world are not equals: you find those who use few words and by whipping you, teach how to reason'.)

12 Family Ties

Drug smuggling brought the links with the United States so close that when in 1952 Vito Genovese—in New York—received the information directly from Lucky Luciano—in Naples—that one of the latter's own 'soldiers', Eugenio Giannini, was giving information to the Bureau of Narcotics, the contract for killing Giannini was commissioned by Genovese and carried out in New York. Luciano, the man behind it, could never be accused: he never moved from Naples.

Remembering the 'good old days', Patsy Lepera, in *Memoirs of a Scam Man*, said:

The only thing they [the Italians] had was their closed mouth between them. My grandmother—you could hit her with an axe, she wouldn't tell you what time it was. Because you were the enemy ... But in those times it was all different. When I was a kid, my father went to jail for fifteen days. The mob gave my mother 150 a week. They didn't say any maybes. A hundred fifty a week ... and when my father came out, they had a five hundred dollar bonus for him—at that time a lot of money. Today you go to jail, instead of taking care of you, they rob you.

In Valachi's day, soldiers had to pay 25 dollars a month tax to the Family, which were reserved for such expenses as hiring lawyers and supporting families of those in prison.

The mentality in the American Cosa Nostra was still based on family nuclei, or on common origins—the same village, region, religion (as also in the case of Jews like Meyer Lansky and Abner Zwillman). Valachi himself said that he refused somebody who wanted to get into the Mob as he was a 'mixbreed', partly Italian and partly German. The network of Families in the States was also undergoing a change. Having been deported to Italy, Lucky Luciano had seemed to be out of the game in the leadership of his former Family. When he suddenly turned up in Havana, with not one, but two Italian passports in perfect order, many Cosa Nostra (or 'Syndicate' or 'Combination' as it began to be called) bosses went to Cuba to see him. It was not until Washington threatened to cut off shipments of medical drugs to Cuba that Havana reluctantly agreed to send Luciano back to Italy.

Vito Genovese had returned to the States. He had ambitions to re-place Frank Costello, still entertaining Tammany Hall leaders at his elegant flat on Central Park West, or at his weekend villa at Sands Point on Long Island.

Costello (real name Francesco Castiglia) was born in Calabria in 1891. He had arrived in the US when only four, and had gone through the classic gangster curriculum—a member of two gangs, the Gobber and the Hudson Duster, often indicted but never convicted except for minor offences. He built his strength by suborning official power, and in 1943 he succeeded in having Judge Thomas Aurelio elected to the New York Supreme Court. Aurelio was the man who had sworn Costello 'eternal loyalty'. Under the 'dubious reign' of Mayor James J. Walker, Costello had opened up the city for slot machines. When Fiorello la Guardia became Mayor and tried to abolish slot machines, Costello's political pull was such that he managed to obtain a court injunction restraining la Guardia from interfering with the machines.

Costello was the organizer of Cosa Nostra, the third generation developing the Family structure, going 'legal' or at least building solid protection from the world of legality. Although he had started, like Al 'Scarface' Capone, in a gang, and had gone through the criminal phase with Genovese, Costello was a real product of a more sophisticated environment: life in the United States had taught him the importance of buying politicians. In fact, in 1929, he and Luciano had come to plan a scheme of non-violence and sharing fields of 'influence'—with Al Capone sitting at the same table. Costello made $4 million a year through the slot-machine racket. He was eventually deprived of American citizenship, but never successfully convicted. Always in the company of powerful politicians, in 1929 he was even received by Mussolini who thought he was a powerful businessman who wanted to invest capital in Italy. They spent an hour together and Costello, presumably a good judge of gangsters, was unimpressed by Mussolini.

As we have said, Costello was against drugs, which he considered dangerous for the good name of Cosa Nostra. Unlike the new mobsters, he had the mafioso conviction of the necessity and legitimacy of his role, the consciousness of being a man of 'order'. Valachi, who belonged to the Genovese Family, said that 'dope' was officially outlawed, and a member of the Family was on his own if arrested for drug pushing. In fact it turned out that Genovese was in the trade.

Early in the 1950s, the Junior Senator from Tennessee, Estes Kefauver, sponsored a resolution to create a Special Senate Committee to investigate organized crime in Interstate Commerce and, when the Committee was organized in May 1950, Kefauver was elected its Chairman. He had an ingenious pre-Watergate idea: lacking a key witness (such as Valachi was to be for the McClellan Committee), the Southern Senator 'invented' live television, and in the sixteen months of the Committee's existence more than six hundred witnesses, from racketeers to officials at every level of government, had to go through the humiliation of being interrogated in front of the nation. Television was just reaching all American homes and 'the program' became the most watched and popular. The Kefauver Committee took testimony in fourteen cities and put on public display the links among crime, politics and business.

Whenever the Committee arrived in a city, handing out subpoenas, the city's major mobsters disappeared: Genovese took a long holiday in the Caribbean sun; even Chicago and Cleveland were deserted. But later, rather than go to jail, they all attended. The television cameras focused on a Cosa Nostra parade which included Frank Costello, Adonis, Lansky, Zwillman, Willie Moretti, Albert Anastasia. Moses Polakoff, Lansky's (and Luciano's) lawyer, was asked: 'How did you become counsel for such a dirty rat as that? Aren't there some ethics in the legal profession?'

The greatest show took place when the Kefauver Committee reached New York: it 'starred' Virginia Hill, the hands of Frank Costello (fearing public exposure, he contested the Committee and obtained the ruling that the television cameras must not show his face) and the former New York City mayor (then Ambassador to Mexico) William O'Dwyer. Virginia Hill had been a kind of real-life Rita Hayworth, had affairs with mobsters and even with Costello. She said nothing to the Committee, but she knew a lot. After attempting suicide several times, she died by swallowing enough sleeping pills in March 1966, and lay down in the Swiss snow. The hearings became even more hypnotic; the husky voice of Costello claiming innocence and his hands playing with cigarettes and nervously twitching became more and more dramatic. I still remember the many cartoons which appeared in all American papers: Costello's hands became a symbol of the Syndicate.

Through the years, Costello had built the 'godfather' image of a kind of elder statesman and public benefactor. His manners had become polished, his clothes elegant, his advice had always been sought after as the voice of moderation within the Syndicate. The hearings shattered that image. After the Kefauver Committee, Costello could never keep the same position in the clandestine councils of the underworld, nor guide organized crimes in the same path of moderation. Indeed, Costello spent the rest of the decade fighting legal battles. He was cited for contempt and sentenced to eighteen months' imprisonment—a real blow for a man of his power and position. He was also convicted for income-tax evasion and received another prison term.

O'Dwyer's testimony was traumatic: his memory, like that of all the other mobsters, proved hazy or contradictory, but he could be reminded of episodes such as when he had willingly accepted $10,000 in cash from a John Crane who testified. One of his men, James Moran (whom O'Dwyer had appointed chief clerk in the District Attorney's office), was convicted and sentenced to five years.

Not only was Costello's power over, but Joe Adonis—real name Giuseppe Doto—who had been controlling part of Luciano's rackets in New York, was indicted and the case against him was so strong that he pleaded guilty. In 1951 he went to prison for two years and paid a $15,000 fine. In 1956, having to choose between a further five years in prison and deportation, he went back to Italy and settled in Milan. The (late) Senator Kefauver had described him as 'one of the most insolent and astute gangsters, and in a sense the most sinister of them all'. Adonis died in 1974 when in exile *al confino* in a tiny village on the Adriatic coast.

With all this turmoil created by 'external' causes, the Families had lost some confidence and a number of leaders. Yet although the American public had been made aware in detail of the existence of organized crime, the McCarthy crusade against the Reds became so strong and obsessive that it made the public forget about the Syndicate. Within months the underworld was operating as if the Kefauver Committee had never existed. In Brooklyn, Anastasia had had enough of being second to his Family and being the underboss to Vincent Mangano. He killed both Vincent and Philip Mangano, who had led that Family since the Thirties. Vincent's body was never found. Valachi and 'Lucky' Luciano stated that the Commissione, or Ruling Council, approved Anastasia, a cruel and dangerous killer, as the new head of the Family.

It was Vito Genovese's turn to rise: on 2 May 1957, Frank Costello was returning home to his Central Park West apartment, having dined at L'Aiglon, a restaurant in Manhattan. 'This is for you, Frank,' said a voice, but the bullet only wounded Costello in the head. Frank Costello was very much in Genovese's way to the top. Although no longer so powerful, his very presence and disapproval of Genovese's irresponsible murderous curriculum made Costello into an enemy. In the same year, Frank Scalice, number two in the Anastasia family, was shot dead. His brother Joseph, who had made vows of revenge, ended up in the same way. Vito Genovese made contacts with an ambitious 'lieutenant' of Anastasia's, Carlo Gambino, who was to become the head of that Family.

At this stage, the Americans needed to consult the Sicilians. They had to discuss the turmoil inside Cosa Nostra and the growing power of Vito Genovese, to settle differences between the new and old *cosche* in Sicily and Families in the States, and to plan and share the new field of narcotics. The 'Americans' needed the 'Italians' then: an exiled boss in Italy could always count on a passport from the Italian authorities, something which was beginning to be difficult in the States after the Kefauver episode. The anti-Genovese bosses needed the *cosche*'s support—which they had: Genovese was a Neapolitan. Lucky Luciano, who although living in Naples was in close contact with the Sicilians, was Costello's man.

A 'Criminal Summit' was called in Palermo. It took place in the most elegant of the city's hotels, the Grand Hotel des Palmes, a former villa which had been built by the English Marsala king, Benjamin Ingham. The mere fact that the summit could be called in such a place gives one an idea of how freely the Mafia could operate in the Fifties. It took place in October 1957. Many bosses were present, but the police had the names of only some: Frank Garofalo was there, and so was Joe Bonanno (Bananas), Vito Vitale, John Bonventre, Cesare Manzella (who was soon to be dispatched by Angelo La Barbera), Joe Di Bella, Carmine Galante, Santo Sorge, Vincenzo Rimi, Calcedonio di Pisa (also later to be murdered by the La Barberas), Mimi' La Fata, Nick Gentile and Genco Russo. The police suspect, but were unable to prove, that

Frank Coppola and Luciano Liggio were also there. There is no record of the Grecos' arrival at the Hotel des Palmes, but their absence would have been unthinkable.

The elimination of Albert Anastasia, a Calabrian who was in everybody's way and was considered excessively violent, had to have the bosses' consent; it must have been discussed at that summit. And in fact a few weeks later, in one of the scenes made famous by films, while Anastasia was at the barbershop of the Park Sheraton Hotel in Manhattan and his bodyguard was strangely away, two gunmen riddled his body with bullets. His murder was a sensation: the press splashed it all over the front pages. Carlo Gambino took over, and the Families began to worry about Vito Genovese. They were delighted that Anastasia, the violent Anastasia whom everybody had feared, had been finally bumped off, but now another violent man was bidding for the overall leadership, which could only be acquired by eliminating other bosses.

At the Grand Hotel des Palmes, another gathering or 'Summit' must have been discussed and planned. Since it had to be called to settle American questions, it was to take place in the States and only among 'Americans'. We have far more details about this Summit because it was described by Valachi. Three weeks after the murder of Albert Anastasia (on 14 November 1957), the mob's conclave met in the little town of Apalachin in New York State. According to Valachi, Genovese would have preferred to have it in Chicago or in a city, where the comings and goings would not have been noticeable, but Maggadino persuaded the mob to stage it in the house of one of his trusted lieutenants, Joseph Barbara, from Castellammare. The meeting was well prepared, and special steaks were ordered (the mafiosi are great meat-eaters, I have always noticed). Reservations were made and the bosses finally arrived, each surrounded by many of his own bodyguards.

It was a serious Council, and several matters had to be decided upon for the sake of maintaining order. Although nobody challenged Genovese as head of his Family, this had to be discussed. Then Genovese was to be charged with the attempted murder of Frank Costello (Genovese's own excuse was that Costello and Anastasia had wanted to eliminate him). Another important point was the Bureau of Narcotics, which was a serious threat to the organizational structure of Cosa Nostra. Some of the bosses wanted to pass a resolution by which drug traffic was to be outlawed for all the Families. But the real reason for the meeting was that Genovese wanted to be elected *capo de capi*, reverting to the old days' practice. Lucky Luciano commented, 'The way Vito organized the Apalachin thing only proves the worst part about him—that he was stupid. He never learnt—he always put his greed in front of common sense. The last thing you wanna do is call attention to yourself. What the hell did Vito think would happen when a bunch of guys from all over the country dressed in fancy city clothes, came drivin' up some country road in their big Cadillacs like it was a fuckin' parade?' (Their 'summit' meeting used to take place by the seaside, five or six of them—Lansky, Costello, Siegel—and they exchanged talk with their feet in the warm sea-water.)

In the little town of Apalachin, a peaceful suburban place, the arrival of many black limousines, containing what were later described as 'suspicious passengers' (big American bosses clad in their best suits, surrounded by their toughest bodyguards, driven by square-jawed chauffeurs), clamoured for the attention of a New York state policeman, Sergeant Edgar D. Cresswell. In the afternoon, after some patient work, he tracked the bosses down at Joseph Barbara's villa. They had not yet settled down to business, and were enjoying a barbecue, in traditional Mafia and American suburban style (eating tons of beefsteak). Spotting the strange group, but having only a vague idea of what it represented, Sergeant Cresswell with three other local policemen decided to set up a road block in order to have an excuse to ask their names. A Syndicate guard burst in to warn the gathering as they were eating in the open air.

The bosses panicked. There were probably up to thirty Families represented at Apalachin, covering every corner of the States and every racket. Several bosses, among them Genovese, decided to go there and then. They were stopped by the road block and taken in for questioning. The police found $300,000 in cash on the people they searched. Others fled into the countryside and were picked up by police reinforcements which had arrived in the meantime. Sixty delegates were caught, and the Justice Department believed that at least another fifty had succeeded in escaping. Chicago's Boss Sam Giancana was among these. A number of those who were stopped and questioned were tried on a charge of conspiring to obstruct justice by refusing to explain why they had all met at Barbara's villa. They were found guilty and fined, but the sentence was reversed on appeal on the grounds that a meeting in a villa did not constitute a crime. In fact, almost all declared that they had gone to see Barbara, who was ill.

In November 1957 the police listened to a telephone conversation between Stefano Maggadino, the boss of Buffalo and Sam Giancana the boss of Chicago.

MAGGADINO. It never would've happened in your place.
GIANCANA. You're fucking right, it wouldn't. This is the right territory for a big meet. We've got three towns just outside Chicago with the police chiefs in our pockets. We got this territory baled up tight.

But Genovese's downfall was near: within a year he was indicted, convicted and sentenced to fifteen years in a narcotic conspiracy case. The Federal police, who had previously tried to get Genovese on so many murder cases, had finally caught him. But from Leavenworth Federal Penitentiary, Vito Genovese went on conducting business, although he could no longer be a *capo* and Cosa Nostra's 'order' was shaken up. Joseph Gallo, a 'soldier' of the Profaci Family in Brooklyn, led a bloody insurrection against his Boss who, however, died of natural causes.

The Justice Department believed that in the late Fifties/early Sixties there were nine to twelve principal Families in the States: Vito Genovese, still in charge of his own Family from the penitentiary; Joseph Bonanno; Joseph Colombo, who succeeded Profaci in Brooklyn; John Scalisi of Cleveland; Joseph Zerilli in Detroit; Salvatore Giancana in Chicago; Stefano Maggadino in Buffalo; Angelo Bruno in Philadelphia; Carlos Marcello in New Orleans, and Raymond Patriarca around Boston. The rackets moved into new areas, air cargo, service industries such as garbage collection, and monopolistic positions in legitimate business. The drain on the national economy of the United States was gigantic.

In Sicily, not all were just watching in fear and in amazement at the bosses' open rule; in 1958 the Palermo Communist newspaper *L'Ora* started to publish an inquiry on the Mafia written by its best journalists. It had never been done before. From the very first instalment the word 'Mafia'—an unmentionable word in those years—appeared in enormous letters spread over the front page.

This totally revolutionary way of tackling the Mafia—which hates that kind of publicity—was due to the arrival in Palermo of a young editor from Calabria. Vittorio Nisticò was a man of personal courage and great journalistic talent. The story of the murder of Almerico and Gioia's behaviour was told. The newspaper also told the story of Navarra and Liggio. Under the photograph of the young bandit, there was a warning: *Pericoloso!*—dangerous. That was the fourth instalment, and Palermo waited for the next, holding its breath. But on the following day the printing presses of the newspaper were blown up. This attack told the whole of Italy that the Mafia was not a fantasy or a colourful exaggeration. It was a daring act (almost certainly ordered by Liggio), but stupid. Again it stressed the total rule of the mafiosi in those years: Liggio certainly counted on some rumour, but on no serious consequence. A special edition of the paper, printed by hand, was rushed onto the streets after the bombing: *L'Ora* had not been intimidated. 'Today's outrage must bring home to the National Parliament the urgent necessity of a Parliamentary inquiry into the Mafia. Such an inquiry must now be in the forefront of every responsible and upright citizen's thoughts.'

Two days later, in the Chamber of Deputies, the Social Democrat leader Giuseppe Saragat repeated the unmentionable word in Parliament. 'Some people maintain that the Mafia doesn't exist. It has taken the attack on *L'Ora* to make us see that there is a Mafia. There must be an inquiry.' Many of those who had been insisting that the Mafia did not exist were sitting there in the Chamber. A month later the Socialists introduced a bill to set up a Parliamentary Committee to investigate the Mafia.

Four years were to elapse before the law could be passed.

PART FOUR

Under Attack

Iu sugno n'eriva ca ntuzzica a ttutti,
eccu mi cogghi num mi po' mmanciari;
mi metti nta la bucca e num m'agghiutti,
eccu m'agghiutti li fazzu affucari.

(I am a herb which poisons all/who picks me cannot eat me./Put me
in your mouth and you won't be able to swallow me/and whoever
swallows me, I suffocate.)

13 The Antimafia Parliamentary Commission

Monsignor Ernest Ruffini, Cardinal of Palermo, whose right-wing sympathies were extreme—even considering the attitude of the Vatican in the Fifties—declared in church that the Mafia, *The Leopard*, and Danilo Dolci had brought dishonour on Sicily. By this Mafia Ruffini meant the publicity around the Mafia. Later he specified: 'A propaganda campaign without limits, through press, the radio and television, has made people believe, not only in Italy, but *abroad*, that the Mafia infects the greater proportion of Sicilians who are pictured as generally speaking mafiosi, thus denigrating the great gifts which place this island among the highest manifestations of the human spirit.'

When the Socialists introduced a bill for the constitution of a special body to inquire into the phenomenon of the Mafia, it was not the first time that exponents of the lay parties had asked for an official parliamentary inquiry. In 1948, Minister Scelba had turned down one such proposal, which had come from the Communists. Regional authorities had repeatedly refused to investigate Mafia matters. In 1958 Mattarella, Gioia and Gullotti had voted against the constitution of a Parliamentary Commission of inquiry into the Mafia. Ministers in Rome repeated that the Mafia did not exist, or that it was an unimportant phenomenon peculiar to Sicily. Most parties were unwilling to lose Sicilian votes, and the regional government was of course too dependent on the grand electors.

But times had changed and in 1962, amidst Palermo gang wars with fifty murders in fifty days, it would have been impossible to deny the evidence. Public opinion, as Cardinal Ruffini had hinted, was by now aware of the way in which the *cosche* operated and had penetrated public life. Even the Sicilian population was now reacting to the openly gangster face of the Mafia, and some followed certain brave examples and went to the legal authorities. The mother of Salvatore Carnevale from Sciara denounced her son's killers to the police. Serafina Battaglia, widow and mother of mafiosi, turned to the police to revenge her husband and son, rather than to the traditional channels of private violence.

This time the proposal came from the Socialists Ferruccio Parri and Simone Gatto: the Commission was to be the first to include the word Mafia in its title, and its terms of reference were to be seen no longer as a solely regional Sicilian problem, but in its national implications. In 1962 the Sicilian Assembly had asked unanimously for an official inquiry; the vote being taken by open ballot, no one felt they could vote against it. Anyway, most of its members, who were deeply implicated with the *cosche*, were confident that they would not be let down by the Roman Parliamentarians.

From the Assemblea Regionale Siciliana, IV Legislation. CCIX debate, 30 March 1962:

> Considering that criminal acts against persons or goods multiply, and in some areas of Sicily make evident the existence of powerful criminal organizations which exercise direct and negative influence on the economic and social life of the island; considering that to overcome the difficulties that are now met in attempting to punish the crimes, it is necessary to clarify which interests are at the basis of such a phenomenon and which are the entities which ensure complicity and help to the delinquent organizations ... we ask that an inquiry on its causes and characteristics promoted by the State should be started immediately and we ask the National Parliament to institute a Parliamentary Commission of Inquiry on the Mafia.

Two days later, the Senate in Rome approved the bill. But it took eight months before the Chamber of Deputies put the law to a vote; unlike the Senate, where the open vote had been unanimous, the ballot in the Chamber was secret, and 35 MPs voted against, 478 being in favour. The Sicilians immediately expressed what they thought in a *canto*:

> *La Cammira delli Dibbutati si pripara*
> *per livari la mafia ura ppi ura;*
> *cerca di sparagnarli li lupara*
> *pi pputarli ncalera, in zipultura.*

(The House of Deputies prepares itself to eliminate the Mafia hour by hour; it tries to spare them the shotgun to bury them instead inside a jail.)

The first commission was formed in February 1963 under the presidency of a Social Democrat, Paolo Rossi; it lasted only three months before the general elections of 28 April. It consisted of fifteen MPs and fifteen Senators, chosen to represent all parties. It took a long time to form, particularly because newspapers and Parliamentarians alike were opposed to the inclusion of Sicilians.

In 1963 the Christian Democrat situation in Sicily was as follows: Gullotti 'ruled' in Messina, Verzotto in Siracusa, Mattarella in Trapani, Gioia and Lima in Palermo, Volpe in Caltanisetta, La Loggia in Agrigento. Gullotti, Mattarella and Volpe belonged to the faction of Moro; Gioia and Lima to that of Fanfani.

The second Commission was under the presidency of Donato Pafundi, and there began the most delicate phase of its work. Secret archives were opened, and to the surprise of many, it became clear that no field in Sicilian life had been immune to Mafia collusion. The Commission had wide powers to investigate the Mafia and to suggest ways to eliminate it. For the first time since Unification, a Parliamentary body could study reports and dossiers prepared by institutions such as the Carabinieri, the PS, the Guardia di Finanza, the Magistrature, the Prefects.

On 30 June 1963 another Mafia outrage stoked up public pressure for positive government action when a car exploded at Ciaculli, four kilometres from Palermo, opposite the house of Totò Greco, L'Ingegnere. Two months earlier another car had exploded, destroying part of his house. The warfare between the 'old' and the 'new' Mafia was going on, in spite of the Antimafia Commission. But in that car two lots of gelignite had been placed, one visible, the other hidden. The success of the plan counted on the mafioso mentality: after the first lot had been found, the designated victim (presumably, L'Ingegnere Greco) would have thought of taking the car away, causing it to disappear from any legal inquiry. A second amount of gelignite, hidden under the seat and linked to the door, would have blown the person up. But on 30 June somebody, having spotted the suspicious Alfa Romeo (it was a period when 'loaded' Alfa Romeos were quite common), telephoned the Carabinieri. Having disconnected the first lot in the back, seven of them approached and opened the door. They were blown to pieces; one of them was Lieutenant Mario Malausa, a brave and honest Carabiniere who had written many dossiers on the *cosche mafiose*.

The Special Laws, hurried through Parliament as a sop to public opinion after the Ciaculli murders, were passed after the first report of the Pafundi Commission to Parliament on 7 August 1963, which asked for urgent penal and administrative measures. All were granted. They were:

1. Preventative measures for those who had been acquitted during the preparations of trials by indicting magistrates, or those who had been acquitted on 'not proven' verdicts for typically Mafia crimes.

2. The institution of the *soggiorno obbligato cautelativo* (exile under surveillance, banishment) and *vigilanza speciale* (special surveillance, see Chapter 7) in places far away from Sicily.

3. A revision of the names of those in possession of arms.

4. Publication of names of all those who possessed arms.

5. A close and overall examination of licences to tender and for administrative concessions.

6. A more careful examination of civil servants in service in the four provinces of Western Sicily: Agrigento, Caltanisetta, Palermo, Trapani.

7. A request to the local State and Regional corporations that they should revise licences and control building activities.

8. That judiciaries should conclude current or pending trials and proceedings.

9. A coordination of the struggle against the Mafia.

To implement nos. 3, 4 and 5, a complete reform of the national electoral system would have been necessary; in fact the mafiosi went on getting jobs in Regional and State offices, and kept their permits to carry arms. To implement nos. 8 and 9 (i.e. close collaboration between police and Carabinieri) an overall reform should have been demanded to change the police system in Italy—a much needed reform, by the way. Therefore the situation remained the same.

The first two measures had originally been introduced during Fascist times. As a result of these an enormous number of people were sent into banishment. Many were innocent; some, like Genco Russo and Giuseppe Di Cristina, were authentic mafiosi. Guilty or not, the measures proved counterproductive. Ordinary Sicilians saw them as state repression, while for the Mafia they were at worst an inconvenience, and easily circumvented.

Nowadays the big bosses, who are clever men, no longer deny the very existence of the *cosche*. Instead they protest against the methods of the police, against the 'Mafia laws', and in that respect their words are likely to find sympathetic ears: these laws are dangerous and un-democratic; banishment under a mere suspicion is an all-purpose weapon in the hands of the police. The ordinary criminal law would often be effective enough, if it were enforced. After being present at too many Mafia trials, one can see that it is not enforced because too often magistrates are weak or corrupt, and that the so-called 'Mafia lawyers' should themselves be indicted. Anyway the direct-dial calls which now connect all Italy, together with the availability of aeroplanes and *autostrade*, have made the idea of banishing somebody to unreachable places a farce.

After Ciaculli, many were banished to towns or villages in Northern and Central Italy, with the naïve thought that they would be detached from their environment and therefore would be put out of action. Those who had less high protection or had lost it, and were particularly dangerous, were sent to faraway islands like Linosa (nearer to Tunisia than Italy), to L'Asinara (a 'closed' island) and to Filicudi, although the population of the last island protested and forced the government to send their unwanted guests on to L'Asinara. But when I went to Filicudi in 1969 I found that many inhabitants had been sad to see them go, since the mafiosi had been a source of income, a badly needed source in the beautiful and forgotten island.

Giuseppe Di Cristina, the Riesi boss, was banished with Giuseppe Sorce and Calogero Sinatra. When I met the latter in 1969 ('Have you ever heard of my relative, Frank Sinatra?'), he was still banished to L'Asinara and complained that they had been let down: they had been the 'grand electors 'of the area. But at that stage the Christian Democrat party had to save its face and could not protect them any longer. Sinatra also complained: 'We have no doctor, no assistance. We haven't seen our families for weeks. It's a terrible injustice, we are not even prisoners; some of us have totally clean records.' Later I played cards with Giacomo Coppola (relation of Frank). 'In Filicudi I was well, I had my family there,' he said. 'We lived in the house of the priest.'

I looked for Gaetano Accardi, who emerged from the sea where he had been swimming all day. Later we sat in his tidy room inside the pink villa where they all lived. He had shaved and changed into a clean shirt (it took him an hour to make himself 'presentable'), and offered me fruit, a rarity at L'Asinara. He had quite a long story to tell:

In '68 they told me that I had to leave Palermo. I was not allowed to go south of Florence, so I started a small engineering business in Turin. Before spending the money to set it up, I asked the local authorities whether I could count on staying there and they assured me I could. But once they give you the mark of mafioso, it's like having the plague. They took me away again to Palermo, saying it would be a formality, without giving me the chance to sell anything. Fortunately my partner was still alive; afterwards he died in a car accident. I was resident in Turin and voted there, but I was tried by a Palermitan court [contrary to the Legal code] and given unjust sentences.

They locked me in prison for forty days and then sent me to banishment at Venaria Reale, near Turin. One night, once again, the *maresciallo* came. He said they wanted to talk to me down in the city. I asked whether I should take a few things with me, he answered that it was unnecessary. They brought me to Messina where I spent five days in the police station, and then to Filicudi. This is nonsense, the sentence says that we are not to meet each other, and here we are, sharing the same house!

Accardi used to be linked to Mancino, Gnoffo and La Barbera in the drug traffic. For one year Angelo La Barbera too had been banished near Turin. In fact the police were beginning to realize that people in banishment continued their links, their traffic, and that most of their telephone calls to their dear mothers asking after their dear families were just a code. Rosario Mancino himself had gone on with his drug traffic dealings from Linosa, under the very eyes of the police!

If hindsight shows that banishment was anything but a solution, and unsafe because it would only really hurt the powerless, much the same can be said of the new special Mafia law introduced in 1965. It decreed that in order to apply the preventative measures (banishment, surveillance, house arrest) there was no need for evidence of guilt; it was enough to state 'a general social danger which could be determined by the personality of the subject or by a specific situation.' This special law gave powers to the police to arrest persons suspected of belonging to or having associations with the Mafia, persons carrying guns without permits, and other infractions of the law. Under these labels almost every Western Sicilian could be put in prison, except for those whose power secured them protection. In Sicilian villages I even came across cases where innocent people had been incriminated because these laws became a weapon for the Mafia itself.

'I would agree that they are dangerous,' a member of the Antimafia Commission told me at the time. 'These laws are left to the discretion of the authorities. In some cases the existing laws turn against us and those who keep a rein on the Mafia activities: those who are behind the curtains, have always escaped. Take Alcamo, for example, a town of twenty thousand inhabitants: thirteen thousand have been in trouble with the law.' In fact I met with strong accusations against the Antimafia Commission, and some even said that it was repeating the Fascist line of punishing 'small fry', leaving those really responsible out of prison.

Signor Marchese, a trade unionist in Palma di Montechiaro (probably the poorest town in Italy: no sanitation, open sewers running through the streets, riddled with trachoma, illiteracy, unemployment, and malnutrition), attacked the Antimafia Commission.

They mostly punish the innocent day labourers, the workers. As long as there is such a government, they can't do otherwise. They should change the special laws, they shouldn't give power to the police. When we have demonstrations and strikes the police, applying that law, takes away our driving licences, pension books; it has become an instrument against us workers.

Signor Scopellitti, a trade unionist from Naro (in the province of Agrigento), said:

Like everything that happens in Italy, the repression against the Mafia turns against the poor. There are more than a hundred people in banishment here; in my way of seeing things, this Commission is not against the Mafia, but against the destitute. They should look for the Mafia where it really is, in the economic centres, in the real-estate industry, in the economic development of a few particular people and in the *regional* government, because the Mafia has become politics.

When the Antimafia Commission arrived in Palermo on 14 January 1964, on an official visit, *L'Ora* published the 'Malausa dossier', which had been kept secret by the Carabinieri. It started one of the greatest Sicilian scandals of the Sixties, and because the resulting investigation called upon all the resources of the Antimafia Commission it will serve to illustrate what the Commission could do, and what (and whom) it was up against.

How *L'Ora* received the document is not known. Based on reports by magistrates and brave witnesses, it read: 'There is a society called VA.LI.GIO. and it is formed by Vassallo, Lima and Gioia.' The dossier was about the illicit building of a large block of flats: Vassallo was the builder and the interested party was Lima, Palermo's mayor. However, Pafundi asked Lapis, the Tributary policeman who was at that stage under the authority of Giovanni Gioia (then undersecretary to the Treasury), to modify the dossier, and Lapis did so. Gioia testified that he himself did not know Vassallo, although the builder was acquainted with his wife. Nor did Gioia know, he said, that the Bank, the Cassa di Risparmio, of which Gioia's father-in-law was President, had given a lot of credit to Vassallo, whose *curriculum vitae* was a cause of concern to the authorities and to the Antimafia Commission.

Vassallo was not strictly a mafioso in the sense that he had never, as far as is known, killed or commissioned murders. He started his life as a messenger boy and cart-pusher, that is, as one of the many destitutes in the poor districts of Palermo. Suddenly, in 1947, he was well-off; he won a contract, in preference to experienced builders, for the plumbing of the city. It was granted by the city's mayor, Giovanni Cusenza, Gioia's father-in-law.

Vassallo went on obtaining contracts against competitors who either faded away at the last moment or were not even considered. Banks always gave him credit, in spite of the fact that in their own dossiers (everybody keeps information dossiers in Italy, from the Carabinieri to large firms) Vassallo was described as a mafioso. In fact, in the Sixties, when the whole of Western Sicily was being 'constructed'—*autostrade*, *superstrade*, blocks of flats—it was impossible to obtain building permits unless one was called Vassallo, Cassina, Moncada or Caruso.*

The Antimafia Commission wrote: 'Vassallo has violated systematically every building permit and regulation.' In a very interesting conversation between Adamoli, a member of the Commission, and Vicari, the head of the Italian police, himself a Sicilian and former head of the Palermo police, Adamoli asked (vol. II, p. 228, 26 Feb. 1969):

* The early Seventies, though, had shocks in store for these men: Cassina, Vassallo and Caruso all had sons kidnapped in mysterious circumstances. And Girolamo Moncada's offices were raided by a Mafia commando which left four corpses on its way (see p. 228).

How is it possible that men in politics, in the administration, in large speculative operations, have never been touched? When it ought to be possible to give the people the sensation of a determined action to fight this phenomenon, how is it that no example can be given, starting from those who are notoriously mafiosi but move in high spheres of politics, building speculation or other activities? Take a concrete case. Among others, we have here a magnificent dossier on Vassallo; if we were to publish it, I'm sure it would be a best-seller: it comes out clearly that Vassallo was counted as a mafioso by important bodies, those same banks who helped him, for example. There is no sector where we haven't encountered him: credit banks, tenders and so on. This character is everywhere in the economic life of Palermo but, strangely, no one worries about who he is and what he does. The fact that his building yards have never been disturbed while those of non-Sicilians have been blown up with dynamite is a counter-proof that this individual enjoys a special position. How is it that no one has ever hit at him?

Salvo Lima had started his career as the organizer of sports and games in the Palermo Christian Democrat party; he was hard-working and energetic, silent and tough. When he was only twenty-eight, he became Borough Surveyor of Palermo; controlling the real estate market of the capital meant controlling the whole situation. It was the Comune, i.e., himself, which recommended the regional development on the north side of the city, La Barbera's area, and indeed both La Barbera brothers, as well as Moncada and Vassallo, were often seen in and out of his office. Lima represented the 'new guard' of the Christian Democrat party, with Gullotti, Gioia, La Loggia, who were taking the place of old notables like Volpe, Restivo and Mattarella. When Gioia was elected MP, Lima became mayor of Palermo (1958) and was confirmed in office in 1960 until 1962. Between Palermo and the Agrigento area, the Fanfani faction had twenty-seven per cent of its national strength.

Lima was re-elected in 1964 and became the provincial secretary of his party. In the first four years after he became mayor, eighty per cent of all building permits went to four people, front-men for La Barbera and Vassallo. Vito Ciancimino was Lima's public-works assessor, the person who handed out the building permits. The Tributary police reported to the Antimafia Commission that Angelo La Barbera helped

Lima to be elected in 1958, and looked after 'the physical protection of his person'. Lima's rule as mayor of Palermo was 'particularly permeable to Mafia penetration'.

In 1967 Lima became Sicilian deputy secretary of the Christian Democrat party. In the general elections of 1968 he was elected in the Palermo, Agrigento, Caltanisetta, Trapani area, with 79,916 preferential votes, ahead of 'notables' like Restivo, Mattarella, Gioia and Volpe, although he had never bothered to make a speech. This success, a Mafia trademark in itself, was publicly remarked upon as scandalous. A Roman magazine commented: 'The success of Signor Lima has deeply wounded public opinion and has created embarrassment and problems for the Christian Democrats.'

In 1970 I went to Palermo, and when I finally found his telephone number (ex-directory) I rang him up at home. He answered himself, and told me that he would expect me the following day at his office. I decided to go early in order to have a good look around. After walking along Palermo's harbour, a mosaic of new buildings and of derelict sites, I arrived at Signor Lima's offices, which were filled with black leather armchairs and slick, elegant, silent young men. While waiting for Lima I thought about what I could ask him. After his split from Gioia and Fanfani, Lima won the control of the Palermo party. The national papers began to talk. *La Stampa* wrote: 'We notice that the real Mafia battles happen in the economic quarters controlled by the new municipality. Struggles between the Palermo gangs for the control of the supermarkets, for illicit buildings, are well known to all. Equally notorious are the struggles for licences to build, indeed for all kinds of licences.' In April 1964 the Antimafia Commission had stressed the need to suspend Lima from his office of Extraordinary Commission for Sicilian Agrarian Reform.

When Lima arrived in his office, dead on time, he was followed by several impeccably dressed young men. Lima, a younger version of Rossano Brazzi, had prematurely grey wavy hair, slightly protruding eyes, a silvery grey suit; he gave me a hard time as an interviewer. Each question of mine was answered by very few words, and he surprised me by striking first: he said that the main problem in Palermo was speculative buildings, some of which were empty although they were let to the regional government. He agreed with the concept that Sicily is used as an Italian colony, exploiting its riches. 'It is a reserve of labour. We need industries, tourism. Mafia?—an exaggeration. In other richer

19. 1967 The first mass Mafia trial, a symptom of public revulsion against a decade of violence
(*Gigi Petyx della Agenzia Scafidi*)

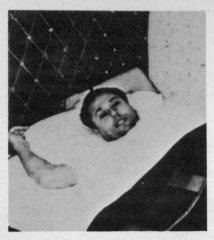

20. 1969 Luciano Liggio, then the most wanted man in Italy, in the hospital of Santissima Annunziata, Taranto

(*Gigi Petyx*)

21. 1971 Pietro Scaglione, Sicily's senior magistrate, a few days before he was shot dead in broad daylight in the centre of Palermo   (*Gigi Petyx*)

22. 1971 Angelo La Barbera and Salvatore Zizzo in *confino* at Linosa   (*Agenzia Scafidi*)

23. 1972 The retrial at Catanzaro: behind the bars, Torretta, Vincenzo Rimi, Vitrano, Philippo Rimi, Badalamenti; foreground (shaking hands), Sirchia, Conforno (with arm outstretched), Calo, Sciarratta (*Gigi Petyx della Agenzia Scafidi*)

24. 1972 The retrial at Catanzaro: the author with Angelo La Barbera (*Gigi Petyx*)

25.   1974 Alberti, the new *capocosca*, under interrogation in the courtroom at Palermo
(*Gigi Petyx della Agenzia Scafidi*)

26.   1974 The women of the new Mafia, Anna Citarda and her daughter Antonietta
(*Gigi Petyx della Agenzia Scafidi*)

27.   1974 Two grandees brought to trial: Mafia boss Frank Coppola (*first on left*) and
Police Chief Mangano   (*Gigi Petyx*)

countries similar phenomena happen. Also the political speculation is exaggerated.' Lima knew what I was up to and played my game. His calm face was only disturbed when I asked him a question which he preferred not to answer (about the split with Gioia). And when he took me to the door, even more polished young men had assembled and all bowed to him, and to me, since I had had the privilege of being alone with him for one hour.

Vito Ciancimino was born in Corleone, Liggio-land, in 1924, He became a protégé of Bernardo Mattarella, who helped both his political and his financial career. In 1950 Ciancimino obtained concessions for all railway transport inside Palermo. The three other firms which had made a bid were put out of the game, since Ciancimino's bid had been accompanied by a letter from Mattarella, who was then Minister of Transport. Ciancimino was not the sole owner of this firm; the other partner was Carmelo La Barba, whose brother was a member of the Liggio *cosca* and finished up in prison. Ciancimino was also a close friend of Canzonieri, the Christian Democrat deputy for Corleone and a supporter of Liggio, who was his 'grand elector'.

Although Ciancimino had been extremely poor, living very modestly, soon after the railway concession he became a rich man, moved house and changed his style of life. A dossier put together by the police (9N 97308/2) was buried in the dusty archives of Chief Public Prosecutor Pietro Scaglione for three years before Scaglione entrusted the Inquiry to a magistrate. In 1959, when Salvo Lima became mayor of Palermo, Ciancimino was given an office in the administration dealing with public works and building permits. That became the peak period of Palermo's atrocious building boom and of warfare among the capital's *cosche* making money in the real-estate business (La Barbera, Torretta, Alberti).

It was also a decade of scandals, and things were coming to public attention since the Antimafia Commission had the power to gather information and publicize its findings. A socialist, Filippo Lentini, started work on an inquiry into public works in Palermo; documents were changed, mismanaged or disappeared from the municipality. Under instruction from cooperative magistrates, indictments, denunciations, accusations, proof against Ciancimino's incredible misconduct, were hidden away in archives. Witnesses retracted, but both the Antimafia Commission and Prefect Bevivino's dossier—an indictment against the Palermo administration which had been shelved by Scaglione—had

scandalous evidence against him. So much so that he was made to withdraw from his official post, retaining the job of Christian Democrat
Commissar of the Comune. His power with the grand electors and within
the party (he belonged, needless to say, to the Fanfani faction) was considerable, especially after his break with Mattarella and after he had found
a new friend in Giovanni Gioia. Gioia needed a man like Ciancimino after
Lima's defection to the Andreotti faction (Lima, it appears, was refused
by Moro).

In 1970, the Christian Democrats advanced Ciancimino's candidature
for the post of mayor of Palermo. In the face of a public scandal, he
was elected with 36 votes against 35: he had the whole Mafia on his side.
The Antimafia Commission called the election 'a provocation which
offended the city of Palermo' and President Cattanei of the Antimafia
attacked him directly.

This episode split the Central Christian Democrat party in Rome:
some were asking that Ciancimino should be dismissed and made to
resign from his new post and that the man 'who at the very least is
indictable of very grave crimes' should be expelled from the party.
But Gioia, and with Gioia, Fanfani, protected Ciancimino.

When the head of the police, Angelo Vicari, went to Palermo, he
declared 'as a private citizen' that he shared the opinion of the Antimafia about Ciancimino. Ciancimino sued the head of the police. (He
lost; Ciancimino also lost a case against *L'Ora*.)

On 7 December, after fifty-six days of office, Ciancimino resigned.
The quarrels and contrasts of interest had taken place, it must be
underlined, not in Sicily, but in Rome. In October 1970 he gave
an interview to an Italian press agency. The following exchanges
occurred:

QUESTION: Does the Mafia exist in Palermo?
CIANCIMINO: One must be clear about what the Mafia is. If an
attempt is made to identify it with the criminal episodes which have
recently happened, it is really a problem of statistics, of murders.
The Mafia is identifiable, I think, with the overbearing bully. It's not
true that the Mafia is only that which kills. The phenomenon existed
before and exists now. The Mafia is a mentality ...
QUESTION: Are there relationships between the Mafia and politics?
CIANCIMINO: On the ground of my personal experience, I shouldn't
say so. It could be that there are ...

QUESTION: And what about the real-estate Mafia, that of building sites?

CIANCIMINO: But what do you mean by the real-estate Mafia? In the five years in which I have been Borough Surveyor I have never felt any pressure from anybody.

After the blowing up of the Alfa Romeo at Ciaculli, a Communist deputy reminded the Sicilian Assembly: 'One can't ignore the fact that the largest part of Socialist and Communist trade unionists have been killed in an area where there have been the largest number of preferential votes for the deputy Canzonieri, lawyer of the *capomafia* and bandit Luciano Liggio.' But Canzonieri's answer in the Regional Assembly was an embarrassment to the Christian Democrats. 'I only know,' he said, 'that Liggio in the past has been accused and unjustly persecuted by the Communists ...' The deputy-president of the Assembly jumped up from his seat and exclaimed: 'How can you defend, here, in this place, Luciano Liggio? You defend a bandit in this Assembly!' Canzonieri meekly answered: 'I believed it was necessary to say this to help the Christian Democrats.'

But the deputy chief of police, Angelo Mangano, had gathered a dossier on Canzonieri from which the judiciaries denounced the M P for murder in 1967. In 1958 a shepherd, Diego Fucarino, had been killed at Prizzi, a village near Corleone (Canzonieri had been mayor of Prizzi). In fact, Mangano's dossier had been completed in 1966 but, as it arrived in the hands of Pietro Scaglione, the Chief Public Prosecutor had kept it for a whole year before giving it in to the magistrates to work on the indictment and prepare the trial. Later, assisted in court by a formidable group of lawyers (Girolamo Bellavista, Giuseppe Sabatini and Giovanni Leone, who had to give up his defence since he had just been elected President of the Italian Republic), Canzonieri was acquitted. His 'partners', the brothers Ramaccia, were also acquitted for 'lack of proof'.

On 6 August 1963, one day before the Mafia laws had been introduced, the *Corriere della Sera* had written:

If the Antimafia Parliamentary Commission will operate with the necessary energy, it will be able to arrive at spectacular, though hardly difficult, conclusions; it will be enough to examine with some attention those preferential votes obtained in some Sicilian areas; to ask why many regional M Ps, who had no following in the party and didn't even bother to hold meetings or make speeches, have gathered two, three, four thousand preferential votes in villages and districts where the 'Notables' are still ruling.

The article concluded by saying: 'The Christian Democratic party is divided into factions and, being always in government, can more easily grant favours.'

By the end of 1964 the Antimafia Commission had all the dossiers from the magistrates of all courts in Sicily, including the report written by Bevivino and the one prepared by Lieutenant Mario Malausa, killed at Ciaculli. Both dealt, as we have seen, with illicit affairs of politicians in collusion with mafiosi. It became clear to the Commission that all sectors of public life had been influenced by the *cosche* and that included all the large State and Regional corporations (*Enti*), like EN I, Montecatini, ERAS, etc. Most Christian Democrat MPs within the Commission were pressed by their party to shelter their colleagues from excessive investigation and public scandal. The same worry spread throughout the political spectrum: all were stained, the Republicans, the Liberals, the Monarchists, the Social Democrats, the Socialists.

These political apprehensions produced pressures on the Commission both from within and without, so that its own history also provides a commentary on the strength of the Mafia's involvement with Italian politics. Senator Cipolla was a Communist Sicilian and part of the Antimafia Commission. He gave me details of documentary evidence which had disappeared or was not made available even to the Antimafia Commission. He also told me about some people who were 'too keen' in the investigations and were given other jobs. Cipolla criticized:

This Commission should have had the effect of encouraging the citizen, to give him the sense that the Mafia was no longer protected by the State. The Sicilian has not so much fear of the Mafia, but of the impunity which is its strength. The lack of trust in the State is more than logical: Mafia people easily obtain passports and have permits to carry arms. On the other hand, one can't say that there haven't been any effects. While, before, the political men looked to the Mafia for support, now this has become impossible.

The Communists were unique in not having had collusion with the mafiosi because their very existence depended on fighting that Sicilian bourgeoisie as represented by the *cosche*. Whenever there had been a

Communist who had been involved, the party had got rid of him. On the other hand, the Communist party had made a great political mistake in allowing and promoting the Milazzo Sicilian government, during which period the *cosche mafiose* had had a field day. The Communists' aim was to demonstrate that the Christian Democrat party could be overruled and that a different coalition, which included the Communists, could rule democratically. The idea came from Emanuele Macaluso, the Sicilian Secretary of the party, a very bright man, who had too large a dose of the Sicilian sense of intrigue to be a Communist politician. He also made a great mistake in persuading one of the few honest Sicilian magistrates, Cesare Terranova, to abandon the magistrature for Parliament: it was a great loss for Sicily, and no gain for Parliament.

The Communist Senator Li Causi once said to the Antimafia Commission: 'I here declare, with full responsibility, in front of this Commission, that if we look at the Christian Democrat list of Western Sicilian candidates we can see that it is a concentration of the Mafia.' But he also told me: 'It is an historical process that is now irreversible; for the first time in the history of our country, Parliament itself works towards the solution of the problem.' He went on to explain:

Of course the Mafia has changed; the old sources of wealth, the rackets of cattle-stealing, water control are no longer so lucrative. Real-estate speculation, banks, the trading of jobs and collusion with power of the State: these are the Mafia's new fields. The Mafia goes where there is power, that is why the Christian Democrat party is riddled with it, not only on a regional level. The high protectors, the ones elected through the power of the Mafia, are in Rome.

In the late Sixties collusion between Mafia and politics became so evident to the public that Rumor, who was then Secretary General of his party, asked Senator Verzotto (!) to inquire into the links between their party and the Mafia. But Verzotto had to protect his grand electors and did not even consider Di Cristina as 'in March 1964 he no longer belonged to the party, because he hadn't renewed his party card.' Verzotto, a Northerner, had quickly learnt the Sicilian cunning: in fact Di Cristina had not been expelled from the party, but had simply been unable to renew his party membership, since he was in banishment.

When Di Cristina came back from *confino* he had no job, the necessary cover-up for his operations. 'Grimly notorious for the many incidents which happened in the province of Agrigento and for having spread his Mafia activities even to Gela', Di Cristina operated in transport, prostitution, sub-contracting jobs, maintenance of roads, car parking, smuggling in cigarettes and drugs. But his deputies owed him a job; so, with a personal recommendation from the Republican MP Gunnella, Di Cristina became the treasurer of the SO.CHI.MI.SI., a Regional Corporation presided over by Verzotto himself. When the Antimafia Commission considered this case, it decided that giving the job to Di Cristina was such a serious act of misconduct that it ordered that the contract should be withdrawn.*

In 1966 Pafundi declared to the press: 'These rooms here are like an ammunition store. In order to give us the chance to go to the very root of the truth we don't want them to explode too soon. We have here a load of dynamite.' But the ammunition store never exploded, and in March 1968 Senator Pafundi summed up to Parliament the efforts of the Commission in three discreet pages. All the documents (1759 on single individuals, 200 on local governments, 24 on public bodies) which had come from the Sicilian Carabinieri, police, Magistrature, and from especially conducted research were locked away.

Pafundi was an elderly Neapolitan and he had become scared at the evidence he was collecting. He told me: 'My dear lady, if I only could talk ... I'd better be silent. I wanted to, but couldn't ... but much was achieved by the special laws we passed sending people to prison, to banishment [exile under surveillance]. The rest will happen through progress and evolution. More than this, I really cannot tell you; but for the prestige of our country, don't go on about these things.'

The man who in 1968 took over the presidency of the Commission after Pafundi was a young Genoese Christian Democrat deputy, Cattanei, a very different man. With a strong sense of uprightness, Cattanei soon grasped the situation and was determined to publish, to denounce, to change, 'to cut off old branches' as he put it to me— branches which had to be lopped from the tree of his own party.

When it became clear that he was not as amenable, or as nervous, as Pafundi, he came under attack from his fellow Christian Democrats. The party's official newspaper, *Il Popolo*, stated that the Antimafia

* This case was first exposed and studied by one of *L'Ora*'s journalists, De Mauro, a man who was to pay dearly for too close a knowledge of some particular Mafia dealings. On 16 September 1970 De Mauro was kidnapped and disappeared forever. His body might easily be inside one of those columns of cement which grace the new city of Palermo. (See p. 261.)

Commission had become an instrument of the Communists. That is, Cattanei should have 'protected' men like Ciancimino for the sole reason that the accused belonged to the same party.

Gossip spread that Cattanei was going to resign. The President of the Antimafia Commission gave an interview to *La Stampa* (December 1970) stating: 'Strangely, a month ago at Genoa, there were individuals who were looking for details of my private life, what I was doing at home, if I had a mistress ...' Everything was tried to get rid of Cattanei and to smear his exceptionally clean reputation, in a thoroughly mafioso way. But the Christian Democrats could not adopt the Mafia solution, and get rid of Cattanei by killing him. In fact, supported by the majority of the Commission and by public opinion he did not resign, in spite of the pressure.

I saw Cattanei in the Antimafia offices, on the top floor of the Italian Parliament building. 'Our objective is to strike at the roots,' he told me. 'In one year we have done a lot. In a month's time we shall give Parliament the first report of our Inquiry and, in one year's time not only will there be an ample report, but all the documents we have here will become public.' I asked Cattanei if he was in a position to hit out, if necessary, at political personalities. 'If the President has proof, he can proceed against anybody.' Did Cattanei think that the Christian Democrat party could risk a thorough inquiry? 'What is needed is courage. It can be done. If it is true that some leaders of the Christian Democrat party are compromised (but this must be verified), the party has everything to gain in prestige by pruning dry branches and erasing the opinion that the whole party is involved. There is, among our young people in Sicily and here, the desire to break with the past.' And what would happen, I asked, if after his reports nothing was to happen? 'I would say, then, that it is no longer the President's fault, but the State's. I should say that, in that case, the State today is not able to take active action against the Mafia.'

That is exactly what happened. 'The Mafia goes with power,' Cattanei told me. 'That is why they say that there is the phenomenon of collusion between the Mafia and the Christian Democrats, but I think that this happens mainly in Sicily and it is difficult to distinguish between organized delinquency and the Mafia. Fear, unwillingness to denounce, is certainly due to the lack of trust that the citizen has in the protection of the State.'

President Cattanei told me that he was going to propose new laws:

confiscation of property acquired through Mafia activities and strong measures against reticent witnesses. That, of course, would have been, and is, the only measure: to fight the essence of the neo-capitalist Mafia; means hitting at its economic roots, the very basis of its existence. There was already a great deal of criticism of the Commission, although the Mafia activities were now better understood, but little was done by the Government. In 1965 Italy was enjoying its short-lived 'boom', but Sicily at the same time had a lower percentage of people employed in industry than fifteen years earlier, despite the injection of new capital. In the Palermo slums, food cost more than in Northern Italy; even oranges which were produced in Sicilian orchards round the corner. On the other hand, on the Eastern side industrialization began to prosper, and Northern industrialists were not afraid to invest in that part of the island where the Mafia did not take cuts.

Between 1960 and 1970, eleven per cent of the population of Southern Italy emigrated. Between 1955 and 1961, 551,000 Sicilians left, and from 1961 to 1971 another 400,000. Details are not precise: about 250,000 are divided between Milan and Turin; the same amount are in Germany. Almost 50,000 are in France; more than 100,000 in Switzerland; the others are dispersed between Belgium, Australia and the United States. Some of them learnt a new way of life, saw that there was no need to bow to the mafioso, to the priest, to the police. But others carried the Mafia seed with them: the phenomenon spread with them.

The great hopes of exposing the Mafia and wiping 'it' out through the new weapon of the Commission were fading. In 1969, Vittorio Nisticò, editor of *L'Ora*, put it to me in a conversation:

The Mafia today is not comparable to what it was ten years ago. Its new aim is to be able to control from an invisible chair. What I mean is that after the establishment of the Antimafia Commission, many have been punished, but the political names, materially linked with the Mafia, remain untouched. The Antimafia's action has been abstract, and if it continues to be conducted in the way it is at present, it does not promise well for the future. There are forces within the Commission that are there to prevent the inquiry from moving towards the political field, which is now the centre of the Mafia. The Christian Democrat party would need courage to allow the truth to come out, because the power of the party here in Sicily is based on the strength of votes that the Mafia has and can procure. The mere existence of the Commission has been a thorn in the flesh of the Mafia, but this is a body designed to disturb, to contain, not to destroy. The Mafia moves where there is money. For example there is new growth around the huge arrival of funds for the reconstruction of the areas destroyed by last year's earthquake. Of course drugs and cigarettes remain a solid field, and the Mafia controls the hiring of men in factories and shipbuilding yards. Organization among the workers is the greatest enemy of the Mafia, but this is still weak, because industrialization is scarce.

Emanuele Macaluso, then leader of the Sicilian PCI, went further:

You see? They've put Gullotti in the Commission with a very precise objective: to prevent the inquiry going too far. Everybody knows that without the political protection the Mafia couldn't act. But it's no good putting in prison people who have minor responsibilities. A real break would be huge: Rumor, Fanfani, had positions from which they could not avoid knowing what was happening. They carry heavy burdens of guilt, not to have done anything to renew their Sicilian political staff.

It is in fact true that various Sicilian Christian Democrat MPs, some even implicated like Matta (his arrival in the Antimafia Commission created a scandal and eventually he had to resign), were introduced within the Commission to stop the inquiry moving too far into the political field.

In its first publication in July 1971, the Antimafia Commission published a group of biographies, exemplary of today's Mafia. It summarized the characteristics of the Mafia:

1. Ruthless elimination of 'awkward' rivals through commissioned murders.
2. Use of threats and intimidation in order to obtain what was wanted.
3. Formal and false respect for authority.
4. Ability to obtain favours and illegal measures whenever they are useful.
5. Continuous and compromising help to the political authorities.
6. Non-proven verdicts.
7. Relationships with people who are able to provide information and collusive administrative concessions.
8. Enrichment achieved by any means.

The volume contained grave words for the authorities. Many real criminals like Di Carlo and Navarra, the Antimafia Commission observed, had clean criminal records. A judge from Trapani stressed the meagre protection that the police were able to give those prepared to testify against the mafiosi. Regular acquittals of prominent mafiosi, even when there had been witnesses against them, scared people into silence— it was not really a question of *omertà*. Every sort of criminal seemed to be able to obtain favours from the Sicilian police, getting passports which should have been impossible for them to retain or renew,* permits to carry arms (ditto), renewals of driving permits (ditto). The Antimafia Commission reported on the weakness or even absence of the State; in the regional corporation and administration, the sons and relatives of the bosses had found easy employment.

'The real-estate speculation in Palermo is not only social robbery, as in other cities', the Commission stressed. 'It has grown inside the frame of Mafia warfare and left behind scores of bodies. Credit concessions from banks to notorious mafiosi have been used to finance, directly or indirectly, illicit trade and traffic with frightening social cost for society as a whole.' The disease could not be solely attributed to the Sicilian environment; behind the concession of a passport to a drug-trafficker, the untruthful reports, the acquittals, 'there is not only the inefficiency of the State and its institutions; there are also crimes and responsibilities which it is our duty to denounce and which other bodies must follow in denouncing and condemning.'

The other institutions (government, police forces, magistrature) did not pursue and denounce. The first volume made fascinating reading, yet very few read the huge grey Parliamentarian volumes which were, in principle, available to all, but were difficult to obtain.

In its later publication (March 1972), the Antimafia Commission stated in its introduction (p. 69, Vol. II): 'Generally speaking magistrates, trade unionists, prefects, journalists and the police authorities expressed an affirmative judgment on the existence of more or less intimate links between Mafia and the public authorities ... some trade

---

* In 1961, when Angelo La Barbera's killer, Tommaso Buscetta, needed a passport, he asked the Questore of the Police, Jacovacci. On the same day a letter had come from Francesco Barbaccia, deputy for the Christian Democrat party: '*Gentilissimo Signor dottore Jacovacci*, I beg you to allow the renewal of a passport to Signor Tommaso Buscetta, a person in whom I am very interested. Being sure that you will comply, I thank and greet you cordially.'

unionists reached the point of saying that "the mafioso is a man of politics".' Naturally there were efforts to try to explain this phenomenon.

The Commander of the Carabinieri in Palermo said: 'The question is essentially an electoral one; given the electoral system I ask myself who on earth can refuse the possibility of obtaining votes. Anyone, even in today's Sicily, who was to take an absolutely anti-Mafia attitude in all likelihood could not obtain any electoral successes.'

One volume, under the title *Relazione sui rapporti tra mafia e banditismo in Sicilia (Report on the relations between the Mafia and banditism in Sicily*, 776 pp., 1971), contained testimonies from all those involved in the 'Giuliano affair'. (In fact, mafiosi like Rimi and Coppola were not interrogated.) It was a very interesting report which left no doubt as to the heavy responsibility that the authorities and some politicians carried for the sad events of Separatist and post-Separatist Sicily. Before the publication of this volume many facts which I have stated in my chapter about Giuliano could not have been revealed, and many others were not known.

Another volume was published in March 1972 under the title *Relazione sui lavori svolti e sullo stato del fenomeno mafioso al termine della V legislature (Report on the state of the Mafia phenomenon at the end of the Fifth legislatura*, 1,262 pages). The Cattanei commission could not complete its work because a general election was called, and many were overjoyed to see the departure of Cattanei. This was a much more delicate volume to compile: some names were skipped, points explained with too many hazy words. Perhaps this criticism can be applied to all Italian official documents: they tend to suffer from the fear of stating something clearly in black and white, so that everything is drowned in a river of words. However, there is interesting information not only in its preliminary text but in the testimonies of many of those who had been interrogated by the Commission (unfortunately the 'conversation' with Scaglione was not printed).

The Commission's main conclusion was that the Mafia was strong because it had penetrated the structure of the State; and not only in Sicily. In many sections the Commission examined the strength of the Mafia in Milan, in Rome—'It is certain that the Mafia has operated in organized forms and with its own men in the territory of Lazlio' (the region around Rome). At times the Magistrature had been of little help: telephone conversations tapped by the police reached the Commission on tapes which had clearly been doctored. 'No one forgets the example of intelligent and brave acts and no one can minimize the difficulties under which the police operate; but this does not detract from the fact that many episodes demonstrate dangerous weaknesses and inadmissible malfunctioning.'

The Commission stated:

> With its extraordinary flexibility, the Mafia has always known how to survive and how to prosper even in surroundings different from those which gave it its origin; it succeeded in doing so as it always asserted itself as a body of autonomous extralegal power and by seeking close links with all forms of power, and in particular with public power, in order to operate within them, to manipulate them to obtain its ends or to penetrate within those structures.

When the volumes were given to Parliament, newspapers published articles for a couple of days, the tone being denigratory of the work of the Commission. One Sicilian newspaper published a comment on its front page under the title 'The Mafia gives thanks', meaning, of course, that nothing of what had been written was a real threat to the *cosche*. The Palermitan *L'Ora* was the only newspaper to reprint great chunks from the volumes.

In its conclusions, the Antimafia Commission made many recommendations and offered much advice to those bodies who were going to take the job on. It criticized some authorities, condemned others. But nothing was done by the government which had promoted the investigation. When the volumes were published, every effort was made to confuse their message and diminish their value, and the work of the Commission was drowned in a sea of slander. Criticism, naturally enough, came from the extreme Right, from the Christian Democrats, from the Mafia (prompt to dismiss it all by saying that it was all inaccurate and misleading). But the Commission was also heavily criticized by the Left, which should instead have prompted it and drawn people's attention to the fact that, in spite of the many interferences, it had worked honestly. Very few read the volumes; they were very long, but they had some extraordinary pages.

Similar difficulties confronted the new Antimafia Commission when they closed down in January 1976. The time came when such a mass of documentation had been amassed that the thirty members of the Commission and its President, Senator Luigi Carraro, decided to call a halt. It was useless to go on acquiring further reports, when a conclusion—the reason for which the Commission had been formed—could be drawn from the thousands of papers which had come into their possession. The Antimafia Commission presented its 'political essay' to Parliament (in March 1976) which was to translate its suggestions into law. The final document consists of three parts: the most important—the one dealing with 'What's to be done'—was approved by the whole Commission (with the exception of the Neo-Fascists). 'Although the Mafia has lost its former prestige with the Sicilian population,' the document says, 'it still thrives and has transformed itself, as is its custom, keeping pace with developments in society at large.' It has implanted its roots in the Northern regions of Italy and penetrated the banking and credit business, the tax-collecting firms (*esattorie*), the wholesale markets and is active in the 'web of unrevealable relations that the Mafia continues to keep with public institutions'.

The Commission proposes the development of the economic structure of the island, the completion of its progress towards genuine political autonomy, the abolition of some of the repressive measures (such as random banishment to different parts of Italy which only resulted in the spreading of the phenomenon, and the confiscation of any wealth which has been acquired by illicit means. It also suggests that a permanent Parliamentary commission should be created 'in order to keep a watchful eye' and to see that laws are implemented.

The other part, which deals with 'Whose fault has it been?', found the Commission divided. The eight Communist members and one independent (Terranova, the former magistrate) produced their own minority report where, as Pio La Torre, the Communist MP from Palermo (and a member of the Commission) specified: 'we mention names. When we say that, for example, Minister Giovanni Gioia is responsible for the political penetration of the Mafia, we think we have proved it.' The minority group (9 out of 31) had to give in on some points in order to be able to present the conclusions which were voted unanimously. ('*We* wrote them,' La Torre said.) President Carraro vetoed the publication of documents and police reports based on hearsay. 'We could not use those reports where police and carabinieri describe facts which they have gathered from *vox populi*. Other "biographies" of characters like Vassallo and Ciancimino have never been concluded, nor have some important enquiries on the *esattorie* and credit institutions,' La Torre added. 'But in 40 pages we develop the history of the links between Mafia and public power in Sicily, what it is, what it has been and why it has not been eliminated.' The majority of the Antimafia Commission instead handed to both Chambers—and to the nation—a document which frankly shows the weaknesses and the lack of courage in denouncing links which all parties have kept with the Mafia, the traditional procurer of votes. But the minority group obtained the gradual publication of all the documents in the Antimafia files, except for those—and they are many—which are based on hearsay and will be buried forever in the archives of the Senate.

I asked La Torre, himself a Sicilian who played a leading role in the confrontation between the Mafia and the peasantry, to summarize for us the work of the last Antimafia Commission. 'The former Commission [under the Presidency of Cattanei] had shown courage: we found an immense number of reports. It was not true that police and carabinieri had sent them spontaneously; they had been asked to make enquiries. When Cattanei had to come to some conclusions a whole year earlier than had been anticipated because the government had fallen many breathed sighs of relief. Our term began very badly, the Christian Democrats were determined not to repeat the mistake they had made with Cattanei. It was a provocation to put a certain MP on the Commission: a man who was the object of enquiries was meant to become an inquisitor. I had to read out to him—in front of the whole embarrassed Commission—all the documents we had on him. I can't describe to you the atmosphere—and the silence! We had to resign—all of us—in order to force him out, but eventually it was a victory. We completed a lot of investigations, on the Mangano-Coppola-Rimi links, the industry of kidnappings and Liggio, the Region of Lazio and Rimi, the real-estate speculations in the Turin-Bardonecchia regions. We completed the enquiry on the hot subject of the Mafia in the industrial triangle and in the capital. We closed the Antimafia Commission because there were not the right conditions for carrying on our work, the political climate does not allow it. But the material we had was enough to enable us to come to important conclusions.'

Although the predictable comments have coloured the front pages of many newspapers—'The State Gives Up' 'Nothing Has Been Done'— the usual attempts to discredit and devalue the work of thirteen years, the Antimafia Commission has achieved a great deal. If its suggestions can be implemented, an enormous step will have been taken towards the annihilation of a criminal phenomenon.

14 The 'High Mafia' and the big trials of the Seventies

On a recent visit to Palermo, I rang up a certain gentleman and asked him whether we could meet. He told me that he was very busy, but ... what was I doing in Palermo anyway? I was there on holiday, on no particular assignment, I answered—which was true. It was a perfect winter weekend, Palermo was warm, the sky bright blue, no coat was needed for walking by the sea at Mondello to eat sea urchins and indigestible pastries. I suggested that he might come to have tea at the Hotel des Palmes, where I was staying. When I had told a few friends that I was going to try to meet him, they had all agreed that he was unlikely to accept. He didn't really like to see people and smelt a rat a mile away, even on the telephone (and even if the rat wasn't there).

When the hotel porter rang to say that my guest had arrived, he was so taken aback to see the man on the other side of the desk that he stuttered and couldn't enunciate either his or my name. He was, of course, very punctual. He kissed my hand; he was very glad to see me again, he said. He was well dressed in a beautifully-cut grey suit with waistcoat. I led him to one of those large drawing-rooms which must once have been the Inghams' ballroom, passing by a bust of Wagner (who composed part of *Parsifal* at the Hotel des Palmes) and a Directoire statue, Canova in style and erotic in message. We talked about England, about the Italian political situation, even about the wonderful weather. But, getting bolder, I started voicing the reason for which I had asked to see him. I was writing a book about the Mafia, I told him, about its historic roots, its development, its purpose and burden on the country.

Pretending not to register the suspicious look which for a second shaded his otherwise impassive blue eyes, I went on telling *him* what I thought that the Mafia was: that in the course of my work I had come to

221

some perhaps controversial conclusions; that the Mafia was not an
organization in the real sense of the word, but a way of thinking (scholars
like Hesse and Sciascia had already said it anyway), and that the nature
of the organization lay only at the level of the *cosca*; that the Mafia filled a
social gap, that of the middle class which in Sicily had scarcely existed;
that the Mafia was not a product of the nineteenth century and of the
introduction of a Piedmontese system on top of an underdeveloped,
feudal society, but similar anomalies could be observed earlier in the
island's history; that the Mafia in Sicily was the normal and accepted
power, and not an alternative to it—for which reason the anomalies
were those people outside it who did not conform.

My guest concurred. Talking about the historic roots of the Mafia,
he pointed out, that Eastern Sicily, which had been Greek and later
Byzantine, had fought against the Arabs (and been cruelly treated by
them) but did not absorb the Mafia mentality—in other words, it did
not absorb the Arabs. Western Sicily, on the contrary, had passed from
Punic into Roman hands, and later had gladly welcomed the Arab
occupation, which enriched Western Sicily with new agricultural
techniques, culture, language and customs, but also gave a new twist to
the mentality. The Mafia, he said, permeated the social strata which,
although functional and productive, lacked the coordination of a power
structure. There was a 'power vacuum', so a substitute had to be found
for the State.

One had to establish, he stressed, *when* the power vacuum began and
when the forces of production started to need a kind of organization.
The Mafia, he said, *is* an organization: there are no effective written
laws, but a code of behaviour which must be respected. Therefore, he
added, one can in fact talk about 'an organization'. Of course I did not
agree with the concept that the Mafia was the outcome of the needs of
the productive strata—on the contrary, its very essence is exploitative,
its role that of an unnecessary broker between capital and labour—but I
did not say that to my guest as I was more interested in his thoughts
than in a debate. To talk with him was, in fact, like sounding out the
Queen of England on the subject of the British monarchy. My guest
would often interrupt our conversation by saying that he really did not
understand why I was asking him that kind of question. In the nicest
possible way he stressed that I should '*registrare non indagare*'—record,
not investigate.

I asked him about the Salvo family (see Chapter 10). He had heard rumours about them, he said, but had I thought what was the base of that family's power? Had I really thought of the source? Who had given the Salvos the privilege of being the only tax collectors in that part of Sicily? Had I looked up Deputy X from Messina? Somebody who could help me, he then told me, was another deputy, Y, who lived in Rome and had written a piece on the early developments of the Mafia. (He mentioned the name of a notorious Sicilian deputy, connected with several *cosche*; he certainly was not mentioning the man for his intellectual gifts, nor did he mean that I should really read his piece. I could have looked him up with that excuse, he added.)

I asked him about Verzotto, President of the Ente Minerario Siciliano since 1968. It has recently emerged that Verzotto was also involved in some shady dealings with the Sicilian financier Sindona. I knew, I told him, that they were friends, but the fact that Verzotto seemed to be implicated with so many notorious names and belonged to the last decades of Sicilian history, of the darkest side of it, made one think that Verzotto was what was called 'High Mafia'. To my surprise, my guest talked about the Christian Democrat Verzotto who had been Mattei's man in Sicily. I should go and see him, he suggested, next time I came to Sicily. He played down Verzotto's Mafia role; anybody in Verzotto's position, he said, had to mix with the important mafiosi who provided votes and MPs. The only difficulty was that he, like so many other politicians, could not say so in as many words. In short, Verzotto was doing what every politician had always done on the island. An odd sort of man, my guest remarked, who tried to trick everybody (I knew that he had even tried to trick *him*, and had failed).

Suddenly he told me an odd little story, the kind of story American tourists are told when they ask about the Mafia. Telling it to me, he was trying to say something else. I thought about it later, wondering what the message was supposed to be. In a beautiful village on the coast—did I know Castellammare? (Oh yes, so beautiful!)—a foreign lady had bought a little boat which she used for going out to sea and for sunbathing. One day she looked out of her hotel window and didn't see her little boat: it had been stolen. So she went and talked to the important man of the place. On the following day, when she woke up and looked out from her window, she saw her little boat in exactly the same place as before. The foreign lady sought out the important man in order to thank him, and asked him how he had actually done it. To which he answered that he was pleased to be thanked, but 'Don't ask me how: the boat is there.'

Well, a parable. Perhaps it was just to stress the *'registrare e non indagare'* concept. When my guest talked about today's Mafia, he was disparaging. It was like listening to some elderly men complaining about the young of today: 'You see, these days there is a massacre. Once they only killed for betrayal, today they shoot for economic reasons, to make more room for others; that's gangsterism, it's no longer Mafia, there is no code of honour. They kill and kill: have you seen this last month? An *ecatombe*: every day there is a new murder.'

My guest was one of those men, who, as Anton Blok puts it so well:

> ... provided the main effective organizational framework that covered the middle ground between the local and national levels ... They controlled the land whose owners lived elsewhere; they dominated the markets and auctions; they alone were able to grant effective production in the countryside; and they 'fixed' elections. Characteristically, however, mafiosi often exercised those functions of brokerage without seeking formal office themselves. In this connection it has been argued that the power and the flexibility of brokers or middlemen can often be maximized by acting informally.

In this passage Blok was describing the role of the countryside mafiosi, the *gabelloti*; but one can see how that pattern has been transferred into the *Enti*, the administration, the State corporations, the private industries which have been given *in gabella* by the new absentee landlords (in this instance the State, the Northern industrialists, the politicians.) One can say that Di Cristina was Senator Verzotto's *manutengolo* in the large estate he controlled. (I am taking Verzotto's case as a prime example out of the many discussed in these chapters.) On the other hand Verzotto added other functions to those of the old absentee landowner (although the role of the preserver of the status quo is the same and so is the need for a stratum which can control and repress demands for reforms). The new absentee landlord plays a more important and active role; he links, he makes and unmakes, he enjoys power. In fact the Mafia can involve non-Sicilians (like Verzotto) who find themselves in the same social conditions and assume the same behaviour: in order to achieve success, they adopt mafioso methods. Industrialists elsewhere used similar methods, and their *gabelloti* employed a different non-physical, kind of violence. A power structure was built through debate, agreements, rather than by the fixing of votes and by conspiratorial means.

My guest defined Senator Verzotto as a person of peasant extraction, and therefore as one who, having achieved power and luxury from total poverty, was particularly keen to cling on to them. On the contrary, my guest was a man of middle-class extraction who seemed to have emerged holding power. Unlike Verzotto, his name has never been connected with criminals and mafiosi. Surprisingly, he was quite open with me about the fact that during the war he had been in Algeria with the Allied forces, thus confirming what had been an open secret for long, that he had been working for British Intelligence. That is probably how he arrived so soon at a position of great unofficial power. Legitimate power? In Sicily, yes.

His sort of power could be related to that of the head of a multinational trust like ITT, a network with so many outlets that it can always escape. *Cosche* and gangsters eliminating each other were a nuisance and drew too much attention; it was a sign of things getting out of control. It was particularly revealing to see how my guest tried to shift continual responsibility on to deputies, political men, rather than on to figures like the Salvos or Verzotto (or like himself), so that the criminal Mafia should appear as an entity led by and made by politicians.

In February 1975 Verzotto's misconduct in bank dealings became public and he had to resign from EMS. Soon afterwards he was the victim of a mysterious attempt on his life; he was badly wounded and his briefcase was stolen. But probably the theft of some papers from his briefcase—which was found later—was a cover-up for the intent of eliminating the person of Verzotto himself. I think that there might have been two conflicting interests: Di Cristina's *cosca* was interested in killing him. Other powers, mainly the man with whom I had tea (and who had advised me to go and see the 'boss' of Syracusa, pointing towards him as an important figure in the Mafia), saw an enemy in Verzotto who was trying to stretch his power too far, invading banking fields which 'belonged' elsewhere, to even higher spheres. The two former friends and associates had become enemies and the best operation was to eliminate Verzotto politically. Papers and details about Verzotto's misconduct were released, he was indicted for fraud in dealing with public funds and 24 hours before being arrested fled to Beirut. Whence, in June 1975, he called for a press conference, asking some Italian journalists to go and see him. But his voice has been effectively silenced: who cares nowadays about a discredited politician?

And it is unlikely that Verzotto will ever disclose important information; it would all point against him.

So Verzotto too is out of the game. Gone are the days when he used to travel about with his private aeroplane, when he could operate and use the *cosche*, when Di Cristina used to call him *compare*. But he will leave a monument to his memory: Syracuse, a city which only fifteen years ago was a gem, is now strangled by oil refineries which surround from all sides (and employ only a handful of men). Real-estate development has been, if possible, even more brutal than in Palermo and while the old city has been left deserted to crumble, a new monster has erased many sights which once made the city famous.

Of course he had been right to complain about the Seventies. In getting out of control, the *cosche* were reflecting the social changes taking place in Western society: overcrowding, a desire of the 'small' man to take an immediate part in the consumer society, a disenchantment with, and a critical attitude towards, any leadership. In the early Seventies we find the *cosche* in the North well-organized after having smelt the rich new fields during the *confino*. The 'new' Northern *cosche* were in communication with each other. The Sicilians bought farmhouses which had been abandoned by the Piedmontese and Lombard farmers, and operated from places where police and civic control was sparse. The traditional rackets they worked included that of kidnapping, in which the Mafia and banditism had centuries-old skill.

The new mafioso became more of a gangster. Rising from the bottom and short-cutting the years of apprenticeship, he did not acquire the Mafia code. There was no time to rehearse the various experiences of underlings, of *campiere*, no time to go through the Cascioferro or even the Greco routine. These men wanted everything at once and they made room for the next generation by murder. But for this reason political protection could not be as open as it had been earlier. Public opinion was by then well aware of the involvement of politicians, patronage, the exchange of votes for favours. For example, after the murder of the Chief Public Prosecutor of the Republic, Judge Pietro Scaglione, all the big Mafia bosses who had been operating quietly *al confino* were banished to remote islands (Linosa, Asinara) in order to allay public opinion.

In 1974, the different factions of the Christian Democrat party could be broken down as follows:

		Deputies	Leaders
Iniziativa Popolare (also called Dorotei)	34·2%	70	Rumor Piccoli
Nuove Cronache (Fanfaniani)	19·8%	50	Fanfani Gioia Forlani
Impegno Democratico	16·5%	38	Andreotti Colombo
Base	10·8%	20	De Mita Granelli
Forze Nuove	10%	18	Donat Cattin
Morotei	8·7%	15	Moro

The new development in Sicilian politics was that after Lima's defection from Fanfaniani and merging with the Andreotti group, Gioia and Lima 'made it up' again and formed a new powerful Sicilian alliance of Christian Democrats between the Fanfaniani and Impegno Democratico.

There were important Mafia trials in the first years of the Seventies, and although they were inconclusive the blame should be put mostly on the complexities of Italian law, on the lack of competence of some judges and public prosecutors and on the reluctance of more experienced judges to handle difficult Mafia trials rather than on corruption and *omertà*. But both police and Carabinieri seemed to be freer from political interference and started gathering evidence against previously untouchable people. The indictments also followed a tougher line; there were more witnesses for the prosecution, more notorious faces on trial. As a younger generation of judges and magistrates emerged, especially outside Sicily, the law seemed to work more efficiently.

Newspapers like *L'Ora* and *Il Paese Sera*, which had always been sued by 'big names' and had always been convicted, began to be acquitted. Personalities who had often been connected with mafiosi and always won lawsuits, began to lose their cases. Minister Gioia (who had always sued and won) lost twice against *L'Ora* and had to pay costs. He also lost a lawsuit against the former Deputy Chairman of the Antimafia Commission, Girolamo Li Causi. So did the former Mayor of Palermo, Vito Ciancimino, and the lawyer Girolamo Bellavista. The heirs of Judge Scaglione also sued *L'Ora*, which had described Scaglione's involvement with mafiosi. The trial took place in Genoa and the defence made a successful request that the Antimafia papers and several secret dispatches from the Carabinieri should be made available at the trial. Again *L'Ora* was acquitted. So, although the Antimafia Parliamentary Commission was dozing, a section of those institutions which had previously been asleep was waking up.

After the 1968 Catanzaro trial (against La Barbera and his gang) there was the appeal in 1973—ninety-two accused (among them Angelo La Barbera, Torretta, Tommaso Buscetta, Gerlando Alberti) indicted for thirty-five murders, two massacres, ten kidnappings; there were also two witnesses who retracted. There was the Via Lazio trial, the trial of the new Mafia (called 'of the 114'), the trial of Di Cristina and the notorious Riesi and Ravanusa *cosche*. I remember that at one of the last big Mafia trials a colleague from *L'Ora* told me: 'Now all those in the dock are new faces for you, not your old friends; you must approach them differently. These are more skilled, they know that journalists like us know everything and they are quite rude, none of that old gentility.'

The era of total disorder among the *cosche* was marked by the 'Via Lazio case', whose story reads like an American film and characterizes the developing gangsterism of the new *cosche*. On 10 December 1969, at seven in the evening, Palermo was busy as ever; the girls had come out for their evening stroll, the rush hour was at its most chaotic. Suddenly there was a burst of gunfire. In an office in Via Lazio, one hundred and eight bullets had been fired and four men were dead: Michele Cavatajo, a forty-six year old Mafia property boss, his friends Tumminello, Domè and Bevilacqua lay in a pool of blood on the floor of the office of the real estate developer Girolamo Moncada, an old friend of Angelo La Barbera. Via Lazio is a modern street in the smart new Northern area of Palermo, and a 'good' private and commercial address. The building of this ugly new district had involved the La Barbera brothers in the struggle for the appropriation of the new city; one of their front men had been Moncada, who had been passed on to the La Barbera 'heirs'. They were tough, ruthless bullies; the protagonists of this story had been acquitted from the first Catanzaro trial. Where the law had failed to condemn them, the other Sicilian 'justice' had succeeded.

On that evening Moncada's two sons Filippo and Angelo had just left their car outside their father's office when several 'policemen' arrived and hustled both boys inside the building with them. Cavatajo was sitting at Moncada's desk. As the 'policemen' walked in he recognized them, grabbed his gun from his desk and fired at the first, who died immediately. A desperate gun battle followed. The two Moncada boys ran for their lives and hid, one under the desk, the other in a small backroom. Both were badly wounded. Filippo Moncada heard somebody shout 'Kill that man!' and as Cavatajo dropped to the floor the fake policemen fled, taking with them a dying companion whom they threw into the boot of one of their cars. 108 bullets had been fired. The 'policemen' boarded two gleaming Alfa Romeos and disappeared through the dense evening traffic. Nobody stopped them. They left behind an arsenal. a 7·65 Beretta pistol, a 7·63 Mauser pistol, a Colt Cobra revolver, a 38A Zanotti shotgun, a 38/49 Beretta machine-gun, and an MP/40 machine-pistol.

In the words of the Antimafia Parliamentary report, Cavatajo, the main target, 'had taken part in the long and bloody struggles of the real-estate Mafia'. The Report also states that 'from the modest position of a taxi driver, in a few years Cavatajo had accumulated a considerable fortune', and that he had been 'tried for the murder or manslaughter of no less than five men in the space of ten days in the summer of 1963. On December 1968, the Assize Court at Catanzaro had sentenced him to four years' jail, ordering the immediate suspension of the sentence.' Like any successful real-estate mafioso, his history of collusion with legal institutions followed the same path of political protection.

At the time of the Via Lazio shooting, it was thought that Cavatajo had worked his way up to the position of boss of the *cosche* which controlled the real-estate developments of Palermo, that is, the position previously occupied by the La Barbera brothers, later by Pietro Torretta (condemned to twenty-six years in prison) and then by Tommaso Buscetta. Against Cavatajo were the old-established groups, such as the Grecos, with their new allies Buscetta and Gerlando Alberti.

It was not until three years later, in September 1972, that the trial for the Via Lazio murders took place. By this time twenty-four defendants had been rounded up. What was new in this case was that somebody talked. Filippo and Angelo Moncada, the builder's sons, were at first imprisoned on suspicion of being party to the plot. In hospital, where he was interned for his gunshot wounds, Filippo started talking about his father's meetings with notorious mafiosi, and described how Cavatajo had gradually become the real boss in Moncada's firm. And he consistently said that he recognized a certain Francesco Sutera as one of the four 'policemen' who had killed Cavatajo. Angelo, his brother, supported what Filippo said. But while he was still in prison, Filippo Moncada received threats to his life. In the yard, one day, there was a message painted on the wall: 'Filippo withdraw your accusations!' The other prisoners would tell him: 'Moncada, don't recognize anybody; you'll be safer!' But Moncada was young. He had been at university and looked like a polished Northerner. Sicilian traditions were not part of his ethos. He recognized Sutera from photographs, and when he was confronted with several men dressed in police uniforms he again pointed to Sutera.

For the Moncada brothers to 'talk' was big news in Sicily. They were released from prison, but their father was placed in custody together with the twenty-four alleged participants in the Via Lazio murders. Most of them had been rounded up on the evidence given by the two brothers. At the trial, in the dock next to Francesco Sutera, I could see Gerlando Alberti, a short man with fierce penetrating eyes. Alberti had been a big catch for the police. He had been in hiding for two years after being suspected of involvement in the execution of Judge Scaglione. Alberti was known to have had contacts with the Via Lazio *cosca*. The Carabinieri discovered that on the day in question he had been in Palermo, although by doing so he had broken the law (he was *al confino* in the North). Needless to say he had not asked for the necessary permit issued by the police, and all his alibis turned out to be false. But the defendant, with true Mafia panache, said that yes, it was true that he had given false alibis. The truth was that he had been in Palermo that night, but he had spent it with a lady, a married lady. Now, since he was a man of honour, could he betray the name of the woman, or disclose any details? He preferred to be locked in jail.

The witnesses for the prosecution looked tense and nervous; faced by the sinister group in the dock, by the lawyers and by the public (mainly composed of families of the mafiosi), it was hardly surprising that their testimonies faltered. Filippo Moncada became less sure of his story and he certainly was not helped by the judges and by the public prosecutor. Sixteen out of twenty-four defendants were found guilty, and eleven of these were subsequently discharged as the result of the 'Valpreda' law. The eight who were released were acquitted on lack of evidence. The final verdict of the jury, after eight hours in conference, was that no evidence could be substantiated to prove that any of the defendants had been directly responsible for the Via Lazio slaughter.

It was impossible for the public prosecutor to ask the jury to convict the accused on the evidence available. Obviously believing them to be guilty, he ordered a totally new case to be prepared by another Counsel for the Prosecution (*giudice istruttore*). But while a retrial may allow time to bring new evidence to light, it will also give witnesses the opportunity to have second thoughts about their original statements; and how could they not, when they see that the State always fails? Yet although Filippo Moncada's courage had not been rewarded, he had set an example and proved that *omertà* was on the wane.

The Via Lazio trial had hardly been a dignified affair: people chattered, exchanging comments and gossip. The acoustics of the large marble hall of the Palermo Palazzo di Giustizia are disastrous: the slightest shuffle or squeak of a chair blotted out the faint voices of the protagonists. Journalists and the usual lawyers for the defence (always the same faces) would often prompt the judge or correct him over some point. At the end of the trial, the judge told me: 'If Sutera did not kill Cavatajo, he can live in peace. But if the jury and the judges have made a mistake in acquitting him, then he will be killed. Not at once, though, because in this part of the world vengeance is a dish people eat cold. It is only a question of time: then part of the truth behind this slaughter will come out.' But in this too the new-style *cosche* had changed. One year later Francesco Sutera was found dead in the Ucciardone infirmary, where he was undergoing treatment for epilepsy. The police said officially that he had died of natural causes, but privately some officials said otherwise. Once again where the law of the State had been unable to mete out justice, the law of the *cosche* had dispensed its own.

Gerlando Alberti was one of the rising stars of the Seventies. A tiny man, totally bald (he wears a *toupé*), 'Paccare', as he is nicknamed, was the son of a fruit-seller and grew up in the derelict Palermitan district of Danisinni. He only went to school for four years, and then was out in the streets, one of the many boys one sees in those Palermitan districts with either a desperate or a criminal future. But lately Paccarè had lived a luxurious life: flats in Milan, in Naples, a green Maserati, evenings at nightclubs with expensive beautiful women and his men. He had an official business of selling textiles, employing a squad of commercial travellers (a wonderful cover) and three expensive Northern lawyers to see to his troubles with the law (he didn't like Sicilian lawyers, he said). Back in 1956 he had been acquitted for lack of evidence in the killing of a barman, Francesco Paolo Scaletta. In 1968, his name had cropped up at the big Catanzaro trial, but there was no evidence against him. He was banished to a Lombard village. He became the boss of a Northern *cosca* (with strong ties in Sicily) specializing in tobacco and drug dealing and in smuggling jewels and works of art. Genoa and Milan were his bastions, rich cities, much better than Palermo. As we saw, in 1970, he was involved in the Via Lazio case.

On 17 June 1970 a group of traffic police stopped a black Alfa Romeo in which five people were travelling. Two gave false names; the others said that they were Gerlando Alberti, Giuseppe Calderone and Gaetano Badalamenti. To those policemen the names meant nothing, but when they were studied at the Central Police Station it emerged that the two others who had given false identity papers were Tommaso Buscetta and Salvatore Greco, 'Ciaschiteddu', both wanted by all the police forces in the world, and both descended on Milan from America on purpose. So Alberti had become a big shot. The group suggested 'big' drug traffic, but also that an important decision had to be taken, so important that other notorious bosses, all wanted by the police, had arrived in Milan to take part in what is known to have been a Mafia tribunal (Luciano Liggio, 'L'Ingegnere' Greco, Joseph Badalamenti from Hamburg were there too). This meeting, the Carabinieri believe, involved the decision to execute the journalist Mauro de Mauro.

Although Alberti was then a wanted man, he had gone to Palermo two months earlier on 30 April, leaving from Naples where he lived under a pseudonym, and came back on 7 May. On 5 May at Via dei Cipressi, in the very district where Alberti was *'ntisu*, the High Judge Pietro Scaglione and his driver were shot dead by an unknown Mafia commando. The confidential source who told the Carabinieri about Gerlando Alberti's presence in Palermo was a barman, Vincenzo Guercio. He too was kidnapped and killed, which shows once again how unsafe secrets are with the Carabinieri.

Alberti was emerging as a tough, dangerous man. Too fast a climb perhaps. He was arrested in Naples by the police, obviously on a tip-off. It was just in time for the trial of the 114, also called the trial against the 'new Mafia'. But due to the mountains of papers involved and the complexity of the case, no judge or public prosecutor wanted to handle it. The prosecution had adopted as principal charge that of guilty by association to commit crime, compounded by the use of firearms (a charge invented by Prefetto Mori to compensate for the difficulties in obtaining evidence against mafiosi in specific types of crimes such as murder). These charges do not carry such heavy penalties as for homicide, but allow more flexibility to the judges in arriving at a verdict. The bulk of the indictment was on tape, and consisted of telephone calls tapped by the police with the consent of the magistrature. These tapes include some interesting documentary material, as well as the *cosca's* vocabulary, some of which is new.

How the police got to tap the telephones of various persons, some of them previously unknown to the Criminalpol, is also an interesting story. On the night of 13 July 1970 a Milanese, Signor Sassi, was woken up by the noise of firearms and a cry of 'Help! They are killing me!' As Sassi rushed to his courtyard he saw a man pressing both his hands on his wounded stomach and leaning on the gates shouting: 'Open! They are killing me.' Behind the wounded man Sassi saw a black car with three or four other persons aboard. The wounded man hid himself under other cars and Sassi, who in the meantime had opened the gates, threw himself on the ground and pulled the wounded man inside the safety of his courtyard. The car stopped still for a few seconds, reversed, and then went off.

The wounded man was taken to the Policlinico hospital in Milan; his name was Benedetto La Cara, born in Palermo in 1929, resident in Milan. He told the police that he had intervened in a quarrel between unknown people and had been mistakenly hit by a bullet. But as La Cara had been taken to the Policlinico, the black car had deposited another wounded man, with no identity papers, and had immediately driven off. The two found themselves in the same ward, both watched by policemen. There was no sign that they knew each other, but the stories of both became more and more improbable. The latter person had been at the cinema, he said, but couldn't remember which cinema; had seen a film, but couldn't remember any detail about the film, and had been shot by unknown people.

As the police worked out a few details, they found that Gerlando Alberti seemed to be behind both shootings, and confidential information established what had happened on that night in July. A Genoa-based company called Pantrasport, a cover for the black market in foreign cigarettes, had had recent thefts to the amount of about 200 million lire both in goods and in trucks. Knowing that the robberies were organized by Alberti's *cosca*, the company decided to act 'mafioso' and engaged Alberti as a protector for 3 million lire a month. But the thefts continued and multiplied, breaking the Mafia code of honour: his connection with the company enabled Alberti to give details of where the trucks would be, and at what time. When, on that night of July, a truck full of cigarettes was stolen, three company men set off by car towards the Milan district in search of the stolen truck. They found both the truck and the cigarettes, and as they assaulted the driver, Benedetto La Cara, another car, the Alfa Romeo which had been covering the truck for protection, joined in the fray. Massimo Calfagna, from the company, was hit by a bullet. In turn he shot and wounded Benedetto La Cara.

Having gathered this information, the police started tapping the telephones of Anna Citarda (the woman with whom Alberti lived in Milan), Francesco Scaglione* and several other suspects. From a sociological point of view, the outcome is very interesting. But it was not much help to the police: the Sicilians hardly spoke on the telephone and, when they did, they rang from public telephones and they almost talked in code. But for the first time a hostile ear had entered the home of the mafiosi, revealing the details of their private lives, fears and domestic problems.

Gerlando Alberti had bought a farmhouse at Cascina dei Pecchi, near Milan. At the beginning of 1970 the *cosca* was building a secret room there, probably intended as a hiding-place for stolen and black market goods, but also for hiding victims of kidnappings. Gerlando Alberti's sister, Sarina, rang up from Palermo (6 November 1970):

SARINA: Hallo. How is Gerlando? [Gerlando Alberti's nephew]. His mother is worried. Why doesn't he ring up?

ANNA CITARDA: But, poor man, he is out in the morning and comes back at midnight.

SARINA: But what is he doing?

ANNA CITARDA: At the moment they are making a villa and only family people can work there.

SARINA: Then how are we to manage christening the baby?

ANNA CITARDA: Now, I pass you on to your brother and you talk about it together.

GERLANDO ALBERTI: Hallo.

SARINA: Ciao, what are they saying?

GERLANDO ALBERTI: We get on.

* Indicted for the murder of Judge Scaglione. Banished to L'Asinara, where I met him in 1974.

SARINA: For the christening, what are we to do?

GERLANDO ALBERTI: What?

SARINA: That his sister has to christen her baby and he cannot come.

GERLANDO ALBERTI: Here we have to complete a villa and others cannot work there ... They would see ... you understand?

SARINA: Yes, and then?

GERLANDO ALBERTI: I am building a room which mustn't be seen. This is it, understand? It is only a matter of days ...

There are several business conversations from which one can detect an atmosphere of danger and suspicion. Often, and even if he answered the telephone himself, Alberti pretended not to be at home. On the same day Cesare d'Amico, a drug courier, rang up:

D'AMICO: Good evening, this is Cesare, I have to bring big stuff. Could you take charge of it? When can we meet?

ALBERTI: I understand. You can come to my house and we can see about that thing ...

D'AMICO: But one is ... the other, marijuana.

ALBERTI: No, that doesn't interest me, I thought you talked about the other stuff, that ...

D'AMICO: The white one ...

ALBERTI: Yes.

D'AMICO: I understand, I haven't got it.

ALBERTI: This doesn't sell in this market. It goes better in Genoa. Have you got samples?

D'AMICO: It is in a whole piece. A sample can be taken off the other. But 'Angel' says it is all in a piece. ['Angel': a man from London.]

ALBERTI: Then come here with him.

D'AMICO: To your house?

ALBERTI: Yes, so we have a chat.

D'AMICO: All right. I'll eat and then I'll come.

ALBERTI: Then bring a small sample ...

D'AMICO: The small sample is with Carrara ...

ALBERTI: I understand. That's how they would tell him what to do with it.

D'AMICO: We come to you so you tell us what you have to say.

ALBERTI: All right.

Great suspicion ran through the following conversation from Palermo between Gerlando Alberti and Giuseppe Romano, also nicknamed

'L'Ingegnere'; Romano was another drug-courier who commuted from the States and was put on trial with the 114 (in absentia).

L'INGEGNERE: Hallo, Paccarè. Are you well? This is L'Ingegnere.

ALBERTI: I'm well, and you?

L'INGEGNERE: I have received that registered letter.

ALBERTI: Good.

L'INGEGNERE: Listen to me. You must know that I have something to tell you.

ALBERTI: Tell me.

L'INGEGNERE: This Martino Scaruto, who's he?

ALBERTI: Yes, I know him, he's from Bagheria ...

L'INGEGNERE: He comes from Bagheria? As I have to make a deal with him ...

ALBERTI: With him? But no! Then they come round with the rotten stuff ... but have you been in contact?

L'INGEGNERE: Yes.

ALBERTI: Look, they must have come to you with fake names. He's been in jail for the last three years ...

L'INGEGNERE: Three years in jail?

ALBERTI: Yes, yes ...

L'INGEGNERE: Martino Scaruto from that district Le Case Nuove?

ALBERTI: From Magliozzo ...

L'INGEGNERE: Magliozzo, that's what I wanted to say ... What kind of type is he?

ALBERTI: But what is it all about? Tell me.

L'INGEGNERE: The usual business of ours ...

ALBERTI: He's my godson ...

L'INGEGNERE: Your godson is he?

ALBERTI: But I want to know before ...

L'INGEGNERE: Do you have to ring him up?

ALBERTI: Then ask him to ring me beforehand ...

L'INGEGNERE: All right.

ALBERTI: Don't you do anything, don't get offended ...

L'INGEGNERE: All right.

ALBERTI: All right. Another thing. Today three people came, perhaps there was also an American, a man called Nicolò ...

L'INGEGNERE: Nicolò?

ALBERTI: There were three of them. In fact I went off and rang and he gave me an appointment for tomorrow. I told him: But I don't know you. I beg your pardon, how can we recognize each other? I don't know ... can you tell me something about them?

L'INGEGNERE: A little bit about Nicolò, Paccarè ...

ALBERTI: I understand ...

L'INGEGNERE: A few things I could tell you about him, but face to face ...

ALBERTI: I understand, all right.

L'INGEGNERE: Ring me up in the morning, at once, if it's the best thing to do.

ALBERTI: Yes, do me this favour.

L'INGEGNERE: All right. Everything is all right.

This time the telephone rang at Scaglione's home. Anna Citarda rang up his sister, Rosaria Battaglia. The '*carrubi*', i.e. the Carabinieri, had broken into the farmhouse on the night between 14 and 15 November, and had found fifty-nine tons of foreign cigarettes. Panic struck the *cosca*: who had talked? Wives, mistresses, sisters, *compari*, relatives rang each other up, talking in half-sentences, to pass on the big news. A novelty here is that the women seem to be very much in the know and actively participating.

Gerlando Alberti stayed away from home. On 28 November he received the news of the failure of an expedition of four men who had been sent to kill Giuseppe Sirchia, in banishment at Castelfranco Veneto. (Sirchia warned the Carabinieri that a car with four men had been sent to kill him. The Carabinieri stopped them and found them armed to the teeth. At the 114 trial, Sirchia withdrew his allegations. See *Angelo La Barbera* (*The Profile of a Mafia Boss.*)

The telephone rang. It was Paccarè:

ALBERTI: Who's there?

ANNA CITARDA: It's me.

ALBERTI: Listen, if 'they' were to come and take you in for questioning, do you know what to do?

ANNA: Tell me ...

ALBERTI: You must bring the child with you, because if they were to go on for long you tell them that you have to go because you must feed your child.

ANNA: All right.

ALBERTI: If they say 'we'll go and buy it', you tell them you have special food for the child, understood?

ANNA: Yes, understood ...

ALBERTI: Then tell me something, did you put all the contracts away?

ANNA: I took almost all.

ALBERTI: And the contracts for the rent?

ANNA: No.

ALBERTI: You must take that away too. They might search the house.

ANNA: And for the telephone numbers?

ALBERTI: But you know what to do with that, the telephone numbers you don't give to them ...

There were a lot of telephone calls from relatives, *compari* and *commari*. From Genoa one lady talked in code ("The bricks are very shiny ... did you clean them?'). Citarda answered that she 'was expecting my cousins' (Mafia slang for expecting the Carabinieri; 'Waiting for my brothers' is expecting the police). Gerlando Alberti rang up home and talked to his daughter Antonietta (from a previous marriage). He asked her to tell anybody who might come to the house that 'uncle left a long time ago'. Alberti and the *cosca* were frightened by the failure of the Sirchia expedition, because he might talk. They also got to know that the Palermo judges were trying to indict them for 'association to commit crimes', a scandalous leakage which only magistrates could pass on. The indictment was being prepared on information given by the Carabinieri regarding the kidnapping of the journalist Mauro de Mauro. Needless to say, not even the press knew about it. But as the date approached, the indictment was dropped, probably for lack of evidence. The *cosca* was frightened, expecting to see '*i carrubi*' at any moment, but then Alberti's lawyer told him that once again he was safe—for the time being.

On 1 December Vincenzo Conti called Anna Citarda. In the following year he was to die in a manner which reminds one of Al Capone's Chicago: his murderers knotted a cord around his neck, linking it to a truck and driving away. This murder was probably due to a 'settlement', since Conti had stolen one of the *cosca*'s trucks, a great '*sgarro*' to the organization.

Alberti rang up while Anna Citarda was out shopping. He talked to his daughter Antonietta. He had a lot of business, had to go to Reggio Emilia and then back to Milan, but wouldn't sleep in his house. The four

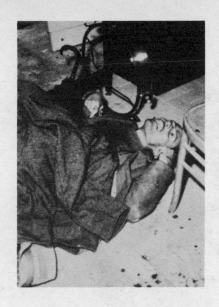

28. 1971–1975 The reality behind the Mafia myth (*Gigi Petyx*)

29. November 1975 A Mafia assassination in the centre of Palermo; the victim's father had been shot in the same way on Christmas Eve the previous year (*Gigi Petyx*)

compari who had been sent to kill Sirchia at Castelvetrano had been jailed. Scaglione warned Citarda that they had been caught 'with problems', i.e. armed.

Benedetto La Cara's wife rang Anna Citarda to complain, asking to speak directly to Alberti. Her husband was in prison and she felt abandoned by all. Alberti said that the woman was breaking 'those things that I cannot mention. I have already paid for his solicitor, what else does she want?' Mrs La Cara also knew that Alberti was *canziato*, in hiding. Who told her? Meanwhile business went on as usual; not only foreign cigarettes, but butter, powdered milk and refrigerators (bought on the black market to profit from EEC laws), narcotics. They were all travelling up and down Italy and the Lombard fog bothered the drivers. La Cara's wife rang up again: she had to borrow money in order to pay her rent. This was another sign of the breakdown of the Mafia code. A *capocosca's* survival as a leader and the *cosca's* survival as an entity depends on the financial protection of its members and families once they have fallen into the hands of the law. The same breakdown had already happened in the USA, as Valachi said.

But while no indictment came from Palermo, it was the Genoese police who acted, suspecting that Gerlando Alberti and his *cosca* were responsible for the black market in foreign cigarettes. Alberti got to know about that as well—in advance—and avoided going back home.

CITARDA: Hallo Gerlando.
ALBERTI: What's happening? What do they say?
CITARDA: Nothing. Have you been at the agency?
ALBERTI: No. Why?
CITARDA: You see, Vincenzo Ferrara rang up.
ALBERTI: Yes, Ferrara ...
CITARDA: He didn't explain to me, but perhaps Totuccio.* He explained everything better to *compare* Totuccio.
ALBERTI: Eh ...
CITARDA: At six o'clock you mustn't go to your appointment.
ALBERTI: Ah ... no?
CITARDA: No. Because there is confusion ...
ALBERTI: I understand.
CITARDA: Anyhow, I think he explained more to Totuccio.

* Totuccio is the nickname of Salvatore Riina, from Corleone. See *Profile of a Mafia Boss.*

ALBERTI: Totuccio?

CITARDA: To the *compare* Totuccio. Now, you ring up the agency and you get it all explained better. All right?

Later Alberti rang Citarda up again warning her that his lawyer wanted him to stay in hiding. 'There is a storm.' She was nervous and didn't believe him. Had he got a woman, perhaps? No, a 'dishonest' person had sent a letter to the police, it seemed.

Francesco Scaglione rang Anna Citarda warning her that the police were about to come to her house. How did he know?

SCAGLIONE: Perhaps it's better for you to get out of your house ...
CITARDA: Now?
SCAGLIONE: Yes.
CITARDA: Tonight?
SCAGLIONE: Now I come to you ...
CITARDA: Yes ... yes ...

On 24 December the 'cousins' came and arrested Alberti, Citarda and many *compari* for trafficking in drugs and tobacco, and for armed theft and robbery. The police still kept tapping the telephones of the few who had remained out of jail. Some began to suspect it, but after inquiries they came to the conclusion that it was a false alarm. Nino Jenna, a *compare*, rang up Alberti's sister with good news. His tone was servile:

NINO JENNA: Hallo, it's me, Nino. Good morning. Listen, he [Alberti] hasn't been interrogated yet by the judge and therefore we can't go and see him until next Monday.
SARINA: All right.
NINO JENNA: After that we must have a talk with doctor Alessandrini. Actually he is a friend of a friend [Mafia way of saying that he belongs]. Eventually, after the holidays, they'll all come back. The chances are ninety-nine out of a hundred. It all depends on Alessandrini ...
SARINA: Yes? ...
NINO JENNA: This Alessandrini is one of ours ...
SARINA: All right.
NINO JENNA: After the holidays ... let's hope, they'll be out. Anyway, signora, take my telephone number, so that when you need something you can call me.
SARINA: All right.
NINO JENNA: Anyway, you can be sure ...

SARINA: Let's hope ...

NINO JENNA: No, no, after the holidays ... don't worry, everything will get settled. Anyway, if you need me, call me. At any time, I'd come ...

SARINA: Yes, thank you ...

NINO JENNA: Yes, because your brother wrote to me, he smuggled a letter through to me ...

SARINA: Yes, my nephew told me about that.

NINO JENNA: Did he get the money?

SARINA: The money in Antonietta's hands?

NINO JENNA: 700,000 lire.

SARINA: No, she gave me 460, and 200,000 were given by that lady who was here ...

NINO JENNA: All right. 40,000 are missing. As he explains, in the letter, that there was 500 plus 200 ... That's it, today or tomorrow I have to receive another letter because there is a *maresciallo* [who was smuggling letters from prison] ...

SARINA: Yes, I understand ... I know ...

NINO JENNA: All right, we'll get in touch later.

In fact, Gerlando Alberti and his men did not get out of jail after the holidays, as promised by Nino Jenna. Only Anna Citarda did, a month after her imprisonment.

After this last conversation, the *compari* and the *commari* received the information that all their telephones were being tapped. Their phrases became therefore even hazier and more mysterious, half words, no names ... But Antonietta, Alberti's daughter, and Rosetta Sedita, the daughter of another *compare*, would sing each other little songs showing their hatred and contempt for the policemen listening in, *'cornuti sbirri'*, *'piedi piatti'* (cuckold coppers, flat feet).

The trial of the 114, nicknamed the trial of the New Mafia, started in February and ended in July 1974. In fact only seventy-five of the accused had been rounded up. Some had been released beforehand for lack of evidence, some were at large, others had been given bail. Most of the Gerlando Alberti *cosca*, many of those we met on the telephone, were on trial. So were people like Di Cristina, Natale Rimi, Tommaso Buscetta (who had been found in South America and arrested), Luciano Liggio and Frank Coppola (both under arrest). It was an inconclusive trial which ended with forty-three acquittals and thirty-two sentences, almost all of which were very light. Gerlando Alberti was given six years, likewise Frank Coppola. Banished to the island of l'Asinara, Alberti was again able to escape in June 1975, and once again the Carabinieri found him (in December 1975) hiding among Sicilians in Northern Italy. His future is predictable: never properly convicted, he will be banished again, and again he will find it easy to escape. Successive trials will be inconclusive, and he will meet his end in the usual Mafia fashion. He knows too much.

For Coppola it was a blow; an old *capomafia* like him—he was then seventy-five—was likely to be out of the game with a prison sentence to serve for six years. (On the other hand, later, when he was meant to be in prison, he was instead in a private room in a luxurious nursing home, paid for by the State.) Gaetano Badalamenti, a very important man, also got six years, much to his horror and surprise: the public prosecutor had asked for his acquittal. Giuseppe Di Cristina, Natale Rimi and Salvatore Riina were acquitted for lack of evidence. Both Salvatore Greco, Nicolò and Paolo Greco had been tried in absentia, and had also been acquitted for lack of proof. The police had intended to strike a blow against the big names of the old and new *cosche* as a reaction to the bold murders of the journalist De Mauro, the police informer Guercio, and the High Court Judge Scaglione and his driver, murders which once again had shown the audacity with which the criminals were able to eliminate people in their path.

I went to the forty-seventh day of the trial, when Giuseppe Di Cristina was being interrogated. The public prosecutor, pale-eyed, the nail of his little finger grown long to clean the others, did not seem capable of expressing himself, let alone of asking pertinent questions. The hall, the same large marble hall where I had been for the trial of the Via Lazio case, was filled by those defence counsels whose faces one had learnt to know. *Primus inter pares* was Girolamo Bellavista, who often walked up to the Court. He represented Di Cristina, Vincenzo and Natale Rimi. The defence objected that the Court should not take the tapes of the above-quoted telephone conversations as evidence, because although the police had obtained the permission of a Milanese magistrate the owners of the telephones had not been warned. As there is a law to this effect, the judge accepted the objection and the tapes, the most valid piece of evidence for the association to commit crime, were dismissed.

Di Cristina declared: 'I have worked all my life.' He knew nobody, had never met Francesco Scaglione or Calogero Sinatra, had 'never called Senator Verzotto *compare*.' The public prosecutor asked Di Cristina whether he could sincerely claim to have led an honourable life: Di Cristina, naturally, answered that he had. At one stage the presiding judge said to the public prosecutor: 'I beg your pardon, but your question was even badly formulated!' They were long, rambling, meaningless questions. But the public prosecutor seemed proud of the fact that he had been a pupil of the lawyer Girolamo Bellavista, and often said so in Court, exchanging jokes and remarks with him. Farce though it was, however, at least the trial had taken place.

But another trial was in store for Giuseppe Di Cristina and the *cosca* of Riesi and Ravanusa, this time in Agrigento. Once again there were powerful witnesses for the prosecution. The story behind it was cruel and archaic, in keeping with the Mafia of the province of Agrigento. It started with the deaths of two men at Ravanusa (the Riesi-Ravanusa *cosca* was responsible for twenty murders in a few years). Stefano Vangelista was hit on the head in a farmhouse near Ravanusa and the farmhouse burnt with the live man inside it. Vito Gattuso was shot at close range with a sawn-off shotgun while he was walking in the centre of the town holding his little son by the hand. Vangelista had committed a *sgarro* against Di Cristina's *cosca* by refusing to house the cigarettes which were shipped clandestinely from the Southern harbours (Porto Empedocle and neighbouring places) on their way to Palermo and the mainland. Gattuso had sided with Vangelista and with another *cosca* (that of the neighbouring town of Canicatti) against Di Cristina's, and his execution had been performed from a red Mini Minor with a Palermo registration number which was seen on the main road by a man who turned out as a witness for the prosecution. A local mafioso, Candido Ciuni, objected strongly to Gattuso's murder.

Three months later, around eight o'clock one October evening, the electricity failed in a small inn on Via Maqueda, one of the central streets which cuts the beautiful old quarter of Palermo into four. It was off just long enough for Ciuni, the owner of the inn, to be knifed. When the light came back on, he was lying in a pool of blood with multiple stab-wounds inflicted by two or three men who had quickly fled. Ciuni was taken to the Ospedale Civico of Palermo, where they succeeded in saving his life, even though his lungs had been punctured.

Six days later, just before midnight, the sleepy night porter of the hospital opened the door to four men dressed as surgeons ready for the operating theatre. One stayed behind with him, a gun pointing at the porter's head. Upstairs, three male nurses were washing the floor. A second 'surgeon' held two of them at gun-point, while the third was dragged along by the remaining two 'surgeons'. 'Show us room number 6,' they demanded. 'They don't open to anybody,' the nurse told them. 'They are locked in.' The surgeons instructed him to say that there was a medical visit.

From under the white uniforms came an axe, in case the door remained closed, and a machine-gun. The nurse, half crying, announced to Ciuni's terrified wife, who never left the side of her ailing husband, that a doctor had come to visit Ciuni. As she unlocked the door the intruders kicked it open and burst in shooting at the wounded man. In a few seconds the four 'surgeons' fled and all traces of them disappeared. Candido Ciuni had been on the point of recovery (on the following day the doctors were due to take out the many stitches in his previous wounds). Now he lay on a blood-soaked bed, disfigured by bullets. There was supposed to be a policeman posted outside Ciuni's door. On the night of 28 October he was conveniently absent.

At the trial, Signora Ciuni said: 'When my husband learnt that Gattuso had been murdered, he knew he had been condemned to die as well.' He was frightened, she said, and even in Palermo, where he had fled and settled, he avoided places where he was known to have gone in the past.

Di Cristina's brothers, who came to stay at the Ciunis' inn, behaved in such a way, she said, that 'he became aware of being in serious danger because Di Cristina wouldn't have tolerated the offence to his prestige which consisted in my husband's refusal; he did not tolerate the fact that Ciuni knew of his designs and, in order to achieve this, he had to eliminate both Ciuni and Gattuso to get rid of obstacles which were in his way to the realization of his association with the Mafia of Canicatti'.

After her husband's murder, she had gone to see Giuseppe di Pasquili, Ciuni's former lawyer, from Ravanusa. But he had told her: 'Don't get involved with those things; those are dangerous people; think of your children. Candido will not come back to life if you become a witness for the prosecution!' Di Pasquali also advised her not to recognize the 'surgeons' whom she had seen in the hospital. Although di Pasquali has been indicted, Ciuni's widow said: 'I don't know if my husband would

approve of what I have done by talking: he was a man of honour.'
At the trial, Ciuni's widow openly accused Di Cristina. 'Murderer!
Why did you have Candido murdered?' Di Cristina pleaded innocence—
he had been staying at the Ciunis' inn as a guest, 'as a son, even'.
But Signora Ciuni showed that she knew the Mafia's customs well: 'This
is the system of the mafiosi with friends; first you eat together, then you
betray.' She made no bones about the fact that her husband was a
mafioso, a good mafioso, a man of honour who 'disliked killing'. Another
woman accuser was Crocefissa Gattuso, whose husband and both her
sons had been killed. And Antonino Cascino accused Raffaele Bove, one
of Di Cristina's agents, who allegedly confided in him that he taken part
in the Ciuni murder and named the other three 'surgeons'. It was all in
vain. When the Agrigento Court deliberated in March 1974 all the
accused were acquitted for lack of proof.

In a way it had been an old-style Mafia trial, because of the ferocity
of the *cosche*, which recalled traditional latifundia methods, and the behaviour of the Agrigento Court. It could not be totally free from the
extremely powerful influence of Di Cristina, who controlled not only the
sources of income but also the men of power in the area.

Signora Ciuni went back to her inn in Palermo: once again a witness's
courage had been wasted. In Court the defence, seeing that she was
determined to go on talking, tried to destroy her reputation. One of the
accused in the dock cried: 'You are a liar, a mythomaniac, you are mad!'
It was the usual Mafia technique of character-assassination, holding up
to ridicule an enemy who could not be killed. (Her murder would be
tantamount to a confession, and Major Russo of the Carabinieri said on
that occasion, 'her talking was like taking out a life insurance'—although
a car accident or a sudden disease could not be ruled out.) The technique
did not work in Antonia Ciuni's case. It was absurd to point to her or
Crocefissa Gattuso as two madwomen seeking publicity: there was no
mistaking the personalities of the two woman who had lived in a
mafioso environment, believed in the old Mafia code and lived in the
shadow of their men. People respected them, nobody sneered at their
'stupidity' in talking, although once again their efforts had brought
nobody to justice. Yet by choosing to cooperate with the law they had
shown that they were avoiding private vendetta, and, by exposing Di
Cristina and his powerful *cosca* they had helped to undermine his power.

One thing comes out clearly from this 'selection' of Mafia trials: there
is a growing crisis in the world of the *cosche*, not only because names are

mentioned and become public, but because the code is no longer respected. The mafioso who has slowly 'matured' into the middle class is disappearing, the Albertis of today have shot their way to the top in too short a span thus disturbing the middle class, a point which was raised by the person who talked to me at the beginning of this chapter. The proletariat of the *cosche* is in revolt as one will see later from the string of kidnappings against that same middle class which once was its base. And the political platform has become more chancy, the Christian Democrats and the other central parties are very exposed and must be more careful about their dealings with the *cosche*. The events and the mood forced the *cosche* to look elsewhere for protection, not understanding that if they move outside 'respectability', outside the middle class, they lose the base, they dig their own grave.

15 The Cosche, the State and the Neo-Fascists

For the first time in history even the Pope talked about the Mafia in his New Year's Day speech for 1974, stressing that the phenomenon had spread. The Pope asked whether the Mafia outlook of 'pseudo-justice, vendettas, all this tragic chain-psychology ...' was deplored as much as it really deserved to be. Pope Paul chose to speak of the Mafia as an Italian citizen, deploring the effect of the phenomenon on 'our good name as a nation, our dignity as a people, our Christian profession as faithful of the Church. Do we not see that it is wrong that such a thing exists still in a country bearing the name of Italy?'

The other novelty in the development of the Mafia was that the whole of Italy seemed to have caught the disease. Earlier the *cosche* could only thrive where there had been a Sicilian population, in a context providing a base for *omertà* and collusion with established power; in the 1970s they could perfectly well operate in a general Italian context, especially in Rome. There the power vacuum, the politics of patronage, the lack of industries, the corruption, had created a parasite city more and more similar to Palermo, in all its manifestations. Western Sicily was having its revenge on the foreign conqueror, instilling its worst aspects within the mother government which had proved totally unable to implant healthy habits and institutions on the island. The Italian industrialist pattern had also become a mechanism of political patronage. In the words of Scalfari and Turani in *Razza padrona*: 'After Mattei's death, the State industry became more and more integrated with political power, at the same time losing its driving spring'.

The process was also due to the phenomenon which we have already examined, the concentration of Southerners, Sicilians especially, in key posts in the police, the *prefetture*, the civil service and the law. Due to their extraordinary drive and intelligence we also find Sicilians in high echelons of Italian industry operating with the kind of Sicilian mentality which we can define as mafioso—as in the case of Sindona and his economic deals.

One of the most interesting moments of the trial of the 114, which we examined in the previous chapter, came in its fifty-third day, when the old mafioso Frank Coppola came to Palermo and faced the Court. Although he could have easily avoided it by claiming that he was ill, he deigned to appear in order to establish in front of the other invisible Court the fact that he had not been the confidant of another important Sicilian character, the police official Angelo Mangano. Facing the Court, but in fact addressing the attentive rows of men in the dock, Coppola insisted vehemently that all that Mangano said about him was a lie. He called him 'a dirty liar, a murderer, a *carogna*'.

MANGANO: Coppola told me that when there was the famous gunfight at Via Lazio, Gerlando Alberti, called 'Paccarè', Riina, Provenzano, Bagarella and others had taken part in it; not only that, but Bagarella had been the one who, when the commando was fleeing, was put inside the boot, dead or wounded.

COPPOLA: He's a liar, a liar!

JUDGE: Coppola, moderate your language ...

MANGANO: And he added that Liggio was the one who had masterminded the commando. Then he also said to me—our meetings with Coppola having been many and in various places; because I went to his house, or we met in other places—so that, always talking about the same crimes, he also talked about the murder of Judge Scaglione, and he said that this too must have been the work of a team formed and masterminded by Liggio.

COPPOLA: He's a liar! It's not true! Murderer! He is diabolical ...

JUDGE: Keep calm!

COPPOLA: I cannot resist, not indeed! Your Excellency, it's not true. He's a *carogna*, *sfacciato*, liar!

MANGANO: And then he indicated some people who had taken part [in the murder of Judge Scaglione], among those Gerlando Alberti.

Mangano added that Coppola had told him about Liggio's involvement in various kidnappings, and that he had offered to give the police precise information about where Liggio was in hiding. In a heated confrontation—to put it mildly—Coppola declared that Mangano had asked him for 50 million lire in exchange for erasing names and embarrassing sentences on several tapes recorded from taps on his telephone. Coppola was trying to get his revenge by sending Mangano to jail as well. The policeman was accusing him of the worst possible crime, that of having talked to a *sbirro*! The old mafioso was livid: it was like being condemned to death and disgrace.

On the other hand, it is unlikely that the others believed what Mangano said. All his information could have easily been gathered by hearsay. Even I could have said that Alberti took part in both the Via Lazio and the Scaglione 'expeditions': it was one of the most open of all Palermitan secrets. But Coppola was also confused, and continued to insult Mangano (whom he never looked at, even when at one stage they were sitting side by side), saying that he was a habitual liar, a man who had lied all his life. But from the vehemence of his insults one could detect that the information contained the truth, although it is very doubtful that it had come from the old mafioso himself. It was as if Coppola wanted to shout that the game was not fair. If a policeman was to behave in an even more mafioso way than the actual criminal, what was poor Coppola to do?

Angelo Mangano is one of those characters whose misconduct greatly exceeds the normal routine of a policeman and whose harsh, illegal methods have always been questionable. Like Coppola, he has always enjoyed the protection of the powerful, and for the same reasons—he knows a lot and has taken part in many 'delicate' operations. The Socialist party organ *Avanti* claimed that Angelo Mangano aided a group of police officers then belonging to the 'special affairs' section, which first started bugging the telephones of politicians in the Fifties, during the brief and shady term of Prime Minister Tambroni (who came to power in a coalition of Christian Democrats and Fascists). Mangano himself confirmed this piece of information.

Mangano was born in 1920 of a poor family living near Catania. He took a degree in law and joined the police in 1945, obtaining quick promotion in the North. In 1959 he came to Rome together with policeman Walter Beneforti. In the Sixties Beneforti, after resigning as deputy police chief of Milan, joined two very important private detective organizations. After Tambroni's departure, Mangano fell into disgrace and was transferred to Frosinone, a small centre near Rome, until Vicari himself, the head of the Italian police and a fellow Sicilian (now retired), called him back and asked him to fight the Mafia.

In 1963 Mangano settled in Partinico, where he used 'tough' methods and set out to capture the notorious Luciano Liggio. One year later, gun in hand, he did catch the big fish and was promoted to *vice-questore* (deputy police chief). When in 1969 Liggio fled from a private nursing home in Rome, Mangano started shadowing the powerful Frank Coppola, whom he believed responsible for Liggio's flight. He visited him several times in order to obtain information about Liggio's hiding-place, and he had Coppola's telephone bugged.

When a Rome magistrate, Luciano Infelizi, announced early in 1973 that his investigations showed that Italy was covered by a vast network of telephone listening devices, a warrant was issued for the arrest of Tom Ponzi, a famous Milanese private detective and a Neo-Fascist. As seems customary in Italy, Ponzi was rushed to a private clinic with a sudden attack of diabetes just as the police were about to arrive with the warrant, leaving the public with the suspicion that he had been tipped off beforehand. Walter Beneforti, the former companion of Angelo Mangano, was put in jail. The bugging scandal was quickly forgotten since all concerned had a vested interest in maintaining silence and further investigations were hushed up. The evidence, which included tapes of bugged telephone calls, remained in the hands of various unscrupulous policemen, private detectives, mafiosi and Neo-Fascists. It was compromising material which could guarantee money and immunity. A telephone official of the SIP, indicted for the tapping of telephones, committed suicide; the magistrate Infelizi was beaten up in his house by men who tried to murder him. Another magistrate investigating the affair, Judge Sica, received threats.

The tapes of Coppola's telephone conversations, recorded for Mangano, probably by Walter Beneforti, were required by the Antimafia Commission. When it finally received them, after long delays and disappearances, they had clearly been cut in places and touched up. Coppola claimed that he had paid Mangano some of the money he was demanding in return for erasing some names. Mangano declared that the highest judge of the land, Spagnuolo (*procuratore generale presso la corte d'appello* of Rome—another Sicilian), had told Coppola that his private telephone was being tapped. Another mafioso, a police informer, added that it was true that Mangano had asked for 50 million from Coppola, and that Mangano had received 18 million on account, but that Judge Spagnuola had been party to the transaction. Coppola denied that Spagnuolo had anything to do with the whole affair, and Spagnuolo sued Mangano.

In a now famous interview (*Il Mondo*, January 1974), Spagnuolo declared: 'The corruption in the police force really started during the Tambroni era. Now it is not easy to erase it.' He explained that within the police 'a secret entity had been created which looked after "reserved affairs" for the secret use of some; a mechanism of blackmail had been built.' According to Spagnuolo, when he had wanted to indict Mangano and put him in jail he had found his hands tied. He said that the police were corrupt and what was needed in Italy was 'to clean up the police force'. What was certain, said the very highest magistrate in Italy, was that the missing conversations had taken place between Coppola and politicians. 'The tapes had reached us with cuts, erasures and breakages, and not even all arrived. Out of forty-one, we received thirty-nine.'*

In 1971 Mangano became *Questore*, police chief, of one section of Rome's criminal police. On 5 April 1973 unknown people attempted to assassinate him. Mangano had just got out of his chauffeur-driven official car and was about to open the gate of his Roman house when shots were fired from another car. He fell to the ground and a man stepped out, shot him again, then drove off. Angelo Mangano was rushed to hospital with six bullet wounds, but after a long operation he recovered. Mangano declared that the men who tried to assassinate him had been Frank Coppola's agents. 'The motivation for this hatred is not clear,' wrote *La Stampa*. One of the two indicted for his attempted murder was a Neo-Fascist. Coppola himself declared: 'For somebody like Mangano, I wouldn't waste half a bullet. It's not worth it.'

The oddity was that for five years Mangano had never revealed, not even to the Antimafia Commission which had questioned him twice, the context of the alleged revelations that Frank Coppola had made to him. He did so only after the attempt on his life and at the Palermo Court: he had to, in order to help explain the hatred between Coppola and himself. A member of the Antimafia Commission declared: 'The revelations of the *questore* have left us surprised, to say the least. We had interrogated him twice in the past and in particular about his relationships with Frank Coppola.' The Commission was the very place, the official

---

* In a very recent report (February 1975), the Antimafia Commission censured the behaviour of both Mangano and Spagnuolo. The latter was linked with Judge Scaglione's friend Jalongo (also a close friend of Frank Coppola) and particularly with the Roman Romolo Pietroni, an investigating judge who was also the legal counsellor of the Antimafia Commission itself, and whose role with the *cosche mafiose* emerges from the report as scandalous.

stressed, where Mangano should have talked in detail about what he knew.

We have referred several times to Frank Coppola, the old mafioso who, in the States, was nicknamed 'Three-Fingered Frank', because two fingers are missing from his left hand. 'It was Vittorio Emanuele Orlando [the former Prime Minister] who advised me to go to the United States,' Coppola recalled. 'I was a close friend of his; I was one of the few men he could count on, and during the Fascist regime the atmosphere became threatening to me.' Coppola is a very short, intelligent man with a thick white beard, easy to talk with, enterprising. He was powerful in Brooklyn as he was powerful in Italy, and he came back as a rich man—and an 'undesirable'. It was certainly not for his own pleasure that he settled the 'Giuliano question': he had been asked to. He settled near Rome, at Pomezia, and invested money in land and land speculation. 'I have always been very interested in politics,' he said. He even declared that he had been 'part of Truman's entourage,' which might be true. From the Sixties onwards he went through several trials, which also indicated that he was losing his grip on power. He was indicted again later for drug traffic, but acquitted. A Palermitan judge said that it was thanks to Coppola that Liggio had succeeded in escaping from his Roman nursing home. In fact it is believed that the sick murderer was hidden in Partinico, where Coppola was born and was the unchallenged boss.

But attempts to incriminate Coppola continued. If he had really been the mastermind of Mangano's attempted assassination, he would never have used two small-fry professional robbers, one of them from a Neo-Fascist background, who, in fact, did the job very badly. Either he would have used professional killers, of which the Mafia has a whole nursery, or more likely he would have waited for his revenge—'since in these parts revenge is a dish people eat cold'—and might have used shrewder means, such as a car accident, a suicide, a sudden 'illness' ...

At 7.15 on the morning of 22 June 1973, three policemen went to Coppola's farm of Tor San Lorenzo at Pomezia to arrest him for the attempted murder of Angelo Mangano. The old *capomafia* stood there in his pyjamas listening to the warrant they read to him. Then he burst out laughing. 'Hurrah!' he said, 'We have caught the murderer!' He did not believe it, nor do we.

The trial, which took place in Florence and ended in November 1975, acquitted Coppola from the accusation of having masterminded the attempt on Mangano's life. In his summing up the Judge said that through the jungle of lies no evidence had emerged against either Coppola or the two alleged 'killers', Ugo Bossi and Sergio Boffi. A lot of time and of public money had thus been thrown away: the only success was further to confuse the public about the already mysterious personality of Police Chief Angelo Mangano.

Coppola did not stay long in prison; it quickly emerged that he was serving his sentence in a private room in a de luxe nursing home—at the State's expense.

It was not only the Italian police who showed their corrupt side. In December 1972 came the third and final report of the Knapp Commission set up in 1970 by the New York mayor, John Lindsay, which had examined police corruption in the city. It concluded that over half of the police force were involved in one form of corruption or another. In most cases the police took small bribes of five to twenty dollars from gambling operators or building contractors, wanting to get round the city regulations. There was a smaller and more serious category where policemen, 'probably only a small percentage of the force, spend a good deal of their working hours aggressively seeking out situations they can exploit for financial gain, including gambling, narcotic and other serious offences, which can yield payments of thousands of dollars.' The biggest sources of corruption were the organized crime syndicates, essentially the Mafia, the report said. These groups controlled gambling, drug traffic, illegal money loans and a number of illegal 'sex-related enterprises', such as late-night homosexual bars and the selling of pornography.

The Commission found that there was some involvement of the New York police in drug-dealing, even murder, and it named senior police officials who simply ignored official reports about specific cases of police corruption. The report stressed that drug trafficking was the most serious problem faced by the police department. In fact the House Select Committee on Crime, which had conducted hearings on the subject, estimated that in 1971 there were from 200,000 to 250,000 heroin addicts in the United States—half of them in New York alone. (Only 65,000 heroin users are officially known to the Federal Bureau of Narcotics and Dangerous Drugs.) Among the activities carried out by the police were financing heroin deals and selling narcotics. The report also told of three specific instances in which the Bureau of Narcotics and Dangerous Drugs, a Federal agency, gave information about the involvement of the New York police in such offences as associating with known criminals, releasing heroin to dealers in return for bribes, selling heroin, and murder. With the affluence and discontent of an upper middle class, the phenomenon of the drug addict is emerging in Italy too. There have been daring articles and protests that the government is doing nothing to stop it. To have drug addicts 'at home' is a guarantee of an easier market for the *cosche* and of trouble for the state: it is a well-known fact that the addict will go to any extreme to find the money for buying hard drugs.

But if part of the New York police was corrupt, the Italian police force was not only corrupt, but obeying the interests of men some of whom were in positions of high authority, able to give orders contrary to the interests of justice and of the law. The difference between the Italian and the American systems basically lay in the fact that the Italian state would not and could not afford to investigate the corruption of its police forces: as we have seen from the Mangano—Coppola—Spagnuolo case, when one single stone was removed too many vermin swarmed out.

The links among criminals have extended to the very institutions of the state, embracing those who should have fought crime, in a frightening illegal liaison. The *cosche* suddenly seemed to proliferate and use— or be used by—illegal extra-Parliamentary fringes: the Italian Neo-Nazi and Neo-Fascist groups which in turn were protected and used by too many legal institutions. In the Seventies came a spate of different but inter-related criminal cases—the telephone bugging scandal, acts of terrorism all over Italy, bombings, illegal arms traffic—all of which have remained unsolved or, when apparently near solution, have been 'transferred' to other inquiring magistrates. The names involved seemed to overlap: Mafiosi, Neo-Fascists, it became difficult to understand who was whose agent, who was in charge at any given moment.

But how could the *cosche* have links with the heirs of the regime which had repressed so many mafiosi? Simply because the moment came when the agents, the thugs employed by both, and sometimes even the leaders, coincided. Money was needed by the Neo-Fascists for their illegal training camps, telephone bugging, criminal activities. Many industrialists had stopped their economic sponsorship of the extreme Right fringe when it became plain that it had been the source of unprecedented violence (bombs in Milan, Brescia, in trains).

First in Sicily and then in the North of Italy kidnappings were organized by the *cosche*, but in many cases as agents of the Neo-Fascists. In some cases the victims had been linked to the extreme Right and some of those kidnappings may have been intended to extract more money from reluctant donors who had stopped financing the illegal groups. The same technique was used in Giuliano's time: when some rich families stopped financing the Separatists, their children would be kidnapped. Count Luciano Tasca used to provide the list of names for Giuliano's gang. More important, he provided information on the habits of the future victims. When it was his turn to be kidnapped (the motivation behind it is still very unclear), the former mayor of Palermo said: 'I don't mind about the millions I had to pay up, nor about having been kidnapped, nor that they broke into my house with machine-guns. But I can't forgive them for coming into the house of Baron Tasca with their hats on. *Cornuti!*'

Records show that even in early Norman times Sicilian bandits raised most of their money from kidnapping and ransoms. The Mafia always pretended to be the go-between. At the turn of the century even the wealthy English were hit. A little daughter of Joss Whitaker, Audrey, was kidnapped and returned for about 100,000 lire, but the family kept very silent about it. Tina Whitaker wrote in her diary: 'Now Joss says it is all an invention'. *Omertà* was hitting the Anglo-Saxons as well.

But, almost traditionally, the feudal landowners and the middle class of Sicily had been left in peace—unless they had committed a *sgarro*, an offence. When their sons were kidnapped they were released unharmed by tacit agreement, without the interference of the police and the law. But in recent years almost all cases of kidnappings have been the sons of the really rich and powerful, those who had always been considered as 'untouchables'. An official of the Carabinieri told me that he believed that the recent outbreak of kidnappings arose out of the fact that many of the Mafia bosses were awaiting trials, which meant expensive lawyers, witnesses to be silenced, jailed underlings whose families had to be kept. Those almost endless trials cost fantastic sums. Another official of the PS Murder Squad (*Criminalpol Squadra Omicidi*) suggested that the new crop of kidnappings of 'untouchables' might have happened because the Mafia had been badly hit and many of its leaders were in prison, banished or in hiding, so that there was no longer a tight rein on the small *cosche*.

Only a few intellectuals then advanced the possibility of a connection between the Neo-Fascists and the *cosche*, but the theory has now become a reality and is being investigated by the police. The kidnapping of Cavaliere Giacomo Caruso's son Antonino was the most astonishing of all the cases involving the 'untouchables'. Antonino was the godson of the late Minister Mattarella, a friend of Judge Scaglione, something which should have guaranteed his 'untouchability'. After this kidnapping, which took place in the province of Trapani on 24 February 1971, Mattarella died of a heart attack. The kidnapping of his godson in the very area where he had been all-powerful came as a blow, a sign of the end of his power. And the fact that anybody would dare to kidnap Mattarella's godson astonished Western Sicily.

Antonino was released a month later for an undisclosed sum. Dealings between the kidnappers and the family took place in total secrecy, his father welcoming any reporter who wanted information with a soaking of icy water. Several months later four people were arrested. Judge Scaglione, had devised a successful method of tracking down the gangsters; all the banknotes had been marked with invisible ink. After being in prison for his refusal to testify, the weak and highly emotional Antonino Caruso was seen to recognize some objects simply because he burst into tears when confronted with them. The police found the house where he had been kept: it belonged to a Neo-Fascist.

On 15 November 1975 the trial for the kidnapping of Antonino Caruso came to an end; seven people were found guilty and two acquitted. Girolamo di Falco was given 15 years, Pitro Barone 14, Rodolfo Collica and Michele Polizzi 13. But in spite of the thoroughness of the trial, the case still remains a mystery and the condemned men chose not to speak. The fact that the important and wealthy Caruso family had to pay its 'tribute' is beyond dispute and the fact that the kidnapping took place in the Alcamo area—the kingdom of the Rimis—leaves doubts on the shifts of power in an area where nothing of the sort could have happened without the knowledge and consent of the Rimis.

In 1972 Pino Vassallo was captured when he was coming home from his office. As he was locking his Fiat 125 in front of his house, two men jumped on him and pushed him to the ground. A friend who tried to help him was stopped by two other men, all armed. The car in which Vassallo was taken away was found two hours later in flames—a common way of destroying all evidence and fingerprints. Pino Vassallo, the son of a tycoon whose name we have already encountered (p. 204), received me in a surprisingly modest office for a man whose hobbies are horses and fast cars; but that is an old Sicilian feature: offices and homes are ugly, it is the exterior which shows and therefore counts. Vassallo's was a long captivity: five months in darkness, locked in a small room.

Where? By whom? Why? These are questions which the authorities have asked many times, as they are convinced that the Vassallos know them, but they remain unanswered. Pino Vassallo told me:

> There was certainly an organization. They were kind in an exaggerated way. How many? I don't know: I had two guardians. Why they kept me for so long, I couldn't say [his father had declared at once that he would have paid the ransom] ... But I was really afraid only when they brought me back to Palermo. They put me inside the boot of a car. I understood that I was going to be released, but I thought that if they met with a police road-block, there were many in Sicily at that time, mainly because of all these kidnappings—they would not stop and the police would shoot at the boot. They left me in a poor district with only a coin for a telephone call.

Later I finally met Pino's notorious father, Francesco Vassallo, once a costermonger, now one of the richest citizens of Sicily. He was very short with black lively eyes and talked thick dialect; his son belonged to a generation which had time and money to become more sophisticated. 'What did they want? Money they wanted. It was a terrible torment, but look, I don't want to think about it any longer: here he is, my Pino!' And he seized his embarrassed son and kissed him fondly.

Why would the *cosche* bother to kidnap people for ransoms which could easily be obtained 'on friendly terms'? Perhaps they wanted to obtain some concessions from the powerful men and intimidate them as well to leave some fields open to the new *cosche*. And certainly so many bosses having disappeared—either in prison, in banishment or in the cemetery—there was no longer any 'respect' imposed for the old guard 'of respect'. Some recent cases of kidnappings happened near Syracuse and Catania, the stronghold of Neo-Fascism, not of the Mafia. When I called on Prince Spadafora Gutierrez, Knight of Malta, whose son Mariano had been kidnapped near Syracuse, he was standing next to a large signed photograph of Mussolini. The Marquis Mariano Spadafora had been kidnapped on 13 May 1971 near his large estates in Eastern Sicily. He was kept tied to a table for seventeen days, in total darkness. Prince Spadafora had been a Minister in the last Republican government of Mussolini, and he is still a strong supporter of the Fascist party; his eldest son is active in the illegal groups of Neo-Fascists and declared to me that Nazism was the only solution. Aldo Palumbo, a rich industrialist from Catania, was also kidnapped on 15 June 1972 and released a month later. The family never disclosed how the ransom money was delivered (it is believed that the ransom was of 107 million lire, £75,000), and Palumbo's wife declared: 'My husband has no enemies.'

In August 1972 it was the turn of another very rich man's son, Luciano Cassina. As he was strolling, three gangsters suddenly blocked his way and seized him. Cassina, who was thirty-seven, was married and had four children, fought back. He was held for 175 days. The son of one of Palermo's most prosperous businessmen, who made his money from property and road construction, Cassina was returned for 1 billion 300 million lire.

The kidnappings spread to the North. In 1974 over forty people were kidnapped in Italy, many of them in the North. After Paul Getty III, who was released for a ransom of 1,290,000 lire, and who had been kidnapped by a group of Calabrians, the victims chosen were of upper middle-class extraction.

After the arrest of many Fascists, it now looks as if the mafiosi have escaped the control of whoever was controlling them. The organization of kidnapping requires men, discipline, silence, cars and hideouts, like the one Gerlando Alberti was building in his farmhouse. It is no easy matter, but is guaranteed by the existence of the system of the *cosche* and by a multitude of agents accustomed to crime and well versed in the art of keeping silent. That's what was wanted by groups which have called themselves by various names and profess the Neo-Nazi and Fascist cause. Until his recent death in Spain, where he had fled, they were under the leadership of Prince Junio Valerio Borghese, who subsequently received a hero's funeral and burial in a chapel of one of Rome's most beautiful churches, Santa Maria del Popolo.

When Andreotti was the Minister of the Interior (1974) he suddenly produced revelations about these groups: who was behind them, what they had done in the past, what they planned to do in the near future, their policy of chaos. (This included bank robberies, bomb-throwing and kidnapping; in the last five years, seven hundred crimes have been their proved responsibilities.) Andreotti told Parliament that not until July 1974 had he seen for the first time a secret fourteen-page document whose title read 'Attempted *coup d'état* under Junio Valerio Borghese (night of 8 December 1970), origins, development and successive repercussions until June 1974.' The details are only partially public because inquiries are being pursued, but everything is being pulled to block these. Clearly the policy of chaos had been pursued by some and protected by others. Following these revelations several people have been arrested. The most sensational name was that of General Vito Miceli, the head of the s i d, the Italian Secret Service.* On the other hand many politicians had got themselves involved by using the Secret Service in a petty policy of blackmailing politicians within the same party, or by accumulating files in order to do so.

In June 1974, the Milan police and magistrates began to voice their suspicions in the direction of links between *cosche* and Neo-Fascists. 'It is not a coincidence,' a Milanese judge said, 'that the Neo-Fascist plots develop mainly in that area of Northern Italy where the Mafia prospers.' And another: 'The Fascist terrorists are flush with gelignite and money, and that money doesn't come only from certain industrialists. Part of the ransom of some kidnappings, we are almost sure, has finished up in the pockets of those Neo-Fascists.'

A young Milanese investigating judge, Giuliano Turone, began to suspect that the kidnappings in the North were the work of a real organization called the 'Anonima Sequestri'. In March 1974, following the track of some suspicious Sicilians and Calabrians (whose form of Mafia is called '*ndrangheta* and is more a nursery for killers than a semi-organized 'institution') banished to the North, he discovered Count Luigi di Montelera who had been kidnapped and hidden in a dark smelly hole in a farmhouse near Bergamo. Turone expected to find not Montelera but another industrialist. When three years earlier the Carabinieri had gone to the same farm to talk to the mafioso Giuseppe Saitta, they had found with him a Calabrian, Vincenzo Mammoliti, who was suspected of playing a key role in the kidnapping of Paul Getty III. In February 1973 immediately after his return from the North Saitta was found inside a Fiat 600, killed by several blows inflicted with a hook, his testicles cut off and pushed inside his mouth. That was to confuse the investigations, as the old Mafia custom indicated that the murder had been performed for a question of honour. In fact Saitta's niece immediately declared that her deceased uncle had raped her.

Officials of the Antimafia said that the only thing they knew about an organization in the North was the fact that there had been a big meeting in May 1972 at the Park Hotel in Zurich, attended by important bosses like 'L'Ingegnere' Greco, Luciano Liggio, Gerlando Alberti and

* The Pike report (1976) on c i a funds in Italy disclosed that the u s Ambassador had channelled c i a money to Miceli to subsidize extreme right-wing movements.

Tommaso Buscetta. Suddenly the idea of banishing mafiosi to the North became unpopular. Eleven murders which had taken place in Milan and Turin in the last years bore the obvious stamp of the Mafia. In 1974 in the whole of Italy there were 1347 men in *soggiorno obbligato*, six hundred of these being mafiosi in the North of Italy. 'In actual fact,' said Cesare Terranova, who after being one of the best Sicilian judges, had joined the Antimafia Commission as a Parliamentarian, 'we Sicilians have exported a lot of bacteria through the *soggiorno obbligato*. Scattering these criminals all over Italy has meant infecting areas which were still uncontaminated by the Mafia.' But a sociologist, Sabino Acquaviva, underlined the reality underneath the phenomenon:

The Mafia, in order to thrive, needs a very precise social and cultural background, mainly characterized by parasitism. Until a few years ago, due to its history, this was a characteristic of the South. Now, little by little, all the country has become Bourbonized; Rome started with its patronage, which quickly spread. It is for this reason that the Mafia can extend itself and find a grip in the North. But it is not so much its own achievement as the lack of achievements in the society which expresses all this.

On 14 November 1975, the enquiring magistrate Dott. Caizzi, from Milan, had finished his investigation of thirty-two people belonging to the 'Anonima Sequestri' and started proceedings. At the head of the association, the notorious Luciano Liggio and other names included Michele Guzzardi, Francesco Guzzardi, Calogero Guzzardi, Giuseppe Ciulla, Salvatore Ugone, Giuseppe Ugone Sr, Francesco Taormina, Giacomo Taormina, Gaetano Quartarano, Giuseppe Pullarà, Agostino Coppola, Domenico Coppola, Ignazio Pullarà, Nello Pernice; as usual the family tie was part of the structure of this particular *cosca*. The 'hot money', Caizzi wrote (enormous sums up to 6 milliards), was invested in legitimate business and was re-cycled with the 'alliance, at different levels of banks and politicians.' Dott. Caizzi wrote that letters from politicians—not only Sicilians, but also from Lombardy—had been found, underlining once again the link between Mafia and politics.

In May 1974, Judge Turone had arrested a priest, Agostino Coppola, a very distant relation of Frank's. Turone believed that Coppola was part of the organization which had probably planned the kidnappings of Antonino Caruso, Pino Vassallo and Luciano Cassina, and had attempted to kidnap Vincenzo Traina, killing him instead. In January 1976 Turone was able to pin down the role that Father Agostino Coppola had played in the Liggio's *cosca*. Not only did he re-cycle 'dirty' money from numerous kidnappings (with the cooperation of the banks), but he kept up political contacts. 'Coppola was the procurer of votes for a very important Sicilian politician.' Among the names in the documents which were found in the priest's house were those of Mario D'Acquisto (public works director for the Region of Sicily), of Giovanni Gioia and the Private Secretary of former Minister Restivo (Christian Democrats).

The trial for the kidnapping of Luciano Cassina took place in November 1975 and Father Coppola was indicted. A young mafioso, Leonardo Vitale, had been 'of considerable help' to the instructing magistrates, and his release from prison was recommended.

But though the Mafia operated in the North, the headquarters were always in Sicily. In the past the *cosche* had acted each of its own accord, but recently there seemed to be a definite systematization for big deals such as kidnappings, the black market in butter, drugs and arms. Could it come from the Neo-Fascists? It was thought that Liggio had been the mastermind of all these operations, but it would be impossible for one man alone to manage all this, and the fact of his arrest shows that he had been betrayed.

But let us go back in time. A very odd episode took place on 31 May 1970: the deputy Nicosia, the only MP belonging to the (official) Fascist party, who was in the Antimafia Parliamentary Commission, was knifed in a central street of Palermo. The wound was deep, and his recovery was slow, but when Nicosia was able to talk he said that the would-be assassin had been a certain George Tsekouris, a Greek who in the meantime had died in a bomb attack at the American Embassy in Athens. The motivation remained mysterious. Dead men cannot talk, and there was no inquiry, just a lot of doubts. But had it really been a Greek—or that particular Greek—who tried to kill the Sicilian deputy? Why? That was the time when the Italian Neo-Fascists were receiving funds and support from the Greek Junta and a coup d'état was being organized by Prince Borghese. Had somebody wanted to dampen Nicosia's enthusiasm for the Antimafia Commission? Had Nicosia stumbled across links between the Neo-Fascists and the *cosche*?

A few months later, the journalist Mauro de Mauro, who had had connections with the extreme Right, was kidnapped and disappeared forever. He was not kidnapped for ransom. On 16 September 1970—it was a hot Palermitan evening—people chatted leaning over the cement balconies against a background of the clatter of dishes and loud television. De Mauro was coming home from his office to his house in the centre of the city. His eldest daughter was also coming home with her fiancé. She saw him leave his car and heard somebody calling his name. He went back to his BMW and it set off at high speed with two or three men inside, bumping along as if driving with difficulty.

De Mauro had been working for *L'Ora*, had 'good contacts' in the Mafia world and had written excellent investigative journalism. He was digging into the death of Mattei, the state industrialist (see Chapter 9) possibly following some track discovered while researching for a film on the subject. At the start of the inquiries it was believed that De Mauro had found a piece of information concerning the 'High Mafia' and its links with Mattei. At least the police believed it, encouraged by De Mauro's widow and by her second daughter Junia (called after Prince Junio Valerio Borghese). The two women talked exclusively to the police (PS), refusing to collaborate with the Carabinieri and with De Mauro's former colleagues. She had few friends in Palermo and a murky political past. But De Mauro knew the Mafia intimately and was well aware that the only safety is never to keep 'Mafia' information to oneself. It was odd that he did not immediately publish what he had found, or talk to his colleagues on *L'Ora*.

De Mauro had belonged to the *Decima Mas*, a group of Fascists who operated in 1944 and 1945 for the last Mussolini government, the Republica di Salò. The *Decima Mas* was led by Prince Borghese, and was the most brutal Fascist force: it killed partisans and civilians suspected of protecting partisans. De Mauro's wife had also been in the *Decima Mas*. After the liberation, the couple fled south. De Mauro spent some years of working under different names for various dubious sources and publications in Palermo before he was recruited by the left-wing daily *L'Ora*. Its editor was probably mistaken in employing a man with a past like De Mauro's, but De Mauro was an excellent journalist and he 'matured politically' or at least Nisticò, *L'Ora's* editor, thinks so. But did his wife?

Shortly before his murder, De Mauro had talked to important politicians like Graziano Verzotto and Vito Guarrasi,* and tried to see

---

* Both men came under suspicion (officially for the first time) following De Mauro's disappearance. Verzotto claimed that De Mauro had been investigating drug-smuggling, whereupon Giuseppe Di Cristina supposedly 'threatened him' for making the disclosure. Verzotto sued Di Cristina, but retracted in 1974.

Alessi, one of the better Christian Democrats in Sicily. It also emerged that he went to see the Chief Public Prosecutor, Pietro Scaglione, who was shot dead by a Mafia commando a few months after this meeting.

The key to De Mauro's murder, and one of the most urgent reasons for Scaglione's, lies in what they said to each other. An official from the police—PS—told me that they now know what was said, but have no proof. De Mauro had got hold of a piece of information concerning the Neo-Fascist groups in Sicily, their connection with the Mafia, with kidnappings, with politics. Of the people connected with the Neo-Fascist groups who have been arrested in Palermo, the psychiatrist Micalizio had been the *mascotte* of the *Decima Mas* when young and knew De Mauro of old connections.

In 1972 another journalist, Giovanni Spampinato, who also worked as a correspondent of *L'Ora*, was shot dead in Ragusa a town riddled with Mafia by Roberto Campria, who belonged to the Neo-Fascists and was the son of the president of the local Tribunale. Spampinato was found dead in his car, killed by six bullets fired from two different revolvers. Campria declared that he alone had killed the journalist because he felt persecuted by him.

In November 1975 the trial of the right-wing Roberto Cambria, of Ragusa, took place at Syracuse, but the case was *'archiviato'*, i.e. 'put in the archives, the sure way to cover documents with the dust of oblivion. The papers, including a report from the Carabinieri, pointed to Cambria as the murderer of Angelo Tumino, a former official of the MSI (fascist party). That year (1972) Giovanni Spampinato who worked for *L'Ora* published articles on the Fascists and on Roberto Cambria. Spampinato was found murdered. Cambria has been accused of perjury. On the other hand, the trial recognized that Spampinato, in his articles, was following the right track, in linking thefts and crimes to the extreme right wing.

At that time Spampinato had been investigating another murder, that of the local Fascist Tumino, and was convinced that it had been a political assassination planned by certain groups of Neo-Fascists from Ragusa and Syracuse who dealt with the *cosche* in the traffic of works of art, cigarettes and drugs. Spampinato believed that Campria knew a lot about Tumino's murder. His murder remains another mystery within the network of Sicilian criminal activities.

'The links between the Neo-Fascists and the *cosche* are several, an official declared, 'and they emerge from investigations into the drug traffic, kidnapping, the illegal money market, and details of meetings between the leaders of the extreme Right. But among the various links, the most important could be that of the traffic in arms. Police Commissar Calabresi was murdered while he was investigating this operation.'*

The areas of the North where there is a maximum concentration of mafiosi were visited by the Neo-Fascist Sicilians Pomar, Micalizio and De Marchi, all of whom have recently been arrested for plotting against the state. In 1974 the same Prince Alliata who had been accused by the bandit Giuliano's cousin Pisciotta as one of the masterminds of the slaughter at Portella delle Ginestre was accused of belonging to the secret Neo-Fascist groups in Sicily. His history could not but confirm his right-wing and mafioso allegiances: in 1946 the Prince was elected to the Palermo county council as a Monarchist, in 1947 he became a regional deputy, and in 1948 he was elected deputy in the national parliament with sixty per cent of his district's votes. Real evidence of Mafia collusion, especially in those days. In 1960 he was expelled by his party for refusing to vote against the Tambroni government. Once again, as one comes near to defining the Mafia, the Hydra slips away, showing another of its many different heads. Different perhaps, but all belonging to the same body.

---

* Calabresi belonged to the Political Branch of the Milanese Police and was involved in dubious political intrigues. He was among the high officials who tried to indict some anarchists like Pinelli and Valpreda, instead of Neo-Fascists against whom there was real evidence. Another name which figures in both stories is that of Captain Varisco of the Carabinieri (see Valpreda's *Memoirs*), who was also mentioned by Judge Spagnuolo as involved with the disappearance of the telephone tapes.

16 Conclusion: The Mafia in Crisis?

The island of Sicily, continually drained by emigration and plagued by desperate unemployment, has clung jealously both to its regional isolation and to its own pagan philosophy which holds the fatalistic view that life is cheap, and that there are worse sins than murder. The combination produced an ideal breeding-ground for the emergence of the phenomenon we have come to call the Mafia. The unique historical process to which the island was subjected brought to rapid maturity the mafioso mentality, attitudes and code of behaviour by pitting individuals against successive waves of foreign invasion. The mafioso has, throughout history, proved able to distort and to adapt to his own ends the ideals and techniques of imported institutions. The Guilds, the Inquisition, the farm agents (*gabelloti*), modern technology have all made their unwilling contribution. The Mafia has harnessed and developed mechanisms introduced by peasant revolts and by the bureaucracy of today. Operating always as anti-social and unnecessary brokers of power at whatever levels were available, the Mafia has proved so successful and so flexible that successive generations have found it difficult to recognize the continuity of the tradition. In the seventeenth century the Marquis of Villabianca failed to see the connection between earlier societies, to all intents and purposes *cosche*, and the criminal life of his own time: modern scholars, similarly deceived, have attributed the 'birth' of the Mafia to the mid-nineteenth century, and have linked its emergence with the introduction of the electoral system.

The mafiosi had achieved Sicily's isolation by monopolizing the meagre capitalistic structures of the large estates and later the State corporations. By choosing to operate through the mafiosi, the State has weakened its institutions in Western Sicily and in Italy which, as we have seen, often overlap with the Mafia as this remains the fundamental broker of power. The problems of management supervision, and of checking or retaining the peasant labour which until 1950 was needed by absentee landowners for their large estates, passed on to the large corporations, either for the absentee State or the absentee private industrialist, or for the absentee political or administrative institutions. While the construction of roads, farms, cottages, provided additional employment in the derelict agricultural areas of Western Sicily and peasants' incomes were supplemented by provisions regarding pensions and social security, access to these rights was only conceivable through personal links with those able to grant favours. This Sicilian and now Italian characteristic enhances the practice of political patronage. Access to State resources and the right connections for mobilizing credits and subsidies is vital and almost automatically makes a Western Sicilian into a person who is *'ntisu*, a mafioso: and this is so because of the island's historic characteristics.

On a lower level, below the urban competition for building contracts, the smaller *cosche* can maintain, with the same mechanism, their hold over markets, transport, and the organization and supervision of labour. This is organized in a plain unglamorous way, through infiltration into any vulnerable industry. It can be compared to the selling of cars, of books, of distribution of food, the only differentiation being the nature of the agents, of the 'distributors', and of the use of intimidation rather than persuasion. Murder is rare, but a 'Mafia' death must be well-timed, well planned and must be recognizable as such: murder is indeed the ultimate form of propaganda which establishes invented rules and codes. The overt executions are part of a PR operation, the murder must not only be recognized as a sentence of death but as a glamorous operation. There are other ways of destroying people, that of gossip and lie, manipulated not only through the natural social channels, but even through the press, which either picks the gossip up or willingly submits to it. This is again a routine operation used by secret services and by public relation offices.

I certainly see the Mafia as a phenomenon which grew and evolved within Sicilian history, habit, kinship. A phenomenon which cannot, therefore, be eradicated by force. The slow development of social change will certainly see its gradual transformation into less brutal and less organized nuclei which should eventually lose their specifically criminal, 'mafioso' characteristics, should wealth become more evenly distributed. Sicily's cultural character is strongly attached to individualistic characteristics which are unlikely to change radically from one century to the next. One step has been taken. In 1975, the Antimafia Parliamentary Commission concluded its work: it had taken thirteen years, the longest time of all Parliamentary commissions which had investigated Sicily and had been the first specifically to study the phenomenon of the Mafia. But although some of its recommendations had been valid, it often repeated Prefect Mori's mistakes by thinking that the Mafia could be defeated by banishing mafiosi and by special laws. Once again some big names were not mentioned nor could they be. They were the power, the government, those whom the Antimafia Commission was actually serving. One must underline the necessity for a reform of the Italian legal code, a purge of the magistrature, reforms in the police forces, new measures to limit some of the Mafia's lawyers' activities; in this way the law could deal effectively with the *cosche*.

In the major context of political protection, the Mafia's proliferation and strength at the moment is the Italian government's responsibility. It is in that central core that the situation has to change radically. If and when Italy changes its system of political patronage, its irresponsibility towards the public (and a total change is vital in Italy to wipe out old Bourbon and Piedmontese structures), then Sicily will change too, and the Mafia will not survive.

But, of course, were the Mafia today unable to get its political protection it would be a minor phenomenon comparable to the Sicilian customs of, say, the cult of the dead or the puppet theatre. That is, if the economic gains were not to be the goal, the violent nature of the *cosche* would disappear. In this the Antimafia Commission's recommendation to punish the mafiosi by confiscating any gains which could not be proved as licit was surely right. The Italian government probably ignored the suggestion, as few people in Western Sicily (or elsewhere in Italy) could show the provenance of their income, and this is also due to the complicated Italian fiscal system and to banks' secrecy. In order to enforce this recommendation, total change, i.e. revolution, is needed in Sicily as well as in Italy. The Mafia is capitalism as applied by a sub-cultural class; were the accumulation of capital impossible as the ultimate and only aim, the phenomenon could not survive in its present form.

The critical situation in which the *cosche* are today is also due to the crisis of the capitalistic system. Although that system never reached Sicily, but in the form of the established Mafia, the philosophy of the Sicilian middle class is undergoing a change. One can detect this by observing a stratum which once would have been reactionary (like a Palermitan real estate builder who is a militant Communist, and young girls who defy traditional taboos and leave for their holidays with their boy-friends) and which presses not only for evolution, but for revolution. And although the Sicilian electoral spectrum remained stable in the last local elections, its behaviour during the referendum on divorce was unexpectedly healthy. Since Sicily was expected to be particularly easy to turn against divorce, the Christian Democrats, the Church, the extreme Right focused their electoral campaign on the island. (In one case, Senator Fanfani, then Secretary of the Christian Democrats, warned Sicilian peasants in the derelict central town of Enna, that had they allowed divorce to remain legal, their wives would have left them … for other ladies! The concept of lesbianism rang particularly absurdly in that sombre and destitute town.) Of course, in that occasion, the *cosche* had not been mobilized: there were no candidates to support, no seats in the Sicilian Assembly or in the Italian Parliament to secure.

There is obviously no single way to 'eliminate the Mafia': the idea in itself is naïve and only regimes which feigned ignorance, such as the Italian and the Fascist, could launch themselves into such mock phraseology. The Mafia cannot be eliminated because, as a single entity, it does not exist, it is not a 'thing', not a secret society. As we have seen, the Western Sicilian political candidates are successful only if their skill is in social manoeuvres and they can supply benefits for those with large kinship affiliations, persons who have a clientele and can provide votes in exchange for which the politician will offer employment in private and public agencies, will distribute agricultural funds and credits, license public works projects.

All illegal channels which can produce an income are allowed as long as political support is provided to the specific political candidate who will be even more badly needed than in the legal or semi-legal operations. Again, as we have seen, the same names seem to crop up and many stories blur or merge into each other in a manner that makes one think that the Mafia today, in its organizational and 'mental' forms, has spread to whatever channel it can find within the Italian institutional structure. Although one can see the logic of the *cosche*–Neo-fascist collaboration, the latter needing large sums of money, the *cosche* can provide the criminal organization in exchange for part of the loot and political protection. But only political protection of a kind: the extreme Right, although tightly clasped to the mechanisms of Italian power—

army, law, secret services—is weakening. In the last regional elections (1975), Italy voted against the existing structure and moved to the Communist party, which gained twelve per cent. The violent Neo-Fascists, although tightly connected with the MSI (the official Parliamentary Fascist party, which has recently changed its name into *Destra Nazionale,* the National Right) have no electoral platform: the *cosche* are thus not vital to them and they are used not in their customary role of providing votes, but as a straightforward criminal organization. This has never happened before: the boss has always known that his stability derived from tying the *cosca* to official power, not to clandestine or semi-clandestine movements.

In this one can analyse a crisis, a beginning of the end: being used by a political group, rather than using it, has always been the role of bandits who ended by being eliminated by their own protectors or by being betrayed to the police. But it is beginning to look as if the Mafia may have overreached itself. The very expansion of the *cosche's* activity throughout Italy should have meant the expansion of political protection at Parliamentary and administrative level. Rome, with its corrupt and 'Southernized' administration, was within the *cosche's* grasp. But this has become public knowledge (cf. Natale Rimi who was employed by the Regional Administration and Frank Coppola settling near Rome). The penetration in the richer fields of Turin, Genoa, Milan, the Veneto region has not been accompanied by securing men in the respective regional administration. Political protection in those regions was only assured through the Neo-Fascists who, in turn, enjoy a degree of political protection from part of the government and the police forces. But it is not real power. Therefore the *cosche* outside Sicily seem to act in an almost desperate way, trying to accumulate capital quickly, without appeasing some of the established local power. The only permanent political guarantee is achieved through the existing semi-democratic machine. The *omertà* which the Christian Democrats have so far imposed on themselves when dealing with misbehaviour within their party, has guaranteed the Christian Democrats' control of Sicily, but for a price which should never have been paid. Yet even there one can see a few changes: Ciancimino was denied a candidature in the last local elections (1975), and was singled out in the Antimafia Report (1976) as a prominent mafioso, Verzotto has been suspended (although not expelled) by the Party and the leadership in Rome now presents some cleaner faces than before the Italian swing to the Left. I have tried to show that the Christian Democrats were (and are) the natural targets because theirs is a party which holds power. All the other parties, with the exception of the Communists, have also been used by the *cosche* and have accepted their votes. When in coalition they shared a slice of the cake of power which, not only in Sicily, is baked with the mechanisms of patronage: State money to pocket, supply of jobs to distribute, building permits, money channelled through the State corporations. By its very aims and base, the Communist party is the enemy of the *status quo* and when it has ruled a region or a city, the Communists have been the banner of honesty: they are the natural enemy of the *cosche*. A radical change in Italy, the participation of the Communists in government which has now become a real possibility, would eliminate the rottennness on which the *cosche* bacteria thrive. The very expansion of the *cosche* has also guaranteed the beginning of the end of the phenomenon of the Mafia, because little by little the *cosche* are detaching themselves from the mentality which produced them, from the *raison d'etre* from which they sprang. Unlike the Sicilians, the American Cosa Nostra learnt to survive in an 'alien' environment and gave itself a real structure, successfully penetrated the legitimate and semi-legitimate business, i.e. was totally absorbed by the American capitalistic structure. Cosa Nostra never chose to co-operate with fringe groups, but with the CIA,, thus sheltering under a real colossus.

The American Mafia has even found a new field: pornography. A *New York Times* enquiry (October 1975) said that today there is no single pornographic film produced in the United States where there is no Mafia money. The Colombo and Bonanno families, for example, put their legitimate money in films like *Deep Throat* and *Wet Rainbow*. Other pornographic films (like the one on the life of the 'Madame' Xaviera Hollander) have been illegally reprinted in several copies and distributed to cinemas of provincial circuits. If the owners of the cinemas object to buying the illegal cheaper copies, means of 'convincing' them are easily found. Also several 'straight' producers who make all sorts of films, i.e. not only pornographic ones, have been mellowed by the tragic end of Jack Molinas. Molinas had been an 'aid' of Joseph Gentile (of the Bonanno family) and had moved to Hollywood. When Molinas had decided to become a legitimate producer and work on his own, he was found on his bed, killed by a single shot. The young lady who was with him, had been spared, but not entirely: her face had been scarred.

The families are also working on the pornographic magazine business: the distribution of *Screw* has been taken over and doubled its circulation since. The American police see the Mafia's expansion in the pornographic films as a climb towards the seizing of the whole Hollywood industry.

We have seen how many of the 'laws' which built up the *cosche*'s strength have been dropped in the haste to accumulate money and in the necessity to make more in a fight against the Law and the police which is actually becoming harsher. The *cosca* is no longer the artichoke with many leaves: everybody is ready to eliminate the core whose only reason to be there at all is to make more money than the others. The family of the henchman who has been caught is not provided for by the *capocosca* (cf. Alberti). The Boss who receives money to 'protect' steals the same goods which he's meant to protect (again cf. Alberti's Genoese episode). People who live in the district and submit to the Boss rule because of fear or passivity or both, no longer seek for his advice, for his 'justice': the *capo* would have no time for that kind of patriarchal nonsense. It is significant that some Bosses who have been caught (Buscetta, Liggio, Alberti) have been betrayed to the police by their people, as used to happen to bandits, but never to a Cascioferro or Vizzini or a Rimi. In their evolution from *capocosca* in Sicily to gangsters in Italy, the *cosche* have as usual followed the tide of the times, ready to absorb chanegs at all levels, including those of ethical values and of the break-up of the family in Sicily as well as in Italy. These elements contribute to the collapse of the substructure which once guaranteed the *cosche*'s well-being.

A cancerous growth, a parallel governmental structure—the opposite and the enemy of the concept of the State—the Hydra has achieved a glamour which it cultivates. But it is the successful side which has been picked up and which is easier to recount in articles, books, films. Indeed the story of a criminal boss makes a better tale than that of the successful policeman (unless the policeman has all the connotations of the gangsters, like James Bond). The mafioso is aware of this over-publicized glamorous image: some bosses try to live up to it, being 'generous', surrounding themselves with luxury, silence and respect. The small fry, the agents, try to achieve power which becomes even more attractive as seen on films and television. Yet it is a tragic life of non-communication: every word spoken is information given away. The mafioso has to live within his own world, which sometimes he yearns to escape, at times even for more interesting company. He questions, he is the recipient of information: the larger his contacts, the stronger he is. But he remains inarticulate, because he has to. Behind the boss there are squalid teams of agents paid for doing something which substitutes an income impossible to achieve by legal means. They collect the *pizzo*, they master the intimidating looks, gestures (rarely phraseology), they are carriers of drugs, of news, of information. They form an immense undergrowth. In some cases they work 'full time', in others they have other jobs, like indeed the one of policemen. The reward comes through better jobs for relatives, or straightforward money if they are in a position to escape suspicion.

But if there is a temptation to sneer at what seems to be an alien and far away phenomenon which could never touch the civilized shores of, say, Britain,* one should stop and analyze the fact that many features seem to coincide with public life in other European countries. This happens as the size of the bureaucracy grows alarmingly and some European middle classes evolve into more reactionary social groups after the effective disappearance of the aristocracy as a class which

* In the South of France, the *caid*, the Marseilles boss, enjoys political protection and so does the Corsican cliques. In Britain there has been 'a Mafia murder', as Scotland Yard put it, and an Italian policeman specialized in the Mafia spent one year at Scotland Yard which, however, would not give any information. A German magazine, *Capital*, dedicated a long feature to Mafia activities in Germany. It said that with the arrival of Italian immigrants, most of them Sicilians, the Mafia grew roots North of the Alps and especially in Germany. The magazine alleged that all Italian restaurants in Düsseldorf, Stuttgart and Munich are under the control of a mafioso from Düsseldorf called Salvatore Gentile, and that two restaurants in Munich, 'da Giovanni' and 'Cortina' were destroyed when they refused to pay the *pizzo*. The overboss and organizer of part of Northern Europe was said to be Luciano Liggio but one can detect the presence of different *cosche* dealings in different areas, rather than the tight network of only one organizer. Anyway Liggio is in prison now. The report went on saying that Saarbrucken was the centre of Mafia activities, such as the smuggling of arms and works of art. An Italian trade unionist in Germany said that by 1963 the *cosche* had taken over from the trade unions as the organizers of work permits and that some of the Italian workers had to pay up to ten per cent of their wages to the *cosche*. This is exactly what had happened in the US. Although the German government seemed to ignore the situation including the bribing of the police forces, *Capital* alleged a tip from Interpol had lead to the arrest of twenty-two people in Frankfurt who dealt in forgery, stolen share certificates, drugs, arms smuggling and even the commission of one murder. In 1973 three Italian restaurants in London were burnt around the same period, but their owners denied to me any connection with a protection racket.

retained power. I have often heard British MPs relating with worry the Mafia to Italy and Italy to the EEC: in fact the EEC could be a real breeding ground for corruption—but corruption of another kind, of the conventional, legalized variety which has no need of the special services of the Mafia to get what it wants. There is no question of *cosche* infiltrating Brussels; the fact is that their primitive subcultural weapons would not do. One needs better training than that, and anyway the fields have already been distributed, the cake is being eaten among bureaucrats.

Britain would be a difficult field for real Mafia penetration because the basis of Mafia power, political protection, would be difficult to buy. Not only because of the interchanging of ruling parties, but because legalized corruption assures clean money for future company directors.

The Mafia does not exist for the mafioso, but it has come to exist for us. We are aware of an entity which operates within anti-social rules and has the connotation of threats, intimidation, of violence. We are all victims, not only when we become tourists in Sicily and forcibly become part of the *pizzo* mechanism, but when we go to a restaurant almost anywhere in Europe and the US (in fact in Canada and Australia too). Even more so in being part of a society which counts many and tragic victims of hard drugs. We tolerate the mafioso because power tolerates him, because the Sicilian middle-class is him, because legal power still merges with him. The vicious circle merges into total identification

APPENDIX 1: A MAFIA GLOSSARY

Ammonizione   Judicial proceeding which imposes specific restrictions on offenders or potential offenders

Anonima Sequestri   Incorporated kidnappings

Associazione a delinquere   A charge 'invented' by Prefetto Mori especially for the mafiosi

Brigadiere   Police, carabinieri and Guardia di Finanza equivalent of the rank of sergeant

Camorra   The Neapolitan entity which, unlike the Sicilian Mafia, was a secret society and in fact does not exist any longer. The Calabrian 'mafia' is generally referred to as L'onorata società, but it has also a variety of names. Many Calabresi are now 'working' for the Mafia

Campiere   Overseer, field-guard

Canziarsi   To go into hiding (from the police)

Capo   Chief of a 'family' (Cosa Nostra)

Capo dei capi   Boss of all bosses (American cosa nostra)

Capomafia   Term used to describe the 'primus inter pares' of several capocosche

Carrubi   Carabinieri

Compare, compà, commare   Old Italian words for somebody who is close to the family (The Merry Wives of Windsor is, in Italian, 'Le allegre commari di Windsor'). It comes from 'cum matrem cum patrem'. In Sicilian *compare* or *commare* are witness to a marriage of godfathers and godmothers, a practice used by the *cosche* to expand the family network.

Componenda   Agreement between the authorities and the criminals for which a portion of the stolen goods is returned to the legitimate owner who, in exchange, does not denounce the theft. The authorities take a percentage of the deal.

Confino (soggiorno obbligato)   Legal banishment

Consorteria   A 'trust', a clique of people linked by the same interests, generally illegal interests. A *cosca*

Cosa bianca   Heroin

Cosa carica   A considerable quantity of drugs

Cosca (*plural: cosche*)—*cacocciula*   Referred etymologically to artichoke (in Sicilian = *cacocciula*) to indicate a clique of mafiosi. *Capocosca* = the leader of a *cosca*

Criminalpol   Branch of the Murder Squad (ps) dealing with the Mafia

Ente   State corporation

Family   American *cosca*

Fare l'associazione   To make the association—slang for: 'the police and the law are trying to indict us for association to commit crimes'

Feudo, feudi   Like *latifundium*

Gabella   The leasehold of a large estate belonging to an absentee landowner

Gabelloto (*gabellotto*)   The leaseholder—the mafioso

Garantire   To guarantee, to protect and give one's word for a 'smaller' man

Guardianeria   Surveillance by mafiosi extended to contingent estates

Latifundum (*pl. Latifundia*)   Extensive properties in central Sicily belonging to absentee landowners

L'Ora   Palermitan evening daily started in 1900 by Ignazio Florio. It is now an unofficial Communist publication (unofficial in the sense that it does not depend directly on the Party)

Lupara   Sawn-off shotgun. Meant for shooting wolves and used by Sicilian criminals for its compactness. It is an ordinary shotgun sawn off at both ends, so that it becomes a kind of long revolver, but a more lethal one, since its bullets contain many lead pellets. It is a fearful and graceful object; some of the shotguns are ornately worked, but most are just smoothed on both sides, the wooden and the metal ends. The belt for the bullets has a beautiful quality and obviously enhances the sense of power of the man who feels its weight.

Mandante   Principal

Mandatario   Agent in a Mafia crime

Manutengolo   Mafioso in his role of accomplice

Maresciallo   The highest nco in the *Carabinieri* C.C.

'nfamita An infamy—for a mafioso, breaking the Mafia 'code'

'ntisu Somebody whose opinion is listened to and is important—a mafioso

Nucleo Investigativo Investigating Bureau of the Carabinieri which deals especially with the Mafia

omertà The Sicilian custom of keeping silent and of not cooperating with the authorities

Onorata Società The Calabrian criminal association. Its archaic denomination of *'ndragheta*—for the society—and *'ndrina* for the cliques. The *'Ndragheta* is unlike the Mafia an organized secret society and the police confirm this. In 1970 policemen broke into a congress of 175 Calabrian criminals at the Aspromonte. The many sentries who were guarding the secret locality armed to the teeth were gagged, and the police were able to take most of the men by surprise. The supreme bosses were wearing masks so that the lesser criminals in the society would not recognize them (a fact which underlines the difference from the Mafia: a Mafia boss has to be seen and known as such). In 1971, 4,600 Calabrians had been hit by police measures such as *l'ammonizione*, and 154 had been banished. *Al confino* they met up with Sicilians and the links with the *cosche* started or were strengthened.

Padrino Godfather; in mafia terms 'sponsor' or guarantor. Also *galantuomo, uomo 'ntisu, di rispetto* (of respect)

Pallettoni The *lupara's* pellets

pezzo da novanta Mafia overboss

pizzo (pizzu) cuccia The tariff required by the *cosca* on any trade. *Fari vagnari u pizzu* = to wet the beak of the bird. The tribute called pizzo or cuccia could consist of wheat or goods or money

Prefetto Prefect. A Fascist official nomination for authorities sent from the central government with special powers over the local authorities. It still exists

Prefettura Official palace of the Prefect

Publica Sicurezza (PS) The Italian Police Force which comes under the Ministry of the Interior

puparo The man who ad-libs the stories of *i pupi* and also manufactures *i pupi*

pupi Sicilian puppets (representing the paladins of the court of Charlemagne)

Questore—Vire Questore Police chief (PS) and deputy Police Chief

Rassettarsi la testa Mafioso slang for keeping quiet

Regime   A crew of mafiosi in the Cosa Nostra organization (American Mafia). *Caporegime* = lieutenant

Sbirro (*pl. Sbirri*)   Southern pejorative for policemen

Scruscio   Noise. *Cose che fanno scruscio* = fire-arms

Sfregio   An offence to the authority of a mafioso, which has to be punished

Sgarro   An offence punishable with death

Soggiorno Obbligato   The same as *al confino*. Legal banishment far from the accused's place of residence

squadra omicidi   Murder squad of the PS (Italian pllice)

subcapo   Underboss (American Cosa Nostra)

Sucività   The society—the Mafia

Vendetta   Revenge

Vossia   Comparable to the English 'thou' and no longer used in current Italian. The Sicilians use it only to address people of respect like the mafiosi

APPENDIX 2:
THE MAFIA IN SICILIAN BALLADS

Lamentu pi la morti di Turiddu Carnivali

E allora, come vedete,
è arrivato lo cantastorie siceliano, Ciccio Busacca:
è venuto a cantarvi la storia
di Turiddu Carnivali,
lo picciotto che morse ammazzato
a Sciara, nella provincia di Palermo,
morse ammazzato della Mafia.
Turiddu chianci su matri e
chianci tutte li povereddi de la Sicilia,
perchè Turiddu morse ammazzato
pè li pane de le poveredde.

Ancilo era e nun avia l'ali,
Santu nun era e miraculi facia
ncelu acchianava sensa cordi e scali
e sensa appidamenti uni scinnia
Era l'amuri lu so capitali
e 'sta ricchizza a tutti la spartia
Turiddu Carnivali nnuminatu
e como Cristu murio ammazzatu.

A Lament for the death of Turiddu Carnivali

And now, as you can see, / the Sicilian ballad singer has arrived: / He has arrived to sing the story / of Turiddu Carnivali, / the young man who was killed / at Sciara, in the province of Palermo, / who was killed by the Mafia. / For Turiddu cries his mother and / cry all the poor of Sicily, / because Turiddu was killed / for the daily bread of the poor. /

He was an angel and had no wings, / He was not a saint but made miracles / He climbed to the sky without ropes or cables / and without help would descend. / Love was his capital / and he shared this wealth with all, / he was called Turiddu Carnivali, / who died, murdered, like Christ. /

Di nicu lu patruzzu nun cunusciu
appi la matre svinturata a latu
cumpagna a lu duluri e lo pinio
e a lu panuzzu nivuru scuttatu;
Cristu di ncielu lu benediciu
ci dissi, 'Figghiu, tu mori ammazzatu
a Sciara li patruna, armi addannati
ammazzanu a cu voli libirtati'.

Turiddu avia li jorna cuntati
ma incuntrava la morti e ci ridia
ca videva li frati cunnannati
sotta li piedi di la tirannia
li carni di travagghiu macinati
sopra la cippu a farinni tunia
e suppurtari nun putia l'abusu
de lu baruni e di lu mafiusu

.... E fici liga di sta carni e pusui
ed arma pi' luttari a li putenti
di ddu paisi esiliatu e scuru
unni la storia avia truvato un muru.
Fatti coraggiu e non aviri scantu
avene 'jornu e scinni lu Misia
lu Sucialismu cu l'ali di mantu
ca porta pani, paci e puesia:
Veni si tu lu voi, si tu si santo,
si si nnimico di la tirannia.

When small he did not know his father, / he lived with his wretched mother, / companion to sorrows and pains / and to burnt black bread; / Christ from above blessed him / She would tell him, 'My son, you will be murdered / at Sciara the landowners, / damned people / kill whoever wants liberty.' /

Turiddu had but numbered days to live / but went towards death and didn't care / as he saw his companions condemned / under the feet of tyranny, / their flesh torn by work / over the gallows like a torture. / and he could not bear the abuse / of the baron and of the mafioso ... /

So he made a union of this peasantry / which is the only way to fight the powerful / of this far away and dark land / where history had found a wall. / Take courage and don't fear / the day of the Messiah will come / blessed Socialism / brings bread, peace and poetry. / Come if you want, if you are good, / if you are an enemy of tyranny. /

Dissi 'La terra e' di cu la travagghia
pigghiati li banneri e li zappuna.'
E prima ancora chi spaccasse l'alba
ficeru conchi e scavaro fussuna.
A addivento la terra una tuvagghia
viva di carni come nna pirsona
e sotto a la russio de li banneru
parsi un giganti ogni jurnateri.

Curreru lesti li carubbineri
con la scupetti mmanu e li catini
Turiddu ci gridau: 'Fatevi arreri
latruna no ci nn'e', mancu assassini
Ci sunnu cà gli afflitti jurnateri
che mancu sangue cian ntre li vini
s'Iddu circati latruna e briganti
palazzo li trovate, a' con l'amante.'

Lo maresciallu se feci n'avanti
dissi: 'Le legge chistu nun lo cunstenti.'
Turiddu ci risposi senza scanti:
'Chista e' la liggi de li priputenti,
ma c'e' una liggi chi nun sbaggia e menti
ca dici: 'Pani a li panzi vacanti,
roba agli gnudi, acqua agli assitati
e a cu travagghia, onori e libertati.'

He said: 'Land belongs to those who work it / take your banners and spades.' / And even before sunrise broke, / they dug and dug the earth. / The field became like a tablecloth / alive with people, like a person / and under the red banners / each casual labourer felt like a giant. /

The Carabinieri were quick to arrive / with guns in their hands and fetters / Turiddu told them: 'Go back, / here there are no thieves, no murderers / Here are only the wretched hired labourers / who don't even have blood inside their veins / if you are looking for thieves and bandits / you'll find them in the palaces, with their mistresses.' /

The head of the Carabinieri walked towards him / and said, 'The law doesn't allow this.' / Turiddu answered without fear: / 'Yours is the law of the bully / but there is a law which doesn't fail / and says, 'Bread to the empty stomach, / clothes to the naked, water to the thirsty / and honour and liberty to the one who works.' /

La mafia pinsava a scupittati;
sta liggi nun garbava a li patruna
ca sunno comu li cani arragliati
cu li denti appizzati alle garruna
Poveru jurnateri sventurati!
ca l'anti di ncoddu a muzzicuna
Na sira torno' dintu senza ali
l'occhi lontani e lu pinsare puru
'Mangia, fighiuzzu miu, cori leali.'
Ma lu guardau e se lu viste scuru
'Figghiu, stu travagghiari ti fa mali.'
Iddu era stata la sera e Turiddu era stato menazzato dalla
Mafia, como vedete, e allora arrevo' a casa pensieroso
e la matre se ne accorse.
'Figghiu, chi fu chi t'amminezzau?
Sung iu matri, un m'ammucciari nenti!'

'Matri, vinni lu jurno,' e sospirau
'che Cristo l'ammazzaro
e fu nnuccentu.'
'Figghiu, 'stu cori miu assincupau
mi ci appizasti tri spati puncenti:
centi ca siti cca faciti vuci!'
La matre se lo vide mortu 'n croce.

The Mafia was planning gunfire; / that law didn't please the landowners / who are like angry dogs with teeth / which want to bite. / Poor wretched daily labourers! / who have them biting their necks. / One evening he came home sad / his glance distant and his thoughts pure / 'Eat up, my little son, loyal soul.' / But she looked at him and saw him sad. / 'My son, this kind of work is bad for you.' / That had been the evening in which Turiddu had been threatened by / the Mafia, as you can see, and so he came back home full of dark thoughts / and his mother realized it. / 'Son, who threatened you? / I am your mother, don't hide anything from me!' /

'Mother, the day has come' and he sighed / 'in which Christ was murdered, / and he was innocent.' / 'Son, this heart of mine has fluttered, / you pinned in it three sharp blades: / People who live here cry out.' / His mother saw him dead on a cross. /

Le mafiose, le mafiose de Palermo, hanno mantenuto
la parola. L'indomani mattina Turiddu era a
travagghiare a la cava, le mafiose lo spettano de
la trazzera dove Turiddu deve passare.
Non appena Turiddu passava, como vedete le
mafiose lo ammazzaro.
E con precisione fu lu 16 maggiu

Sidici Majo l'alba ncelu luci
E lu casteddu autu di Sciara
tagliava lu mari chi stralluci
comu n'altaru supra di na vara
E tra stu mari e casteddu na gran croce
si vitti dde matina all'aria chiara
sottu dde croci un mortu, e cu l'aceddi
lu chiantu rutte de li puviretti.

The mafiosi, the mafiosi of Palermo had kept / their word. On the following day,
Turiddu had gone / to work in the case, the mafiosi wait for him / on the track where
he used to pass. / As soon as Turiddu came by, as you can see, / the mafiosi killed
him. / And, to be precise, it was the 16th of May. /

16th of May, the sunrise lit the sky / and the high castle of Sciara / cut out from the
shimmering sea / like an altar, over a coffin. / And between the sea and the castle a
large cross / was to be seen in the morning, in the clean air / under the cross a dead
man, and with the birds / the broken sobbing of the poor. /

Stanzas from *The Story of Giuliano*

E allora, comu vedete,
Ciccio Busacca ve fa sentire
un episodiu di la storia de Giuliano
quando Giuliano se presenta
dalla cuntissa di Pratoameno,
una cuntissa riccona.
Turiddu, quando eva a rubare,
non ci eva mai con le pistole,
specialmente quando se presentava
a quste grandi signore,
ci eva elegantissimu.
Sentite la storia de Giuliano quando
ci robba i gioielli a la cuntissa:

La cuntissa ci fu di Pratoameno
ricca di terri, di giuielli e grano
ca n' giorno, in casa sua, niente di meno
vidi spuntari a Turi Giuliano
vistuto elegante veramenti
e cu n'aspetto allegro e risulenti.
Basandoce la mano in quell'istante
come s'usa tra li nobili genti
quando una dama ci sta davante
'Vussia cuntissa, mi divi scusari
s'iddu mancu mi fici annunziari.'

And now, as you can see, / Ciccio Busacca tells you about / an episode of the story of Giuliano / when Giuliano goes to see / the Countess of Pratoameno, a rich countess. / Salvatore Giuliano when he went to rob, / never went with a gun, / especially when he was paying a visit / to these grand ladies, / he dressed extremely smartly. / Now hear the story of Giuliano when / he steals the jewels from the countess: /

There lived the countess of Pratoameno / rich with land, jewels and wheat / who one day, in her house, / saw coming none else but Turi Giuliano / dressed up really smartly / and with a happy and smiling look. / Kissing her hand in that moment / as they used to do among noble people / he said 'Countess you must forgive me / if I didn't even announce myself.' /

... Giuliano mai si faciva annunziari
perche' non entrava mai dalla porta, traseva
sempre dalle finestre, como vedete.
'Contessa, mi Voglia scusare, ma ora mi ci
vogghiu presentare. Sono Giuliano.' 'Oh,
caro amico miu, ma da' tanto piaceri, tuo
patre como sta lu generale? un gran sempa-
teconc c gcniali.' 'Mio patre generale?
contessa, lei si sbaglia.' 'No? non siete
l'inceniere Giuliano lu figgiu de lu generale?'
'No, no, cuntissa, io sungu lu banditu tali e
quali
che lu destinu miu cussi' voli
Turi Giuliano, intisu lu banditu
cercato da la liggi in ogni situ.'

'Non scherzare giovanotto arditu.'
'Dicu la verita', gleilu confidu
dicendoce perche' sungu venuto.'
'E perche' siete venuto?'
'Per rubare li giuielli tutti
se nun vuoli suffrire peni e brutti.'
La cuntissa sbattio gli occhi
a bianca diventao comu lu latti
tra po' ci disse due paroli rutti

.. Giuliano never announced his arrival / because he never came in from doors, he / always used the windows, as you can see. / 'Countess, I must beg your pardon, but / now I must introduce myself. I am / Giuliano.' 'Oh, dear friend, it gives me / great pleasure, how is your father the / General? such a nice and friendly man.' / 'My father General? countess, you must / bc mistaken.' 'No? Aren't you the / engineer Giuliano, the General's son?' / 'No, no countess, I am the bandit / that my destiny so decided / Salvatore Giuliano, called the bandit, / wanted by the law everywhere.' /

'Don't joke, daring young man.' / 'I say the truth, and I am going to tell you / why I have come to see you.' / 'And why have you come to see me?' / 'To steal all your jewels, / if you don't want to have a bad time.' / The countess blinked and became white / as milk, and said a few broken words: /

'Le miei gioielli non ce l'aiu
sunnu a Palermo ntra a cassaforti
a lu sicuru de la brutta sorti.'
'Lo dice lei, cuntissa, ma qua mi risulta
che i gioielli sun da 'nantra parti e chiusu
dintro locali fatti a parti.' ...

'Allora me ne vajo e nun m'en curu
pero' l'avverto e ce lo dice chiaro
li miei compagni, con lo cuore duru
li su nipiti diggia' sequetraro
e si vussia non vuole piu' danno
mi dava li gioielli e io ci manno.'

'I haven't got my jewels, / they are in Palermo, in a safe, / guarded from bad events.' /
'You say so, countess, but here they / tell me that your jewels are somewhere / else
and locked in these rooms on the side.' ... /

'So I shall be gone and will not care, / but I must warn you and I tell you clearly /
my rough friends have already / kidnapped your nephews / and if you don't want any
more harm / give me your jewels and I will send your nephews back.' /

The Ballad of Luciano Liggio

Liggio has even had the honour of being the subject of a ballad called 'The Prince of the Mafia'. In it we find the usage of the word 'Killer', by now adopted by the Sicilian dialect whenever referring to the Mafia.

Signori miei, voglio raccontarvi la completa storia del capo mafia siciliano Luciano Leggio (detto Liggio):

I

Quannu muriu Calogero Lo Bui,
Lu capu di la mafia lucali
a Corlionici fu un fui fui
pp'acquistari ddu titulu ... riali:
ma cci appi cchiu putiri e fermu pusu
don Micheli Navarra, mafiusu.

II

... Luciano Liggiu ancora era un mucciusu
un carusiddu a chinnicianni appena
siccu, arruganti, agili, mpignusu
di pruvatu curaggiu e longa lena
ca spurtusava, ccu la so pistola
un palancuni ca nta l'aria vola.

Good people, I want to tell you the complete story of the Sicilian head of the Mafia, Luciano Leggio (called Liggio):

I

When Calogero Lo Bui, head / of the local Mafia died / at Corleone there was a rush / to conquer the 'royal' title: / but the one who had real power and strength / was Don Michele Navarra, the mafioso. /

II

... Luciano Liggio was still a boy / a youngster of fifteen only / lean, arrogant, agile and overbearing / of great courage and energy / who killed with his pistol / a bird which flies in the air. /

III

Ma la so puverta' non lu consola
e cuminciau la vita di banditu
ccussi', a vint'anni, dopo bona scola ...
addivintau assassinu rifinitu ...
ed ammazzau la guardia giurata
Calogeru Calajanni numinata

Il Colajanni fu ucciso perche' aveva denunciato Liggio per un furto di covoni di grani e l'aveva fatto rinchiudere in prigione.

IV

Ppi ddu dilittu non cci vinni data
nudda cunnanna, ca non cci fu prova
e Luciano fici la so entrata
nta la famigghia di la mafia nova
suttapostu a Navarra, lu dutturi,
comu killer, fidatu esecuturi.

V

In cuntrata Strasattuintantu, mori
Stanislau Punzu, un ottimu camperi
siccu allampatu ccu ncorpu a lu cori
e l'assassinu e' ignotu fucileri;
Luciano Liggiu vosi, ad ogni costu,
sustituirlu e ottinni lu so postu.

III

He was not consoled by his poverty / and started the life of a bandit / and so, at twenty, after a good school / he became a refined murderer / and killed a guard / called Calogero Colajanni /
Colajanni was killed because he had denounced Liggio for a theft of wheat and had him locked up.

IV

For this crime he did not get / any sentence, as there was no proof / and Luciano made his entrance / into the family of the new Mafia / under Navarra, the doctor, / as a killer, trusted executioner. /

V

At the locality of Strasatta then / Stanislao Punzu died, an excellent *campiere* / lean, thin, his heart in the right place / and the murderer is an unknown gunman; / Luciano Liggio wanted at all costs / to substitute for him, and got the job. /

VI

L'incaricu trimendu cci appi tostu
di Micheli Navarra, lu picciottu,
di siquisttrari e teniri nascostu
lu paisanu Placidu Rizzottu:
nascostu, si', ma ca non fussi vivu
nt'on lucali d'entrata affattu privu.

VII

E Lucianu Liggiu, sinsitivu
e a lu so capu sempri ubbidienti,
senza mancu sapiri lu mutivu
a Rizzotto ammazzau, immediatamenti
e a lu so corpu sipultura tocca
nta na spacca profunna di la Rocca.

VIII

Un pastureddu di la lingua sciocca
dissi d'aviri vistu l'assassinu,
ma la so virita' prestu lu stocca
e va finici mortu nt'on littinu,
ccu na mistiriusa gnizzioni
mentr'era in ospidali a Corleoni.

VI

Soon the picciotto had the terrible mandate / from Michele Navarra / to kidnap and keep hidden / Placido Rizzotto, the peasant, / yes, hidden, but that he should not be alive /

VII

And sensible Luciano Liggio / always obedient to his chief / without even knowing the reason / killed Rizzotto at once / and it happened that his body got / inside the deep hole of the Rocca. /

VIII

A little shepherd with a naive tongue / said he had seen the murderer / but his truth soon lost him / and he has finished as a corpse in his small bed / with a mysterious injection / while he was in hospital at Corleone.

IX

Scanza la guista carcerazioni
l'assassinu Lucianu prucissatu:
ma la magistratura lu proponi
e lu cunanna a soggiornu obbligatu
insemi ccu lu medicu Navarra
ppi ddi dilitti chiamatu a la sbarra.

X

Sett'anni doppu, Liggiu s'incaparra
ancora n'autru orribili dilittu
e lu birsagghiu so certu non sgarra
canta la vucca nserta, rittu, rittu
e don Splendidu Claudiu cadia
un cunfidenti di la pulizia.

XI

Navarra, intantu, teniri vulia
di capu mafiusu lu pristiggiu
ca jornu doppu jornu si stintia
la cuncurrenza di Luciano Liggiu;
percio'tra li du coschi mafiusi
cuminciaru tichetti e autri abusi.

IX

He avoids the just imprisonment / murderer Luciano on trial / but the magistrates condemn / him to be banished / together with the doctor Navarra / called to trial for that murder. /

X

Seven years later Liggio is guilty / of another horrible murder / and the target he didn't mistake / to stop the mouth ... / and Don Claudio Splendido fell / he was a spy for the police. /

XI

In the meantime Navarra wanted to keep / the prestige of the mafia boss / as day after day he felt / the rivalry with Luciano Liggio: / and so between the two coschi mafiose / started quarrels and other abuses. /

XII

Ppi Navarra assai brutta si cunchiusi
Ca lu rivali sonterra lu stisi;
Centudeci pallottuli chiummusi
in corpu cci cintrau, tutti, precisi
mentri, nta n'automobili, passava
ccu Gianni Russu ca l'accimpagnava.

XIII

Diddu dilitti non si cuntentava
Liggiu, ch'era assitatu di cumannu,
e Corleoni na notti assaltava
ccu la so banda, siminannu dannu:
ogni seguaci di don Michilinu
vinni ammazzatu, comu un beccaccinu!

XIV

Mariu e Giuvanni, fratelli Marinu,
Ninu Streva e Giuvanni Pruvinzanu,
fidili a lu difuntu malandrinu,
foru tutti sparati, a mmanu a mmanu;
e n'antri vinti morti, certamenti
cci foru a Corleoni a ddu presenti.

XII

It finished up badly for Navarra / as his rival killed him / 110 bullets entered / his body, all well-aimed / as he was passing by in a car / with Gianni Russo, who accompanied him. /

XIII

Liggio was not content with / this deed as he was thirsty with power / and assaulted Corleone one night / with his gang, disseminating murder: / all followers of Navarra were killed / like small birds. /

XIV

Mario and Giovanni, the Marino brothers, / Nino Streva and Giovanni Provenzanu / the faithful of the dead mafioso / were all, little by little, killed: / and certainly there were another / twenty dead at Corleone at that time. /

XV

Lucianu Liggiu, ormai, era punenti,
incuntrastatu capu mafiusu,
ma ricircatu cuntinuamenti
ppi mittirlu ngalera, fora d'usa
ccu puru ch'era invalidu e malatu
di lu morbu di Pott straziatu.

XVI

Intra un spitali s'ha ricuviratu
ccu lu fasullu nomi Centineu,
ma, finalmente, poi, vinni attruvatu
e ammanittatu, comu nu babbeu,
nta l'abitazioni di l'amanti
Sorisi Leoluchina, nta dd'istanti.

XVII

E, ppi cinc'anni, non fu latitanti
ma mprigioni ristau, beddu rinchiusu;
poi vinni assoltu tanti voti e tanti,
comu in Italia, troppo spissu e' d'su;
ed a Palermu, Bari e Catanzaru,
comu nuccenti, non lu cunnannaru.

XV

Luciano Liggio was by then powerful / unopposed capo mafia / but the police were always looking for him / to put him in prison, out of use: / and he was also an invalid, ill / with Pott's disease.

XVI

He went into hospitals / with the fake name of Centineo, / but finally he was found / and locked in, like a fool, / in the house of his mistress / Leoluchina Sorisi.

XVII

And for five years he was not at large / but stayed in prison, well locked up: / then he was acquitted many times / as in Italy too often is done: / and in Palermo, Bari and Catanzaro / he was acquitted as innocent. /

XVIII

Ma l'appello di Bari fu cchiu' amaru,
all'innocenza so nuddu cci cridi
e la galera a vita, in modo chiaru
la curti di li judici dicidi
fu piantunatu di la polizia
ma scappa e nuddu sapi unn'e' ca sia!

XIX

Poi la Finanza scopri' la so scia
ppi puru casu, propriu a Milanu;
ma si fu casu o puru fu na spia,
nuddu po dirlo con li provi ammanu:
di cettu c'e' ca vinni ammanittatu
e a lu carciri, a Lodi, fu ntirnatu.

XX

Di Scaglioni, lu judici ammazzatu
di Mauro de Mauro, giornalista,
di lu quisturi Manganu, sparatu
cchi sapi Liggiu? Auturi fu o rigista
o puru di sti fatti iddu e nuccenti
e non sappi ppi daveru nenti?

XVIII

But the Appeal trial in Bari was more bitter, / and didn't believe in his innocence / and the court of judges decided / in a clear way to give him a life sentence: / the sentries were beside him / but he fled and no-one knew where he was. /

XIX

Then the police discovered his traces / by pure chance, in Milan: / but if it were chance or a spy / no one can say with proof: / what is certain was that he was imprisoned / and was interned in the prisons of Lodi. /

XX

What does Liggio know about Scaglione / the murdered Judge? Or Mauro de Mauro, / the journalist, or the policeman Mangano, / who was shot at? Was he the author or the director? / or of these deeds is he innocent / and really doesn't know anything? /

BIBLIOGRAPHY

I Manuscript sources

Quaderni del Centro Documentazione, Agrigento 1972—*Michele Pantaleone un personaggio scomodo*

Foreign Office Papers—Public Record Office—FO371 / 37307 / 37308 / 37309 / 77310 / 37356 / 43815 / 37325 / 37327 / 37328

War Office File 204 Secret and Top Secret (USA and UK)

Tesi di Laurea, Palermo 1973, Sala, Concetta—*Quando occupavano i feudi*

Corte di Appello di Palermo—Sezione di accusa—sentenze processi

Museo Pitrè (La Favorita, Palermo) Archivio fotografico—Lettere di estorsione

Museo Pitrè—Tesi di Laurea

Archivo di Stato di Palermo—Gabinetto di Prefettura

Archivio di Stato di Palermo—Archivio generale di questura

Danilo Dolci—Franco Alasia—*Un fondamentale impedimento allo sviluppo democratico della Sicilia Occidentale*—Contributo alla Commissione Parlamentare antimafia, Settembre 1965, Partinico

Camera dei Deputati, Roma 1965, Senatore Morino, A.—*Relazione sul caso Zizzo alla Commissione parlamentare d'inchiesta sul fenomeno della Mafia in Sicilia*

Camera dei Deputati—*Relazione su Giuseppe Genco Russo alla Commissione Parlamentare d'inchiesta sul fenomeno della Mafia in Sicilia*—Senatore Cipolla, Nicolò—Roma, 1969

Camera dei Deputati—*Relazione del Presidente Cattanei Francesco alla Commissione Antimafia sul viaggio di presidenza in Sicilia*—svolta nella seduta del 6 maggio 1969, Roma

Camera dei Deputati—*Relazione Comitato Enti Locali svolta dal Senatore Cipolla Nicolo alla Commissione parlamentare d'inchiesta sul fenomeno della mafia in Sicilia*, 1969

Camera dei Deputati—*Proposte per un piano di lavoro della commissione parlamentare d'inchiesta sul fenomeno della mafia in Sicilia approvate dal consiglio di presidenza l'11 del 12 1968*

Camera dei Deputati—Della Briotta, Libero—*Relazione sul traffico degli stupefacenti e sul caso Mancino*—6. 10 1965 alla Commissione parlamentare d'inchiesta sul fenomeno della mafia in Sicilia

II Printed sources

Camera dei Deputati—*Atti Parlementari* (Rome, various dates)

Carte di Polizia B 15061—Gabinetto di Prefettura—Archivo di Stato di Palermo

295

Relazione della Commissione Parlamentare d'Inchiesta sul fenomeno della mafia in Sicilia—Termine V legislatura 1972—Allegato—Brancato, Francesco

Camera dei Deputati V Legislazione Doc. XXIII N2—quater Commissione Parlamentare Presidente Francseco Cattanei deputato sul fenomeno della mafia in Sicilia—*Relazione sull'indagine riguardante casi di singoli mafiosi*—Rome

Camera dei Deputati Doc. XXIII N2—sexies Commissione Parlamentare Presidente Francesco Cattanei Deputato sul fenomeno della mafia in Sicilia—*Relazione sui rapporti tra la mafia e il banditismo in Sicilia*—Rome

Camera dei Deputati—Presidente Francesco Cattanei Deputato. Commissione Parlamentare d'inchiesta sul fenomeno della mafia in Sicilia—2 Septies—Doc XXIII—*Relazione sui lavori svolti e sullo stato del fenomeno mafioso al termine della quinta legislature*—Rome

Real Camera dei Deputati, Di Rudinì—*Interpellanza riguardo le proposte fatte dalla commissione d'inchiesta in Sicilia*—Rome 1877

Real Camera dei Deputati, Bonfantini—*Relazioni della giunta per l'inchiesta sulle condizioni della Sicilia*—Rome 1876

Real Camera dei Deputati, De Pretis, Agostino—*Risposte alle interpellanze dei deputati di Rudini*—Rome 1877

Real Camera dei Deputati, Professor Lorenzoni, Giuseppe—*Relazione del delegato tecnico—Inchiesta parlamentare sulla condizione dei contadini nelle provincie meridionali e della Sicilia*—Vol. VIIe Capitolo IX della parte II (Delinquenza in Sicilia)—Rome 1910

Manchester University—Session 1959–60—Prof. Waller, Ross, D.—*Danilo Dolci from Vol. 102 of 'Memoirs and Proceedings of the Manchester Literary and Philosophical Society'.*

III   Books

ACTON, Harold: *The Bourbons of Naples* (London, 1956)
   More Memoirs of an Aesthete (London, 1972)

ALLUM, Percy: *Italy: Republic without Government?* (London, 1973)

ALONGI, Giuseppe: *La Mafia nei suoi fattori e nelle sue manifestazioni, Studio delle classi pericolose della Sicilia* (Turin, 1887)
   L'abigeato in Sicilia, Studii di patologia sociale (Marsala, 1891)

BARRESE, Orazio: *I complici, gli anni dell'Antimafia* (Milan, 1973)

BARZINI, Luigi: *The Italians* (London, 1964)
   From Caesar to the Mafia (London, 1971)

BELLINI, Fulvio: *L'assassinio di Enrico Mattei* (Milan, 1970)

BLOK, Anton: *The Mafia of a Sicilian Village 1860–1960* (Oxford, 1974)

BRAUDEL, Fernand: *La Méditerranée et le Monde Méditerranéen à l'époque de Philippe II* (Paris, 1966)

BRANCATO, Francesco: *Storia della Sicilia post-unificazione—La Sicilia nel primo ventennio del regno d'Italia*, Parte I (Bologna, 1956)

BRUCCOLERI, Giuseppe: *La Sicilia di oggi* (Rome, 1913)

BRUNO, Cesare: *La Sicilia e la mafia* (Rome, 1900)

BRYDONE, Patrick: *A tour through Sicily and Malta in a series of letters to William Beckford Esq., of Somerley in Suffolk* (London, 1773)

BUTTITTA, Antonino: *Ideologica e folklore* (Palermo, 1971)

CANDIDA, Renato: *Questa mafia* (Caltanisetta, 1956)
CAPUANA, L.: *La Sicilia e il brigantaggio* (Rome, 1892)
CARBONE, Salvatore and GRISPO, Renato: *L'inchiesta sulle condizioni sociali ed economiche della Sicilia, 1875–1876*, 2 Vols., (Bologna, 1969)
CARINI, I.: *La questione sociale in Sicilia* (Rome, 1894)
CARLYLE, Margaret: *The Awakening of Southern Italy* (Oxford, 1962)
CHILANTI, Felice: *Rapporto sulla mafia* (Palermo, 1964)
COLAJANNI, Napoleone: *La delinquenza della Sicilia* (Palermo, 1885)
Nel regno della mafia (Palermo, 1903)
Cronache e storia (Palermo, 1904)
La Sicilia dai Borboni ai Sabaudi (Milan, 1951)
CROCE, Benedetto: *Uomini e cose della vecchia Italia* (Bari, 1956)
CUTRERA, Antonio: *La mafia e i mafiosi* (Palermo, 1900)
D'ALESSANDRO, Enzo: *Brigantaggio e mafia in Sicilia* (Messina, Florence, 1959)
DE FELICE, G.: *Mafia e delinquenza in Sicilia* (Milan, 1900)
DE ROBERTO, F.: *I Viceré* (Milan, 1962)
DE STEFANO, Francesco and ODDO, Francesco Luigi: *Storia della Sicilia dal 1860 al 1910* (Bari, 1963)
DOLCI, Danilo: *Banditi a Partinico* (Bari, 1955)
Spreco (Turin, 1960)
Inchiesta a Palermo (Turin, 1962)
Conversazioni (Turin, 1962)
Chi gioca solo (Turin, 1967)
Inventare il futuro (Bari, 1968)
D'ORSI, Angelo: *Il Potere repressivo: la polizia* (Milan, 1972)
FALZONE, Gaetano: *Histoire de la Mafia* (Paris, 1973)
FARINELLA, Mario and CHILANTI, Felice: *Rapporto sulla Mafia* (Palermo, 1964)
FAVA, Giuseppe: *La violenza* (Palermo, 1969)
FINLEY, Moses I.: *A History of Sicily (Ancient Sicily to the Arab Conquest)* (London, 1968)
FRANCHETTI, Leopoldo: *Condizioni politiche ed amministrative della Sicilia nel 1876* (Florence, 1877)
FRANCHETTI, Leopoldo and SONNINO, Sydney: *La Sicilia nel 1876* (Florence, 1925)
GABRIELI, Francesco: *Normanni e Arabi* (Bari,)
GAJA, Filippo: *L'esercito della lupara. Baroni e banditi siciliani nella guerriglia contro l'Italia* (Milan, 1962)
GALT, William (Natoli): *I beati Paoli*, Vol. I and II (Palermo, 1970, reprint)
GARUFI, C. A.: *Contributo alla storia dell'inquisizione in Sicilia nei secoli XVIeXVII* (Palermo, 1920)
GENTILE, Nick: *Vita di un capomafia* (Rome, 1963)
GIACHERY, Luigi: *Piazza Marina ed alberghi di Palermo nel secolo scorso* (Palermo, 1923)
GOETHE, Wolfgang Johann von: *Italian Journey* (London, 1962)
GONZAGA, Ferrando D.: *Relazione delle cose di Sicilia fatta all'imperatore Carlo V 1546* (Palermo, 1896)
GOODMAN, Walter: See LEPERA, Patsy Anthony
GOSCH, Martin and HAMMEL, Richard, *Tje Last Testament of Lucky Luciano* (London, 1975)
GRASSO, Franco: *A Montelepre hanno piantato una croce* (Milan-Rome, 1956)
GRIECO, Raffaele: *Perche' il fascismo combattè la mafia*—from *l'Antologia della Mafia* (Palermo, 1964)
GRISPO, Renato: See CARBONE, Salvatore

298   Bibliography

HAMMER, Richard: See GOSCH, Martin

HESSE, Henner: *Mafia* (Bari, 1973)

HOBSBAWM, Eric J.: *Primitive Rebels: Studies in archaic forms of social movement in the 19th and 20th centuries* (Manchester, 1959)
Bandits (London, 1969)

HOUEL, F.: *Voyage pictoresque des îsles de Sicile, de Malte et de Lipari* (Paris, 1782)

INCHIESTA, Jacini: *Redatta da Gabriele Damiani 1877–1885*, Vol. XIII—I and II

INCHIESTA, Lorenzoni: *Inchiesta Parlamentare sulle condizioni dei contadini nelle provincie meridionali* (Rome, 1909)

KEFAUVER, Estes: *Crime in America* (New York, 1958)

KENNEDY, Robert F.: *The Enemy Within* (New York, 1960)

LAMPEDUSA, Giuseppe Tomassi di: *Il Gattopardo* (Milan, 1958)

LANZA, Gioacchino: Tomasi *Castelli e monasteri siciliani* (Palermo, 1968)

LEPERA, Patsy Anthony and GOODMAN, Walter: *Memoirs of a Scam Man* (New York, 1974)

LEWIS, Norman: *The Honoured Society* (London, 1964)

LI GOTTI, Ettore: *Il teatro dei pupi* (Florence, 1958)

LIONTI, Ferdinando: *Antiche maestranze della citta di Palermo* (Palermo, 1887)

LOSCHIAVO, Guido Giuseppe: *100 anni di mafia* (Rome, 1962)

MAAS, Peter: *The Valachi Papers* (London, 1969)

MACALUSO, Emanuele: *La mafia e lo stato* (Rome, 1971)

MACK SMITH, Denis: *Italy, a Modern History* (Michigan, 1959)
The Making of Italy 1796–1870 (New York, 1968)
A History of Sicily, Vol. I, *800 1713* (London, 1969)
A History of Sicily, Vol. II, *From 1713 to Modern Sicily* (London, 1969)

McNEISH, James: *Fire under the Ashes* (London, 1965)

MADEO, Alfonso (editor): *Testo integrale della relazione della Commissione parlamentare d'inchiesta sul fenemeno della mafia in Sicilia* (testimonanze On. Francesco Cattenei, On. Libero della Briotta, On. Pio La Torre)

MARCHELLO, Claudia and Gianni: *Palermo dal basso* (Palermo, 1957)

MARINO, Giuseppe Carlo: *L'opposizione mafiosa. Baroni e mafia contro lo stato liberale* (Palermo, 1964)

MAXWELL, Gavin: *God Protect Me from My Friends* (London, 1956)
The Ten Pains of Death (London, 1959)

MAZZAMUTO, Pietro: *La mafia nella letteratura* (Palermo, 1970)

MERLINO, F. S.: *L'Italie telle qu'elle est* (Paris, 1890)

MORI, Cesare: *Tra le zagare oltre la foschia* (Forence, 1935)
Con la mafia ai ferri corti (Verona, 1932)
Ordinanza del Prefetto Mori per ristabilire la sicurezza pubblica nelle campagne siciliane—1926—*Antologia della mafia* (Palermo, 1964)

MOSCA, Gaetano: *Partiti e sindacati nella crisi del regime parlamentare* (Bari, 1900)
Che cos'è la mafia?—1900—*Antologia della mafia* (Palermo, 1964)

MUSSOLINI, Benito: *Discorso dell'Ascensione*—*Antologia della mafia* (Palermo, 1964)

NATOLI, Luigi (GALT, William): *I beati Paoli*, Vol. I and II (Palermo, 1971—reprint)

NOTARBARTOLO, LEOPOLDO: *Memorie della vita di mio padre Emanuele Notarbartolo di San Giovanni* (Pistoia, 1949)

NOVACCO, Domenico: *Inchiesta sulla mafia* (Milan, 1963)
Mafia ieri, mafia oggi (Milan, 1972)

ODDO, Francesco: See DE STEFANO, Francesco

PAGANA, G.: *La Sicilia nel 1876–77*—*Antologia della Mafia* (Palermo, 1964)

PAGANO, Roberto: *Scarlatti* (Rome, 1972)

PALAZZOLI, Claude: *Le régionalisme italien: constitution à l'étude de la centralisation politique* (Paris, 1965)

L'ambiente insulare italiano e i suoi problemi in Sicilia e Sardegna (Palermo, 1965)

PALAZZOLO, Salvatore: *La mafia delle coppole storte* (Florence, 1958)

PALIZZOLO, Raffaele: *Dai ricordi del carcere* (Palermo, 1908)

PANTALEONE, Michele: *Mafia e politica 1943–62* (Turin, 1962)

Mafia e droga (Turin, 1966)

Antimafia occasione mancata (Turin, 1969)

Il sasso in bocca (Bologna, 1971)

PASLEY, F. D.: *Al Capone* (London, 1931)

PEDICINI WHITAKER, Manfred: *A record of English families in Sicily* (Palermo, 1970)

PETACCO, Arrigo: *Joe Petrosino* (London, 1974)

PITRÈ, Giuseppe: *La famiglia, la casa, la vita del popolo siciliano* (Palermo, 1889)

Studi di poesie popolari (Palermo, 1889)

Usi e costumi e credenze e pregiudizi del popolo siciliano (Palermo, 1889)

Del Sant Officio a Palermo (Rome 1970)

PONTIERI, Ernesto: *Il riformismo del baronaggio siciliano* (Firenze, 1943)

Il reformismo borbonico nella Sicilia del sette e dell'ottocento (Rome, 1945)

PREVIDI, Alessandro and BELLINI, Fulvio: *L'assassinio di Enrico Mattei* (Milan, 1970)

PUZO, Mario: *The Godfather* (London, 1969)

RADICE, Benedetto: *Memorie storiche di Bronte*, Vol. I and II (Bronte, 1906)

REID, Ed: *Mafia* (New York, 1954)

RENDA, Francesco: *L'emigrazione in Sicilia* (Palermo, 1963)

Risorgimento e classi popolari in Sicilia 1820–21 (Milan, 1968)

RICCI, Aldo and SALERNO, Giulio: *Il carcere in Italia* (Turin. 1971)

RIZZOTTO, Giuseppe: *I mafiusi de la Vicaria di Palermo—100 anni di Mafia* (Rome 1964)

ROMANO, Salvatore F.: *Storia della mafia* (Turin, 1963)

Sul brigantaggio e sulla mafia (Messina, 1952)

Storia dei fasci siciliani (Bari, 1959)

Storia della mafia (Milan, 1963)

RUNCIMAN, Steven: *The Sicilian Vespers* (Cambridge, 1958)

SALADINO, Giuliana: *De Mauro* (Milan, 1970)

SALAPARUTA Enrico Alliata Duca di: *Cucina vegetariana e naturismo crudo* (introduzione di Giocchino Lanza Tomasi) (Palermo 1971)

SALERNO, Giulio and RICCI, Aldo: *Il carcere in Italia* (Turin, 1971)

SALVEMINI, Gaetano: *Scritti sulla questione meridionale* (Turin, 1955)

Il ministro della mala vita e altri scritti sull'Italia gioilittiana (Milan, 1962)

SANTAMAURA BRAIDA, Silvana: *Palermo viva* (Palermo, 1972)

SCALFARI, Eugenio and TURANI, Giuseppe: *Razza padrona* (Milan, 1974)

SCIASCIA, Leonardo: *Il giorno della civetta* (Turin, 1961)

Todo modo (Turin, 1974)

SERENI, Emilio: *Il capitalismo nelle campagne 1860–1900* (Turin, 1947)

SERVADIO, Gaia: *Angelo La Barbera: Profile of a Mafia Boss* (London, 1974)

SONNINO, Sydney and FRANCHETTI, Leopoldo: *La Sicilia nel 1876* (Florence, 1925)

TACCARI, Mario: *Palermo l'altro ieri* (Palermo, 1966)

I Florio (Caltanisetta, 1967)

TAJANI, DIEGO: *Discorsi Parlamentari—Antologia della mafia* (Palermo, 1964)

TARROW, Sydney: *Peasant Communism in Southern Italy* (Yale, 1967)

TITONE, Virgilio: *Considerazioni sulla mafia* (Palermo, 1964)

La Sicilia dalla dominazione spagnola all'unita' d'Italia (Palermo 1969)
Storie della vecchia Sicilia (Milan, 1971)
TOCCO, Matteo: *Libro nero di Sicilia* (Milan, 1971)
TOMMASI CRUDELI, C.: *La Sicilia nel 1871* (Perugia, 1872)
Il mattino di un mezzadro-Racconti (Milan, 1961)
TREVELYAN, G. M.: *Garibaldi's Defence of the Roman Republic* (London, 1907)
Garibaldi and the Making of Italy (London, 1911)
TREVELYAN, Raleigh: *Princes under the Volcano* (London, 1972)
TURANI, Giuseppe and SCALFARI, Eugenio: *Razza padrona* (Milan, 1974)
TUZET, H.: *La Sicile au XVIIIe siècle vue par les voyageurs étrangers* (Strasbourg, 1955)
UCCELLO, Antonino: *Carcere e mafia nei canti popolari* (Bari, 1974)
VACCARO, M. A.: *La Mafia* (Rome, 1899)
VALPREDA, Pietro: *TheValpreda Papers* (London, 1975)
VILLABIANCA, Marchese di: *Diario palermitano*—biblioteca comunale di Palermo, Vol.
    XIX (Palermo, 1975)
VILLARI, Pasquale: *La mafia* (Turin, 1878)
Lettere meridionali (Rome, 1885)
VITTORINI, Elio: *Conversazione in Sicilia* (Turin, 1946)
VOLPES, Nicola: *Tenente Petrosino* (Palermo, 1972)
ZULLINO, Pietro: *Guida ai misteri e ai piaceri di Palermo* (Milan, 1973)
ZANNER, Don Benedetto: *Sulle condizioni della Sicilia—lettere di un Italiano* (Milan,
    1863)

IV   Articles and periodicals

ALASIA, Franco: 'La Mafia: un fondamentale impedimento allo sviluppo della Sicilia
    occidentale', *Ulisse*, 1969, Vol. LXIV
'Aspetti psicologici del banditismo', *Quaderni di Ulisse*, 1969, Vol. LXIV
BANDINI, Franco: 'Lo sbarco in Sicilia', *Storia Illustrata*, Jan. 1974
BAUDO, Roberto: 'La pista parte dai Rimi', *L'Ora*, 16 July 1971
    L'Ora, 13 Oct., 15 Oct., and 7 Nov. 1973
BERTI, G.: 'Discorso al Senato sulla mafia', *Cronache Meridionali*, Sept. 1960
BLOK, Anton: 'Mafia and peasant rebellion as contributing factors in Sicilian lati-
    fundia', *Archives Européennes de Sociologie*, 1969
BOCCA, Giorgio: 'La criminalità cittadinà', *Ulisse*, 1969, Vol. LXIV
BOISSEVAIN, Jeremy: 'Patronage in Sicily', *Anthropology Institute*, 1833
BRANCATO, Francesco: 'Genesi e psicologia della mafia', *Nuovi quaderni del Meridione*
    (numero speciale sulla mafia) 1964
CAMMARERI SCURTI, Sebastiano: 'La lotta di classe nei proverbi siciliani', *Critica
    Sociale*, 1 Aug. 1896
CAPPATO, G.: 'Luciano Liggio ha parlato', *ABC*, 1969
CIMINO, Marcello: 'Se Buttafuoco é colpevole non e' la figure principale', *L'Ora*, 21
    Oct. 1970
'E lei che ne pensa Senatore Verzotto?' *L'Ora*, 23 Oct. 1970
'I sequestri e la politica', *L'Ora*, 28 Aug. 1972
L'Ora, 2, 13, 16, 20, 23 June 1973
Paeae Sera, 9, 12, 14, 17, 19, 24 July 1973
'Quel 10 luglio in Sicilia', *L'Ora*, 10 July 1973
'Il mezzogiorno sotto il fascismo', *L'Ora*, 28 Oct. 1973

COSTANZA, Salvatore and GANGI, Massimo: 'La mafia nel giudizio di Napoleone Colajanni', *Nuovi quaderni del Meridione* (numero speciale nulla mafia) 1964

CUTRERA, Antonio: 'Perche esiste la mafia', *Antologia della mafia* (il Punto), 1964

FRIEDMANN, Frederic G.: 'The Rap Gangsters Fear Most', *Saturday Evening Post*, Aug. 1958

GANCI, M.: 'Il movimento dei fasci nella provincia di Palermo', *Movimento Operaio*, 1817–92, 1954

GANGI, Massimo and COSTANZA, Salvatore: 'La mafia nel giudizio di Napoleone Colajanni', *Nuovi quaderni del Meridione* (numero speciale sulla mafia) 1964

GATTO, Simone: 'Lo stato Brigante', *L'Astrolabio*, 1971

GENCO, Mario: *L'Ora*, 19 June, 1974

GHIROTTI, Gigi: 'La rivalita storica tra le forze dell'ordine', *I problemi di Ulisse*, Vol. LXIV, April 1969

GIORDANO, A.: 'La mafia nelle relazioni inaugurali degli anni giudiziari dall'unita' d'Italia ad oggi', *Nuovi quaderni del Meridione* (numero speciale sulla mafia) 1964

GOODWIN, John: 'Progress of the two Sicilies under the Bourbons', *Journal of the Royal Statistical Society*, Vol. V, London, 1842

GUIDI, Guido: 'Profilo della criminalita in cifre', *I problemi di Ulisse*, Vol. LXIV, April 1969

La Stampa, 31 July–23 Aug. 1974, 4 Jan. 1974, 4 June, 1974

HAMMER, Richard: 'A little light on the Syndicate', *Playboy*, April 1974

HOBSBAWM, Eric J.: 'Social Bandits. A Comment', *Comparative Studies in Society and History*, 1970

JANNUZZI, Lino: 'I grandi protettori', *L'Espresso*, 11 April 1965

'I nomi della mafia', *L'Espresso*, 4 April 1965

'Vostro Onore', *L'Espresso*, 16 May 1965

LOSHIAVO, Giuseppe Guido: 'La delinquenza nella societa italiana in trasformazione', *Ulisse*, Vol. LXIV, April 1969

McDONALD, J. S.: 'Italy's Rural Social Structure and Emigration', *Occidente*, 1956

MATTARELLA, Bernardo: 'Dei Separatisti', *Il Popolo*, 24 Sept. 1944

'Uno sviluppo equilibrato delle aree economiale', *Trapani Sera* supplement without date

MAZZAMUTO, Pietro: 'Mafia nella letteratura', *Nuovi quaderni del Meridione* (numero speciale sulla mafia) 1964

MELIS BASSU, Giuseppe: 'Il rapporto tra banditismo e apparato giudiziario', *Ulisse*, April 1969

MONTALBANO, Giuseppe: 'Brigantaggio e mafia nella societa siciliana', *Rinascita*, Oct. 1953

'La mafia a occhio nudo', *Il Mondo*, 9 Nov. 1958

NOVACCO, Domenico: 'Bibliografia della mafia', *Nuovi quaderni del Meridione* (numero speciale sulla mafia) 1964

'Considerazioni sulla fortuna del termine mafia', *Belfagor*, 1959

'Profilo storico della mafia', *I Problemi di Ulisse*, 1969, Vol. LXIV

Intercettazioni telefoniche, *L'Ora*, 14, 17, 19, 27, 29 May 1973, 7, 12, 16, 26 June 1973, 12 July 1973

PALUMBO, Mario: 'La mafià nel cinema'

PANZA, Gianpaolo: *La Stampa*, 23 Sept. 1972

PESCE, Livio: 'Come lottare contro la mafia', *Ulisse*, Vol. LXIV, April, 1969

PITRE, Giuseppe: 'L'omerta', *Archivo di Psichiatria*, Vol. X, 1889

REECE, J. E.: 'Fascism, the Mafia and the emergence of Sicilian separatism', *Journal of Modern History*, June 1973

SALA (Saladino) Giulia: 'Scaglione un mese dopo', *L'Ora*, 5 June 1971
  'Scaglione sapeva chi c'era dietro Giuliano', *L'Ora*, 8 June 1971, 4 May 1973
SARDO SPAGNOLO, Nina: 'Una inchiesta poco nota sulla mafia', *Nuovi quaderni de Meridione* (numero speciale sulla mafia) 1964
SCIANNA, Francesco: 'Lucky Luciano una storia che si ripete', *Europeo*, 1973
SCIASCIA, Leonardo: 'Appunto sulla mafia e letteratura', *Nuovi quaderni del Meridione* (numero speciale sulla mafia), 1964
SCIOTINO, Salvatore A.: 'Dello stato in Sicilia e della mafia', *Nuovi quaderni del Meridione* (numero speciale sulla mafia) 1964
SERVADIO, Gaia: 'Wall of silence in the war against the mafia', *The Times*, 26 Feb. 1970
  'The political untouchables who protect the mafia', *The Times*, 29 Sept. 1972
  'The real victims of the mafia', *Evening Standard*, 27 March 1972
  'The kidnapping industry', *Evening Standard*, 5 July, 1974
  'The island of sinners', *The Sunday Times*, 29 May, 1974
  'Sicily: Epitaph for the élite', *The Sunday Times*, 3 March 1974
  'Islands of exile', *Daily Telegraph Magazine*, October 1971
  'Law misfires over Mafia's inner war', *Sunday Telegraph*, 27 Feb. 1972
SORGI, Antonino: 'Quindici anni di lotte contadine', *Il Ponte*, 1959
SPAZZANO, Francesco: 'La commissione parlamentare antimafia', *Quaderni di Ulisse*, Vol. LXIV, 1969
STABILE, Alberto: *L'Ora*, 14 Feb. 1974, 23 March 1973, 12 Feb. 1974, 23 May 1974
TITONE, Virgilio: 'Radici e caretteri della criminalità in Italia', *Ulisse*, Vol. LXIV April 1969
TOCCO, Matteo: 'La mafia. Origine e carattere del fenomeno nel quadro politico e dell'ordine pubblico in Sicilia', *Quaderni della Sala d'Ercole*, n10*III, 1959

INDEX